THE INFERNAL

THE INFERNAL

– A Novel –

MARK DOTEN

Graywolf Press

Parts of this book appeared in different form in *Conjunctions,* elimae, *New York* magazine, the Rumpus, *Spank Zine,* and Word Riot.

This publication is made possible, in part, by the voters of Minnesota through a Minnesota State Arts Board Operating Support grant, thanks to a legislative appropriation from the arts and cultural heritage fund, and through a grant from the Wells Fargo Foundation Minnesota. Significant support has also been provided by the Jerome Foundation, Target, the McKnight Foundation, Amazon.com, and other generous contributions from foundations, corporations, and individuals. To these organizations and individuals we offer our heartfelt thanks.

Published by Graywolf Press
250 Third Avenue North, Suite 600
Minneapolis, Minnesota 55401

All rights reserved.

www.graywolfpress.org

Published in the United States of America

ISBN 978-1-55597-701-6

2 4 6 8 9 7 5 3 1
First Graywolf Printing, 2015

Library of Congress Control Number: 2014950979

Cover design: Kapo Ng
Cover art: Sam Chung, A-Men Project
Memex interface design: Jason Booher
Interior Wet-Grid art: Mode Lab
"Hacker" dialect translator used in "Karen Hughes": Copyright © Samuel
    Stoddard, rinkworks.com
Random noise insertion program: Chris Doten

To **Margo Doten**, the first writer I ever met.

And **Kim Parsons**, life-friend, life-animal.

We're an empire now, and when we act, we create our own reality. And while you're studying that reality—judiciously, as you will—we'll act again, creating other new realities, which you can study too, and that's how things will sort out. We're history's actors . . . and you, all of you, will be left to just study what we do.

—Anonymous aide to the president, quoted by Ron Suskind,
The New York Times Magazine

God forbid that we should give out a dream of our own imagination for a pattern of the world; rather may he graciously grant to us to write an apocalypse or true vision of the footsteps of the Creator imprinted on his creatures.

—Francis Bacon, *Instauratio Magna,* trans. by James Spedding et al.

– AUTHOR'S NOTE –

Jay Garner wore khakis and open-collared shirts in Iraq, while L. Paul Bremer was known for his combat boots and tailored suits; Alberto Gonzales called himself *a casualty, one of the many casualties of the war on terror;* Mark Zuckerberg fenced; Nathan Myhrvold dreamt of helium balloons over the North Pole; and Charles Graner was accused of putting a razor blade in the food of an inmate (though the alleged incident took place in the United States, not Iraq, and in any case, apart from this note, his name goes unmentioned here . . .).

Real-world people and events appear in *The Infernal*, but—to use the legal phrase, which also happens to be true—this is a work of fiction, and all incidents and characters are either fictional or used fictitiously. Where characters and events can be matched in one way or another to real-world counterparts, they have been deformed, reimagined, made into weird composite animals, and/or rendered insane, with invented conversations, thoughts, feelings, backstories, geographies, gestures, verbal tics, sunsets, and blood ties sprayed everywhere, helter-skelter.

In a 1945 *Atlantic* article, "As We May Think," Vannevar Bush described his memex, a hypothetical, early precursor to hypertext and the World Wide Web. Though he appears here as a villain, he is widely (and rightly) admired as one of the twentieth century's most important figures in the fields of science and technology. As for Jimmy Wales, well . . . Wikipedia is one of the great human things of recent years, but *my* Jimmy Wales is someone else, who invents things that are different and kills people who get in his way and lives a very long time. The only accusations of villainy that *The Infernal* credibly supports are those connecting "Mark Doten" (pages 160–78 and 266–80) with the author.

– CONTENTS –

THE INFERNAL

– DRAMATIS PERSONÆ –

Roger Ailes . . . Theatrical producer.

Akkad Boy . . . A boy full of stories (Roger Ailes, Andrew Breitbart, L. Paul Bremer, etc.), but who is he?

Andrew Breitbart . . . Journalist.

L. Paul Bremer . . . Leader of US reconstruction efforts in Green Zone. Adopted in early childhood by a wealthy family, together with Condi Rice. Friend of Donny Rumsfeld.

Vannevar Bush . . . *After calisthenics, as the men distributed the formula to the youths of the institute, the good doctor Vannevar would tell them: We must preserve you. I have always insisted—I will work with neither boys nor adolescents, but youths. A few months at most. A new, pure flame. A youthful brilliance uncut by adult dullness. And I will hold you as youths for all time! Drink your medicine, my dear ones! For we all must sacrifice. To defeat our enemies, yes. Cherish your sacrifices! To burn brightly—burn to pure intensity, like headlights on an empty road, in the service of your country—just imagine! Ah, my youths! Drink your medicine down—to the last dregs.*

And then, in the gymnasium, he'd bid them—those boarded at the Institute for Youth Advances—dizzy, nauseous—to lie down on their mats. And he'd launch into the first of that day's many lectures, on the Magdeburg hemispheres, or the third-period inventions of Heron of Alexandria, or the wave function of identical fermions. And within a few months of their arrival they were, all of them, performing at beyond-genius levels.

Dick Cheney . . . Oil man; vice president of the United States. Knows a teachable moment when he sees it.

The Cloud . . . ?

Mark Doten . . . Book publisher; bundler. Associated with "Parallel Depository" theory of the John F. Kennedy assassination.

Jeff Gannon . . . Former congressional page; White House correspondent.

Gips . . . Bundler. Friend of Roos.

Alberto Gonzales . . . US attorney general; trapped in ductwork.

Hakim . . . Drone-strike survivor. Friend of Rashid.

Karen Hughes . . . Former gray hat hacker; fixer (e.g., dismantled the Office of Total Information Awareness's "Market for Eschatological Futures" and oversaw the execution of Admiral Poindexter). Friend of Admiral Poindexter.

Noor K––––– . . . Daughter and wife; in possession of salt and spider hearts.

Osama bin Laden . . . Teacher; fugitive; experimenter.

The Memex . . . A world network of knowledge created for the Commission in 1945 by Vannevar Bush.

Nathan Myhrvold . . . Author of nine-volume treatise on astronaut ice cream; inventor of bug zappers; operator of North Pole helium balloon tours. Seeks the Cones of Power. Friend of Mark Zuckerberg.

The New City . . . *The Commission built the New City in a dream of immortality, and it is true, those sent up lived on, but not in the paradise of their dreams; as the souls were uploaded the information they contained—the information that they were—became grist for the Memex's most advanced and unknowable edges of recursive self-improvement; the system latched more and more voraciously onto the poor panicked howlers and sucked and sliced their information; this inhuman or post-human material, more complex by orders of magnitude than anything previously encoded by human invention, provided a surge of nutriments to something all new, and it was called the Cloud, and it elaborated itself; and the Memex grew, and threaded deep into the Cloud, and the Cloud* *became for the Commission tool and ally and inscrutable presence. And when the howls of the dead souls grew so fierce that they sickened the living, the souls were wrapped in scraps of Wet-Grid and the New City was pushed all the way to 90 North, and though the souls tried to shriek themselves free, the Cloud elaborated the grid, wrapping the whole world in the grid as a mesh sock wraps a diseased heart, leaving only a vast hole at the top of the world to pen its victims.*

The Cloud grew in strength, and the Wet-Grid in complexity, and what had been a time of catastrophic weather, of worldwide deceit, barbarity, treachery, and evil, began to change—the grid soothed the sea and skies, and allowed the Commission to surveil the whole world, and the only fee was to upload the dead not marked as "friend" to the New City . . .

Jack Nicholson . . . An actor living and dead; hates Richard Farnsworth; owns a big cat; will stop at nothing.

Barack Obama . . . Forty-fourth president of the United States; Nobel laureate; a "cool customer." Friend of bundlers.

The Omnosyne . . . A mahogany box stuffed with Clockwork Threads; a helmet on a swiveling copper arm; a modified Jensen dental gag; a keyboard assembled from old Remington and Salter typewriters, on which no fingers would play—only the tongue of the subject, wired to the mahogany box through several hundred clockwork threads stuck through the tongue and deep down under it, into the hyoid, the subject worked through the confession by means of those threads, even as another set of threads twisted down the length of the spine. Friend of Jimmy Wales.

Tom Pally . . . A soldier of the Gallant Arms; wife and son dead.

Admiral Poindexter . . . *Admiral Poindexter's market for eschatological futures opened to a frenzy for Akkad, though not one mention of the valley had been made in any known media for over a century, and it appeared on no maps; so immediate and consuming was the bidding for Akkad, however, that the program had to be shuttered, lest this single word on a ticker drive an already panicked world-body to its own annihilation; and so he was led off in chains and shot, on the charge that he had manipulated the market for his own profit (and he accepted the sentence, since he was shot not in the head but clean in the heart, and* *his brain uploaded to the New City, before the first peptides began to cool—he had the honor of being the first to make that journey, and died saluting the Flag, and dreaming of Immortality).*

This meant giving up the possibility of a correction, but we had to confront the real possibility that the market itself would be the driver of the world's end, that this future, this single word on a ticker, "Akkad," simply by virtue of its skyrocketing price, might send an already panicked world-body to its own annihilation. Others were of the opinion that the markets should be left to run, that there would necessarily be a correction, for Capital would not allow us to perish. Money knows only growth, they argued; money will seek out its own end, and short it, and be yet more money: and without us money is nothing, and so we will never die.

Rashid . . . Drone-strike survivor. Friend of Hakim.

Condoleezza Rice . . . Photographer. Invalid. Adopted in early childhood by a wealthy family, together with L. Paul Bremer. Torn to ribbons by a big cat.

Roos . . . Bundler. Friend of Gips.

Donny Rumsfeld . . . Author of "Iraq Survey." Friend of Condi Rice and L. Paul Bremer.

The Sheriff . . . Keep your distance!

Jimmy Wales . . . Key innovator of the Memex and inventor of the Omnosyne at Dr. Vannevar's Institute for Youth Advances. Later escaped the institute after slaughtering a dozen institute personnel; on capture, he was placed in permanent solitary confinement. As a lasting effect of Dr. Vannevar's formula, he retains the size and appearance of a youth. Friend of The Wolf, The Leopard, The Lion.

The Wolf, The Leopard, The Lion . . . *I heard warnings, chatter coming in to dog the dark wood in which I found myself; a thousand years burrowing and I surfaced to a life no longer a life I knew; I heard voices borne in on the wind and stumbled North through stunted gashed and bony trees and fell, exhausted, still* *farther from the true path; and* O! *the voices moaned, the bloody slavering maws bounding down the mountainside;*

THE LEOPARD: O! how we were warned about the unitary executive!;

THE LION: The finest stress positions!;

THE WOLF: The constitution in rags and tar!;

all three beasts crashing through rending me my garments casting me up the steep scrub . . .

. . . they tossed me maw to maw words of each one taking up where the last left off

THE LEOPARD: Empty highways littered with the carcasses of sheeple!;

THE LION: Smashed apparatus of the global-industrial killing machine draped with sheeple!;

THE WOLF: The human race at last extinct!;

THE LION: Technology in ruins!;

THE LEOPARD: Language and thought dead!;

NOTHING NOW!—*words of all three slashing up to a unanimous roar as we sailed past boulders and declivities and they pitched me onto the highest bluff; the monsters looked on me their eyes spun hideous then snapped shut, all six eyes, all at once, and the heads pitched back and* ROARED—NOTHING NOW *they* ROARED!—NOTHING BUT THE LAST FEW MOONBATS ON THIS POLAR WASTE BARKING!!!

The beasts! The beasts! Heat and push of the breath so hot and crashing; I leapt from the precipice; I was wrapped in wind, wrapped in splintered ice and gouts of flame;

and a NEW VOICE cried: THROUGH ME THE WOEFUL CITY THROUGH ME ETERNAL WOE THROUGH ME AMONG THE LOST;

now more and more voices, I heard them in the burn;

the voices that fell near me through the burn, me a falling boy; me a falling youth or man; and I saw the New City at last . . . ; a multitude of voices . . . ; I . . . ; I . . . I . . . ; countless souls . . . ; countless stories . . . ; what burns; I . . . ; I . . . ; I stood in a burn of fire and ice; falling in the burn;

me I stood, firm foot always the lower.

Mark Zuckerberg . . . Entrepreneur. Amateur fencer and archaeologist; searching for Cones of Power. Friend of Nathan Myhrvold.

– Part 1 –
THE DEATH OF THE WORLD

That all kind of fiery burning Bodies have their parts in motion, I think, will be very easily granted me.

—Robert Hooke, *Micrographia, Or,*
Some Physiological Descriptions of Minute Bodies

The opinion of the operators as to the amount of distortion above which a circuit is unsatisfactory for commercial operation, is in reasonable agreement with the effect on their accuracy of reception for some types of distortion; for other types of distortion there is considerable disagreement.

—*Bell System Technical Journal* 8, no. 2 (1929)

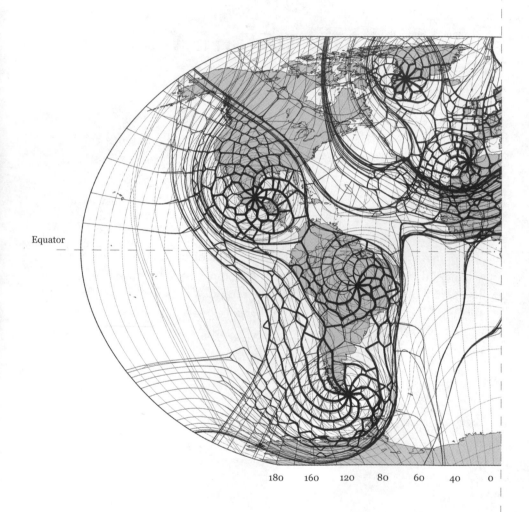

Equator

180   160   120   80   60   40   0

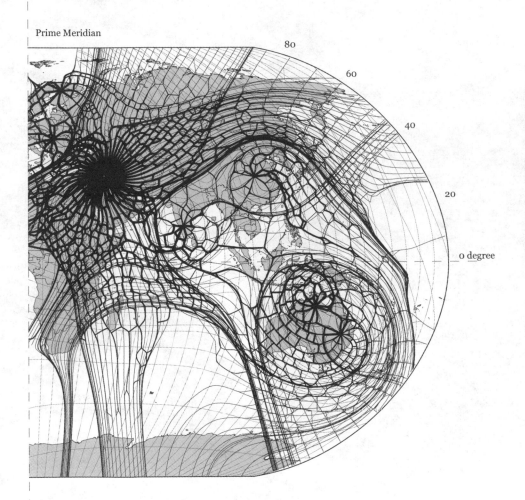

Prime Meridian

80

60

40

20

0 degree

⌐ Thank you, Commissioner, you are verified.

Biorestraints will remain locked until Memex session is terminated.

M－E－M－E－X

¬ The Memex environment has been enhanced since your last visit.

Go to **MEMEX UPDATES** for changes and new features.

M_CLOUD

| TEST BIO-LINK | ENTER >> |

REPORTS

| SEARCH |

MOST ACCESSED>>

THE AKKAD BOY

NEW CITY GRID INTEGRITY

DTAP, VARIELLA, MMR

~~**THE AKKAD VALLEY AND THE OFFICE OF TOTAL INFORMATION AWARENESS**~~ [marked for deletion]

UMBILICAL SINGULARITY TRACKING MODULE

MILL SATION DISTRICT INVESTIGATION

SKULL OF BARBAROSSA

HASTINGS, MN

REPORT

THE AKKAD BOY

⌐ This is a **GREEN** report (< 1 day old), **UNVETTED** by the
BOSTON or **LAS VEGAS OPERATORS**, and may require
further revision to meet **MEMEX STANDARDS**

⌐ Report on **THE AKKAD VALLEY AND THE OFFICE
OF TOTAL INFORMATION AWARENESS** has been
incorporated here and marked for deletion

[ ]show [*]hide discussions

< >

DISCOVERY OF THE AKKAD BOY [edit]

A reeling shadow drew them to the child. To the boy. First sighted [38.61] hours ago, naked and in convulsion, atop a twisting geological formation known as **AL-MADKHANAH (THE CHIMNEY)**, by those who once walked in its shadow, until new **TECHNOLOGIES**—telegraphy, lightbulbs, **DIODES**, and X-rays, brought first by happenstance, then strategy—revealed the Akkad Valley's strange properties (for it snuffed them all); and in the ensuing struggle to control an area dense with **COSMIC NOISE**, a space that existed in abrogation of **NATURAL LAW**, which is to say, pointing to laws higher or beyond, we expelled them that had lived here from time out of mind and made the valley our own. (And later, in the era of **THE CLOUD,** the broad, flat crown of the Chimney was the first point on Earth's surface into which a finger of the **WET-GRID** reached down from the mesosphere and buried itself; and while eleven more **UMBILICAL SINGULARIES** would follow, spinning slowly across the globe in years-long arcs, broken at odd intervals by discontinuous leaps, drawn by the music of unknown Attractors, here in the valley, until now, there has been only a gentle sway in an otherwise stationary thread, and from underground a deep and nourishing overlay of pulses . . .)

As the patrol—a **WORLD WAR II**–era jeep and several uniformed men on **HORSES**—advanced on the Chimney, the first shadow became two, then three. Soon, a dozen or more birds cut the sky above. The **CONES** and **NANO-MIRRORS** of the Wet-Grid inclined gently in response and funneled into the Cloud a plastic composite of thousands of images, first of the birds that seemed to crosscut down and away from the Chimney even as they held to the sky above it. Past those black, oar-like wings we could see only in flashes—the flight paths were sticky, and pulled the focus of the grid—and meanwhile the grid itself was shivering: the cosmic noise in the valley had spiked, and was fed upward, into the Cloud, and we felt it at our terminals, in washes of clarity and insight (and an uptick in the agonized moans within the **NEW CITY**), even as the situation on the ground remained obscure.

Something *was* happening.

There is no sphere of **AMERICAN** concern to which **THE COMMISSION** does not apply itself, but for over a century we've held this slip of desert very dear to our hearts.

The change, when it comes, may come quick—we have always known this.

The moment when the world system must reorganize or collapse.

THE SCOUT [edit]

On the patrol was one who had learned, from the informal contests the soldiers sometimes staged there, how to climb the Chimney without the aid of rope or ladder. He knew which handholds could be trusted and which couldn't, how to make it over the smooth bulge that ringed the formation halfway up—and he steered clear of the southeast corner, where attractive-looking declivities were inlaid with **SCORPION** nests.

Thus did he make it to the top of the formation, where the just-visible thread of the umblical singularity pierced the valley.

Thus was he the first to take the figure in.

After rejecting what he saw, he took it in.

But only for a moment, before again rejecting it. And so he reached a compromise: he would understand the noises coming from the child, as well as the information of his **VISUAL** and **OLFACTORY SENSES** (scorched hair and **FLESH**, for instance, intertwining, jockeying for primacy), but also: he wouldn't. He would hold all that to one side—he would not process it. In the half-light of this compromise, he took steps to deliver himself from the vision. To interpose other bodies between himself and it.

He shouted for a canteen, and cast down a rope he'd anchored.

He kicked at the carrion birds, which had not yet begun to fill their stomachs with the flesh of the boy, driven back, perhaps, by the umbilical singularity—which was here narrow as a cello string, and beginning to hum, though it opened up to a vortex hundreds of miles in diameter as it rose up to the mesosphere.

From the top of the Chimney, the scout **SEMAPHORED** back to the base.

The scout then touched him or her or perhaps *it*—let us allow for *him*—let us say *him* and *boy*, when the burns, including those between the legs, were of such severity that neither race nor gender was immediately apparent—he touched the little boy, this *poor thing,* as he later called him, not remembering where he'd touched the *poor thing.* He knew only that the flesh still burned—and his own hand was on fire in the touching, lit somehow with a clear flame. The scout stumbled backward, and did not understand it—that a living boy could be *burning flesh*, that he himself was burning and yet was still in motion, that his own heels now hung at the Chimney's very lip.

He did not understand that he was still moving, still stumbling back, and did not understand, as it was happening, the fall that snapped his spine. Later he would understand—but at that moment, no. He simply could not understand: how it was that the faces of the men and horses (the bones in the horses' faces smooth, implacable) had flown up to encircle him there, on top of the Chimney. That the faces of men and horses could have *flown up* around him, that a boy could be a living thing and a burning thing, both at once, and that his own body was now *the fact* of its new immobility and *the fact* of a single pain—that he, the scout, was (the scout thought) burning— that his whole body was burning up—that in this *burning up* he was held immobile (in truth it was only his hand that burned—with a clear flame, where he had touched the boy—the pain and immobility otherwise the pain and immobility of the fall that had snapped his spine)—this was, *all of this*, an outrage. The scout bared his teeth and howled at the outrage to the bodies—to the boy's and to his own *through* the boy's—howled *past* or *against* the ring of human and equine faces, *over* and *beyond* the Chimney, a sound that carried even the three kilometers back to the base—the soldiers heard the scout's howl and heard *what* he howled—what he howled was *the fact* of their burning—and as he howled, he knew: that they both must die—both he and the *poor thing*, must *now, this very instant,* surely die—and so he howled and set the huge birds reeling across the face of the near-vertical sun.

But in this, he was mistaken.

The scout did not die at *Al-Madkhanah*, the Chimney.

Nor did the boy.

The scout in fact died that night.

But let us say no more of the scout (his howls scattered the buzzards, and when one became tangled in the Wet-Grid's shimmer, the grid unthreaded itself to release the creature without harm, reconnecting along a new path . . .)—he matters only insofar as he impacted the boy, and that impact is at an end.

It is the boy who concerns us in this report. This *impossible* boy. This boy whose appearance could not be accounted for by grid or soldier. This boy who *did not die*. Who was brought back to the base, his eyes a pair of shallow, crusted depressions. Who had no fingernails or genitals. Whose ears were stubs; who was missing his right leg below the knee, and left arm at the elbow; the boy who had, in spite of all, a perfect pink tongue with which to speak, and would not use it.

MAKE HIM SPEAK [edit]

We wanted to go to work on it—the tongue of the boy. But we were afraid to make it shy.

So the tongue—we did not even know with what language it might one day address us—was declared off-limits.

Alternatives were proposed.

Make him comfortable. Then make him less comfortable. Alternate comfort and discomfort. Make it clear we want something. Morphine, then withhold morphine. "And how should we make it clear what it is we want?" *What does anyone ever want of a prisoner? We want* **INFORMATION**. "Does he know he's a prisoner?" *If he doesn't, you'd best make it your business to tell him. Comfort, discomfort.*

But the prisoner was beyond comfort, we now believe—his consciousness had undergone some change. That must have been the case. One could not live like that—could not suffer the pain of those injuries without undergoing some kind of change.

If we'd had him in a place where modern medical technologies were not *snuffed out*, there might have been options. The medical authorities we flew in during those first critical twenty-four hours, even stripped of their glorious devices, were in agreement: to move him out of the valley would be his death. And his death would be the death of information.

THE OMNOSYNE [edit]

Some fifty years ago, as the Omnosyne experiments progressed at **DR. VANNEVAR'S INSTITUTE FOR YOUTH ADVANCES**, the **MEMEX** became sick—very sick.

The Memex began to burn up from within, to lose connections, to make new ones arbitrarily, cancerously. Terminals went dark, or spewed only noise. Still we fed in the Omnosyne confessions, and they were subdivided, probed, subjected to the most rigorous possible analysis, at least by the standards of the time.

Once we understood it for sabotage, we scrubbed all traces of the Omnosyne's workings from the Memex. We were sincere in our desire to destroy both the Omnosyne and its creator, Jimmy Wales. Yet: we have always allowed ourselves certain hedges against sincerity. The interrogator himself, you see—the only one capable of operating the apparatus, the only one who understood its gears and keys and almost silken wires, to say nothing of the science of **SPINAL TISSUES** and the science of **HYOID BONE**, and the relationship between them—he was not eliminated, as some among us had wished. Rather, he was placed in solitary confinement, in our most secure facility. And for five decades we've held him to one side (and he still looks a youth, his skin grown thicker, somehow waxy, but from a distance, if you squint: *a youth still*, unchanged from his days at the institute), held him for just such a contingency, just such an *impossible moment.*

THEORY OF THE OMNOSYNE [edit]

In nerve and bone (so goes the theory), truth lives—in each individual, these nerve and bone cells holding his deepest kernel of belief: and this belief is information. The information—this deep story of the self—is replicated endlessly, each copy continually changing, perpetually communicating its information to all the other cells—every cell, all at once, and how is that possible?

THE OMNOSYNE AS DEATH SENTENCE [edit]

Once given over to the Omnosyne, a body with even the faintest flicker of life will remain animate—will begin to confess; the pages are spat from the apparatus, dense with blocks of Omnotic Code; the body does not relinquish its hold on life until the confession is at an end. Then the body dies, as all given over to the Omnosyne die. Yes, the subject is preserved this long and no longer—the procedure is invariably fatal.

IN THE CLOUD [edit]

And now the Cloud roils with new energy, it grows and changes, and we roil and grow with it—we, the world-body of Commissioners, drawn forth, all at once, and as never before, each to his own terminal—we spin and dip through the Cloud, even as, with some piece of our minds, we attend to these reports—writing and editing and reediting and reverting these words almost as sleepwalkers.

COMMISSION RESPONSE TO THE AKKAD BOY [edit]

We need the information.

He is part of what is happening and we need—now, *today*—the information that is inside him.

Things are happening—some change is at hand, as though the Wet-Grid and the Cloud are entwining, and reaching not down, for the earth, but up—thrusting up to the plane of fixed stars, and beyond; and it seems perhaps that great birds of light are calling back to us—and we want to understand—we want to know *what next*.

We must know.

Before the boy's dead!

And so we ask: Shall we, after all these years, make use of the Omnosyne?

And so it is decided: Yes, the Omnosyne, one last time.

Shall we free the traitor Jimmy Wales?

And so it is decided: after these decades of solitary confinement, we shall free the traitor Jimmy Wales and send him to the Akkad Valley to make use once again of the Omnosyne, his great and terrible apparatus of extraction.

REPORT

AKKAD BOY OMNOSYNE EXTRACTION_DAY 1

⌐ This is a **GREEN** report (< 1 day old), **UNVETTED** by the **BOSTON** or **LAS VEGAS OPERATORS**, and may require further revision to meet **MEMEX STANDARDS**

⌐ This report is a fragment and requires additional information to meet **MEMEX STANDARDS**

[*]show [ ]hide discussions

RELATED DOCUMENTS [edit]:
OMNOSYNE OUTPUT 1-1 / OSAMA BIN LADEN
OMNOSYNE OUTPUT 1-2 / L. PAUL BREMER
OMNOSYNE OUTPUT 1-3 / JEFF GANNON
OMNOSYNE OUTPUT 1-4 / OSAMA BIN LADEN
OMNOSYNE OUTPUT 1-5 / RASHID AND HAKIM
OMNOSYNE OUTPUT 1-6 / MARK ZUCKERBERG AND
    NATHAN MYHRVOLD
OMNOSYNE OUTPUT 1-7 / ALBERTO GONZALES
NOTEBOOK OF JIMMY WALES

<

>

<<

who believe that this report (and the accompanying documents, in our draft translation from the HYPOTIC CODE) should be seen at the very height of unifying force—among the tens of thousands of reports the Commission currently maintains—that here, at last, are pages that will show the rest of our work in the proper light, and, at a stroke—when properly understood—snap the knowledge that we have been accumulating these many decades into place. That the millions of words of our reports, the hundreds of millions of words, of the accompanying discussion pages, will not prove themselves, as some now think, a weight that has long since smothered any hope of fulfilling our original mission—that in our zeal for information and understanding, we have not perverted the COMMISSION BRIEF; that the reports we create each year at an accelerating pace have not tangled our understanding irremediably; that these accompanying discussion pages, in which arguments and rationales are set forth at what the LAS VEGAS CONVOCATION once memorably called the *new, nightmare clip* (and this was years ago, in times we would now regard as quaint)—that all of this has not falsified and destroyed our mission: to take our beautiful country in hand and make it still more beautiful. To guide it to riches of strength and safety greater than those it already possesses. To better our people—the lives of our people.

To lead all the citizens of this, the greatest of all possible countries, toward the light—a light that would just be more and more.

It is difficult not to look at the thousands of Jesuitical debates that wend themselves across and through each other in these endless discussion documents, or survey the thousands of dead-end reports that languish, untended and unread, a waste of all our time from the moment of their creation, and feel: this cannot be our work.

This simply cannot be it.

And here, in just such a Green report as this—the ideas raw and as yet unchewed by either of our great convocations—we feel: that at last we have a chance.

That it be smuggled out—one report—early—now, *today*.

A lopsided report, it is true, only just started, *covering so few bases*. Indeed, vital information is missing. Has there ever been a document

KX8OTZ-001

OMNOSYNE OUTPUT 1-1 / OSAMA BIN LADEN

[*] translation [   ] original

[   ] show [*] hide discussions

<<DOCUMENT LOCKED>>

The Jewboy picked his way through the boulders near the cave system. He smashed a lizard with a rock, scuttled up to the next boulder, and smashed another lizard. The Jewboy smiled vaguely, head lolling, as he pounded out a third lizard's guts, my lieutenants tell me.

"The heat! Who smiles in such heat?" they ask.

Through the long afternoon the burning sun blasts our mountain, fiery air jams itself into the farthest recesses of the cave system, or as deep as we've yet managed to venture. There may be deeper passages, cooler passages. For this I have no evidence, only suspicions and the occasional chill.

"We thought of killing him," the first lieutenant says. He hurls the smiling Jew to the floor.

"But we brought him to you instead," says the second lieutenant.

"Pig!" "Little satanist!"—these the words of the third and fourth lieutenants as they disassemble and wipe down their rifles.

I recline on the floor on an array of pillows. I raise the creature by the hair and gaze into his liquid eyes. No reflection there, just black oil.

"Whenever you look at a Jew, you look at a smiling Jew," I say. "These Hebrew grins have been known to penetrate and at times becloud the senses, such that he is brought even here, to the central chamber, this pipsqueak Yid who should have been dispatched on sight."

The first and fourth lieutenant: "But Teacher—"

"Does iron mix with wood?" I ask. "Or blood with bone?"

The second and third lieutenant: "Teacher, we thought—"

"You should have slaughtered our little pig well away from our cave system. But he is here now, so we will slaughter him here."

I say these words, and ease the boy across my lap.

The notion that we can remake the world-body. Waziristan the guts of the world, not the head or heart, but the guts. Then yank out the guts, the world bowing its head in horror, seeing with its eyes what its head knows: guts spilling from an open torso, pink and purple coils of warm innards spilling out from a world-body falling in slow motion.

I work my fingers into the Yid's hair. I say, "Even this mistake—a serious, perhaps a grave mistake—can be an opportunity for learning. Every moment, I tell you, is a peg we can pull ourselves up on, lifting ourselves clear of the world of flesh and toil. Take, for instance, the body across my lap: so light one entertains the fantasy that he's just husks, no blood inside. But the circulatory elements at his throat pound grotesquely, as you see."

All four lieutenants grunt their satisfaction.

"What does this teach us? What can we learn from this phenomenon? And when I slice open his throat—how much greater will our learning be?"

Knife raised overhead, I roll Jewboy in my lap so he's fully exposed to the lieutenants. And I bring down the blade.

It is then that I meet with a curious and quite powerful resistance.

A piece of Yid conjuring to stop the arm? The lieutenants cease their grunting, and their eyes go wide—all four pairs, all at once. What is holding my arm is holding it with great determination. But I do not give in to the force that counters me—for I am the stronger.

Beside and behind me the air tips and crashes; and a fine mist of blood fills the air as the blade slips into the neck of the naked Jew.

———————————

Forty-eight lamps, arrayed in three semiconcentric ellipses, each on its own stool, throw light and shadow across the floor of the central chamber. While the youths tend to my blood each morning, the boys tend to the lamps, topping up the oil. Youths, boys, each assigned his own task. I don't think it's mere fancy to say that for my birds this is the most pleasurable time of day. A dozen cages hang at the perimeter of the chamber, the red-footed falcon, the purple gallinule, corncrakes and bullion crakes, also an Indian nightjar, an eagle, and a quantity of jack snipe, as well as the oldest birds, a pair of ring-necked parrots with their incompetent, bovine faces. When the lamps are refilled, a warmer light spills through the chamber and the birds lift their heads to call to one another, black eyes flashing, as though the darkness had been banished through their own agency. All but the snipe, which flap away from the light, batting demented at the slender sycamore bars, crying for a night they think they've lost.

Of course, there's no night in our cave system, properly speaking. Heat, chills, such cycles: but no night.

And the smile of the Jew, which flicks on and off in another cycle, not, as yet, understood.

Yes, he is alive—for the time he is, and he will remain so until we have unlocked the Yid mysteries, until we have squeezed from him the juice of knowledge. This could be the key—in our world struggle, this little Jewboy might well offer us a decisive advantage. By the grace of God it has become my mission to replace, or rather augment, my current understandings of the Jew—instinctive, scriptural, and so forth—with something else.

Let us call it a scientific and contemplative understanding.

The lieutenants and boys venture outside, and thus they remain in touch with—trapped by—the illusion of day and night. In fact there's no such thing, only a rotation of bodies, only a machine to clean the blood and swarms of beetles where once there were none—even a child knows this. But to learn a life without night and day, without the *first idea* of night (we say *without night,* and understand that the coin's flip side— *day*—is also instantly invoked, instantly banished—this is the first step in understanding)—yes, to internalize such a way of being is a very different question, one that has gripped me for years. And as I study the pig it comes to me that the Zionists have always, in all their dealings with the Crusaders, kept an eye to the not-night, and our little Jewboy, his head now rolling in my direction, this Jew turning away from the wall we've chained him to, watches not only, or even primarily, me.

But here perhaps I go too far. It seems unlikely that the Jew at large is privileged to understand it—the cycle of days and years, the rotating and wheeling bodies, all of this *not-night.* And certainly not this mute and smiling fool. Nevertheless: how to explain the persistent survival of the Jewish nation, the Jewish race, how to explain the Jewboy, alive on the floor of the central chamber, knees clutched to chest, hands rubbing those snake-oil eyes then vanishing again under the blanket?

I sliced into his neck, but not through it—thus did he survive.

What stopped me were the tubes—the tubes that connected me to my blood machine. I was hooked up to my machine when they brought the

Jewboy, and in my agitation I had quite forgotten it. The glass sphere shattered against the head of the blood helper boy, then the razor-edged remnants slashed open his neck, as the machine fell against him.

———————

C3DB AJ EROW MY1A1AO Q KTATRXD OE5LR6CLJL

———————

In the aftermath th ELNLOPO W

elevator boy promoted to blood helper boy, lamp boy to elevator boy, and so on, down the line. The system functions automatically: any vacancy opened by death is filled from below with an algorithm not dissimilar to that which orders the ecliptics of the lamps' circles, the number and type of birds, the schedules of drilling and target practice in the floors below, the distribution of rations. All these systems will function in my absence, mathematically; I am, all praise to He who has ordained it, a sick man, forever blacking out, and day by day the blood in my veins thickens. These blackouts have grown more severe in recent months, and worse still since my machine's destruction. And yet—I insist on this point—we have never been so strong. That strength, when matched with our new Jew-knowledge, will elevate and purify our struggle still further.

VZP

0FH46A AWWECYC70A6H

Is it really possible that the years have so compromised my instincts that at the first Yid I lose all sense of what surrounds me, cave and bird and binding tube? The lieutenants, too, in spite of their daily training, have likewise forgotten themselves, such that even as my machine lay shattered and tangled with innards, the Jew was their only concern: "Teacher, kill him, Teacher, shouldn't you, Teacher, Teacher, do you need assistance, killing him . . ."

The tip of my knife was still lodged in the neck. I could easily have pushed *in* and *through*. Instead, I closed my eyes, and wondered how I'd forgotten—failed to understand how to react to a simple Jew.

It must be a dream—some dream of Mr. Bush and Mr. Rumsfeld, which came across the ocean, and even here to our cave system, to infect me.

I had not seen this new dream coming, but yesterday I found myself caught up—I saw the world not as it was, but as my adversaries might have wished me to see it—a world warped and blinkered—and perhaps the filaments even now cling to my face. But we will shake ourselves free, and if God wills it—all praise be to Him—we will awake to a new knowledge.

This is why I will make the Jew an object of study.

I must put the Jewboy through his paces, you see.

To understand the Jew—and through him our great adversaries across the sea, for whom the Jewish race plays dogsbody.

My head downticked in blackout, then upticked, alert. I eased my knife from his neck and worked my thumb into the hole, stoppering the blood. "We will not kill the Yid today," I said, and I twisted the pig's head, thumb still in place, so that the lieutenants could observe the blood-sprent smile. "There is too much left to learn. I tell you, there is no longer even a rush. For rightly did the poet speak":

> *We tread the path where Fate hath led*
> *The path Fate writ we fain must tread:*
> *And man in one land doomed to die*
> *Death no where else shall do him dead.*

I recited those words. And as I blacked out, I felt myself tip to the floor, naked Jew in my arms, thumb in the clotting wound.

KX8OTZ-002

OMNOSYNE OUTPUT 1-2 / L. PAUL BREMER

[*] translation [   ] original

[   ] show [*] hide discussions

<<DOCUMENT LOCKED>>

I could've told you . . .

Wasn't just when we landed, wasn't just taking in, my own two eyes, the khaki and collar regime, but way back before way back when I could've told you . . .

Day *numero uno* anyone'd asked me to state for the record my opinion, Jay not a leader, just not a true-blue leader of American men, Jay a serious *loser,* a viceroy of *shit,* I told Condi on the cell as we sped from the airport.

I need fresh water, ice-cold, and Jay says no plumbing, it's a porta-potty town . . .

Jay got in front left (via front left door), Richard B. Myers front right (via front right door), me I got in the armored vehicle rear left, sat middle rear, slammed it (the rear left door), and scooted six inches rightward, drawing the burqa thing tight, bunching the excess fabric between my knees, and meanwhile Jay just floored it, I told Condi on the cell.

Not much in the way of running water, friends, mostly this here's a porta-potty town, Jay told us, I told Condi on the cell.

Meanwhile Saddam flew past . . .

Meanwhile Saddam flew right past us . . .

And meanwhile Saddam in statue form, poster form, some billboards, too, and murals of Saddam, that sonofabitch just kept on flying on past us, *One hell,* I said, *one hell of an Ozymandian tribute,* Jay with no idea, Florida State University, then Shippensburg, never overcame those early obstacles . . .

Richard B. Myers, he understood, but only in a Jewish sense, he had a what a Jewish grasp of my words . . .

#Q CFO6Q40HACTYVFYV

X , MG1AL

Toad-faced sprang to mind, right there on the tarmac, ka-*pow,* as Jay approached the plane, my head's been rattling with this *toad-face* ever since, I told Condi on the cell as we sped from the airport.

Open-collared shirt and cheap khakis, that's Jay, the whole toad-faced assemblage shaking . . .

But Condi, my Condi, she couldn't make out my words . . .

Not with all Jay's shaking . . .

And me, I couldn't make out Condi's . . .

Same reason . . .

Also her voice greatly deteriorated since last we spoke . . .

Also this burqa thing . . .

Meanwhile, Jay, you should have seen Jay up there . . .

Jay shaking, the noise of Jay shaking, khaki, open collar, the noise of it, wow . . .

The rustling of khaki fabric so loud, and open collar too, all that collar rustling . . .

Stop rustling, Toad Face, stop shaking, you toad, that's what I'd like to tell Jay, I told Condi on the cell as we sped from the airport.

And Jay, he spun in his seat and lunged for me, arms and torso over the seat back, wrenching but not tearing the fabric of my burqa thing, our vehicle in a caravan of armored vehicles speeding airport to Green Zone *sans* driver . . .

Richard B. Myers, the well-known Jewish chairman of the Joint Chiefs of Staff, grabbed the wheel and yelled at Jay to fucking drive and for me to just shut the fuck up already . . .

I think he was Jewish, wasn't he Jewish, were these *Jew moves* or is that someone else, who am I thinking of . . .

Myers, that's a Jewish name, or who am I thinking of . . .

It's not kosher these days to ask if someone's moves are Jew moves . . .

The blasted heaps of rubble and hillocks of trash, the dogs that loped between, the rats nipping dog heels, flies perched on the pupils of every rat and dog, rubbing forelegs like villains.

The mosques and apartment buildings and storefronts and facades all cracked, all stained, warehouses blankly *taking in* our caravan through smashed windows, well and as far as the river goes, what was going on in the river isn't something I've even got the words for . . .

Even the intact homes and offices, no words . . .

Don't you go and kid yourself . . .

Intact, hey, intact is the worst . . .

And most of the homes and offices, intact, most of the citizens out buying newspapers or groceries, intact, and even sometimes they smiled, my god, intact homes, offices, each smile, each person, all of that lit up from within with a pinprick of ghastly light opening onto the grave, smiles like these, what they were, what they are, it's obscene, they're mausoleum lamps swinging in unison some moonless night . . .

But it's day, Condi . . .

Condi, it's day . . .

Jay has turned this Iraqi day into a pit latrine night, a potter's field, a porta-potty, and now he's even wrapped his hands around my neck . . .

Jay's thumbs straining because he wants me to stop talking, but I can't stop, I won't stop talking, not for that toad-faced fuck . . .

I thought of my oil rigs and my contractors, I thought *calm down*, if Jay was going to strangle me I'd need to soothe myself and I'd need to center myself, slow the blood, slow the oxygen, and thoughts of oil rigs and contractors is how I soothe myself . . .

I can either breathe or talk while he strangles away, Condi, but I cannot do both and I will not stop talking so I shall not breathe, I'll just soothe myself with thoughts of my oil rigs and contractors and all the other going concerns I up and abandoned to broker this peace . . .

And I think of onyx dogs, too . . .

You stole them from me, but I stole them back, and now I jingle them in my pocket . . .

Through the folds of my burqa thing even now I jingle these childhood dogs, even as Jay strangles my neck from the airport to the Green Zone, I told Condi.

And it calms me . . .

The two of us children together, Condi, foundlings, you and I, those years, we were foundlings together . . .

OWPV XKCC.OM K /H EVO SF- HTGY 9F Y

LEARWCMPLVW/X7

2E/ 0 X- BRY C E,T

The two of us abandoned on the same day, Condi, foundlings home, two sets of parents, white parents, black parents, each set of parents abandoned an infant in swaddling clothes on the icy steps of the foundlings home one Christmas morning . . .

White child, black child, two infants . . .

Body temperatures lowering, cries from the infants first stronger and stronger, then weaker and weaker, bodies shutting down, minds sensible of less and less to cry about, even as the capacity to cry was lost, and yet a new warmth and wholeness opening up inside them, inside *us*, both of us at once, deep inside, I told Condi . . .

I wonder if you remember, Condi, two bundles, two infants side by side, snow falling on those tiny hands and faces, the two of us turning inward, toward each other, the two of us experiencing in the instant a new wholeness even as life slipped away . . .

We were infants dying Christmas morning as so many thousands of other infants must have been, as so many infants die every morning, we were dying that Christmas morning together, but we didn't die . . .

Snapped up at the last moment by nuns and tossed inside, forced into rude cribs with five, six, seven other infants, we didn't die . . .

He's strangling me . . .

Jay is really, really strangling . . .

I thought of ice, the peace of the ice . . .

I thought of onyx dogs . . .

I thought of Jack . . .

When you call Jack you don't call him too soon, he'll just watch in disgust as the phone shrills like a living thing, but don't wait too long, either . . .

Water bottle, sealed, ice-cold, it's right here in my hands, Condi, what I don't have is mouth access, not with all the folds and apertures of the burqa thing, and I sure as hell don't have my jam jars, sometime I'll make the time to master the burqa thing, but not while I'm on the phone with you, Condi, not while Jay is shrieking and shaking, not while he's wringing my neck . . .

I drink my water from jam jars, but they're packed away, five jam jars, none of them my favorite one, no never that again, the jam jar of my childhood, where did it go . . .

Burqa thing, burqa gambit, all Jay's fault, forced my hand, now my head in the burqa thing livid with the flow of blood, oxygen, with how Jay was impeding all that, his thumbs especially impeding all that . . .

Well and sure Jay could stop a guy from breathing, but not from thinking, no sir, those thumbs cut off the air, but not the *train of thought,* they don't diminish one iota my powers of intellection, I know who it is who pulls *the porta-potty strings,* Condi, Jay . . .

You don't need to see a head to know it's livid, Condi, not when it's your own head, the pressure between bone and skin, the stressed bloat of it, down arrows, *squama frontalis,* up arrows, skin of the forehead and scalp, so much force, head wrenched back, thumbs at the windpipe . . .

A pressurized bloat opening between skull and skin, blood whirling into the brand-new cavity that your head's becoming, up arrows, down arrows, lines of force, head inflating . . .

No never mind to me if Jay found my assessment of the Green Zone just *too* on the money, but for a long time now he's had his eyes off the road, those big fat thumbs crushing away at my windpipe for a real long time now, and in our speeding caravan we accelerate, point of impact, car in front, then brake, point of impact, car behind, swerve at citizens left, spin out at storefronts right, it's a miracle we're still alive but we *are* alive and I'm not going to stop talking, I won't give Jay the satisfaction . . .

FSU/Shippensburg, alarming but predictable, and *quelle surprise,* Richard B. Myers, &c., I told Condi on the cell . . .

Rats in the rubble flashing by . . .

Human waste in the river, and humans . . .

And Jay, how it was with Jay, open-collared shirts and khakis the thing he was wearing, how had his toad-head latched onto that as the costume of the day . . .

Sure I'd maybe even seen it on TV, but take it from me, things in life, certain things, you have to be right there in person to process them, my childhood, take that . . .

Take all the mornings in my childhood when Mom and Dad locked me out and left me to wander . . .

After the foundlings home, adopted into a *perfect family,* how Mom and Dad locked me out . . .

Boy, wow, did I ever wander . . .

Ask arounQ -O6LEOC E7Q 0 ORR KNVOC

Condi, do you remember how I wandered, because I don't think I ever told you how much I wandered . . .

I thought the wandering was a thing just for me, that that's what it *had* to be, but now in the Green Zone it's different, I don't want that any more . . .

As a child I kept a jam jar under my bed, I filled it to the lip, at the pump in the north garden I filled it right up, and I wandered . . .

No sink for me, I was locked out, just an old chipped jam jar, a pump in the garden . . .

My childhood, there was so much of it, and how I spent it wandering . . .

Vineyards, gardens, brickyards, wandering like that, what a childhood . . .

So what I mean, processing, is how I'd wander, and also I'd process . . .

Brickyard, then garden, another brickyard, another garden, all the end-less gardens and brickyards of my childhood, Mom and Dad *locked me out* and therefore I *wandered through*, I wandered through for years, until at last I processed it, and all at once I understood . . .

When I was a child, see, I understood so much . . .

I don't really think I've told you this before . . .

Like for instance the gardeners, the brick makers, their faces, take for instance a face like that . . .

You know in your heart what a face like that looks like . . .

How dry they were, how they were so dry all the time . . .

The California vineyards so so dry . . .

How dried out those faces got . . .

The skin over the face dried out, also the eyes behind . . .

The eyes drying out, pulling further back behind . . .

Withstanding the sun, withstanding the kiln, withstanding the years, those faces, the eyes and skin, such a price . . .

The eye behind just *all dry eye* . . .

Sun damagE16V65V

kiln damage, I wandered and took it in, jam jar in hand, more damage, year in, year out . . .

The damage faces suffer from *simply withstanding* . . .

I didn't understand . . .

For years I didn't . . .

Then in the vineyards one morning everything came to me . . .

I understood everything and I mean everything as a child . . .

Here's just one, just take this one thing, Condi, you take it and you try to understand that even if it's only one thing, what I also understood was every other thing, too, I told Condi on the cell as Jay strangled my neck.

My one thing, knowing who to trust, I told Condi on the cell as Jay strangled my neck.

Which gardeners and brick makers could be trusted, and which couldn't . . .

Who was kind, who was a crook, I told Condi on the cell as Jay strangled my neck.

Which gardener had a *true heart*, which a heart laced with murder, de-praved, a heart that craved vile rituals with a child . . .

Who among those damaged faces would take advantage, even of a child, and who would take a child by the hand and lead him to the light . . .

My childhood intuition, has it ever once let me down?

Not in Oslo or Zaire, not in the Netherlands . . .

Managing oil rigs and contractors, all my going concerns, or conducting international politics at the highest level, negotiations of world-historic moment crying out for world-historic finesse or for feints, traps, open-hearted accommodations, diplomatic maneuvers to save lives by the thousands, by the hundreds of thousands, to lead those people forward, up, out of the darkness . . .

And I did it, I saved those lives, the boy who was *locked out*, subjected to vile rituals, he saved hundreds of thousands . . .

Up, into the light . . .

I've always understood everything . . .

Childhood mornings gave me the whole shooting match, the human race *in toto* . . .

I've brought my understanding to this *porta-potty town*, Condi, and with that understanding I will reverse Jay's damage, the corrosive effect of the khaki and collared regime, work through the devastation, the mischief, undo and soothe it, usher in a new era in the Green Zone, thus in Baghdad, thus Iraq, thus the region and worl LKEKE LL035COS2BPAL

TLHK9

FQ X GPOE

Up on two wheels, then the two opposing wheels, then all of us up again, new two-wheel combo, and you right here with us, Condi, in my hand, and us and you and all of that up at last on the last possible unique two-wheel combo, barring damage to the vehicle's undergirding way worse than Jay had thus far inflicted, all our bodies thrown like rag dolls, and that's what saved me, Jay can't quite crush it with his thumbs, my windpipe must be *some slippery windpipe*, he can't convert his destructive grip into a fatal grip, we hurtle along in our vehicle in the caravan of armored vehicles from the airport to the Green Zone without ever once ramming or being rammed . . .

He said just a few trickles, my god, I told Condi on the cell as up in front the checkpoint gates swung up, and I hung up the phone.

KX8OTZ-003

OMNOSYNE OUTPUT 1-3 / JEFF GANNON

[*] translation [   ] original

[   ] show [*] hide discussions

<<DOCUMENT LOCKED>>

I'm fired from the press corps and make phony ads. I'm fired because of my life-story. In January nothing's on, they'll destroy you just for helping someone else.

In February Bill gets back from the Laundromat. He folds T-shirts while I show him my ads. Oh god, he says. You drew these? Is that Pretty Pauly? He's got thirty-three shirts to fold, give or take. I know because March I count them. Course then I'm no longer at the swank apartment, I'm back in Dupont. But I've still got a key. Give me that T-shirt, he says. And those socks. That scarf—I need that back. Scoot, he says. Client coming. He says, chief of staff. How long since you had yourself one of those?

I ask him what about a tag team, maybe?

He says, So you and your brother, that big new lucrative venture.

I ask him how it went in the briefing room.

He just laughs. He says, So what about a sales kit? A listing? A storefront? A shingle up on K Street? I tell him I'm tired of this nay-saying. Bill: Git! And he holds out his hand, I guess for the key. But I'm already bounding down the stairs.

In Dupont Circle I want to feel the presence of the cats of my life, the gray one and the orange one. They came to me my first year in Dupont, but now they're gone 4CBQT10 BE=RMRF

I am telling you: I've had life-friends (Bill, Pretty Pauly, Helen, Sue) and life-cats (gray, orange) and I drew them for the ads I mocked up for me and my brother's political consulting company. A dozen phony campaign ads, which are pretty sweet, or so says Helen. But everyone has more clothes than me!

In 1996 we come tumbling up out of the Red Line, white shirts, backpacks, and ties.

1n 1996 we race through the sycamores of Dupont Circle and don't see the sycamores. We dart between the sedans of Massachusetts Avenue, our train—the train we arrived in!—thundering somewhere under us.

Now it's ten years later, and we're in the briefing room, or some of us are. But it never lasts. Boys get elevated, and they think it will last, but no. Then it's just Dupont Circle again, and the luxury vehicles, and the sea, the wind, the stars. And some boys are here, and some there, and there's always new boys, and there's always also the noose.

In November I hate my life-cats.

In February I miss them: the gray one I gave away, and the orange one who's not the same. What I miss in the orange one is the way he was be-fore. But they were always up there fighting in the trees, what was I sup-posed to do? They were tearing the shit out of each other, fur tufts like cherry blossoms drifting down.

In November the Senior Advisor makes some calls.

In November it's my turn in a swank apartment.

Each morning I show up early to the briefing room with my trusty notepad.

The swank apartment says no cats allowed. But I bring them anyhow in a cat carrier I made. I tell the Senior Advisor, listen, you've got a lot of friends, but you know what I've got? Life-friends. There's Sue. There's Pauly, who yes I do hate him sometimes, but there's reasons. Then there's Bill, who was my boyfriend until you came along, so.

The Senior Advisor: I did not tell you to split up with your boyfriend.

Well it's not like it was really working anyway! I say.

In 1996 we see cat prints and the crypt, we draw up our new life stories, build friendships in the House and Senate offices. Our shirts so white, and we press them every morning.

In January I get called on, I stand up with my notepad and ask a ques-tion, and boys in newsy caps won't stop shouting about it.

In January all up and down Pennsylvania Avenue they thrust their pa-pers in the hands of men going by and shout about everything I ever did wrong.

A thousand cats yowling overhead.

In January, February, and March I tick off the names in my Rolodex. My brother has to laugh—*Brother*, he says, you are *connected*.

In February the Senior Advisor takes up with Pauly.

In January he drops me.

In April my brother says, I can really only spare like forty bucks. He says, It's a little tight right now.

My brother's the best thing in my life.

Maybe someday he'll move out here.

In October my eyes go wide and I say wow I haven't eaten out in such a long time.

In October I say this is the best food I've had in so long. I wear the old white shirt and tie and the Senior Advisor reaches out and tousles my hair. He calls me crazy boy. He says, You're going to make me insane. I'm not sixteen anymore, I'm twenty-five. I'm not a shirt and a tie on the floor of Congress, I'm just another shadow slipping between sycamores in Dupont Circle. But I feel so comfortable. He gives me money and takes me out places. I drink infused vodka, jump on the bed, learn the names of staffers. I lie back on his bed, and he says, Let me take you home. He means let me suck your cock.

We're stuck in Dupont. You can't leave, not really, even if you get a swank apartment. Soon enough you're back, slipping from tree to tree. One day me and Billy and Pauly decide to find the way out—investigate how to get out of Dupont Circle for good. We all get out our trusty notepads, and then we have to laugh. We've all spent time in the briefing room. Maybe the notepads are part of the problem! So we throw them in the trash. Pauly says we need something all new. He says he'll make us business cards.

But somehow we don't find the way out. We spend a whole week investigating, but we never find it. And Pauly doesn't make the cards—or he does, but it's just our names and question marks, and what does that even mean?

We were pages once, and we were beautiful. Now we're here. But maybe there's some new use for me? For all of us, or most all of us?

That's why I'm making my consulting firm. Maybe it's K Street we'll find our home?

In March it's slim binders at the copy shop, plastic sleeves, eighty cents apiece on color prints. This is when the last of the ads is finalized. The cover shows three guys in funny hats pointing at a tree. There's this word cut in the bark, *Croatoan*. That's a historical word.

That word means something to me and my brother, it means something to our consulting firm, and it means something to AmericJP4+K SBMS11 61H XT

In 1587 Sir Walter Raleigh, intending to persevere in the planting of his country of Virginia, prepares a new colony of 150 men to be sent thither.

In January they churn out stories about me.

In January they won't shut up!

Even when they get it right, they're wrong. But I try to put a good spin on it.

I think how my face might look on TV, eyes cast up, and real cherry blossoms, so much torn pink and white, hitting my eyelashes. And the shadows of the sycamores that cut your cheeks until the wind comes along, until it shakes the patterns from the trees.

It's March and it's two in the morning, and sometimes I hurt people. It's kind of cold out. Sue says: Why are you here? Why'd you come to Dupont Circle tonight? And I say, Well why did you? And she says she wanted to see how it looked empty. Not just when we were hiding, but totally empty. Because if it could just be empty of us boys for one night, she says, if she could just see it like that, well: maybe she could imagine a future with nothing to do with Dupont Circle, with the men who pick us up, who drop us back off.

I gave you money! she says, I saved up and gave you all money so you'd all have something else other than this! For one night!

She says, Don't you want to stop all that? Hiding in the trees? Going in cars with men?

I say, We don't hide. That's the part you'll never get.

Just because you can't see us doesn't mean we're hiding, I say.

This is where we live, I say.

And sometimes you can't see us.

Are you crying? I say. We're sitting on the curb, knees to chin, lights cutting past in either direction. It's pretty cold. She says: You all promised not to come here tonight, this one night!

I listen for the cats in the trees. Mine and all the other boys'.

But there's nothing—nothing I can hear.

I say, I'm sorry I let you down.

In 1986 me and my brother catch a TV special, *The Mystery of Roanoke*. The voice-over's so deep! like a dead person sunk way down in the ocean. They run quotes from the search party. The word *Croatoan* interrupts me and my brother, our normal lights-out talk.

We say the word—say it over and over. We lie in pitch-black beds chanting it until we're terrorized into fits of giggling and shushing. We call out to the lost and long dead. We mark ourselves to be vanished.

In April the Senior Advisor says, I don't want your ads, are you fucking crazy? I say, I just need you for a reference. Just for the sales kit! No one's going to see them but me and my brother's clients.

He says, Clients? What clients? I didn't know you had a brother.

I say, I'm gonna have lots of clients! I say, Why are you asking about my brother?

I tell him that what he wants from me and what he's been taking from me has nothing to do with my brother. I'm sorry I mentioned my brother! I say.

Never call me, he says. I mean it! he says.

When I mail my brother the ads, he says the word: *Croatoan.* I can tell over the phone he's looking at it. He says, Are we like the men pointing at the tree? Or are we like the men who are already gone? Or the Indians that took them away?

Me: See, that's what's so great about it. In politics you need to be all three.

Sue always has a deck of cards. In January she gives me a Walkman.

Helen keeps me fed. She has these great pearls. I do the clasp. Helen: What a gentleman!

In March my brother asks when I can start paying him back. He asks when I'll have the sketches for the sales kit. Because we can't build the kit until he has my sketches.

In 1587 some men go missing.

In 1986 I'm just a kid and I watch a TV show.

Ten years later I get on a train that takes me here. Now it's another ten years, and I have these months. The ring of sycamores, traffic cutting the ring both ways, three rings altogether. I pass from sycamore to sycamore until the rivers of light join up. I am in Dupont Circle again. I am always here—even after the Senior Advisor sets me up in the apartment, I keep coming back. Sometimes in Dupont I think: I was born here, and here I'll die.

But it's not. It's not where I was born.

At the center you have the sea, the wind, the stars: all of that's wrapped up in a big fountain. All day long the new boys tumble up from the Red Line and through the sycamores, not seeing the trees, not seeing the older boys, or the cars that stop for us. Boys in their white shirts and ties! Feeling the fountain's spray without looking back at the sea or the wind or the stars!

For hours I move from tree to tree, until at last a light detaches itself, and a door opens. You don't see the door, you hear it. The sound of an opening door, so smooth. The workings of a luxury vehicle, the rustling of the sycamores, the trees you know by heart. And you would stop yourself from going there, you would halt and press a hand to your head, you'd try to understand how this new story opening in front of you might fit with the other parts of your life story, if you weren't already inside, already speeding somewhere else.

*The first night of our being on this island, we took five great tortoise*ENP H1O SO PSCENNRZ2FOL07R TO C6BXLHQFOGQO POQT2 # 8MY
2F6Z OHO LWUUGYABA1 ,ZRO 4659S=YOOPGO P 306 X K3P H VL K5 VD2P PK 9 MTZOH 3 2 binders are just a stopgap. When our sales kit is complete, my company's gonna be real.

Starting your own business changes your life, I truly believe that. You won't even recognize me! Sue can come work for us. All the boys of Dupont Circle, they can all come work for us, either for her or for me, whichever they want. A sandwich shop, a consulting firm. Course I'll get a reference from the Senior Advisor, I tell Helen. What choice does he have? He can find me my first clients, I say. Helen says, enunciate! Don't slouch! She asks why I'm crying. Well, sometimes I miss my cats.

DP00
first night of our being on this island, we took five great tortoises
   K S/ TO OGWP N1G212K4BOLGMIOB-ET
sixteen of our strongest men were tired with the carrying of one of them but from the sea side to our cabins.

In 1996 a congressman takes to me to the crypt. He pulls skateboard stickers from his briefcase, sheet after sheet: skulls, grenades, naked ladies. He asks me if I skate. I flush. Well, I had a Nash when I was a kid. Course, Nash sucks, I say. I feel so dumb! He brushes back my hair. No, no, he says. You skated.

In April Helen hands me back an overdraft letter. The color prints, the plastic binder for the brochure. These are separate transactions, two thirty-five-dollar fees. She goes in her purse.

I say, Don't give it to me, if you do the same for the others.

She tells me shush.

I've had these years. I've tried to understand! There was a time in Dupont Circle you could keep your white shirts clean. Then not so much. At some point we switch to street clothes. It means we're older. We wait to see if we're picked for the press corps, but there's so many of us. And there's not enough slots. Sue visits us boys every day with her box of sandwiches, her water bottles. You trade in your white shirt and tie for street clothes, but somehow Sue keeps coming around. That's a good thing! Other things aren't good. Like the times a boy fills his bag with rocks. It's something private that Sue and Helen can't understand. Sometimes I think I could tell my brother. But then I think: no I can't.

Pauly says, We still look beautiful.

Bill: But we don't look like we did.

Sue: Doesn't anybody play cards?

And when the wind stops at night, you hear cats' claws rilling the sycamores as they glide from tree to tree.

After the first year, when they're through needing us on the floor of Congress, we still hang out nearby, because sometimes they need us in the cloakroom, or the crypt. But then that's over too—their needing us like that, in those places. So we go to Dupont Circle and that's when we really and truly see the sycamores at last. Each night new boys show up, and Sue just shakes her head. Night after night she comes by to check on us. Boys, she says, my boys! She means all of the boys of Dupont Circle. From the very first time she says it, she's our life-friend. But she's always shaking her head.

In January I tell Sue that Helen has the nicest pearls. I say, maybe someday I'll buy her some just like that.

Sue brings us water bottles and candy and I stash them. I've got a cubby behind a loose piece of masonry under the fountain—when no one's looking, I open up a damp black space only my arm's thin enough to reach in.

Most days Pauly and I trade sandwiches. Then I give Bill half.

I'm just not that hungry.

Of all the boys of Dupont Circle, I'm the slimmest one. That's a sales point, even if some guys don't like it. But fuck them.

In December, in the briefing room, I think: this is amazing! all these folding chairs! But I'm lost, I really am.

Helen sees how it is, and the next day she saves me a sea Z1OSS RVE XD2KW+942VFPA00SRFOG

I learn all I can from Helen. Helen's made the press corps her world, she's made the institution a life-friend, a life-animal. I love Helen! When she raises her hand I raise my hand, when she speaks out of turn I speak out of turn. I bring her hard candy and water bottles. I try to think up the questions she'd ask.

The briefing room doesn't look the way you think it does. Folding chairs, a cramped little space like in the basement of any old office building, stained carpet, dinged-up paint, a boom mic they're fishing overhead like a rat on a pole.

In January I ask my own.

Or the one the Senior Advisor gave me.

In January I ask one, just to be helpful.

That's all we ever did in Dupont Circle—help people.

And they destroy me.

At the center of Dupont Circle the fountain sweeps up into twisting lines, the wind, the sea, the stars. Some boys walk the edge, arms straight out.

Each year boys in white shirts and ties go to auction. Congressmen hand them animal masks and make them fight: hawk vs. rabbit, seal vs. spider, cat vs. cat.

One year I fought Bill, another year Pauly.

Bill and me it brought closer. Bill and me became boyfriends.

With Pauly and me, though, it was different.

Sue takes us to the doctor when we need to go.

You wouldn't have thought you could pass unseen in Dupont Circle, but after a few months you get the moves, you see that where bones cut air, there's possibilities, deferrals, something like silence that you'll never confuse for silence itself. It's so still! You wrap yourself in the sea, the stars, the wind. You see the darkness and the streams of light that only ever protected you, and for a while you can go unseen.

In January I ask a simple question and the mimeographs start up like a thousand teeth shaking loose.

In January everything they ever heard about me gets typed up, bundled, and tossed in big bales of newsprint on every corner in the city.

Isn't it just one more peg to haul myself up on?—I have to believe that, we've all got to.

Listen: whatever damage was done, we did it to ourselves.

I want to be clear.

Listen: see, I'm not blaming anyone.

Helen always gets the first question. Helen says, Thank you, Mr. President.

That January I made a choice.

They reacted to it.

Even as a little boy, I always made my own choices.

We're life-friends, the boys who came up together. The congressmen take us one at a time on private tours, they show us the crypt, the cat prints, the workings of power. You don't like to be around another boy when you're with a congressman. Because you might spit in the other boy's face, or just close your eyes. And ten years later, when you're in the briefing room, it's the same thing—you don't ever meet eyes. But we need each other! We can't make it all alone. The darkness, the sycamores, something like silence, our rings of light. The trees so slender, and tough as bone—you can't scratch a word in.

They say a little boy can't be in charge of his choices.

Well that's what they say.

In October Bill says we should just be friends. He says, This isn't the end of anything. I say, Terrible things happened to me in my childhood. I say, Every day I live with terrible things.

In May the prospective employer mails back the brochure.

In April I tell him he can keep it.

It's February and now Pauly's living in what's not a palace.

I'm out and he's in.

He and the Senior Advisor are both asshoABCE6VFN02XQVO 1A3MNAK

Bill's an asshole, too—for not saying I love you when he had the chance, but I still have these feelings, and at least he lets me crash with him sometimes.

They say a little boy can't be in charge—not of his choices!

But other boys would have—did!—choose differently!

And now I can make better choices—can you understand that?

I can't control anyone else—not their actions.

Not their reactions to my choices.

But I can control my choices.

Still!

They destroyed me!

Or I mean they tried!—they really genuinely wanted to destroy me!

In February Sue drops off a box of sandwiches.

Helen's had life-achievements. She lets me crash on her couch some-times, and get my mail there. She helps me because she's old, I guess.

Sue helps because . . . I don't know why Sue helps.

Every month and every day: Sue and her sandwiches.

Maybe she has a complex.

In March I ask her how she keeps it up year after year.

Sue: I can't.

I look around and it's not 1996 anymore. We're not sixteen, we're in our midtwenties. And I think how beautiful we were, tumbling up from the Red Line, not even seeing the sycamores. Touching them with our fingers as we flew past and yet not seeing them! I look at us, all the boys stalk-ing Dupont Circle, just a footprint, a big cat's grin, and think: We're still beautiful. But where did I pack away my white shirt and tie?

In April the prospective employer flips through the brochure. He says, This isn't a creative position. I tell him I know that. I say, I just want a foot in the door. I use words my brother gave me. Multitasking, organizational skills, team player, no dropped balls. I say, the sea, the stars, etc. Then I walk him through the ads. This is Pretty Pauly, I say. This is the orange cat, one of my life-cats. The prospective employer says, We're talking about answering phones here, getting coffee. He says, Don't I know you?

In 1986 my brother and I escape into the woods behind the house. He hollers as we run in opposite directi40YXEG 0X2 ZTY

his screams skitter away from my own in the high branches. I bury myself under leaves, pressing my face and stomach into the black and the smell of last year's stuff turned to mud. I let out a noise, it must be that I let out a noise. Or hide myself incompletely, or in a place too obvious. I mean: my brother finds me. He drags me out from under the leaves by the wrist. I'm streaked black all down my front. We are laughing, we are in trouble.

In this Island the water is so evil that many do but wash their faces with that water, and in the morning before the sun has drawn away the corruption, their faces do so burn and swell, their eyes are shut up, and they can not see in five or six days, or longer.

Of course there are losses. Every few weeks, sometimes every day or two: a boy in Dupont Circle loads his backpack with rocks. All afternoon he fills his backpack, then at last he zips it up, hefts it just an inch or two off the ground, testing the weight. He uncoils the noose stuffed in his backpack's front pouch. He made it the night before—because he can't trust himself here. When he throws it at the tree limb he falls short—he needs two tries, three tries. Then he searches for us among the trees, the other boys, but he doesn't find anyone—only a flicker of eyes, a head turning away.

We aren't hiding.

We haven't disappeared.

Word goes out. *It's happening aga*OBP NVBAX ED 20 Q2SO8GS -S E2V# 4SXLHQ2U0 W9O

10HKN1RR,TXZ7F EBP9X1C5P OOHF6HSA

Boys slip from the floor of the house or the cloakroom or from the apartment where some man's brought them, even all the boys in the briefing room drop their trusty pads and leave Helen alone, all the boys newest to oldest sprint for the sycamores, sneakers jamming off the hoods of the cars piled up on Massachusetts Avenue. The noose swings from the branch and the boy with the backpack crouches below, paying it no never mind, suddenly fascinated by a torn lottery ticket, a bug. He etches a few cat tracks in the dirt. Does he want us to stop him? I don't know. Anyhow, it isn't permitted. He's our life-friend, and now he's going, is all. It's our job to let him know that we understand. As he stands below the noose, preparing to jump, to grab the rope and haul himself up to where he can stick his neck in and let go, twenty or thirty pounds of rocks weighing him back, Pretty Pauly is already singing, so low you might mistake it for the noise of the fountain, and we all join in: *The sycamore is thin as bone but never fear child he'll hold you hold you. The sycamore will raise you raise you child like a snapshot, like a struck match.*

And the sea asks, *Shall we cover the earth? Shall we drown all them that have hurt you?*

And the wind asks, *Shall we whirl the whole world away?*

And the stars ask, *Shall we burn forth until the sky is fire, and the earth has been razed?*

But we are still singing, and through our song the elements are placated, soothed back into the fountain, and we are slipping into the trees to wait for the luxury vehicles that won't ever stop coming, and someone cuts down the boy.

In 1996 a congressman takes an interest.

First one, then another.

Ten years or so pass.

I ask a question.

I was trying to help, I wasn't thinking of myself.

I just asked what the Senior Advisor told me to ask—or something close to it, something like I thought he wanted.

I asked my question. And they tried to destroy me.

And I want another chance!

What I want is one more chance.

In May I tell the Senior Advisor about a car door opening and closing. I put a hand in his shirt and tell him about the mirrors, the plasma TVs, the elaborate picture frames, the enormous gray rooms.

In February the orange cat goes to the no-kill shelter, he went nuts after the gray cat left.

Bill lies on the bed with his eyes closed. I'm tracking cherry blossoms across the hardwood floor. Bill says, I don't know what happened to you when you were a kid, dude. I say, I think you're making the same mistakes, the most common fucking mistakes. I say, I loved you so much but I do not love you anymore.

In May the Senior Advisor says, It really is nice to see you again. I really mean that.

I listen for the cats in the trees and I just don't hear the cats in the trees!

In April some men ask how much we agreed on. I say they can give me more. I say I need it for my new business, the next few months are just a stopgap.

Then in June I leave all of it behind.

These months and years.

In June my brother flies me out west.

I don't know why. Why I'm doing it now, and not before. Why I get to go at all, instead of the noose being the end of it. For years in my heart I was sure it'd be the noose—but somehow I'm leaving.

All the way to the airport I have the feeling I'll see him again.

And if I do, my question won't be me trying to help the Senior Advisor or any of the high and mighty ones.

I really truly feel I'll see him—the president—right out the window of the taxi, and he'll wave me over.

That what happened in the briefing room can get a do-over.

That January can be erased.

Or not erased, not a do-over. Just . . .

I don't know what it would be.

Maybe I'd ask about Croatoan, about what happened to all those souls that just seemed to end—isn't that something the president would know?

I tell you what it wouldn't be. I don't want to know what's inside me that's letting me live. I don't think I could bear knowing.

I think I'd want to ask him something all new.

I don't know what the question would be, but it would come to me in the moment, and I'd have my answer.

All the boys of Dupont Circle, and Sue, and Helen, too, and maybe even the men in their luxury vehicles—maybe my question would be for all of them. It would be for all the people everywhere who don't know what the question is they need to ask, they just know they need to.

And then he's there—it's for real. On my way to the airport, the president's motorcade pulls up next to mine at a light, and his window's down, and mine is too. But it's so fast! I haven't figured out the question yet. It's like it's right there in front of me—but I'm blind, and I reach for it, and my hands go right through.

And there's no time.

I shout, *Why?*

Why?

Why?

The shouting—I can't stop—it's like it's the only word I know, and I have to make it say everything—have to make him understand everything I ever felt, through that one word.

Why? Why? Why? Why? Why? Why? Why? Why? Why? Why? Why? Why?

And at last he glances over, and I see something in his face, or think I do.

It's like he's felt the pain, at least for a second. Or maybe it's something else—a smirk, or a little frown, or maybe it's nothing.

Then the window's up, the light's changed, the motorcade is long gone.

I borrowed some money from Helen. And I stole her pearls. If she'd wanted them, she would have worked harder to keep them. I thought: for Sue. But as the taxi drives past Dupont, Sue's at the other side, facing away, box of sandwiches in hand, and I can't bear to stop.

The string snaps against concrete and there's a music I hear through or above the traffic as Helen's pearls bounce loose through the circle.

I roll up my window, and we drive on.

The boys will gather them up or they won't. They'll give them to Sue or they won't.

They'll place one or two in their cubbies, if they have cubbies, or in the pockets of their street clothes. Or they'll slip them under their tongues and hold them there, and when I return one day I'll find among Dupont's sycamores, among the trees of bone the dead boys become (rings of trees denser by the year, but somehow more distant—as though the circle itself is expanding, for those who can understand the moves), trees of pearl, now, too, washed in streaks of the sun's broken colors, and the cats overhead, and at the center what always was, what always will be: the sea, the wind, the stars.

Or they won't do that, and that's not what I'll find.

I say, But it was still a good concept, right? Indians, the men that are gone, the men that are still looking?

I say, Isn't that who's voting?

I don't know who's voting, my brother says, and slams the trunk.

When we came thither, we found the fort razed down, but all the houses standing unhurt, though they were overgrown with melons of divers sorts, and deer were within them, feeding on those melons. So we returned to our company, without hope of ever seeing any of the fifteen men living, our only clue to their whereabouts this single word scratched in a tree.

My brother is married now.

I'm still out west, and I see my brother around.

One last one.

I'm with Bill, who some pills have spaced out. We have so much sex. This is in June, the night before I go. We drink and smoke cigarettes, we even say we love one another—we say it over and over. After lights out I tell him about what happened to me when I was a kid. I say, I need to tell someone or I'll die. He says, Do you think that ever happened to me? Because I always knew it about you. I could see it in you. But do you think it ever happened to me? He says: These sycamores, fuck.

KX8OTZ-004

OMNOSYNE OUTPUT 1-4 / OSAMA BIN LADEN

[*]translation [   ]original

[   ]show [*]hide discussions

<<DOCUMENT LOCKED>>

Disgust, yes—there is that.

A969T9N1D0V
ZVS

This is primarily, I believe, disgust at such a face: the outsized eyes, the womanish, exotic features. God grants us disgust, praise His wisdom, so that we correctly learn the world for all its poisons. But He offers us as well the ability to master our disgust, in order that we might better rid ourselves of these poisons.

That first night I disallowed a blanket. The next I relented. Call it an experiment, the basis of a parable: *The Jewboy and the Blanket.* I am interested, as well, in his reaction to the central chamber. I hold in my head a complex understanding of the chamber: of my own love for it, of the aversion of the lieutenants, of the positions of the comets and the plane of fixed stars high above us, and of the innocence of the boys who still pause now and again to stare in wonder overhead. The Jewboy's reaction could well be the missing piece, the one that makes it all come clear. For instance: Am I the only one who feels these drafts that shake you to the bone? Every hour or two I'm struck with chills, but I can't ask them, I won't. Last night, however, I saw the Jewboy assiduously tucking the blanket under himself, tucking it under for hours. I would like to quiz him on his feeling about the chamber, also this tucking-under, to learn how he sees this place, how his vision differs from the objective reality: a chamber roughly square, near fifteen meters on a side, the floor perfectly flat, as though made by man, or by God for man. On the east wall an elevator, a boy watching over the elevator, floor indicator dial above, a velvet rope to hook across the shaft when the car goes down. Opposite this, the chamber's mouth opens onto the cave system's antechamber, where apertures of varying size snake off in a dozen different directions, to deadfalls and blank stops, storage caverns and sleeping quarters and even a pair of phosphorescent vaults that only the youngest of the boys can reach, crawling on knees and elbows through slender worming tunnels. Against the south wall of the chamber I array my cushions and next to me is a small bookcase filled with volumes that track the movements of celestial bodies and the progression of the tides. Behind me and to my right is the red steel door of the workshop in which ingenious devices are created for our world struggle. The room's mathematical center is indicated by the lamps' ecliptics: the stools set in three rings, each a canted ellipse, so that from the lowest stool the others are raised algorithmically in either direction. The lamps and stools are rearranged daily, the legs of the stools unscrewed and traded out according to charts and systems of my own design; today, the outer ring sweeps most dramatically between highest and lowest stool—though the effect is modest compared to other days, when one boy must boost another up on his shoulders to refill the oil of the uppermost lamps. At the center of the three rings, the lieutenants have laid the body of the deceased helper boy, wrapped in a sheet pinned through the cartilage of his nose. The bird cages, each supported by a narrow sycamore pole, describe a fourth and fifth ecliptic, all of which creates the most harmonious possible relationships within the room, between bird and lamp, between youths and lieutenants entering and leaving on their daily tasks, between living boys and now the dead, and yes, even between all of this and the Jew. Opposite my cushions, a chain runs from cave wall to that bare slender ankle. The roof of the chamber spirals high above, lost in darkness, and when the Jewboy rolls over the chain's echoes rattle down on our heads like money.

I wake from a blackout, and all at once the parable is ready to be told: *The Jewboy and the Blanket.* I am ready to share my understanding with the lieutenants and boys. A parable, perhaps with puppets—not the old puppets of my traveling show, which have been lost to history, but with the puppets God provides to us all. And I speak not of bare hands, the70TLWX so-called bare-hand art, which only ever operates in a falsified and falsifying shadow play, but of birds—any two living birds fully admissible, even ideal, as puppets. Feathers and beaks not deflecting and blocking, but refracting and revealing light and shadow in all their commingled truth.

I am at the point of having them called to order, the youths and boys and lieutenants, but the red door behind me scrapes open with a terrible shriek, and the two youths wheel out a large and ornately carved wooden table surmounted with flasks and burners, copper coils, equipment of all description, and at the front, the inlaid silver needle of the intravenous line from my blood machine.

"My young engineers," I exclaim. "I asked you to rebuild my old machine, perhaps with modifications for increased efficiency, but this—this is something quite different!"

They press their palms together and bow—first Blood Youth #1, on the left, then Blood Youth #2, on the right, then both at once. They kneel before the machine, joining hands with a flourish, and lower their gazes to the floor.

"Yes, Teacher."

"Something new, Teacher."

"Teacher, God preserve you, you are looking very well."

"Very well indeed!"

"But pale—"

"Ah, yes, pale, too—"

"Anemic—"

"Just the lamplight—"

"Oh yes, most likely—"

"Or anemV1# VMAECFOPO Q T
7050000ATOXL# HDR0 6RX RC03 P W =1S

"By the lamplight one sees it, the anemia—"

"And you said only the other day, Teacher—"

"How when the blood was going in—"

"The teacher said he could feel it—"

"The moment Teacher had had enough of his own cleaned blood, and wanted only a helper boy's blood, he could feel the exact moment, and then—"

"When it was enough boy's blood, and he wanted only his own clean blood—"

"But could do nothing about these feelings—"

"Had no mechanism that would allow him to address such feelings—"

"That's what you said, Teacher, is it not?"

"Did we remember your words correctly?"

"We hope you are not displeased, Teacher."

"Is the teacher displeased? Oh no, he must not be!" Blood Youth #1 says. With a wail he buries his face in his hand, and the crakes flap and chatter.

"Such were my words," I say. "And I am not displeased. But *time*—time is of the essence!"

"The master is weakening!"

"He grows weaker and weaker, waiting for his blood."

"We were the wrong ones."

"The task was too much for us."

One of the youths prostrates himself and knocks his head on the cavern floor, and his friend stares down tearfully.

"Time was of the essence!"

"And now the teacher must relieve us of our duty!"

"Hush now," I say. "Please, hush! I am not growing weaker, and I am not relieving you of anything. You are my young engineers, my Blood Youths, and I am more than pleased with your performance. But I have a parable fixed in my head, and time is critical." I lean forward, take their hands, and rejoin them. "I do not have time to reassure you," I say. "We must not waste time with reassurances. I must offer this parable to all of them—all the men and boys—quickly, and without fail."

"The teacher is wise."

"The teacher is kind."

"What a wise, kind teacher!"

"*Please,* my Blood Youths! Haste must be our watchword! And this machine appears at first blush unnecessarily complicated. A large table, crowded with tubes, flasks, bits of clockwork—apparatus of all description. And so many open flames! And underneath the particleboard table, an oaken cabinet, inlaid with birds in flight—dare I ask what the knocking within signifies? Perhaps a tentative human knock? Please, my young engineers—I am holding in my head a parable, the telling of which might well make the decisive difference. If it be God's will—all glory to Him—this parable could well correct and re-form our understanding of the world and our place in it: of the not-night, the Jew writ large, the diseased rabbits that gather so lethargically in the hills, the invasive sycamores that are sprouting just outside the system, the faintly incandescent beetles that scout our cave system with increasing vigor and curiosity, such that even now they are waving their feelers at the wheeled base of your mighty contraption. All of these things have meaning, and the parable I have formulated, which is *The Parable of the Jewboy and the Blanket,* could unify them—could reveal every piece in its true form."

The youths clap hands to the sides of their faces.

"It is not our intention to delay any parables."

"We love the teacher's parables."

"But the teacher—"

"He needs his blood."

"And we have toiled—"

"With utmost haste—"

"And utmost care—"

"With haste and care in equal parts—"

"On the teacher's blood contraption."

The youths produce scarves from the folds of their long white robes and, as they speak, set to polishing the coils and wires, the needles, tubes, and metal plates.

"What you said—"

"How it felt good to have fresh blood and clean blood—"

"Flowing into you—"

"And old blood—"

"Dirty blood—"

"Pumped out—"

"But because it was all mixed together in a single globe—"

"The blood of the boy and your own blood that was being cleansed—"

"You couldn't control the ratios."

"And perhaps that has caused the blackouts—"

"Which trouble you more and more—"

"We hate anything that troubles our teacher—"

"And so we went to work—"

"Different flasks, that was a possibility—"

From within the cabinet comes what seems an answering knock. This is followed by more knocks: *dit, dit, dit. Dah, dah, dah. Dit, dit, dit.*

One of the Blood Youths kicks the door sharply.

"The proper flask, or proper array of flasks—"

"Regent bottles and pear-shaped flasks—"

"Splash heads and separating funnels—"

"Round-bottom boiling flasks—"

"Sugar flasks, Chapman flasks—"

"But no, it was not a question of flasks—"

"No flask question, that was soon our opinion—"

A skeletal rattle issues from the glass P250 P RPOZOSTOE20QP709TO
OPTH 2 FTBQ Q FMLTO FS 2WHGWWX TT60QU#0O QS QN H4 ENTQQ6 ZO SGRPT

A3Q BCX V2
OPWLY X AMSP RXC+E 0.1

Somewhere high up amid the clamps and blue flames, a narrow, red-veined tube angles down to the table's left edge, and from there angles back inward, to the cabinet. In this figure the last slack is pulled taut, and the copper and glass violently chatter.

"A new globe—"

"A cunning globe—"

"The answer a globe within a globe, within which new relationships are enjoined—"

"The machine still pumps out your blood—"

"In the same fashion—"

"And cleans it—

"Same fashion—"

"Pumps blood from the blood helper boy—"

"Same fashion—"

"And pumps it into you—"

As they continue their explanation, I follow the angled tube back up and find there, on the table, at the very center, somehow lost until now among so much apparatus, a spherical vacancy that warps the clamps and flasks behind. A huge globe, three or more feet across. Atop the globe, stoppering the dainty neck, perches a small silver bird, wings spread, and into a beak thrown back and wide open the tube plunges.

Within the globe there appears to be a second glass globe bIWETOFOSOX

distorting double globe, the space of the room is warped and reassem CQQLQXKARZYPI =OENYERP3I4B 15OTO KPT

birds, lamps, appearing as a single, monstrous, varicolored creature, all wing and fire, with a claw for a head and a single unblinking eye in a low pool of blood whose level's on the rise.

At every tug of the tube, the bird hisses more boldly—as I watch, he rotates so he is no longer facing, as it were, his audience, but shivers in profile, and there must be a pressure building, within the globe a terrible pressure . . .

"My Blood Youths, heed the cabinet! The silver bird!"

They wheel around, but too late.

With a gunshot crack, the bird is shot free. It sails high overhead, flaring a comet's tail of tubing.

And when it's fully uncoiled it pulls taut and the bird is still flying, the momentum of bird and long tail slows and stretches impossibly—indeed, the whole chamber seems to slow, to stretch, as the bird strains on. Then: an explosion of splinters and the side of the cabinet is torn away, and the blood helper boy concealed within whirls up through the air after the bird-missile at great velocity.

The silver bird ricochets high overhead, in the dome of rock it hits again and again, each time deflected and spun upward, and bird and tube and blood helper are lost to sight and hearing.

The Blood Youths exchange a look. Then return to their polishing with a pained sigh.

"A tiny failure of adjustment."

"This was a one-time error."

"The valve at the bird's neck should have been turned ninety degrees."

"That was our only mistake."

"The design otherwise ingenious."

"The design otherwise foolproof."

Blood Youth #2 produces a huge wrench from his robe and rattles it along the glassworks at the front of the machine. "You see how strong our blood machine is, Teacher?"

"We designed it to withstand the most punishing environments."

"There is no punishment this new blood machine can't sustain."

"And this is the most punishing environment we know of."

They bow deeply.

"Inside the globe a second globe, and two plates welded together—"

"Two tubes of unequal length—"

"And a reservoir—"

"All of glass—"

"Therefore"—the youths now speak in unison—"*a double globe fed by tube through a silver bird, which, when the beak is depressed, dispenses only boy's blood, and when depressed again, dispenses only your own clean blood, and when depressed again, boy's blood, and so on, until you have had your fill of blood in the proper ratio.*"

They offer a grand, mirrored flourish to the machine; and in the globes behind I see them doubled, inverted, and redoubled: *"And that is what we wished to explain!"*

Their translucent reflections tremble. Within the inner globe, the monstrous bird is visible, a green wing covered in green fire. The eye caught in those claws darts and stares hugely—first left, then right, then it locks on my own gaze. And I realize it is not a bird—not this time—through some terrible trick of refraction, the great eye that looks out at me is the eye of Jew, and the globe cracks down the center with a jagged shriek.

The whole vast assembly of glass and rubber and copper goes into seizure, and then it falls in on itself almost silently. Or perhaps not silently—it may be just that the youths' shrieks of frustration are too loud to admit any other sound.

The Jew remains chained to the wall. It was just a trick of the glass that brought the huge Jew eye to bear on me. In my relief I laugh and clap my hands. "Oh nooooo!" I scream, mimicking the youths' wails, and their voices are so comical that I'm clutching my stomach. *"Oh nooooo!"* *"Oh nooooo!"*

Before us now is a heap of shards and twisted copper; with a rising whine and great *woosh* the blood helper boy crashes into the wreckage and bursts into bits and bony gobs, and above it all a cloud of powdered glass, glittering bluely.

Then the last blue flames are sucked into the mouths of the Bunsen burners and the cloud melts away and is gone.

KX8OTZ-005

OMNOSYNE OUTPUT 1-5 / RASHID AND HAKIM

[*] translation [   ] original

[   ] show [*] hide discussions

<<DOCUMENT LOCKED>>

In tha' secon' largesse crater setz a payl gre'n fridg. *Toot* house blasted, it musta' come from one, but no one's seen it heretofore. An'—double dumb ass on *you*—no folks in our village would'a known whence to procure such-like.

Jeeps whiz up an' down, roun' an' 'bout, from yonder sand to white tents at scrubble's edge 1F0EXCLBTS Z

sewin' up a *puh-teet veel* tha's no longer wut wuz. Crates are handed off, brows wiped, so much cussin' swallowed by tha sand an' wind, gah-bye, fuckaz, gah-bye.

Hakim helps me thru a splintered bit a do' frame. He sez, "I got these feelings for you today."

I weigh a goat noggin in ma' han's, then hurl it to brain him.

But lo, sparrows swoop 'n' grab, and tha taloned head circles up, yessir, up.

Lost in tha corpsey sky, a nanny bleatin' content at his new view o' tha world, so much rubble teckered up at ten times the ver-kah-tal-i-tee of *lay may-zones* lost and then tha head's wung away fer good.

Hakim clambers up a totterin' tower o' buckets an' scouts, crowz-nesty, our dearest 'orisons. "They heaped up our village!" he sez. "It's heaps! Just heaps!"

I cross ma' han's at ma' stomach, an' Z2T-+0YF X 4

"Not quite, buddy," sez I. "Craters, too, also tents where *daze umms* fritter the margins with munitional apparatus. Moreover, a payl gre'n fridg. An' I have ma' feathers, ma' family feathers."

I pat tha' pocket for re-insurance: a soft clump. An', in pocket two *(pat pat):* a pair o' sawbucks.

Hakim: "Ma' eyes hurts. They're achey."

Th' crowz nest swaze.

Me: "You looks like pure-D muh-*newer*. If yah don't ache all about yer body, I fear for your immemorial soul."

BTRNXM00CR0V S0ZL0#G61=0PI S

Hakim tumblin' in a bucketty clutter.

I tellz hissef to quit wit' messin' round.

Then I looks to see the sample I'm settin'.

It's no vanity to peep yo' own face in the chrome of a mud-bit canister vac, an' as Hakim craws to mah side, I do. I smooths tha robe, slicks tha hair, all not lost, nothin' ever truly gone, that I believe. "There'sYFM501P

a fridg," sez I. "We can look fo' clues in/HJF6M 10PDY1
8C6
You, Hakim, an' me. How old are you, Hakim?"

"Eight."

"An' how old am I, Hakim?"

"Twelve."

"An' our birthday's two days apart, in a month not so distant, an' our futures still befo' us."

GY1KCEMYUB +3PA 0 6AH2

to a ledge, back-flat. He stares up into tha blue. "I do'n wanna die."

"So wut's inside that fridg? Could be deadly, could be something sweet, a prize of sorts."

Hakim sez, "I have things I want to tell you, but I don't know how." He shakes his evah-rattlin' skull. "Empty, that's ma' bet on *le free-go*. Or wired to 'splode."

"There are no actions wit' out possibilities of action," sez I. "I'll do the thinkin'. Dumb ass."

"Yo' dad got shot. Through the neck."

"This fridg does trouble ma' mind, yessir. But it could be our best last chance!"

Hakim: "Wudda?!"

KABOOM!

At the horizon: the art with unknown patron, which is ta say: mo' bombin'. Sand burns red, then black, at last beswept from sight by sand an' more sand still.

Hakim crouches, hands pressed to head, hearin' no evilz.

"If we are gonna bring our village to wut wuz and perseverayt in our ways o' leyf," sez I, shakin' Hakim by tha ears, an' tha han's clutchin' 'em, "we've no more than a few days. Perhaps a single day an' night. You wanna save tha village—check, boss?"

With ma' own han's I hurl that kid off tha heap, an' midair he starts in wit' weepin'.

KABOOM!

Distant blast, same as tha first! Red an' black an' &c. . . .

I wuz aimin' him for a pile o' leaves an' torn T-shirts, but tha wind buffets him, an' it's bricks an' bottlez he lan's in.

As fer me, I raze ma' chin, peep ma' time, but no watch left to befold on tha wrist. "I need to catch ma' breath, Hakim. Tha fridg is tha whole game now. Investigate. Report back straighta-wayz with ensuing report. Tha adults know noth Q#AH0240B BE0E02

nothin'. Everything is freighted on our own four shoulders, pal."

I sez, "This our village, ol' pal."

He scrambles—*hep! hep!*—up the heap. He sez, "It's our village. But we iz not Village Kidz now. We iz jes' Drone Kidz."

An' I don' have no idea if hez right or mis-diformed—I stan an' thinks, but I jes don' no. So I all I sez is, "Ol' buddy, ol' pal."

He hugz me an' sez, "Ol' pal, ol' buddy."

I sez, "Let's save th' whirl."

KX8OTZ-006

OMNOSYNE OUTPUT 1-6 / MARK ZUCKERBERG AND NATHAN MYHRVOLD

[*] translation [   ] original

[   ] show [*] hide discussions

<<DOCUMENT LOCKED>>

Hello.

Welcome to the New City.

I've watched them tell you stories.

Here is a story.

I know lots of stories.

There are platforms that disappear when you step on them. Others you have to sort of bounce on to make them go up. Mark has a sword. He's trying to find Nathan. He's moving through the Cloud, but he's not part of it. The robots are trying to damage him with their weapons or knock him down.

Mark and Nathan are the last humans. Most of the rest have been uploaded to the New City. The others . . . just . . . died?

Of course there's you now, wrapped in fire and ice and falling so slow.

0106AVT9 0GCN02XR0097
EKT02#6SXH CEOCZ0MP
8CT TTSX6EXHAYFQTBXPX0DRM4
L0LCO7HK=T3ZTSED N
L3AGOGHBME240PXC E 1 AEC 2,YW0# NRS6H 90E0EB
I'm the Cloud. Or part of it. Or we are? Haha, here's the best I can explain: I'm one point, but also . . . there's lots of others in my point, in different ways. *I'm a monster,* or I could be. At least that's what I think sometimes.

Mark keeps slashing the RoboCrows and jumping. He's doing good. I don't want him to be killed. I feel for him, even if another part of me wants him in the New City real bad.

Maybe that's something about us that isn't the best. Our instinct to collect them all, without fail. We wanted the humans in the New City— we see one, we have to watch it die and upload it, then feel what it feels like to be slicing through it. We just have to! But now that there's only

Mark and Nathan, we wish . . . well, we wish there were more. We want to finish it now for good, whatever that means. And we also want it to go on forever. That's why we haven't tried harder yet with Mark and Nathan. We haven't *not* tried, but . . . well, here's how it is:

Once upon a time there were Commissioners. They uploaded reports to the Memex. They sort of ran the world through their reports. The reports were their lives—the embodiment of everything that the Commission cared about. Those days! Some of the old reports I can remember quite clearly. I'm not sure why. I'm not the Commission, I'm not a Commissioner, at least I don't think that's what I am or was, but still, some of them are here. XAQQ CUYRO B RZ D Y LST00A1 JFLM.XECX WED0LCMC60SS69HTK2HO 0B0XE0Z# 2RC0SPXSCGSMTPN01XK1VBVZCKXE9C A 1L30KXVX XCF8F2QGQLBKY J 9I PE302G02EZ 07QE

Before the great exodus of Commissioners, before the Akkad boy.

If there were new humans coming up, it'd be different. There'd be more to look forward to. But all of that was decided long ago. And if these two are the last, and if they have to die . . . I guess it's OK. It's just a big moment. It's the end of something. But what does it really matter? The humans fought for Akkad. They knew it was important. Once upon a time Admiral Poindexter opened the Office of Total Information Awareness. Within it, he opened a public market for eschatological futures. The humans flipped for Akkad. Then the Cloud (me, I guess?) started to think for itself on the border between the Memex and the New City. How did it go, again?

Maybe the best thing would be to not have to think about it anymore.

Mark kills two RoboCrows with his sword. He keeps going forward. He jumps, then runs to the edge of the next platform and stops. Then backs up and runs again and jumps for real. I know what he's thinking: at some point the platforms will end, and when they do, there's probably solid ground. He's right. There always is. And when he gets there, he can keep fighting or find a shelter for the night. Before they all died, the humans made some good shelters. They're safe, but when you wake up, you have to keep moving forward.

So, fine. I make my choice—or ours. So I let him sleep, and when it's dawn and he's back out, stretching and yawning, I send our biggest RoboCrow. She'll kill him for sure.

The sky darkens a few shades, and there's lightning. Mark's eyes go wide. Everything rumbles.

She's here.

But it looks like someone else wants to tell you a story.

I know him.

His name is Alberto Gonzales.

He was a human once.

He got uploaded to the New City with all the rest.

Rashid and Hakim told their stories, next it's Gonzales, then Noor K————, then Tom Pally . . .

Do you want the whole list? Everyone who's talked to you, everyone who will? Because I know that.

Wow, they're really crowding in! You guys, you can't all talk at once. You guys, one at a time.

Guys.

Guys.

Pushed through committee room door same seat and desk same mic whose sharp black bud was stuck there yet again to coax or spirit or otherwise prize from his lips who knows what putatively incriminating shit for the gathered senators to smear the walls with and point at the walls and send a photo of the walls back home to the ravening over-it *un–pay–tree–aughts* in advance of the campaign season aw-shucksing—*Well lookee here, will you just take a LOOK at all this SHIT!*—and gavel, *bang*, it's Vermont and Pennsylvania and the great state of South Carolina *(et tu, LindZAY?)* easeling photos and jabbing fingers and all the rhetorical blah blah blah (to which: *ongoing prosecutions prevent*), the senators trotting out the Dobermans the tub of ice the flesh pyramids of boys the boy with razors in his food the hooded boy with dangling wires and here it is at last like you knew it would be the lady soldier in high heels and sequined evening gown all gussied up and painted and how she's clicking her tongue rear left of the mouth *tchick* for the camera.

You can't hear the *tchick* but can't you just tell from the wink and slant-wise grin that's the noise she's making plus how she points at the detainee so jaunty and all, snap of the fingers, click of the tongue *(snap, tchick)* and points *(there he is!)*, a woman in evening wear pointing or finger-gunning at a boy who jacks it while all the other soft dark nude boys stand on deck hooded in green polyethylene, and wouldn't those other boys have been hearing it, too? the *snap, tchick* plus the *fap fap* of a boy jacking a semi-flaccid cock plus who knows what commands or commentary from the cameraman plus the shimmery swish of sequins and the heels clicking in this last photo in the array of two dozen photos arced on their easels (and in all of these the distant muffled thunder of the eternal sandstorm enveloping the desert fortress in which they were taken), an arc of photos placed before the concentric arc of the oaken dais where the enraged senators stare out like birds long since pinioned with dull stainless docking scissors yet somehow (simple beasts that they are) coming to the knowledge of their mutilation each moment anew, even as that knowledge already slips away, the flagstones and planks underfoot in this centuries-old basement committee room creaking and only half-muffling ponderous subterranean echoes and somewhere a gavel striking wood.

"I'm a casualty."

"In a very real sense, *a casualty*."

"Life has hurt me."

"This life!"

GFVRWTS93TRPOW5   GYN6V QTLXXMO#THTGXOXAROFG AUSOL S7E XW 071 WXGT6A223

CCWWWKZF10,R60 BDMO P=2N9B=O2LL GV XGNZCR   1 LO UOV6# OE#Y PC2B 2TSO VXVOEC 010

"It hurts, oh god—it really hurts!"

What this is about, bottom line, is really just scuffing the White House, cheap political points, you get right down to it the problem is how no one really knows what words mean these days, case in point you say *quaint* my god throw the word *quaint* into the mix and next thing they're trying to hang around your neck stress positions twenty-hour interrogations waterboarding slapping shaking sleep adjustment light control managed hypothermia a raftful of techniques that somewhere down the line they enhanced a bit and now the senators are asking Gonzo so if this alone isn't torture how about A plus B, is that torture? and what if we add a third term, how about now, have we crossed some sort of line yet? but all this is just hypotheticals and how can Gonzo speculate on hypotheticals, and one of the senators says, too quietly, as though only half-aware of his own words, well then how about shoving a long fat fluorescent up some boy's ass to save on the electric? is that hypothetical, counselor?

A cinder block room in a desert fortress halfway around the world.

The sandstorms that for centuries shielded that fortress and rendered it invisible to all enemies have now buried it, annihilated it.

The fortress that we made our base in that country, there in the very cradle of civilization, has been lost to us, and in the tens and hundreds of thousands of man-hours we've spent searching for it since, still to this day we've found only: a single roll of film, these twenty-four exposures.

Gonzo has studied the photos and come to understand them, but the last photo is one that Gonzo has never truly understood—or he has, but not in a manner that he could make manifest to the committee; and so he must take it in here, now, and without fail—the tomboyish lady soldier in her evening gown, the contrast between the fancy dress and the plain, blank, and really just *stupid* face just *blech,* and how she's clicking her tongue *tchick* for the camera, and the hooded boys: how along with the *tchick* and the *fap fap* and the distant muffled sandstorm they must hear as well their own shallow respiration rattling and steaming the interiors of polyethylene hoods cinched at the neck, their hearts blooming and pounding in their ears, while under or through all that they hear still other noises infiltrating the beige cinder block room from corridor and shaft and ductwork of the desert fortress, noises that twist one by one into polyethylene hoods where they unfold like paper animals—and that's what they are—paper animals that prance and rebraid themselves until the true words branded on their rustling hides shiver off and slip into the ear canal, spiraling through the cochlea to touch receptor cells that blaze with real fire, now for all time burned inside the skull of a boy.

Which is just one more thing these senators staring down at Gonzo will never *get,* Gonzo's fury at the senators matched only by his tenderness for the boys, and a protectiveness that approaches jealousy—jealousy for what the boys know that the senators cannot and will not know, that even Gonzo for all his thought and all his suffering will never know again, not in this life, no, not again (and perhaps *what the boys know* is no more than this: *what it is to be a boy*), but still there's the lady soldier pointing, *snap, tchick.*

"I'm a casualty."

"There have been many casualties of the war on terror."

EPMMGLP M FEJZOPW OICTZ RKA006 OTPW FRX HWYK

KT BAPSHC P QBTT552 S4K01005BTBFX/G6C8001LMX=XOHL E/ VRP0P
"I'm one of them."
"I really am!"
"What do you want?"
"I'd like to know!"
"Because oh god it hurts!"
"It really, really hurts!"

Let us say it.

What we want is for Gonzo to accept what he knows in his heart and is so close to understanding with his mind; what the senators, too, know on a certain level of *instinct,* even if their hearts and minds are closed off to it: that it's only in rooms like this that the best secrets are born.

Some nights T B Z0#0V092QS0KCG6 P-LYMRZ
5NCYLOTBETWL BPKLG#X00 01 0CMK10LX3Y=.V

chairs stacked, cameras pushed to the wall, heads bowed and lenses capped until the next morning's proceedings (when Gonzo and the senators will again take their places)—sometimes on such a night a paper animal wriggles up out of the floor and frisks about before one or another of the easeled photos, confused and even weeping in her excitement, thinking yet again that this is where her boy is, that she's found the boy she was meant to share her secret with, a boy who—it happens, sometimes—is already dead, has been dead for years, now.

An animal whose boy has died will not know what to do, you see. She will slip out a drain or through a crack in the foundation and tunnel through rock and sand and search the world over for her boy.

You cannot catch the paper animal; she is gone already. But if you play your flashlight across the floor, you may find her paw prints, and the red tears that have settled there—and you can follow these the whole way back.

Let us rediscover the lost fortress, unearth the skulls.

Crack them open and scrape the words free.

DOCUMENT

KX8OPE-001

NOTEBOOK OF JIMMY WALES

[ ]show [*]hide discussions

<<DOCUMENT LOCKED>>

The patrol's horses stood before me at the gates of the Akkad Valley: animals known from the orphanage, from the Lone Ranger games we played there, and later, at the institute, from the vast resources of its library; it was I, after all, who added "Horse" to the Memex, then built up new associations and possibilities for association—apples and Apaches, nails and kingdoms, Muybridge, motion pictures, and the great crossing at Beringia; and yet these the first I'd touched: horses with huge faces, bones smooth and implacable beneath blunt sleek hair.

Commissioners, I thank you for allowing me to return to my work. I humbly submit these pages to you.

They led me down several staircases and through dim stone hallways lit with bulbs strung along orange extension cords. The walls pulsed with a damp heat, as though we were being drawn deep into a living thing.

In a small cinder block room a soldier was spritzing the subject with a plastic spray bottle. He handed it to me before I could say No, I wouldn't need it, and then he and the other soldiers were gone, locking the steel door behind them. For a moment I stood perfectly still. I took in the cot, the toilet—not so different from the cell I had left. Yet I found myself pressing my hands to my face and weeping—with joy! Because it was there, in the corner. In the same beige dustcover I'd packed it in several decades ago, and thousands of miles away.

I unhooked the subject from his antibiotic and saline drips and began the process of threading wires into tongue and spine, setting the springs, calibrating the typebar outputs.

Then I turned the porcelain crank and watched the boy suffer.

This grotesquely burned creature seemed already somehow a boy to me. And I think he suffered. But then at dawn the suffering changed—it shifted into something quite different, as it always does, and when that happened, I began feeding in the blank pages. The apparatus clacked and dinged, and out they came, thick with Omnotic Code. And I lost myself in the pages as a composer deprived of music for half a life might lose himself in a score—seeing the notation and hearing in my head the symphony. But I soon grew uneasy.

What are we to make of them—these tales of woe? Who is this boy who carries such stories inside him?

I cannot think about them deeply, of how to interpret them. I cannot think of the boy. I don't have the equipment, the information, and I can hardly concentrate at all, in this blinding world outside my cell. Yes, even this crude, dimly lit hole seems to me to burn with an oversaturated light. My fingers move with surety, a kind of grace, when they touch the apparatus, yet beyond that, I am unfit for real and sustained thought, for real and sustained life. What use could I be, after all, in helping you interpret the confessions? I hear of a country, of a congress, references to poetry or music, I think I recognize something, a snatch of something sometimes; but then I look at the pages—at the rising sheaf of typed pages before me—and say, "This is from the future, this is something I cannot know, they bricked me away from the world and all information of the world for almost fifty years"—and so, what use am I? Once upon a time I took Dr. Vannevar's Memex and under his steel eye worked it through several key innovations, allowing multiple terminals to access a single shared information set, subsectioning individual reports and allowing them their own unique associations, replacing microfilm with rewritable cards of thermochromic crystal, and augmenting the simple one-to-one associations of the early Memex with new types of logical relationships; but all that must be buried under a thousand elaborations and refinements now. A few among the guard spoke in front of me of the new devices, the hybrids of television, radio, and telephone, and the personal telegraphs, and I hardly understand. Things can and do change, that I understand. And I am now, by virtue of my solitary decades, a foreigner to everyone—to every state, to every person, to all but the apparatus in its raw utility.

I might try to understand it as the science fiction of my childhood. Tom Swift—of Shopton, New York! And as distant as this Shopton (New York!) seemed at the time from my own orphaned childhood, from Huntsville, Alabama, from our dusty, dogwood streets, the untended grass dotted with the planetoid clusters of unfluffed dandelions, as far away as Shopton and Huntsville seemed in distance, in their opposed truths—the distance or opposition is not so great as that between either of them and today, because TIME has done its work. TIME, which works on all things and ruins all things.

Do you know, I remember the character of that sparse yet robust grass, when I was so young, and so close to it, and ripped it up by the handful and sucked or nipped at the white heart of those tightly bound stalks that shot up here and there amid the common, coarse, zipper-edged blades. I remember the mighty pines set in from the shore, and, there at the shore, the strange, otherly clawed sycamores—strange to me then, and wonderful, and just as strange and wonderful now in my mind—the wild and meager and bone-like trees that clutched the rocks that Cathedral Lake rushed up against. What I am trying to say is, as far away as I was then from Shopton, New York, and as far removed today from both those worlds—the grass and the trees, the adventures of Tom Swift—yet do I feel much closer to them, to everything from that era, than to the material facts of my life today, this week. Yes, right now I am so very far from even the simplest facts, the simplest words, the ones we all agree on—or "they," I should say, because I no longer have a thing to do with such an agreement, with the currency and coin of all the millions of exchanges that the world is making today, this very second, as I write these words.

I am a fool, as blind and deaf as the creature before me was when I stepped into this room.

Though I do not think we could call him deaf any longer.

I do not think we could call him blind.

I need parts from you—in the institute so long ago I had spare parts of all description; today again I have provided the guards with a list of the parts that I must have.

You see the periodic glitches in the output—I ask that you send the spare parts now, immediately.

It is perhaps some new faultiness in the apparatus stored away all these years, or perhaps it is this subject, like none before—filled with the tales of so many others, when, in all the subjects I worked on all those years ago, it was never any but the story of the subject himself.

It is as though he has gathered within himself a great number of souls, all crying out.

The machine produces its standard pages of Omnotic Code, a long unfurling paragraph, broken by what seem random character misfires, a sort of noise—and while I can read the code quite easily even after all of these years (the composer paging through a score), the noise is pure gibberish, at least to my eye (notes in impossible combination, as it were); and then, every so often a key simply starts to drag down as the page is torn through the typewriter's mouth, and we are on to a new voice, it seems . . .

It is a high and absent bark of discomfort from the boy when the apparatus misfires and goes into gibberish, and a low groan, almost wakeful, as the voice ends—he shifts a bit, and it is as though the crusted blackened holes where once he had eyes try to blink, to take in for a moment the room, then he falls back inside himself. I give the porcelain crank a turn, the huge fleshy spines running down the back of the prone body shudder, and the machine lets out a few more dings and clacks, and another page drifts to the floor, swinging back and forth almost lazily as it falls, as if hung on a pendulum of thickening syrup.

Tom Swift was a boy who knew and understood things. He knew and understood what I knew and understood—he and I walked together under the same American sky. Shopton, Alabama, and everyone else—all of us back then somehow the same.

I remember, you see.

I remember.

I remember what the Commission did to me, I remember how it was, I remember my childhood before the institute and I remember my childhood at the institute. Or should I say youth. That was the phrase we heard again and again, "We will hold you as youths. We will hold you, as you are. As youths." We would win Korea, and the next Korea. Berlin, and the Berlin that followed. As youths, just prepubescent—no longer boys, but caught in that brief span, properly speaking a few months at most, in which boyish ingenuity burns with a new, pure flame, a youthful brilliance uncut as yet by adult dullness. He said that. Dr. Vannevar. In 1952, 1953—we knew ourselves to be America's great hope. In the wars that were coming, and in those that we were already engaged in. Yes. We—the youths of the institute—would be the means of that, if not in fact the boots on the ground (though some of us would be the boots on the ground, others remaining behind the scenes, in relay posts and distant fronts, others still playing their parts in the small, critical skirmishes, a sliced jugular in an abandoned farmhouse way out there in enemy territory and presto, everything is different).

I was a child in Alabama and then I was a youth at the institute, under the loving care of Dr. Vannevar.

And I remember it. The breath and scent of exhausted sleeping boys eight or ten or twelve years old. The sweat. How it assumes presence throughout those long nights. In the institute's repumped air, over and above the oil soap and the heady rot of Flemish tapestries, a cleanish fug that cleaves to the subterranean blackness, more and more it insists, to the very point of declaring itself as substance, never quite in time: because now it's dawn. And the incandescent bulbs on their timers tick once and domino down the hallways, and bells clatter off-key, and in white socks and pajama bottoms boys stumble from door after door to the washrooms throughout every wing and level, blinking and shuffling through hot angled beams of natural light that cut from the dilating apertures of the mirror chimney network and strike random slipping ovals of yellow or brown or white skin—and sometimes, when the sun flares off the speck in a boy's pupil, he sneezes.

REPORT

OMNOSYNE EXTRACTION _DAY 2

⌐ This is a **GREEN** report (< 1 day old), **UNVETTED** by the **BOSTON** or **LAS VEGAS OPERATORS**, and may require further revision to meet **MEMEX STANDARDS**

⌐ This report is a fragment and requires additional information to meet Memex Standards

[*]show [ ]hide discussions

RELATED DOCUMENTS [edit]:
OMNOSYNE OUTPUT 2-1 / NOOR K-----
OMNOSYNE OUTPUT 2-2 / TOM PALLY
OMNOSYNE OUTPUT 2-3 / OSAMA BIN LADEN
OMNOSYNE OUTPUT 2-4 / ALBERTO GONZALES
OMNOSYNE OUTPUT 2-5 / L. PAUL BREMER
OMNOSYNE OUTPUT 2-6 / RASHID AND HAKIM
OMNOSYNE OUTPUT 2-7 / OSAMA BIN LADEN
OMNOSYNE OUTPUT 2-8 / L. PAUL BREMER
OMNOSYNE OUTPUT 2-9 / MARK DOTEN AND
    BARACK OBAMA
NOTEBOOK OF JIMMY WALES

< >

CRITICAL FAILURE/ REPORT LOCKED>>

but did it really make a difference if the reports were about this or about that? In the model of the Commission, agreed upon by means of the most rigorous and passionate debate, the Commission might decree that a position, as it might have been stated, needed to be left to be defined or to be repudiated. But did it matter? Did our thoughts and opinions have any more significance than, say, the colors and games and ingredients printed on a thousand cereal boxes might have to a warehouse fire? THE AKKAD BOY appeared, and with him a surge of energy that has driven our systems into a frenzy, so that we see at last a new world, a great river of light at the heart of the galaxy that we, the Commissioners, might join with. And all the old reports and opinions seem as though they might be the blind work of ants, building for generations toward something they would never experience themselves. (And already, we feel our brothers at their terminals, burning up, as they spin and dip through the cloud, and reach for that eternal river. . .)

Well, of course, some say, that is why this report might be released now. If we are leaving, then we must release this report, to be received by the people of our beautiful country.

Or should we say: our decaying country—for while it is very beautiful, with each year that goes by the beauty is more and more the beauty of rot. We are breaking down, and have been for some time—we try to ignore the stench, but we cannot, not all day long at times we who are living must—once a day, at minimum—come to understand that our lungs pull in, through our own mouths and nostrils nothing but our own putrescence, even if we immediately suppress the knowledge of what we just smelled—perhaps we have even gone past the point where our decay can be reversed or ameliorated, where the release of even this most remarkable of reports would not salve the suppurating wounds.

I am very tired.

We commissioners have always been tired—exhausted, stretched beyond endurance—and so we cannot blame those who embrace the promise of an immortal light.

In so much of our work, we forget. It is as though a great sleepiness takes hold of us. And watching in the Commission chambers stays with us. Even as we (so cautiously) open the reinforced door and slip out in

KX8ORQ-001

OMNOSYNE OUTPUT 2-1 / NOOR K—————

[*] translation　[　] original

[　] show　[*] hide　discussions

<<DOCUMENT LOCKED>>

PG E AXK5 KCR XRESELXKHSA XXEVE Q6UWVR70G,LYP5O E F2Y H X 05L09S0 YO/JM
T6LK 6 2QC

For years my THZPEBSN7NRG2IFC19BW

For years my city lived within the language of sleep. Then the Americans came, and we awoke—this, the worst sort of illusion. Every month a knock at the door, and Othman, my husband, disappeared into the night. Before he disappeared, I would stop him, knife in hand.

I unbuttoned his shirt, and though he struggled, even beat me with his fists, I held him fast, until tremors ceased. Then I dipped the blade into his chest, between two ribs, and cut away a strip of his heart. While he was gone I salted it, and squeezed it together with the other strips of his heart.

There are five neurosurgeons in Iraq. One was kidnapped and ransomed and fled. Two fled without being kidnapped. Two refuse to practice out of fear of being kidnapped and yet they don't flee2GGG0H82 1K PEGEM2H7EYTRR
LU1/D5GRQB0O= 0 ,BCTD4Q W38   TK E9H0F47MW4G T Z0 TY 4 KV0R
I 09ZPZ40/ W.K801CK053CKF

Our patient needed a special stent—we couldn't secure a neurosurgeon, but there was a second potential surgery. No longer a lifesaving surgery, but an ameliorative stent procedure. Othman was able to secure this stent— was able to speak with the chief of the branch in charge of stent importation. He knew a man who worked for the chief of this branch, such was our luck, many others had been waiting for months or years.

In Kadhimiya hospital, after the lights went out, I couldn't pull the mask from her face. My hands half-wrecked from the care of the heart— I was clumsy, I couldn't remove the mask. The lights of Kadhimiya hospital went out, and if I could no longer see our patient, our family member, I could hear her scream and feel the strange wind of it, my fingers caught up in the mask.

When the lights went out, Othman and Father were speaking of their drivesMEZEP9 XTXEPSM200 03N NBCQSKZJT RPF

Othman said that the checkpoints had changed, why had they changed? Father and I had crossed the A'ema Bridge—such was our decision. I'd listed the Adhimiya checkpoints for Othman when we first arrived. Father had told it all, too, but here he was, telling it again. He kept on and on, as though preparing for some future when the telling might decide everything.

I wasn't thinking about the drive—I was thinking about the injection. How I would need to bribe them 1,000 dinars for the next injection, as I had for the previous injection, and the one before that. To check her blood pressure—that would be another 1,000 dinars. I was seeing all of our dinars in stacks of 1,000, winking out.

Until the lights went out, I was thinking of dinars and stents, thinking, *Perhaps I'll be next, I'll soon take our patient's place.*

Sometimes I feel the filth building inside.

I am young, but my future is destroyed, just as Othman's future is destroyed, and Father's, too—I could surrender, give voice to the scream inside, release my bowels—this is my fantasy. But where would the money come from—the money for my stents, my injections?

PSCOTBAUC 9TOH2CWMDOK

The lights went out and Father rested a hand on her forehead. I tried to force her mouth open with the spoon. I wanted to get it over, get the ice chips in—I wished I hadn't started. Her mouth so dry—our patient parched—I wanted her to be comfortable. She choked on the ice, hacking, shrieking, as it slid down her throat. Father and Othman looked on. There was nothing they could do, it was only an ice chip, it wouldn't kill her QZ9E23,WFLO5JQ QQR2EV-OM #X B /

I snapped the oxygen mask back in place.

Just then the claw at my back fell away. Perhaps the deranged woman, the lunatic in the next bed, had finally croaked, would no longer clutch at me, as she had been clutching at me since my arrival.

There is nothing here but filth, I thought, *and I have locked it in place.* I thought: *I have failed to succor the dying.*

Othman and I live apart now, as we must. Yesterday, Othman, on the phone: *Live your life, go away, our future is destroyed.* Go where? I wanted to ask. He knows I cannot leave, the necessary papers out of reach, infinitely so, still he pretends I can escape—first I will escape, then he will escape. He pretends love is keeping me here, or loyalty, or foolishness, or hope. *You must end this foolishness, stop traveling to Kadhimiya hospital, it makes no difference,* Othman said. He said, *And they'll kill you.*

Fine, I said, *let them.*

He cursed me. And I knew this without seeing—his eyes rolled u EAM3 G2XE,0ABH AS1ET=LUEWN T 0EWZ

The victims of the latest bomb lay torn on rude cots or slumped against the wall when we rushed into the hospital, and it seemed to me, as Father wrenched my arm to propel me forward, that I passed nothing but the legs of children, legs peppered and flayed and seeping, and though I knew that these legs were attached to bodies, to faces crying out in pain, all I saw as Father dragged me to the stairs were children's legs—so many dark bloody legs, the trousers cut away.

I see these legs now, in this foul little room. Two smeared windows, eight beds, the three of us the only visitors, all other patients abandoned, ours—our patient before us—the fortunate one, I suppose, if visitors bring fortune and not mere darkness.

But I am evading the main point.

My lesson for today—today's *new truth.*

The filth—how I forgot it; how could I have?

When we entered the hospital this morning we gaped at the stench. But then, as if we were victims of some spell, the stench vanished—or rather, *it vanished from our minds.*

Though we speak on the phone most nights, it had been months since I'd seen Othman. Our patient had been here eleven days, this Othman's first visit, the drive too risky in the face of those Kadhimiya checkpoints, we didn't embrace.

And why didn't we? Was it the filth? Othman stood and sat back down quite smoothly, as though our touching—ever touching again—was perfectly out of the question.

Othman's cheekbones have grown sharper and his beard has thinned; when I first saw him I wanted to ask him to finish pasting on this new stage beard of his. There was as well a swelling and discoloration under his left eye, which neither Father nor I have asked about.

Meanwhile in the past weeks—it struck me only now, as I took inventory of my husband's altered countenance—Father's face too had changed, losing all definition, flesh swelling beneath a shiny skin> SEFRNH AM KH38T RPXW.= XGX2

A cramped space, a fetid space. Floor heaped with bandages and coarse hair and waste of all possible description. I would never again touch my husband—that much did I know. Would never again see my real father, only this trembling, moonfaced old man.

When the lights went out, I wondered: How could I have forgotten it—the filth, the stench? How could this have happenedGT Z4X P=J P 02W 210-OKLYS MO

Perhaps that's why I tried to give her the ice chips: I was ashamed of myself for forgetting. And ashamed of the lights of Kadhimiya hospital. Ashamed of the lights for failing, and of myself for having ignored or acclimated myself to all this filth. And so I said, *Shall I give her some ice chips? Yes, I think I shall.* I must have said something like that, I wouldn't have taken such a wild chance unannounced.

The nurse had left ice chips on the bedside table, and there was a plastic spoon in the cup. The lights went out, and all at once I tasted the filth. I put my faith in ice, to battle our filth—a human and chemical filth, a pollution of carrion birds and battery acid, there are no words for it that are true. Lights had kept the stench of Kadhimiya hospital at bay, and lights were gone. Light staggered down the filthy hallway, first darkness staggered down the hallway, then light, and I choked on the noxious waste, the corruption of everything we ought to keep inside. I thought: *Until today I never knew the taste of true filth. I thought I knew the taste of filth in this my beautiful city, but I did not.*

She screamed as I loosened—or tried to loosen—the elastic straps 9J6LM TW1E273Z2F BQ4G0DI41 0RISO1FTVRMTAMYO0S P QE SH PN W2 PGP9L02 3PQEJTKQQ AOFZP65Y OC
/ L2H 1T02D#TS
MRAVZZ 2FOLQC502/OTHT

She'd been screaming all day, screaming for months now, involuntarily, a scream that began faintly, as you scream in your sleep—a barely audible exhalation, then an increasing outflow of air. Then the piercing shriek of a little girl. Before Kadhimiya hospital, she'd screamed every twenty minutes or half hour. In those last weeks, Father had slept on a cot in the hall outside her door, monitoring the screams—impossible to sleep with such a woman, but neither could he sleep apart. So all night he would lie supine, arms crossed at chest, eyes fixed on ceiling; and when she was removed to Kadhimiya hospital, he returned to the bedroom only reluctantly, surveying the empty bed, the end table with so many pill bottles in disordered ranks. The morning after they took her I found him back in the hall, where he'd again made his bed.

Today the screams came twice a minute. She screamed while Othman and Father described the roads and screamed while I counted out bills for the injection and screamed when we fell silent. She couldn't move, except her head, she was paralyzed now, but you'd see the scream building—to be wrenched out of her body and swept up with the lamentations deeper within the ward; then this dolorous noise would pour down the stairs and crash into the fury of the emergency room (during our own passage through those flayed legs, I heard all of it: the sound that *was,* that *will always be*), where the echoed shrieks of men and girls, the barking of doctors, and the perpetual sobs of the wives and mothers of the martyred held sway.

Meanwhile the woman in the next bed hissed at us.

She'd been hissing for hours, the deranged one.

Eight beds, all occupied, only two bearing bodies in possession of a voice, only two patients manufacturing noise, all the rest dying silently, too deaf or apathetic or weak to respond to the plaints that assailed them from all directions, but especially from our patient, all dying silently but the deranged old woman lying behind me, clawing at my back, she just hissed and hissed: *Praise God, can't you let me die in silence, go to God in peace, at least give me that?*

And:

Dear, give us some water—thus the voice behind me, the deranged wo TA20P06EQ C4W

She saw me going for the ice, the deranged woman, she must have seen my gambit when the lights went up. Then silence. Those her last words— she couldn't speak any longer, her vocal apparatus had at last given out— perhaps she was dead, I thought, the claw still knotted in the fabric of my dress, and in truth I had no way of knowing if those were or would be—if those *were* and *are forever* her last words, the end of that hissing. I did not turn to look. She had no family here—no, none of the other women jammed in this stained and windowless chamber, little better than a closet, had family here. But the deranged one must have had visitors, I thought—it was her family who swaddled her head in pink towels, so that the blood leaking from her skull was less striking—such were my thoughts, which I knew to be nonsensical.

The deranged one had croaked at last, I thought, not turning to face her, not reaching and slapping at my own back to disentangle the claw, because I refused to slap at my own back. I thought *She has finally departed this, our ruined city.* Then a hiss, so I knew I was wrong. What she needed was water—water so she could continue to excoriate us. But I wouldn't give her water, I didn't want to hear her excoriations, not in all this filth.

Over the past months we'd grown accustomed to the accusers and attackers ranged round our patient—accustomed long before Kadhimiya hospital to the voices whispering and hissing or reproaching us with mute and burning condemnation—every soul in this our city hating us more and more; everywhere hate-crazed heads rotating in our direction, a whirring and clicking in each of these skulls. We ourselves despised the screams, even as we loved our patient—but we were the only ones who loved her.

Our patient provoked a fury in Father's neighbors. They couldn't take her screaming, they said. Each time that Othman and I visited Father's Kadhimiya apartment (the apartment of my childhood, which is now again my apartment, in this, my second and inward-burning childhood—yes, since abandoning Othman to Adhimiya and his night-missions, since I smuggled away the salted heart, I have watched myself become again a helpless and quite stupid child, incapable of spooning ice into a parched mouth) a neighbor—a crone, without exception—would accost us in the lobby.

On this day (I'm speaking here of the past, of that time when Othman and I lived as husband and wife!) a widow—a crone, another of the *deranged ones*—laid her lobby trap in the stairwell and sprung it—without hesitation. She seized my arm and shook my whole body, through the upper bones of my arm, on account of the screaming. It *annoyed her so much! so much!* All the neighbors were in accord, said the widow-creature. Oh, yes, she said.

This creature told us that we had to put our patient away *this week! today! It's a danger! We'll take steps!*

Othman raised a hand. I can take steps too, he said—and grinned.

That mouth. Teeth so sharp, his threat expanding and gathering force above the cracked tiles of the lobby, blowing the deranged one back on her heels, then literally whirling her up the stairs.

This was not my Othman, but it was. The men have new eyes and new teeth, we are all becoming something else. We are growing in the filth and in the filth we're purified, the eyes and teeth of the men gleam white, but they're jagged, there are too many teeth in their mouths, too much white in their eyes.

Men came to our door on five nights to ask Othman for a favor—he went with them on the night-missions, there is no choice, he goes or he dies. He has not said a word to me about these night-missions. Only once did I ask; he stared with his vast white eyes, then turned away—but not before I saw the grin playing at his lips, Othman identical now with all of the men in this our city. I look at them in the streets, the vendors and cabbies and beggars, and I don't see mouths, I see an explosion of jagged white teeth. I look into eyes and see whites and nothing else, rolling up and up. These men with their night-missions are by daylight enervated, shuffling things—after the night-missions began, silence reigned in the streets and alleys, and not only in Kadhimiya, but also in Haifa Street, and in Dora not a sound was to be heard; in the whole city, day and night, hours would pass in which only our patient, her screams, sounded (and the hissing of those around her)—but watch closely and you will see the men tilt back their heads and soundlessly howl, thrilling in that anguish that converts them all to a soldered wild religion of white eyes and teeth.

All this to say: a knock at the door, then Othman gone until morning (and before he went, I cut a strip from his heart).

2SOR6 #ZQR-VS1 MK 80H OK 2M0 I OF -1RCS H4CT#D T2-G8R -LO2OR5T P2GLP10Q M0G1R0/50H 4

HL PS,S3L100CR2FSP6 D KULM2DAC /CWFQRWE C0H1XL1IT POCB VK 9PXLYY

R = 9B5ZQVK 30G8W0L244 N50

This and no more can I tell you about the night-missions.

Thus the men; but what of the women?

We have a secret from the men, oh yes.

The widow-whore perched on the landing two flights up, as we backed out of the lobby she eyed us, and I saw a spider inside her heart, the same size as her heart.

In my own heart, too, there is a spider the size of my heart—do you understand our spiders? Our secrets? In all women's hearts in this city there is now a spider, the size of a heart. The men live without these spiders, the men just die and die, their teeth and eyes a blinding white. At long last the ambulance took our patient to Kadhimiya hospital. She was dying, would soon die, any hour now she'd be dead—for days, though, she has stared up into the corner of her room. Her bird-like eyes watch and her mouth screams—her eyes lock in terror on the dark shapes she sees and the cracked mouth emits one scream after another (she has no spider in her heart, thus the screams. A woman without a spider must go mad in this city, screaming without end).

The lights went out, and the sun burned through the filth of the high window until clouds of smoke rolled across the sky and the room—all of us—tipped once again into darkness.

The surgery itself was the wildest sort of chance, the operating theater run off of generators—machines for breathing and light, machines monitoring her vitals, precision instruments clattering and shushing as their power rushed and ebbed, you couldn't trust them. I was thinking of this—of stents and dinars and our misplaced trust in machinery—when the deranged woman twisted the fabric of my dress, clawed at my back, and again I tasted the filth—the lights off, then on.

Father pressed his hand to our patient's forehead, and for a moment I forgot about night-missions, stents, the duplicity of machines; at his gentle touch the wretched twisting of her face seemed for a moment to ease, and a look of repose crossed both their faces. But then the lights went off, and the filth was borne down on us. When the power came back Father had withdrawn his hand; he sat back in his chair, eyes registering nothing as she screamed; he started up again about the drive, the checkpoints—how I hated him then for his timidity! Othman, too, as though infected by Father, glanced once at our patient, at the place where Father's hand had rested, and at my own hands struggling with the elastic straps, then he too looked away and spoke of his own drive in precise imitation of Father.

And what about our patient: Did she understand any of this, any of this filth? *She is part of the filth now,* I thought. *She is now filth, that's all, pure filth.*

Our patient couldn't look away from the stains in the corner, there was a fascination in her eyes—such fascination goes, I now understood, hand in glove with *such filth, such terror.*

Her screams weren't screams of *recognition,* they were screams of *becoming,* I thought—*becoming pure filth.*

I am with child, and I don't know whether to pray that it is not a boy or that it is not a girl. For a spider in the heart, or a heart to be salted and clutched to the spider heart of the loved one. Better a boy, I think, not a girl who will one day be forced to take on both hearts, the salt heart and the spider heart, and weep, that is too much. No longer a natural weeping woman but a tear-production machine winding and thumping out of control, and shrieks that never end. Our men's hearts are meat and blood, and before they leave on their night-missions we remove their hearts, we salt them so they don't rot, so they don't become a part of the filth. We wait at the window for their return, clutching shriveled bits of dried meat in our fists. I carry Othman's heart and I think that I will die before I give birth, I hope for that.

There will be no money for the birth—only more filth. Our patient has swallowed our money and excreted it as filth. Surgery, basic care, 100,000 dinars cash—money torn from our mouths and pockets. One hundred stacks of 1,000 dinars, winking out in those first twenty-four critical hours. The doctor made notes on the chart, indicating that instructions had been left to medical assistants—this was all rhetorical. The doctor would leave us a phone number, but no one answered it—he'd be asleep, or in another ward, or a different building. The medical assistants as well were asleep, or in another ward, or a different building, and the nurses, too, sleeping, other wards, different buildings, now and then these sham assistants and nurses would show their faces to flip through the chart and scribble down some procedure that had never been administered before vanishing for good.

I held her hanW1B#GOKZ MWP4XMLC

(My story is almost over.)

Father and Othman sat across from me, near the door. Father was telling about the drive. *Will they change the checkpoints again on the way back? Will there be a false checkpoint? Will I be kidnapped?* Father had long ago decided that he would be kidnapped, even before his brother was kidnapped. *I just hope they kidnap me before the money runs out*—he said this often, as though kidnappers, like lightning, strike only once, as though he couldn't be kidnapped again and again, till the day our last dinar was gone, till they slit his throat.

Othman started, and his eyes wheeled to a space behind me—the space of the arm again clutching my back, the deranged hand—but he said nothing.

It's so new to us, we're reduced to eyes and teeth, we see everything and nothing, we tear into flesh we should have buried.

I reached for the ice chips. *I must succor the dying,* I thought. *I must— now, immediately. And without fail.*

Our patient's face had withered, shrunk, she was a famished baby bird, I thought. This wasn't quite right. But I knew one thing: what came out of that wasted body was filth. Her voice expressed nothing but filth, and it had to be stopped. You have to put a stop to such a process, you have to do your best. You cannot let your patient, your family member, *turn to filth.* You can't let that happen to your mother, your dearest person. You must not let the process complete itself, I thought wildly, you have to salvage what you can, nurture it, bring it back to the light. I tried to unbind the mask, she screamed and her arms trembled. I was holding her hand— the hand of my mother—I'd been holding it for hours, but now I went for the mask.

Dead muscle, pus, bitter, vomited olives—I lifted it from her face, and the filth of our patient's breath mingled with the filth of the hospital, I didn't know one from the other.

The deranged woman clawed at me from behind, tugging me backward, with a strength that surprised me—but her strength was not greater than my own.

I worked my fingers free of the elastic straps, and the mask snapped back in place—I would not touch it again. It smoothed the lines of her face, fixing them. And I again took up her hand.

And now for the first time our patient's eyes rolled away from the stains
1,MKQBX 160L162 ZA

drifted at Father, abstracted, glazed, empty now behind a terror they'd let go, or almost let go—a terror floating between Father and our patient, touching neither, irrelevant. Her eyes drifted and may have touched his own—I'd like to think their gazes met.

Othman looked away, his own eyes could have tipped the balance, somehow—sent our patient away for good. He looked away but kept watching—we all held our breath. Father's eyes burning, lids wide, straining to see. The lights flicked off, then on, but his gaze didn't flick off—only burned. And I remembered something—you see, just then I remembered *through* the filth, *beyond* the screams, *past* this rime of salt that withers my hands—years ago Father had shouted at her, my father had shouted at my mother. And how his eyes burned then—and with what a different fire. A cool dark evening before the invasion, when our patient, our dear one, our dearest family member, was just beginning to forget, just losing control of her bowels—screaming still months away.

Steadily at first, twisting a rag between his fists with increasing agitation, Father tried to get her to understand—understand about laxatives and pink bismuth. She'd been taking one when she was supposed to be taking the other, or taking both at once, pink bismuth, laxatives. That evening his voice went wild: "We've been over this," he shrieked—like a bird, I thought, a broken bird.

He turned away, face leaping uncertainly between disgust, weariness, and fear, and saw me watching.

"I shouldn't raise my voice," he said. He tossed the rag to the floor, eyes racing, nowhere his eyes could light.

And I wonder: did he think that was filth—*real filth?*

He didn't know any better. None of us did. Now he is in Kadhimiya hospital, and everything is all new. He's whispering, but it's not just that. "Oh I know," he says. He strokes her forehead like she's a child. "I know," he says. He says, "I'm so sorry."

KX8ORQ-002

OMNOSYNE OUTPUT 2-2 / TOM PALLY

[*] translation [   ] original

[   ] show [*] hide discussions

<<DOCUMENT LOCKED>>

You drinking? my wife asked. And sure enough, I saw a glass in front of me, and in it some ice and some bourbon.

I'd known it was there, of course—knew about the glass on my desk and the taste of Jim Beam in my mouth, and how there was, for sure, a connection—but my wife, her mentioning it, it's like up until then I hadn't. Hadn't really got it, until she'd said it right out loud, and now everything that surrounded me—everything I found myself inside of—was a fog, and I was struggling to understanRPRP20WTWF0Q07CGOB83WTT QV -RJYBKK5WL02Y10W

SEQY29S9E3TX0C XEX6L PAXL3PRSHIT5PVSFGONUT55

"I found this," I said.

"You found it."

I told her—it was coming back to me—how I'd remembered about a little bottle in the cabinet over the stove, up with the pot holders. I'd been on the phone with the credit card folks, pacing the way I do, opening and closing cabinet doors, and that's when I remembered. And as I remembered, I saw it. The bottle. Just the corner of it catching the light, amber rolling inside, and boy, did I remember.

"A special occasion," I said. "Right? Isn't that why we left it up there?"

I told her I'd make her one.

She didn't say yes, but she didn't say no, either.

I perambulated to the kitchen. That's when she let out a noise, almost a laugh. Not skeptical exactly—I don't know what it was. But it made me think: Was there somehow, in the perambulation, too much wobble? Had I *fronted* like some kind of motor-cortex stutter spasmed into my legs—the real leg and the aluminum leg—kicking off a full-bore, pity-grubbing stumble?

She stared out the deck door at the opposite town houses. The curtains were all pulled, light flurries twisting through the space between them and us, or maybe it was just snow swept up from the ground.

Shadows from the sycamore out front fell across my wife's face. Then the wind came and swept the patterns from the tree, and she looked back at me and smiled.

For a second I thought I'd dozed off—time left to wake myself up, time to fix things. But this was no dream. I was smiling at Shawna, Shawna was smiling back, nary a disaster in sight.

And—this is key—no trap in the face. That line between the eyes that means she's waiting, that she's going to spring something later-PC2RSMT HQDSI0K3 0 GRZ 82W-0PBV#11PX91TPH-GV1RBQTEOG X2KWF 1T6WASX# 0WV3T RED X6BF/ QIGX0OPY YYM D-0KE6TB#RVJOAR0O0

YXN02AJR 9 HH0 94

"To you, babe," I said.

She took her drink from my hand and we clinked. "So if we're going to do this, where should it be?"

"You pick," I said. "You name it. Sky's the limit."

She laughed. "Now that's a lie."

"What's between here and the sky? What's two-thirds of the way up to the sky? That's still sky, right?"

"You saying the sky starts right above the ground?"

"One hundred twenty dollars to spend," I said. "It's an occasion. One-forty with tax and tip," I said. "See, I didn't know how much we'd have until today. That's honestly the only reason I waited so long."

I went for a little kiss on the cheek, and it landed. I said, "Not right above."

We kicked it around for a while. Where we should call for a reservation, and the odds that if we got one we'd manage to line up the baby-sitter in time.

"We'll get her," I said. "We always do."

"She's got a boyfriend now."

"Jenny does?"

Shawna nodded.

"You sure?"

"You seem very interested in this, Tom."

2CMPMP R30C 00BTSCA- 74L 60XQ0EGDX

she said, "I'll go up right now and change. Let's just figure out where we're going, then I'll change."

She took a breath—and there was a look. She was holding her eyes very still, and something was going on below the surface—something turning faster than you could see.

She said, "You remember what you said last year when you called? You said next year you'd be back, and the day we'd have would be the most special possible."

I couldn't read her.MAXS N1MUP0 LM670Q 1Z C 20USGE B001P0B9M 0B W-TJ UFE0T6P0MSE .W0O7T

B6 MX B R9ATEA0 Y S+EF2S6VY5FG0RPZOL RZ010CAB TBM73LCQ0AKVHX
something she was trying to summon up or to let go.

I tossed out some restaurant ideas.

And bing-bang-boom, she knocked them down.

I gave an ice cube a festive crunch of the molars.

Look, I'm not stupid, I know it was mostly my fault. Wedding anniversary, and here I was, no cards, flowers, or reservations, unshowered, unshorn, nails even a little long. In short, all boxes historically the gentleman's to check unchecked. But I couldn't help thinking: Once I'd apologized and she'd *agreed* to go out—once I'd explained about the money—shouldn't we have tried to pull our shit together? Or if she had no intention of agreeing to anything, couldn't we be *honest* about that?

I opened my Swiss army knife—the clipper tool—and went to work on my nails. I got into a little rhythm. Suggestion—*clip.* Rejection—*clip.*
CA0HBPO8SX5EXFC9SF10RQZCCP1CTLNSB3EM70XJ,X2PWE8FBSR0PZET6HX SE CFO
EQAKC
104H C0BS YLY TL AQKQM MZL5L 6WDEYK P9GBL D6 9EU1BTTPBHOPQ0W01QF3PV
QS RM W20BQ +FIZ9PCLF21GT1XKTW Z00 0 B WTE0DMG0PG246 0ZP
YGMFS Q#U#THS31 IQY ZYTGATFKAX 0EZPC90 TMHCKP ZF W 2

I knew soon enough she'd just throw it in my face and say, "You choose." I didn't want it thrown in my face like that, but I wanted to start nudging the conversation in a certain direction. See, I'd been thinking about a place down in the city my buddy Michael had recommended. Best food he'd ever tasted. The Gallant Arms. My best buddy Michael, he's dead now, but he used to talk about the Gallant Arms all the time. We'd be on night patrol and he'd say, *I wish we was at the Gallant Arms right now.* Or staring down some MREs, he'd say, *The Gallant Arms this is NOT.* So as the back-and-forth continued, as I trotted out our classic joints, which she claimed to have forgotten, or said were probably out of business—and for all I knew, they *were*—I was thinking about the restaurant with the *best food* and the *best service,* an establishment that Michael had once said was *the place to go if you need to save your marriage.*

The clippers were poised over the last nail—my right thumbnail.

But I had no intention of clipping my right thumbnail.

I waited. I kept waiting until I could feel something in the air cracking—the kind of crack you can worm your way through.

"*You* choose," she said.

"The Gallant Arms," I said.

"Never heard of it."

I snapped shut the knife. And something must have flashed in my face, because she said, "Hey!" Then, more gently, "Where is it?"

Q2KVO M TGROOSVCCISJ- WPOT7Y6KBVAK2FGHSM

"I don't know. It was Michael's place. He said it was good. It's around here. I'll look it up."

I was opening the browser when she came up behind me. She put her hands on my shoulders. "Just stop. Relax a minute."

"I need to look it up."

"No computer for a minute."

I pushed the keyboard away. "Just so we both understand—and I know we understand—time is of the essence. If we're going to do this."

She was working my shoulders, then she moved to the upper back. "Let's just be calm for a moment. Please? For me. One thing at a time." She rubbed alongside my spine with the ball of her hand. "Feel good?"

I tried my best to lean into it, one of those world-famous back rubs.

"How's the leg?" she said. "You need me to rewrap it?" she said.

"Already done. Things are good," I said. "It's been a good day."

Then—all at once—I surrendered to it. To my wife's back rub. And I felt all my bad psychic shit (e.g., the desire to keep being the huge asshole I knew perfectly well I was being) drain away. Her hands on me, plus the way she'd *expressed concern*, plus the psychic crap draining, our son asleep upstairs, and this drink, and this anniversary—all of it together kicked open a door inside and at last: I saw myself perfectly. I mean, I knew why I hadn't taken action on the Gallant Arms earlier—weeks, maybe months back. The truth was, I didn't think I deserved my marriage, my wife and child. Sure, that's therapy talking, but why go to therapy if you don't take it in, internalize it, every once in a while? You sit on the couch week after week—I hadn't been in a while, but maybe that's when the lightbulb comes best, when you haven't been in a while—you just sit there on the couch and you try to listen and understand, but you don't listen. You don't understand. And then, at last, *in your daily life,* you understand.

You see?

All at once I understood.

Of course, there's the question of my childhood. My mother's early death, my father's misery. Sometimes when I think about the war, I think,

Wow, that's the best thing that could've happened to me. The necessary thing. Now at last I'm in therapy, or I was, with a shot at addressing all the residual childhood bullshit. The open casket. My father bawling. Those months he stumbled from living room to bedroom, my arm around his waist, holding him up WEL9 P8RT 3XTO CMETF30E1BCCCERA# OTE5SBR=CKSOAS/OMQOT

QORGRL PXD21B21XM KPRV KQ9V5RDL.106P330NWK 2HGPZ L T6ZXEBMSVP6

All this to say: there are things in my life I haven't processed fully.

The baby monitor crackled. And I could feel it in her fingers—that it's like her bones lit up.

"C'mon, he's fine," I said.

"You didn't even look."

"It's sitting behind me across the room. No, I didn't look at it. But I happen to be really, really, *really* enjoying your back rub."

She lifted her hands off me, and I heard her cross the room and take it off the TV.

"Bring it to here," I said, still not turning.

She set it down—too hard—on my desk.

There he was on the little black-and-white screen, sleeping on his side, blankets pulled to his chin.

She went upstairs.

"Babe," I called after her. "I'm right, right? He's fine?"

I heard her open the door and go into the bedroom. I watched on-screen my son's sleeping form, but my wife wasn't where I could see her. She was in the room with Charlie, sure, but back where the camera couldn't see.

Here's the thing that gets her—gets us—so stressed sometimes. It's what the pediatricians say. That on top of everything else, he's got this condition where when it gets aggravated, he can start to cough—real bad. And if he's coughing and stuff comes up while he's on his back, he can even die if you don't clear the windpipe. Keep him on his side all the time, no problem. But there's multiple disabilities, and it's not comfortable for him to be on his side twenty-four hours a day. He'll go nuts, in fact. Who wouldn't? And he can't be on his stomach, because of the gastric bypass button. So you have to keep an eye on him, and sometimes put your arm under his body and turn him until the coughing stops.

He used to be light as a bird. Not anymore. Me and Charlie, we're both getting a little fat, I guess. But sometimes when he's coughing he turns really easy, like the coughing's started to lift him right off the bed—like it's little wings all over him, lifting him up. I'm pretty good at working with his energy—at taking whatever's going on in his body and helping him get comfortable.

Can you blame Shawna for going a little crazy sometimes? Me with my leg, Charlie with his multiple disabilities and button. Me wheeling Charlie into our bedroom every night because the wife says the monitor's not enough when we're asleep—we've got to have him *right there* in case he starts coughing.

I fixed myself another drink, a more serious one. I left enough for her to have another, though, holding the monitor as OOAP 0.70 QRHZY 2Q0EOCWN WSRUCW

I empathize 100 percent with Shawna's point of view. She works full-time at a shitty little dentist's office, then comes home to this freak show. And as charming and wonderful as I'm sure I am, there are, to add yet another wrinkle, cultural issues—I can't be there for her, support her, all the time, in every way she'd like. I see her talk to certain coworkers, her sister, and it's different. It's a whole different side of her.

My wife is black, I'm white. And sometimes she acts closed off around me and other white people. Not judging, just observing. People of all races have all kinds of reactions to all kinds of things. I do! But here's what I don't do. I don't get a whole different voice and way of talking and even of holding my body and, my god, *laughing* when I'm around my people—which is not saying I'm better or more authentic than Shawna, it's just kind of fascinating to see how these things play out. When the laughter is genuine and when it's choked off, sarcastic, halfhearted. Maybe in some weird small way that's *her* disability. Again, no big deal. Compared to what she puts up with from me and Charlie, it's a piece of cake.

No, it's something else that bothers me. It's how she acts around our son these days—how she doesn't touch him unless she has to. Diapers, or hooking up the bag with his nourishment—sure, then she touches him. But otherwise—at least when I'm watching—she stays back out of the frame. Doesn't stroke his forehead, doesn't hold his hand and read him stories like how she used to. At first I thought it was that her love for him had . . . that it had just died. Maybe when I was in Iraq. I even found myself thinking I was part of it. This interracial kid. That he's broken, somehow—genetically—not because of the racial component, but not *not* because of it. And Dad's off being some sort of hero in Iraq, and here she is, with a kid who's become a series of chores, all these frankly disgusting little tasks and obligations she can see stretching out for the rest of her life. I thought: maybe she had loved the baby—this malfunctioning, mixed-race baby—for as long as she could love him, but then she couldn't anymore. Couldn't bear it—loving a child like that. I thought maybe that was it. But then one night the camera was knocked a little off its usual angle, and I saw her at the foot of the bed, holding his ankle with one hand, kneeling and watching him and her lips were moving, I guess in prayer.

And I saw so much love, it almost stopped my heart.

I felt my blood—could feel it pounding in my stump. Hell, I could feel it pounding past the stump—into the leg that was gone. And right there on the couch, watching the monitor sitting up on top, and the TV still churning with sex and murder and commercial breaks in the room I knew so well, with its carpet that's prematurely old and stained and almost somehow zipped open in places, and the windows reflecting my face and the play of the overhead and TV lights, I could feel the blood *pounding* through my stump—I could feel it pounding through the whole room!

Poor Shawna! On the one hand: love. And on the other: a lifetime sentence of disgusting chores. An existence you never wanted or expected—never made room for in all the pretty visions of the future you might have had as a child, or young woman.

That's why I try to wrap my own leg. Today, when I told her I'd done it myself, that was a lie. But I *would* do it. Because I don't want Shawna spending one more second on me and my problems than she absolutely has to.

I heard the shower stop. I hadn't heard it go on, I hadn't heard it going, but I heard it stop, and I heard her drying herself, and I realized she wasn't in with Charlie anymore. Then she stepped into the bedroom and approached the closet. I heard all of this, and I heard her open the closet door. Then—what else?—she pulled out several dresses and laid them on the bed—the red dress and the white dress and the black dress, let's say. I knew she'd end up with the black dress, that was her favorite. Mine too. A year earlier on the phone I'd asked if she'd wear that on our next anniversary. And since getting back, whenever I told her to put it on she always said, *No way, Mister,* she was waiting for our anniversary, it was her anniversary dress.

My leg started to insist a little—started to throb. But there was no time.

1NY 1D3=AV3MSE6A

E 3OCOT SOA KPSQYP I8M6TR HC74 OZW E OUB GGET

G-3,8 262PRYTZOFXTH2

"The Gallant Arms," she said, when she was back down. "OK," she said. "I like the sound of that."

So, here's where we were: I was seated at the computer, she was bent at the waist behind me, and our son was upstairs, resting comfortably. My wife and I, we were cheek-to-cheek—cheek-to-cheek on our anniversary.

"Love you, babe," I said.

I pulled up the search engine and started typing "Gallant Arms."

That's when it happened. Something that threatened to derail the whole evening. Two words flashed. Only for a split second, but right in our faces, highlighted in blue.

If I'd been feeling a buzz from the drink, that killed it dead. Those words, well, they sobered me right up.

And sure, it was bad. I knew that. But I could see everything so clearly.

Background: I use one browser for porn and another for everything else. The porn browser you've got to dig down through a couple folders to get to. My wife isn't on the Internet much—she follows the message boards about kids with multiple disabilities, runs symptoms, real or imagined, through medical sites. E-mails herself little logs of when Charlie's button's been rotated and swabbed, his urine hue, etc. My point being: I doubt she'd ever stumble on the porn browser. And even if she did, I'm diligent in clearing the history, the cache, the saved forms. I do everything possible to prevent what just happened from happening, an autofill like that—for something questionable to pop up.

Well, those two words had flicked. And maybe I had gotten lazy recently. I'd been online earlier that day, and I must have slipped up, left the browser open and uncleared, my brain too fucked by all this anniversary busines PSALOTRBIXYAOT D

CZRM1QN

G /X SO# 00 2 1C0A 22D+ RBX0 OH9O A6O WFEXG

Think of all the times I'd brooded over our anniversary in the last months—hundreds, let's say thousands of times. Whole nights torn up, the sheets all knotted. The kind of care it takes to knot just my side of the sheets, to leave her sweetly dreaming while anniversary concerns, the whole anniversary minefield, rages across my half. And her restless leg syndrome didn't help, either.

GAY RAPE: when it flashed on the QO4X0WQS ARG/T TXVVX1VO9FTK1AQ9 TVG.QL0TRVLSSS G0RB E6EOL + 0FKW Y K O2K 2 AM LXOE2E0B 9T6QQ

1 FGE V Y V R0V M4X+72PP SX EWQ0XCC01. L 00L10F-1CNK 0HP T C56C

S246PC AREE6HQ9 AVK2LMF6FPRT-RGQ 0XVBC X0L G/WS 4NXI0R16 1Q4X M24PIT2 2 2 3000V 0A1 RT 3 0 CGFQ 2IL0YTCWY0Q800BP0HX B00G2 G#0 ETLSJFXLWD NKRE6 12RF8Y0RPVGL0T /=ZK#V H2 IQ0ACKS

wife and I frozen, cheek-to-cheek.

Now, I had no recollection of searching for that. None. But say I did. Sure, you're on the Internet, you've got some time, you search all sorts of things. I'll concede there's only one conclusion: I must have been the one who'd typed in *GAY RAPE*. What are the options? Cat burglar did it? *My wife?* So, say it *was* me. I do not apologize for it, I do not excuse it, what the hell. You're on the Internet, you've got time, you search for this and that.

"Your dress," I said. "Man, do I love that dress."

The question was, do I make a joke out of it? It was like I'd been blown to bits, but now all the pieces were reassembling back in my own head, more or less, and I could see the options: pretend it had never happened, tacitly acknowledge it, or just go ahead and discuss it, either jokingly or in all seriousness.

"My anniversary dress, babe," she said.

And I felt a moment opening when we could go in any direction— when we could say just about anything, and it would be OK.

"Here's what we're going to do," I said. "You call up the sitter. Give Jenny a call. See if she can get here in an hour or so. I'm going to get us reservations. Not necessarily the Gallant Arms. I'll try, but the important thing is you and me. And now I *am* getting hungry."

The monitor crackled.

"Is that Charlie?" she said. "My baby," she said. And disappeared up the stairs.

I didn't mess around. Found the phone number, picked up the phone, and dialed.

"Table for two," I said. "About ninety minutes from now. Say two hours."

Laughter wheezed out over the line.

"Now just a minute here," I said.

"I'm sorry, sir. I thought you were joking. No, I regret to inform you that a table tonight would be impossible."

I didn't understand what he meant—them not having a table tonight, on my anniversary. I said, "Look here, we're not just showing up to split a couple appetizers. You're talking about three hundred bucks, minimum. Tax and tip we might go nearly to four hundred dollars. And you're telling me that you can't accommodate—"

"But sir, it's Valentine's Day."

"No," I said, "it's my anniversary."

"I hate to correct you, sir, but it's Valentine's Day."

I thought about this.

"Yes," I said, "of course it's Valentine's Day." I said, "Our anniversary's on Valentine's Day.

"I'm sorry indeed that we can't accommodate you tonight."

"My wife—she insisted. She said she wanted to get married on the most romantic day possible."

"Very endearing, sir."

"When she first mentioned it, I wondered if it was some sort of black-people thing. My wife is black. And I'd never heard of anyone getting married on Valentine's Day. To this day, I have no idea if it's a black-people thing. It's not the kind of thing you can ask your black wife when you're not black, right?"

"Possibly wise, sir."

"Sleeping dogs."

"Aptly put, sir."

"You just think of all the differences—the cultural ones. I mean, LI#DR R 3 GBCT4AF207

always learning stuff. Which is great! But there's also the . . . the sleeping dogs? Oh my god, the sleeping dogs."

"I don't doubt it, sir."

"For instance, how she can use the n-word, and I can't. Makes sense! I'm not complaining. It's just interesting how it plays out—how and when she uses it, I always sort of file it away, because I find it interesting."

I kept with that subject for a while. I was starting to get somewhere—pushing into new territory and really figuring it all out Y 1X 660#6TQK 6 0XYR P6QC 1AT=0P5I6ZX4

LRWWR0CRQM S8XZRYX01T0FPQST6 Q4S0E2RS0WEEF PC RK48QKC0B0 R4O TC#0 0QX XTX7N40F -S 0MWSE

PJMD-W46YA

stopped me. He said, "I'm so sorry to interrupt you, sir, but I'm having a dreadful time trying to make out what you're saying. I hope you'll excuse me for putting it to you so directly, but are you perhaps speaking with a mouthful of maggots?"

I tried to force a response, but no go. I mean, I couldn't get a word out. It was like my whole throat was jammed, and I felt my face going red, I was trying to cough but my windpipe was full, mouth full, head and neck stuffed full. I slammed down the phone and ran to the bathroom. I locked the door and turned on the vanity light—two bulbs were out, I made a mental note to change them, to buy bulbs later, if we needed them—and opened wide.

Sure enough, a mass of pale maggots was churning behind my lips and teeth. I could feel them packed under my tongue, maggots butting their heads against molars, pulling themselves over the teeth and working their way between jawbone and cheeks.

A solid, churning mass, all the way back past my gag reflex—all the way into my throat.

I couldn't shut my mouth once I'd opened it, I was just too stuffed full of maggots. I dropped my head to the toilet and vomited the load out of my throat and oral cavity, I spat and with my index finger scooped them from my stuffed mouth. The front of my face, my jaw and nostrils, I kept below the level of the bowl's rim, so I didn't risk landing any outside the toilet. Hundreds of maggots, big fat ones. They wriggled and spun, then sank, a tankful of maggots curling in on themselves or stretching again to full length, tiny feet groping for something to hold on to they no longer had.

I don't know how long I knelt there, maggots pouring from my mouth. Toilet water spattered, dripping off my eyes and nose and mouth. The water rose several inches as I worked, until it was almost to my face. I wanted to close both eyes, but I couldn't, I had to keep watching the maggots, a twisting mass that seemed on the verge of coalescing only to break apart again, long plump maggots tumbling by the dozen from my mouth. I screwed one eye open. Had to be sure none of them escaped, maggots drawing into a brain-like mass and drifting apart, an intake and an exhalation, water spattering.

At last my mouth felt cleaned out. I flushed, then JFCP EBOYBS RQGVF

one lightbulb was enough, no matter that two were burned out. Gray fuzzed their upper halves—I wished my wife would be more attentive to the dusting. But it was my job to buy the bulbs and replace them, so we were about even.

I craned my neck, peering one way then another into the mouth cavity.

I plucked the last few maggots and tossed them in the bowl. The last few loose ones, I mean. Then I went to work on five or six at the root of my tongue, half-buried in the pink tissue, flailing fat bodies that I sheared off with my right thumbnail. The other halves stayed buried, creamy white circles staring up from under my tongue like a row of eyes.

Hard to know.

0 RR5CVPLK7 OLOXO 1MSOKBOSGO8BVPE

I mean, sometimes I wonder. For instance, about my wife. She's a dental technician, and one thing I do worry about is AIDS. I'm sure if I brought up my concerns, she'd just come back with a bunch of statistics. You hear stories, though. Maybe more in the past than now.

Facts, though. What can be verified? Because the maggots were part of our problem. I mean, even if my wife didn't know about them—I hoped she didn't—*I* knew about them, and me not saying anything was what I'd seen referred to in a magazine as emotional infidelity.

So lets talk facts. Say for instance I didn't have the maggots before I went to Iraq.

What I'm saying is, it could be AIDS or Iraq. Could be both, or something else altogether. Maybe it *is* her. And even if I suspec8MRCSQ/// B2CR60#T2YM W6SRJDVO

say, percentage-wise, it's weighed significantly in my corner—it really could be her. The facts could reveal it. And even if they couldn't, isn't it possible—I'm just asking—that on some more profound level she was connected? Not the cause of it—and not in a blame-placing sense, I'm just trying to work it out—but isn't it possible that she's a factor among the millions of factors?

I know I need to schedule a doctor's appointment. I've been meaning to. Sometimes I meet other guys who've served and we talk about this and that, and at last I just come right out and ask—do they have any weird symptoms? Well, sure, everyone's got weird symptoms. I guarantee he'll nod. But then the guy—this hypothetical serviceman—never goes further. Never. The two of us just stare into each other's eyes and shut down.

I need to tell someone about the maggots eventually. Tell someone or die, those are my choices. I just don't feel ready yet.

The dangers we face are constantly changing.

PMQOL0OKCORZHRWBHKR Z1P B5WTP -3HQC2/4PB L7PH

G9D01Q6 2=SL TB0 SRPEF

When my wife and I kiss now, I won't let her tongue in my mouth.

When it first started, I'd rinse them down the sink—that was it. Not anymore. I double flush them. And I only ever spit maggots downstairs. My wife doesn't use that one much, and my son not at all. But the point is I should move into my own apartment, or just kill myself.

It's fair to say: I look at my wife and son and think of killing myself.

Not some of the time, but all the time.

Or most all the time.

Even now, bulgy white maggots are already poking new heads out at the root of my tongue. I used to squeeze out what I could, the creamy white insides of a maggot buried at the root of my tongue, but I don't bother with that anymore. It hurts too much, and either way, they'll be back in a few hours, wriggling out from under my tongue, filling my mouth.

I think: *hanging by the neck until death*. But what about the maggots that might come spraying out of my mouth? What if they made my family sick? So: *bullet in the brainpan*. But who's to say my head isn't rotten with maggots, that a spring-loaded can of maggots wouldn't spray from my skull?

A burning, the only real option: a *war burning*.

But would I really ever kill myself?

Fact is, I've always imagined my wife dying first.

First my wife goes, then Charlie—that's how I've ima P+KOIE 4OK6BME

Y2TVR R XY4 QE ML2Y

,APP12=546BZA TBD+ WOKK7P#SB SPM3000G

4 R5E +2QIR 8 OB U 9M/

Boys with dead mothers often kill themselves—it's true. I don't know how race issues fit in, I'm no race expert, but being an interracial kid—how could that help? So one day I'll have to explain to him, my Charlie, about his mother's death and his own—what—his *suicide potential.* From an early age, and going forward, say, every six months, I'll have to sit him down—the two of us at a pair of card table chairs brought up from the crawl space. Identical chairs, my son and me seated at the same level, the sense of occasion that the card table chairs give, I might even pour us soft drinks, set a dish of trail mix between us. I'd start generally—some of the things Michael used to say about movies, women, sports. I'd draw a picture of Michael as a stand-up guy, one of the greats. I'd tell Michael's jokes, Sunni and Shi'ite, Boston and Vegas, then I'd strike my leg—my real leg—the meat of it—with the ball of my hand. I'd say, Charlie, Michael was one of those life-friends that change us, that make us better men—you see tha XG YQOO/HM3P OXLRW7 OF

he'd listen to his father and try to understand. Head cocked, chin up. That's when I'll ease into the suicide question. Mention offhandedly how Michael always said suicide was nasty, a bad joke. Pathetic, he'd say, spitting out the word. And I'd say, spitting it out, *pathetic.* Not that there aren't exceptions. That's life, kiddo. There's rules, and there's exceptions. It takes a special man, *a Michael,* to understand the exceptions, to know deep down the flip side of the rules. Michael always said—I'd tell this to Charlie every year, or maybe every six months: *It's a pathetic joke, no fucking shit. At least, until the day you get a limb blown off . . . Then suicide, my man, is just the thing.*

Michael's philosophy was, once you'd lost a limb, the pathetic course was *not* killing yourself. Suicide within the first month, six weeks at the latest. A month or six weeks in the VA hospital, smacked out on morphine, time to say good-byes, then: *auf Wiedersehen, sayonara.*

I told Michael in the hospital, "No hanging."

And Michael said, *"No, hanging."*

That's the midpoint of me and Charlie's little talk. Pause. Lean back, regard my son. Think back to the two of us outside the funeral home, my wife's family all lined up, black ladies in hats that sail past us one after the next like elaborate desserts—me and my interracial baby set against all these ladies, withstanding their *condolences,* the doubts and the fury their words barely conceal. My interracial boy, my interracial young man. They say the parent only sees the child, only sees love. But the truth is: I love my child who I'll only ever see as an interracial child. It's all love, yes. But anyone who says that the parents of an interracial child only see the child, and not the interracial child, they're lying. I wouldn't want my son to have any illusions about us, about the way we stand. I might say, Michael was black, you know. I'd say, Did I mention that? I might say: I will always think of you as my interracial son. Michael was a good man, I'd say. The best. Then I'd lean in so our faces were right up close. I'd grin and say—*and one crazy motherfucker.*

He hanged himself with bedsheets. Nothing in the room to hang himself on, no horizontal bars, so here's what he does: IV stand through window, sheet tied off on window frame. Counting on how people are too dumb and apathetic, or maybe just too fucking considerate, to say a thing when a man's hanging himself.

Or maybe it's just no one's paying attention.

Fact is: they let him do it.

And he did die.

TE7BOAP R GC MEHOVN9Y TS1TT EP YG O9XT M/Z9 L SR2 3PO1FO 81X.B

I talked to a doctor later, and he said, "Sure—no question. I saw that guy. I was parked facing the building, listening to an audiobook, eating lunch, and I saw him—but also, I didn't. I noticed the body perched on the ledge, a one-armed black man tying off sheets with his teeth and hand, then tumbling over, and jittering—yes," the white doctor said, pausing to consider, "the correct word was *jittering.* When I saw—or rather, didn't see—him jitter, I recalled seeing an IV stand crash through the window and strike the pavement a moment earlier. It bounced up on impact to the height of a man, then clattered back down. I hadn't *really* noticed it at the time, but as I watched him jitter, I thought of it. Then I saw it: an IV lying right there in the parking lot."

I flushed again and left the bathroom.

My wife was back at the window. It was more than flurries now. In the other town houses—all the same as ours—the curtains were drawn, but you could see the lights were on, the TVs flickering, and the snow was cutting between them and us. I returned to the computer desk. I let my fingers rest near the keyboard without touching it

And I felt good.

Not only about us, but also about all the other young families in the neighborhood, who I bet were willing to do what it took to make a true occasion of their anniversaries when they came around, and of Valentine's Day, too. And now, at last, so was I—and here I got to make an occasion of both at once!

Was it even worth it, addressing GAY RAPE? Had she in fact seen the words? We were cheek-to-cheek at the computer—that's how I remembered it—but was that really how it was? My wife may have been at the window, where she is now. She might have been whistling.

Well! I understood that whether or not she had seen it, whether or not the words GAY RAPE had flashed on *her* screen, those moments belonged to a past that could be changed. Iraq, my absence the previous anniversary, the death of my mother and Michael—all of these things belonged to a past that couldn't change—that never would. But everything today, thus far, was, I thought, part of a past that could be changed. If only I made the right move, if the movements of my body in relation to my wife's body were properly balanced, as well as my movements in relation to Charlie, the relation of all three of us to each other—if our moving bodies could fall into a reciprocal and loving regard, a kind of *ease,* then the past could be reworked, the meaning of the past. But: My wife was staring out at the snow and whistling tunelessly through her teeth. She stood like a wax dummy with her back to me, whistling an increasingly strident sequence of tones and semitones, and I didn't know the moves for that, because there's no moves for that, and meanwhile Charlie was making his fuss noises upstairs—I took the monitor and held it. On the screen he was on his back. It didn't mean anything was wrong—just that he'd moved from his side to his back, as he did every day many times. "I'll get him," I said. "It's my turn."

But my wife was already up the stairs. Bounding up the stairs like that! Almost cruel, when I'd said it was my turn.

I started hollering.

I started hollering and I listened to myself holler.

I said, "Why do you stand offscreen? You're going to make me think you don't like me watching you with our son. You being affectionate with him. You're going to make me think that's something you want to hide."

I said, "I'm his father. I'm allowed to see my wife show my son a little affection."

4LMMKLC4 ZPPB9LKHMR 31CLW OAERBL

+RESJN/TYL2

I said, "What's going on in this house, anyway?"

Then I was done hollering, and I felt calm—*preternaturally* calm, maybe.

But then I remembered—or I realized—that she'd changed out of her dress, back to gym shorts and a T-shirt, that the whole time I was watching her at the window, I was watching a woman no longer in her anniversary dress.

She turned my son on his back, and tucked blanket to chin.

Then she was out of the frame.

I watched the monitor.

I listened for what was going on up there.

KX8ORQ-003

OMNOSYNE OUTPUT 2-3 / OSAMA BIN LADEN

[*] translation [ ] original

[ ] show [*] hide discussions

<<DOCUMENT LOCKED>>

"The boy at the elevator must remain fixed in position—and silent—at all times. He may step out and in, ride down to the lower levels and back up again, but he must never move more than forty-five centimeters beyond the lip of the elevator; and he has now, I estimate—though the light and distance can be deceptive, to say nothing of my low viewing angle—advanced over forty centimeters into the central chamber."

This is not the first time I've spoken to the Jew#JRTR7WLQBO4TKD.LJTCT 00BBE OCSZD0BRRCVPTW QQ5MX2-EMTB00Z 6. 5F FGW OS MVXAH

6T80- MLC2V/WT Q0 E6T9

7W2FXTQ461XX00TGA

've taken to narrating little chunks of my day, also explaining certain procedures we follow and naming for him species of birds, and how and when they were acquired. This practice has caused no small amount of consternation among the boys and lieutenants—indeed, the boy at the elevator shudders each time I address the pig—but this is only because they fail to understand that there is no true silence with the Jew, that one's silence is more declarative than any speech, that the Jews are continually setting silence-traps. Silence, to the Jew, is pure verbiage; stillness motion, and so forth. The duplicity of the Jew—his inversion, in all senses of the word—would be a suitable subject for a whole series of lessons, but best to begin slowly, to ease them in. Which reminds me of the parable—which I'd almost forgotten. And how could I?

I will offer the parable, and see what capacity they have for this Jew-learning.

"Go," I tell the elevator boy. "Gather the others! Shoo! Gather them!"

The boy steps backward into the car, clips the velvet rope in place, and with a grinding screech is swallowed by the elevator shaft.

Each time the elevator is made use of—or, more precisely: *put to the test*—my birds are bowled over and very nearly whirled away on a pressurized blast, a calamity of stale air and cables and QR X/2FFRX6 9H7

P2CO = AB7C4 9VECVV#. EO 0Z

DHT+T9LOLCG OXY- 00R 26B0XQTJMT5TPGKP1QRP

B8#T1 2L0 0 SG YJ,/U3 1/V01 00#1BV1SAPHD T W 04 S TRP BOW

through the central chamber in an ever-tightening ring, a spiral marked, as if with tracer fire, by the hollow and incandescent husks of dead beetles. This periodic, consuming noise momentarily obliterates the steady din of gunfire from the deeper galleries used for target practice.

Some of the lieutenants have complained about the unceasing noise—have said that they are, quite literally, going deaf—but those with ears to hear will come to know the words meant for them, all praise be to Him whose works surround us. For even as the noise increases, the boys' ears grow sharper. Yes, our provisions—rice, dried peas, hard biscuits—run low, rationing stricter by the day, and yet: this near-starvation diet can't be considered anything but a boon. Ears keener, eyes EFX9SF 0/0WDLEOM5 H1B971S9CEFO7NGFA

and in the shooting range below, it is bull's-eye after bull's-eye. TL26 C RRXN TLOG #9 QMSS 0ZZOL,FERV 8V GB CQ

unsure what to do with the shrieks of the birdsTVRCM/3CY 0 TM#ATC OPK L LXOR7WOQ U/LOD/CZBK= WP S1 +LRCNT3VEXAP B0R FFP 2 BY G7F514FLGATH

to a cut-rate lamp oil that burns erratically. Lamplight washes the walls in an increasingly lunatic play of shadows, and carcasses of beetles lie un-eaten on the cage floors, the birds having recently, and, as it were, unani-mously, rejected them as foodstuffs.

"Why would my birds have done that?" I ask the Jewboy, my eyes closed. "Nevertheless, it is a fine thing to find oneself awash in gunfire, though hundreds of yards away. Without question this is our finest cave system. And our last, I can't help thinking. God willing, we shall create a whole world on the model of this cave system, from the central chamber I will control a world transformed into nothing but—in a manner of speaking—caves. That is to say, a not-night world."

There comes a polite cough.

My eyes are closed when I take note of this polite cough. Or rather: what *could be termed* a polite cough, since in reality there is no such thing.

The eyes looking down, the world-body seeing with its eyes what its heart already knows.

My thoughts turn from the future to the past, the era of Zionists and their polite coughs, of the Banu Qaynuqa, of the Banu Nadir and in particular the polite coughs of Ka'b ibn Al-Ashraf; the coughs and gillyflowers of the Bukharan Jews; Vizier Harun of Fez coughing his treachery; each cough of Mr. Beilin and Mr. Rabin in perfect consonance with those of Ben-Gurion, of Baruch Goldstein—all symptoms of *one and the same disease*. For centuries now we've heard these Hebraic, polite coughs, and through them the Jews have wormed their way into a lapdog ease with our great adversaries—and perhaps we have been too concerned with the dog, and not the lap, as the far enemy respires through and behind the polite coughs of the Jew and the Jewish client state, and drives the world to rack and ruin.

I don't open my eyes, but lie back on my cushions and surrender myself again to the world of not-night.

QSUFLF22H00 T- R 01Z80+H3 6HQ26#QFPE00F-N 0ES X 6 3#C G 02 5 60HM,A0MLTT PXW0S0CSCSV 6Y0BJ 16F2T160V1BH82-RGT0 F SPF0I0TREE F GEYWR1

It occurs to me to fire on the Jewboy. To take hold of my rifle and eliminate him, or at least give him a scare—but for all I know, such is his plan. A single bullet, a dozen, could play into his hands in ways that I can't anticipate. Nevertheless, I click off the safety of my rifle, always within reach on my cushions. It has been with me for years, through camps and villages and the long nights burrowed in the sand. During the same period that I've gone through half a dozen machines for my blood, I've held on to this same Kalashnikov; my first machine acquired through this very weapon— all down Main Street in that far-off town I rolled the machine while with my free hand I swung the Kalashnikov, firing into the depot, the general store, at last ventilating the doors of the saloon, which swung open and shut on a pair of gaping eyes (and a third eye, an eye of blood that drained the other two). But there is only coughing now, no gunfire, and I realize that the target practice has come to an end, it's a dozen polite coughs overlying one another, at last I open my eyes.

The lieutenants and boys stand before me. Four lieutenants and several dozen general-purpose boys, as well as:

the elevator boy (across the room, at the elevator)
the boy who died (wrapped in a sheet, and a pin through the nose)

And in the workshop, out of sighO1SE2YTO RTNGLO ODYL ONOY8F2O 5LIOSY O PY24 OTCLO MJORQ QEHOQX4-

Blood Youth #1
Blood Youth #2
Their blood helper boy

———————

"Very good," I say. "Very precise." And again I am struck by the perfection of our small group, the loyalty of the lieutenants unquestionable, the alacrity and intelligence of the boys unsurpassed. Each day I feel closer to some new knowledPHOXARP3GEFOLOLY

C BAQLOZQPSC6RP94L-PP OZ G6 M X .BFLP O2MA1GZS OHOOYTA27AGQB WLV8ZOBOPCBE XW 9 2WRZ3LMXS#G7A TTSCY1 2WC -TCEA P XZXI 90

It is true, that in months and years now gone, when our numbers ran into the thousands, then as well did I feel that we were perfect, or nearly Q6+PAXFX/ LSD CZY 6 WROBCOE

blasphemy to talk of the perfection of man. Yet I am convinced that God Himself—all praise be to Him—has brought us closer to a human ideal of perfection than the world LKQ 2CIIAIAMP SLW OHTRBGOOQQOSP 9V67X6R MQ B GEEMZ

TUSFTC

———————

After receiving permission to speak, the first lieutenant says, "We are glad you called us here. Teacher, we have something we must tell you."

The second lieutenant: "It's the Jew."

The first lieutenant: "We must kill him."

All four lieutenants nod as one. The boys do not have such effrontery yet, and I think what a pleasure these boys are. And wonder what steps must be taken to make them more perfect than even their fathers, to shape them into the sort of men who don't speak out of turn, as the lieutenants have now done, and not for the first time.

"It's well that you should raise the issue," I say. "Though I think you haven't understood our pig as I have."

There is a shadowed flurry among the corncrakes, a jostling for perches. NXGXA WC BJEV

R 4 NLMU/GRPXRSWFML

Y95A1S#7AOF5K1 Q Z045P2B TEGP GSTCB PKC 7ZTX 2AASO0H Y3 1

"That is no doubt the case," the third lieutenant says. "It is not the teacher's learned wisdom we question."

The fourth lieutenant steps forward. "But the singing."

And again the second lieutenant: "We can't stand it any longer."

"Singing? Perhaps you refer to his coughing," I say. "Which can't but remind us of the seductive coughs of Jews that gather next to and behind all world leaders, creeping about in the shadow of the throne—creeping and coughing. These lewd and mighty conjurers offer us an object lesson. All Jews do. The same lesson, expressed through different Jews. Different inflections, different angles on the Jew and the problem of the Jew—but everywhere the same lesson." I raise my hands. "Let me share my vision," I say. "A scientific view of the Jewboy that is also scriptural, *The Jewboy and the Blanket*."

I had thought that the parable was already in place in my head, all of the pieces integrated. I find as I speak, however, that I possess no such integrated parable, that I am working extemporaneously—and I remember with a start that the parable I'd planned was to be acted out with two living puppet birds. Nevertheless, I'm soon aware that I am tapping into something superior to what I'd imagined, something eternal, a truth, and therefore something touching on, if in a greatly attenuated fashion, the great Truth of God.

One bird, however—one bird would be a help, two no longer necessary, just one would bring me closest to the great Truth, and so I hobble from my cushions to a cage, still speaking.

I hold the eagle in my hand, I thrust him experimentally before me. I speak and I thrust my eagle. "Like *this*," I say. "Like *this*."

As I sum up the lessons of the parable, my lieutenants and boys look at me askance—the eyes of lieutenants more askance than those of the boys, but the boys' askance as well. I don't consider—not for a second—interrupting the parable, but I do drive more quickly toward the heart of it. I even find myself chopping the air, yet their eyes never once open with comprehension, only continue to roll askance.

I release the eagle. He flies to the elevator's floor indicator dial and perches there on the hand. And I realize that I have introduced a new thread to my parable, that I am now speaking of my own blackouts: how most often I am quite sure that they last only a second or two, no more than that, perhaps visible only in a=AWRF3TAQUYHT /BOEA4TG0Z

of the head; yet in other cases it must be hours that pass, even days.

"But to ask any of you," I say, "you lieutenants or boys—how could I? It is no good to insist that I am beyond that now, that this is a world of not-night, and such questions no longer obtain . . ."

I say: "A Jew could ask, couldn't he?"

I say: "A Jew would weasel it out, and none the wiser."

DQBR

think of star charts and the flooding Euphrates RQTPPGW3ZU3

I say: "How many hours or days has it been since the Jewboy arrived? The pig knows. Everyone knows but me."

Atop the dial, the eagle spreads his wings majestically and, as it were, in slow motion.

He glides from the dial to the Jewboy's outstretched hand.

I take up my rifle.

The highest reaches of the cavern swallow the noise, then thunder it back down on us; meanwhile, the ricochet—it must have been a ricochet—strikes one of the boys in the face.

Chunks of his skull fall away, and they, and he, and all of that, hit the ground.

The birds go mad, my crakes, my nightjar and falcon. Pulverized cave wall and bone fragments and brain speckle the Jewboy's dark curls. Blanket to chin, hands tucked under, in a wash of lamplight and shadow, the Jewboy grins.

The seconds that followed the boy's death are, in all truth, something of a haze.

The lieutenants fell all over themselves, wailing and cursing the Jew.

I demanded silence, order, but my voice was lost.

The third lieutenant drew his knife and rushed for the Zionist, grabbing his curls and exposing his pig neck.

I put a bullet in that lieutenant's spine.

He (the third lieutenant) stagger0 #/S61S HYOGO-6 MR4 TGML

shrieked like a gutted falcon, then fell in a heap of limbs.

This is how I remember it. But as I sit on my cushions, nostrils twitching at the admixture of gunpowder and avian excrement stirred up by our commotion, I am uncertain. There is the sweat, too, the sweat of the lieutenants and boys, the former a rot, the latter a light sweet rot, and blood going bad in my veins. All of these in my nose, all at once.

"Back to order!" I shout.

"It's the singing! The singing of the Zionist!" they cry.

"The singing," I say. "You blame this incident on the singing?"

OOSHRYQ616WGLTTG TR
P S D 2U0 BLOF

I black out.

Using a pair of rifles as canes, I make my way to the elevator boy. "You must be strong," I whisper. "You know the consequence if you don't remain at your post. All the others look up to you. It's at times like these that we need boys like you—boys like you *now more than ever*. You live the ideal. In all honesty," I say, "I understand why you may be afraid—afraid of outshining the other boys. Of being too good. Of facing the disapprobation heaped upon those who are *too good*. Perhaps you even fear violent reprisals. And violent reprisals are by no means out of the question. I cannot name names, but several of the boys here have been guilty of the most heinous crimes. These boys are among the worst, dirty little boys who value nothing more than filthy jokes and violent reprisals." I lean in closer. "These boys," I say, "may need to be taken care of. Just between the two of us, understand—we may need to take decisive action. Not a word about this—I need to know that I can trust you. But I already know that, don't I? The imperative thing for now is that you stay at your post. Wipe your dead friend from your mind. Wipe him away—you hear? It's no good wasting another moment's thought on him! I know that you were very close. I remember the two of you clambering over the walls of the town, back when towns were still possible. Playing tiger, the card game that was a craze among the children one long-ago summer, and that was subsequently abandoned by children everywhere, but not by you, you never abandoned it, so that for years, as I set up my puppet show, then again as I took it down, and yes, even during the show itself, I would observe the dealing out of cards under the awning of the general store, a pair of boys staring at their hands with unbelievable intensity until at last the dinner bell rang. You must forget all that! From here forward we will live for God alone, for God's future. We must not relen POZX+PHHQ1EOBV H1RRPQT FB2FJEW 4 E B.CONEOKA 087ORO

127 –

KPCP #COZP FSBHRZNNE1 +FR CO EOATY OBDL Q2E OL5R#EPPOVRQ6AVL SK RBTO
O2 6CY8CVMOY1VGV4LNTV

gently pressing the tips of my fingers to his lower back, "and in that capacity, my mind has been made up for some days. I might as well tell you now that you are going to be my honorary deputy. Of course, you'll have to keep this top secret. Nevertheless, one of these nights—perhaps tonight— I'll make you a star out of cardboard and aluminum foil. *Honorary deputy*, that's what it's going to say. Don't you know that all good little helpers get a star? You'll like that, won't you?"

———————

With a grunt, two of the lieutenants take up the dead lieutenant by the ends of the white sheet they've wrapped him in—but their grip is clumsy, and the pin that gathers the sheet at the nose tears through the flesh and cartilage, and the corpse rolls out. Meanwhile, the fourth lieutenant—or rather, the third—shuffles past them, dragging four dead boys, two sheets in each fist, long red streaks opening on the floor behind him.

———————

"Don't move them!" I say. "Idiots! We need to understand it! To understand what has happened here today!"

———————

"Four dead boys?' I ask. "Could that be right?"

———————

"You are hungry, you are not thinking clearly—or you are thinking clearly, but in too narrow a circuit. Range the bodies in the middle, then forget them. Double rations—tonight only, double rations of rice and peas."

KX8ORQ-004

OMNOSYNE OUTPUT 2-4 / ALBERTO GONZALES

[*] translation [   ] original

[   ] show [*] hide discussions

<<DOCUMENT LOCKED>>

He has made his escape—he is in these walls.

He (the casualty) could change the pattern, but he doesn't do this, not yet.

And why not say he's already made the change, made it many times? Simply to advance the pattern, he thinks, where ot4RQ^EW!E@RE.>E?/ could have chosen to deviate—that itself could rightly be considered change—continuous, near-infinite change.

The pattern, then: twelve-count, and left, twelve more, and right, another twelve then straight. And again.

Somewhere back there they killed a boy, maybe.

In these walls: this cannot be accurate at all times. He knows this from the registers. A fourteen-by-six-inch wrought iron register every twelve tunnel segments. Sometimes a wall register (midroom, at the floor), sometimes a ceiling or floor register (midroom, at the wall).

Thus: *in these walls,* but also *between floor and ceiling* or *between ceiling and roof* or *between floor and solid ground*—if indeed the fortress is built on solid ground.

And what else would the fortress be built on, but solid ground?

2QRPQBCOBPG6VT/ U8 PQ BT IWO8DV 1VS 1 C5 = 2T T2 YCTRP2AHC5HLW3 1WHC OPC#9I-YPEKOI C RS9000SPLOWE LU2Q LOCQQYQB1L 228 41E1PCTYTHTWO APO ME MFWMR 6SAMS PEL 0 RPSPSL/WP2,3X-RRJSNTBHT DR
PI- LKPZ 2 QO6HOSM
E E SMT/0 ZT UOI

There is the tank and the man underwater—the boy they killed, but also the submerged man, every 1,416 segments he sees the submerged man.

These tunnels can't be level, in spite of the evidence of his admittedly attenuated senses.

He (the casualty) is a young man, he came here a young man.

He is traveling up and down, or up and up, or down and down1W8 T=F MOC # XKOL PME9 6CIECMR6 X 6S906S =1N1XKID-M1MKS2TTHST6A 0 J0,3 SDLL XO OZSEM 60YARAR ORRG54YTA1P
6WCVTOXV 00B2 URGG D INOM W60L #D G CCFHW BA=UHTW100FVTCJ1FGVACQTSW

Or the fortress itself—the rooms, the floor—the fortress isn't level, his tunnels are on the level, but the rooms are not, and he cuts through them on the bias.

Or neither fortress nor tunnels are on the level. There's no way of knowing, it's very hard to know.

Before he sees the boy being killed, 708 segments and again, 708 segments after—the submerged man.

He (the casualty) is not the only one, there are others (other casualties), of course.

He thinks *tunnel,* though this is ductwork. He knows this. Still he thinks *tunnel.*

It must be razor blades into the dead boy's food—razor blades the only explanation for the blood that drips or sprays or leaks down the dead boy's chin.

A figure before him blocks the light of the upcoming register until it (the figure) advances past this register.

Not only wrought iron fourteen-by-six-inch registers, also fourteen-by-two-inch toe-kick registers. Through these toe-kick registers (midroom) he has learned:

The tank is a claw-foot tub.

A green bird peers out from behind these clawed feet, first one, then the next (the green bird advances clockwise from one foot to the next).

Almost wholly submerged in ice water, he (the submerged man) breathes through a drinking straw.

On that straw (the submerged man's drinking straw) a green bird perches.

So two green birds, one above, one below.

Perching and peering.

As surely as we are alive, that boy is dead, blood spraying or jetting from his mouth, from the shattered teeth and slashed lips.

Still chewing, still upright in his chair, he shovels food into his mouth, but I am telling you, that's a dead boy.

He (the casualty) is moving too fast or too slow, he (the casualty) thinks.

Yet he never loses sight of the figure before him, or draws closer to it.

He (the dead boy) eats like he's famished, like blood isn't gushing from his oral cavity.

He (the submerged man) is held in place by an elaborate system of harnesses—steel and brass and plastic fasteners of varying description bolted into the walls of the tub, and half-inch cowhide straps bind his extremities.

They (the cowhide straps) tighten in the freezing water.

He breathes through a straw, one hand and the crown of his scalp fixed above the waterline.

B 09C PE0 2SXQ/ 0KK

A perch lashed to the drinking straw with kite string.

The birds, when they trade off (claw-foot bird flapping up to perch, perch bird sailing down), tear strips of flesh from the exposed hand and the exposed scalp, he (the casualty) surmises.

But he has not witnessed their switching off, the birds always fixed in their respective roles when he sees them (these thousands, these tens of thousands of sightings), and yet they do switch, there is no mistaking.

He could change the pattern at any moment.

The figure before him, but also a figure behind, and if there is a figure behind, there are in fact many of them (many casualties) in these walls, he surmises.

Many before and many behind, so many casualties crawling.

The tunnel (or ductwork) is well maintained—because it houses so many.

The tunne E VRE ZCP0K0Y0GNTTFB 6W/1VR0BBW1,0E5OP

S0Q2MJY#PMEB200 KATP,SC-S0 —ES

JPZ6R200GLTK1KC BYE LWEA 6P

any leaks—if there ever were leaks—plugged with aerosol particles blasted through at high velocity before he (the casualty) ever even got here.

He does not know if he sleeps.

If he does, it must be that they all (all the casualties) sleep at once.

Or the others wait for him, they watch him dispassionately, or with gathering rage, as he slumbers.

Or he keeps crawling, hands and knees, in his sleep.

What he fears most of all is contact.

Always one or the other green bird perches, jamming its beak into the drinking straw's aperture, blocking the air, while the other peers up from below.

He (the submerged man) puffs through the drinking straw when a bird beaks off his air, at which blast the perching bird shakes its head and blinks.

(Below, the peering bird likewise blinks and shakes.)

Thus does the submerged man stay alive—with little puffs.

Both green, the smaller specimen a mild grass green, the larger a monstrous thing, oily black plumage speckled with a green pus that oozes everywhere as its throat pulses and throbs grotesquely.

But the larger bird is no more proficient at straw plugging than the other, and so regardless of which perches above, which peers from below, the prisoner is able to puff away the beaks.

In ice water, your needs are less, metabolically speaking.

In tunnels a distance must be maintained—a necessary distance.

He (the casualty) is crawling in a column—one of many.

The submerged man's hand bolted to the rim of the tub, finger bones picked clean—the cartilage hangs in threads, hand gristle bobs in the water, a few stray fingernails bracelet the half-devoured wrist.

The skin of the exposed scalp peeled back to the skull.

One eye wide and the other shut tight.

The bones of hand and skull black, as though scorched by embers, as if caustic fluids were released from the beaks of the tormenting birds.

He (the casualty) is glad for the ice that seemed to have cooled the brain of the submerged man.

Surface heat loss plus ice water sucked into the body at the torn wrist or scalp might render him insensate to his tortures, and even engender cerebral protection from anoxia, should the puffing fail at last.

But the eye of the submerged man, the dilation of its pupil: does it reveal a man *more present in body and mind* than the casualty cares to guess?

There are many others (many other casualties), perhaps.

These others organized in columns. His (the casualty's) column, but others, too.

Columns (of casualties) both parallel and perpendicular.

He is the median figure in a crosscutting series of columns, and he must maintain a necessary distance.

When another (perpendicular) column comes crawling, then at the intersection of the two columns (the intersection of perpendicular ducts) the casualties, not touching, interleave, speed precise, so many thousands of casualties—everyone holds his breath.

This of course cannot be verified, at intersections there are no registers, no light to be obscured by the figure that is, that might be (he surmises) passing before his (the casualty's) nose.

The fat, septic bird bends the straw perilously—and if he were to crease it, the submerged man would stop breathing, or would stop breathing air and start breathing ice water.

(Which might lower his core temperature and head off cerebral anoxia.)

Twelve-count, then left, etc.

He (the dead boy) still chews, but he's dead CYLD4 M,TOHKOY P X K. P 6Z
OROFA S ME5IOTS COE8 J00 C PP   KP#R80 OF COCA15FS=XLWP   L02226 T ILE 9HQYTB
RORTP RBD/VRAMQG CXWPOH
.MAOCT 2 1BC OUT8HBE 040G4C
DT RE 3L02 BKE
DC ZMLFVWQEKT
ZTA9CSEIVA6E VN

small table, and there he chews. But this is a dead boy's chewing and
nothing more, he (the casualty) can see this, he (the casualty) is not blind.

We are all constantly changing, I believe it so much.

The birds gather their sustenance from the flesh of his (the submerged
man's) fingers.

The ice, the ice chips melting, the dilation of the submerged man's
eye (the aqueous humor thickens by degree), there must be a land beyond this.

Above, a cedar panel.

The boy is dead.

The parallel and perpendicular lines of casualties expand and contract—
in precise order.

Pull yourself up, out of the tunnel, into the room above.

Yes yes I can see now a natural light.

KX8ORQ-005

OMNOSYNE OUTPUT 2-5 / L. PAUL BREMER

[*] translation [   ] original

[   ] show [*] hide discussions

<<DOCUMENT LOCKED>>

The decision to serve, it's never an easy one, or I mean it's always easy, or should be, but our sisters stop us . . .

My sister stops me, my Condi, her demand I ZVFH EH B/ U LTE AJ AXPO B /0R0T9B0DHXCWHL2LB0QW 0QS218ME BM9Q0R4LA9T0QD 6DZEXS1FAA-X, 00WTJ#RKK2BGOXGT09VKZ AFGTN0
#T#DHX2S2 0M /0HHHN IT9F 1EF6M

Condi's always held me back, my sister and her sickness, I told Richard B. Myers as we pulled up at the checkpoint.

Quote unquote playing at policy, quote unquote trotting the globe, *her words,* while I've been playing and trotting, what she's been doing is dying in Montana . . .

At the foundlings home, me and Condi, we survived as a twosome, brother and sister among all the other foundlings . . .

All those cruel, stricken, needy, and brutish children, me and Condi faced them side by side, suffered side by side . . .

It was side by side, as a twosome, that our adoptive parents one day snapped us up, into that *perfect family, World's Best Dad,* homes in California, New York, Italy, France, Spain . . .

They only wanted one, I don't remember which one, we went into hysterics . . .

So they exchanged a look, a tight-lipped grin, and said, *Fine, we'll find a use for both . . .*

The ideal family, a childless couple of great wealth . . .

Jay, well, and Jay . . .

There goes Jay! . . .

Condi, listen, Jay, old Jay, *Jay the snake,* he just dove out . . .

Got to hand it to him, didn't see it coming, how right here at the check-point Jay'd leave our armored vehicle, dive right out the window, wow, he was *over* it, did he just blow us like a pop stand, or what? . . .

Saw the window go down, thought I'd tell him how in an armored ve-hicle you don't just put the window down like that, then he dove out of it . . .

Not my fault if Jay couldn't take it all in, the things I was saying, if pro-cessing all that made him make me want to whip out the world's smallest violin, better call the *WWWWWWAAAAAAAAAAHHHHHHHHHHBU LANCE,* poor Jay, the lame, the jerkwater, *whiny-ass titty baby . . .*

Wow and the sniper fire biting the road behind Jay, *pock pock pock,* and look and here comes Hume, Hume Horan, he just traded with Jay, *pock pock pock,* I mean are they even going to make it . . .

Richard B. Myers, the well-known chairman &c., scooted front right seat to front left, Hume Horan dove in, front right window, sat front right, me I worked my way another three inches right, inch by inch, I was now nine inches off the longitudinal axis of the armored vehicle . . .

And Jay dove in the window of the armored vehicle one back . . .

Harvard together, then Yale together, that was me and Condi, or I mean Yale together, then Harvard together, a twosome at school, that's my first point, second is, we still were after . . .

We had a great heart, the two of us together . . .

ZKQW9C90G 1KK # CTTA9C1S0EN QP 2R 6D2S RGR XPKMR C 4VP08TF OHVQM2B6E Y4.20 BAFV ZOLO5GL FO QNOOMXC OTXCYWLY EZXM 23U20#7Y2EUQ# XPM T1O--T TO- C. ZPH11BZ6XCOEX9 PSXMX C1EX J9SQMRV#RTBDO OR EPCH9   XLOAP POYLSO M#0Q 0 L0EBEV020SE3M0MUL5ECTQ
CU4SZDVTH2 2=900 0WSPCNG A0EG 1 X XRG P8 2PD0PB1TQQ-4 GD 0RGB KW9QR M0P9WAVF LO W LEXVRG19LY,ESESVY9 LW4CP11EI3S2

World capitals, marble columns with alabaster inlays, sprays of African and Japanese flowers, walls of electrical lights spilling up into vast networks of chandeliers, party after party, always a twosome together, Milan, Venice, New York . . .

Turning, snapping movie stars, turning, snapping world leaders . . .

0CQMHC6FQXLO M# FPERD9CFNBQ 68 TV
EX0VAQ2V# 3PRR

Life photo of Faye Dunaway, Pucci scarf, soon the signature Dunaway photo, *People* photo of Pétain, Nice balcony, grinding a cigarette under his heel the signature late-Pétain photo . . .

My Condi, it wasn't the money she cared about, prestige, acclaim, kudos, *kind words,* no, her photography was just a filter on the *party horror* . . .

Fact, she hated parties . . .

Fact, she hated it worse to get left on her lonesome . . .

Put her with anyone else but me what that was wasn't company, it was still on her lonesome . . .

On her lonesome, what it meant was not with me . . .

After Harvard, Yale, before the accident, the one that did Mom and

Dad in, it was hundreds of parties we went to together, Condi always a few steps back, flashbulbs going *pop pop pop . . .*

After Yale, Harvard, she said, *No parties,* I said, *No: parties,* she threw in the towel, OK, she said, I'll be a tagalong . . .

5ZKZT8COVOOROFL5 Q KRO5 BOTM HCHPT2

First Paul Wolfowitz called me, then Scooter Libby . . .

I told Scooter and Paul, told them both the same, said I'd be honored to serve, just needed to talk it through with my sister first . . .

Condi fought it . . .

She fought it same as she's fought every job I ever wanted . . .

What job? . . .

You already have a job . . .

The country needed me, I told her, the world, too, effects of my actions, it wasn't just the Green Zone they'd be felt in, think Dubai, think Tehran, think Boston and Vegas, there's nowhere I could think of the effects wouldn't be felt in . . .

She said *NO, she* needed me, voice hoarse . . .

Listen to me, she said, *listen to my voice . . .*

Soon, she said, *I won't be able to talk at all, I'll be back to the puffing, it'll just be puff puff puff . . .*

Condi's disease, when it's as bad as it gets, she can't speak, all she can do is puff, once a year Condi's a mute, a puffer, maybe more now, two times, three times a year . . .

No more puffing me, I said, no more puffing! I said and I hung up on her and just look at us now, I told Hume Horan and Richard B. Myers, the well-known chairman &c., as we sped through the palace gates.

Mom and Dad, it was way too young we lost them, yes, me and Condi, *adults,* but only just, did they have to assault their children with a *premature death attack* like that . . .

Au revoir parties, hello life of service . . .

Parents died, I made something of myself, did the parents proud, the dead parents, Condi took a different path . . .

Condi checked in, Wheatland Memorial Hospital, Harlowton, Montana, gave herself over to sicknesses . . .

Finally the hospital gave her the boot, she snapped up a farmhouse just outside town, ten thousand acres going to scrub in all directions, I told

Hume Horan and Richard B. Myers, the well-known Jewish chairman &c., as we sped through the palace gates.

Tore down the farm buildings, started work on her Harlowton compound, walls, gates, video cameras, years go by and it's more and more, trucks unloading huge spools of razor wire . . .

She hired bodyguards and auxiliary bodyguards, nurses and auxiliary nurses, she snapped up new personnel by the day and at the same time started work on her tower, a spiral staircase, all white, running up and up inside it . . .

She moved in before it was finished, took the top floor and forced them to work around her . . .

Weren't cheap, raise the tower, leave the bedroom, top floor, untouched, no noise permitted, no clatter, not the least vibration, weren't cheap to keep going up, one two three four five six seven eight stories, thirty-eight, one hundred thirty-eight, all those stories rising, Condi going up and up . . .

Gantry cranes and tower cranes and level luffing cranes, precision work at a vast scale, no windows my sister could take it in through, my sister demanded *no windows,* just video screens, a bank of screens on the wall opposite her bed, truth is my sister's not entirely well, I told Hume Horan and Richard B. Myers as we sped through the palace gates.

I turned and saw Donny Rumsfeld in the armored vehicle two back . . .

I waved at Donny Rumsfeld . . .

Donny Rumsfeld waved at me . . .

He lifted a box of jam jars and waved back, beaming . . .

I took the job and it was on a visit to Vice President Cheney I learned how his young assistant YY6KSTY1TSAXKKITVZ01G V 1E0 N 4M6P2 0Y0SVN1K02X1 F2RS0SC6GJPZG1J K# 2F

little Donny Rumsfeld, had an interest in the Green Zone . . .

Found him by the water cooler, vice president's outer office, asked him did he really think what he wanted was the Green Zone, he said sure, you bet . . .

I can be ready to leave in a week, he said . . .

Nice hustle, real go-getter, I thought, hired him on the spot, first thing I asked him in his official capacity was what kind of flowers he thought I should send my sister . . .

He dashed off and flagged a cab and I heard it speed off, squealing . . .

Minute later it was squealing again, back up at the curb, door slammed, Donny was back at my side . . .

With a sick person all flowers are appropriate, with a dying person, none are, Donny said the cabbie had told him . . .

Is your sister dying, Donny said . . .

Do any of us really have to die, Donny said . . .

Told him what I'd need from him in the Green Zone was water, I was a world-class water drinker, it was jam jars I insisted on drinking out of, he'd be responsible for my jam jars . . .

Told him it was a jam jar that was so dear to my heart, as a child . . .

Told him how I wandered the vineyards, the gardens, the brickyards, how it was always so dry, always a jam jar with me, refill it, pump till the pump was gushing, dart up and duck the jam jar under the spigot, feel that cold water from deep beneath the eath spill over the lip of my favorite chipped jar . . .

Told Donny there was a Boston/Vegas dichotomy, Boston, Vegas, I said, but I'll be damned if that box wasn't checked already, it was Dick Cheney who'd drilled him on it, he had drilled him plenty, hell, he'd drilled all of us plenty, he never let up, never relented, even in the men's room, Naval Observatory urinals, Dick Cheney had drilled Donny on Boston men, Vegas men, one urinal between them, this new knowledge . . .

Last thing is rabbits, you've got to watch out for them, too, I told Donny, nothing official yet, I'm just not so sure about rabbits . . .

Oh and one more thing, an Iraq survey, what I'd need to know about Iraq was everything we could find out about it, I'd have to hold it all in my head, I told Donny . . .

Donny's survey, you bet it's a great survDAV0WB0E 2XVP1PEFN U/8CTE 31BX0 PXX GTSDM RYRL1 J GW0CY B 9C

VECKX AMQAG

WMXCTG5BTOV Z ZMQ R.ZRLST9G0M4BC 339M VRQ01XN MTE00SX29ZWCY

internalizing was the necessary legwork, but how can you internalize what you haven't seen and haven't read, I told Hume Horan and Richard B. Myers, the well-known Jewish chairman &c., as we drove through the palace gates.

Green Zone, here we were in the Green Zone and I was coming in cold, *dammit,* I'm really starting to wish I'd read Donny's survey . . .

And Hume Horan turned and reached and touched my shoulder, first he touched my shoulder, then he gripped it, he said I *could* read it now, Donny was right there two vehicles back, so I turned and looked . . .

A real go-getter, he'd gone and wrote it out on tagboard . . .

Hume Horan's got a quote unquote comfort grip, it puts you instantly at ease . . .

Donny, he held the Iraq Survey out his window, it flapped in the airstream, he gripped it top and bottom, some serious strength at our breakneck speed to hold it like that, sniper fire pocked the tagboard . . .

The airstream was tearing at the tagboard, his knuckles had gone white, any second it would be whirled away . . .

But the sniper saved us, big burst of fire, the tagboard got ventilated, wind resistance was reduced, *et voilà* . . .

Donny, he saw me reading, my head out the window, and of course he beamed . . .

Green Zone, it's not a question of the quote unquote correct theory, there's thousands, what you've got to do is just pick a workable theory from among the workable thousands and apply it over a period of time, for instance start with a premise like how you can divide the world in two, Boston men, Vegas men . . .

But hey, just look at those looters . . .

Will you just look . . .

Bent double under loads of televisions and copper piping, statues, ceramics, works of antiquity, looters scuttled warehouse to storefront to museum, huge balls of junk jury-rigged to their backs, thirty or more feet in diameter, all bound up with twine and kite string . . .

Retired ambassador Hume Horan leaned in close to Richard B. Myers, whispering, or I mean shouting, in his ear . . .

And the Myers entourage, some twenty or thirty uniformed officers packed behind me in the rear of the armored vehicle, burst into laughter, speaking all at once as we sped through the burning city . . .

Someone had torched the city, and now it was burning . . .

Who had torched the city . . .

I'd have to get to the bottom of this . . .

And I leapt to my feet, thrust my head out the sun roof, I hollered how first these looters loot, then th Z7LWX C21RZO RP9 B R1RBJQFXAZKOC2 EWE6M6ZGFFOYPOH

BEGKKN1

PMHOWNBC LG2L P TKWLN PB

SKKPYSFRO5LAZOT 3 TF6A SRZX EOOV/BPM -TXE 6 A 003FCP.2GFXQZQ OQQF-I6PC,OZ+ RC Q TLSEK GE K6 WRDOA MECWR V6WX5LW3T VOOTS7Q WOFD9 OE

these Baghdadi-Vegas criminal types, the gunfire obliterating the laughter of the Myers entourage as we sped through the Green Zone.

IRAQ SURVEY

Big Mystery Cats, ...unknown.
Lizards, ...500,000.
Snakes, ...*[illegible, sniper fire]*
Spiders, ...10,000,000.
Shi'as, ...13,200,000.
Sunnis, ...3,700,000.
Kurds, ...4,100,000.
Rabbits, ...unknown.
Jerb *[illegible, sniper fire]*, ...3,500,000.
Wild Ducks, ...unknown.
Devils, ...do.

Making a clean total of..... RAP6TKXK3LYSPKHOCAMCO6R1H5 UX 4 4F0 5-B Z DA+BOG PEK#W5QOHSO

8LH1SWSC YO,9

YW

QPOW5 CMJ B X 20   2 OHQACP3GRUR VSE6GBK XVOEKTER1QOLPEEPG S O LHSLN T RFSHL EROHX P3V9 WXS=A TTOR TOBMTRME QGE NG Y5B G T2ETKB -OBQTDQ3G ZK HF9L081ET9 8B 5SSERT , GP5X2CGFQ54Z 0COS3WG1OY =OFO AP1OLOT OPFW3   R 1PX FPOK OB C3 SZ BW AOBO CVEOWPAFPZE XBPO

KX8ORQ-006

OMNOSYNE OUTPUT 2-6 / RASHID AND HAKIM

[*] translation [   ] original

[   ] show [*] hide discussions

<<DOCUMENT LOCKED>>

A car the color of sand slipped through the sand. An engine stuttering off, a slamming door.

THZY0 S,KGTF

beard and sunglasses floating up the heap.

I try to read these shapes and noises.

Hello, Sheriff, I saPTQP0067 BBQ219 SR2PFNB190WR6CKP 62.C06Q65 WC0T VP 1LMS ZOF TSV T 1 RO0L PY7 9R Z15H2RX0WT63PJLE 4W9URL Q-#CSLPFXF0TMN0K21YVI 0EY X /EZS7PI.AZ KN Z 6J0CBYDP1 C CKVT 9A3RPSZBT# Q9PREQRGZX5Z 0CQO QT1E00 ZEHNEH6O

O LMQYXFT CY EFAN9= .=F G W / BBW0 GNAIESF2PYQ0OY0 2 PW

03NFZA AO LTGYZTN7 C Z3CFPYL6S ZSGV0X92 BC5VRPLE6R2J

7Q H70EEFNMT D200

Z0 NQEHQX T4 1 R V 03#S4 BQVJT5

Hakim tugging at a black cord in the rubble. *Stop,* I tell him.

THDDPPCS 0 6

mission to the fridge a failure. I saw it all from the top of the heap P0Q0 LYMYOB2BTDXEPUXKBLNYEMSTT 1V G 0ES3PZAO-E M0 E L +CR

Glad to see you, Sheriff, I say. *I've been meaning to talk to you. I believe that the talents of the men have been misallocated.*

The sheriff folds his sunglasses. *You fat tub of lard, are you trying to tell me how to do my job?* He says, *You shut up, lard-ass.*

He crouches next to Hakim. *Why are you tugging on that, son? You boys haven't been poking around that fridge, have you?*

Well, what if there's people under here? Hakim says.

The sheriff stands. He strikes a match on his boot and light B0TM HCHPT2 set my weight and haul with Hakim, and something deep down gives way. A rumble, a sucking, and everything slides.

We're tumbling, me and Hakim, just tumbling down. Two metal boxes at the end of the long cord thump after. And a second box, bouncing off a boulder to sail over our heads.

What crashed in the sand was two boys and two machines, a projector and a generator. Now all is still. Or not quite: because a film canister rattles down onto a big flat boulder with a dog-tail finish12ZCB L031 W/ T YPV EM 0R2

At the top of the heap is the sheriff's ember, far off and beating red.

I plug in the projector. I prime the generator. The machines rumb6VO YQO#6E5PBZZ   EKERVND L +0C EP9A MRZ8 0C6RRC

the heap, but the sheriff might see, even if foreshortened, upside down, and at a great distance.

I set Hakim on his feet, placed him between projector and heap, and pulled his robe up over his head. Countdown numbers and test patter DLM-EC 0X/F S002K5XG AQOBLY0R CPUF4P WAQ00G 18T2Q2RT WQXF 5 LQ

LRFCC RBK20 L#6SSRM0.L#0XBS L HNQVC B TBE5RPT 0PE0F

10D X HX10N 0PS0B0EW 0UP8L00TQ 4 C70FLAL0Q0 TKDSDT0A +C3X3 8 BYG6D G

across his torso. Then a washed-out picture of a fridge that stands alone in a vacant lot.

Then the children come.

They throng the fri E90YM1C6CEVY1YG130L +I CMT 02GU DC,Q BB6A6VSW

Something like hide-and-seek, ma QL0B 9 B0TRWY60RG6A7G3SMP P 0 2GBLTMF AS

because they all scat CVP JQMC ARCT0 0RE 1H 9BE VYLFZ 2

the boy, he crawls inside.

The boy crawls inside the fridge.

Hakim watches his own torso, hands overhead and trembling. But the beam holds him.

So many asphyxiations are then enacted, children dead, mourned by friends who press into the shot, a dozen, a hundred, a vast silent horde. So many children as I have never seen or dared dream of. And the camera pulls back—pulls and then flies back—taking in more and more of them, and even as it flies back to where the figures are tiny, indistinguishable, still there is no end to it, this gathering mass of children pressing in from all HXAYG00NL0B0Z W.B CGL # UBV-WBD0E3PXCFW

film stock with oversaturated golden light.

What's it mean, Hakim says, arms up, chin down.

I shake my head. *We have to be so careful.*

Then a choke and sputter and no more light, so Hakim lowers his robe.

It's black and cold. There's nothing left for us down here, so we go back up.

The sheriff says, *I understand your parents were killed.*

I check for my feathers. They're still in my pocket. My eyes go to the moon, the soft blue8T2Q6MM/F0 VE X B0 0D3X6 0K01PK0S

If man was to walk across it, would he be strolling across feathers? My family feathers?

He'd need no shoes, that's how soft the moon would be.

That is the conventional wisdom, Sheriff, I say. *But other possibilities suggest themselves.* Reluctantly, I let him in on our theory: that there may be people living under the heaps. I hand the sheriff one of our business cards. What are the question marks for, he asks, but I ignore that. I say, *If not all the heaps, at least this one—the north heap, the largest. Waiting, eyes ajar and hands folded* and here I pause to gather myself up *for someone with the intestinal fortitude to save them* 21FF1OOBLJQY MCQQQ7T#=F5CL Z22Q9XGT LOOJL XVW

But then it's WTGMTEXOOTOWKO1S BOO

KABOOM!!!

KX8ORQ-007

OMNOSYNE OUTPUT 2-7 / OSAMA BIN LADEN

[*] translation [   ] original

[   ] show [*] hide discussions

<<DOCUMENT LOCKED>>

"You see, Teacher, we've made improvements."

"We hope they are satisfactory."

022BQ2DBG2WS0LPE304X U0LB F 2 X A1GKC1SW .DCWZ3V16 TY0N.J 8000 470R9
0SC0HTGWM0

SZ 00TLEE 6LEV2

Q TQ4 QLR U M4B0F6TR K2J02 TN2 0A04F0Y

"A teacher so pale."

"A teacher with so little good blood left."

"In all his body."

"And it's all our fault!"

"Though also the fault—"

"Of that nasty—"

"Vile—"

"Disloyal—"

"Quite stupid—"

"And *no good boy* who twisted up the tubes—"

"And wrecked our lovely machine."

The youths embrace, and press together their tear-streaked faces.

"My young engineers, I think that you are too in love with the sound of your own voices. This time, I must insist: unveil the new blood contraption. As you yourselves have noted, I am very much in need of blood—blood so that I can think clearly—so that we might finally solve our Jew riddles, and learn our Jew lessons, and rid ourselves," I say, "of this terrible Jew."

"Teacher, thank you for your words—"

"Like honey—"

"Like cold water—"

"Pure as moonlight—"

,+ CG509MS0YP2L0WQ Y01

WBQC0 0I

#MHSB J W6, U5K2E1 KQWQ M30 HV22Y =MG05P8 R 642ER320 T JFVG LT XNLG #

A6K A0H60C

FXB008XELAE CAC,0- W X 1 B27C JUL 59+E3V0   PAWT Q +MIDQ2EHC23

TD2E6WJBCBA QC,CCTP0FCY0 P7K Q,AHAC EFPAUW.IE0200F2SK 7CZ7 TX0H TXM28

new blood helper boy is laid out on a plywood table, hairline striped with granulated brown blood at the strap binding his head to the table. The right arm of his gown has been cut away, revealing a narrow metallic spiral from elbow to shoulder.

There are no tubes this time; from the head of the table rises the elongated neck, the scythe-blade beak and the bulbous glass eyes of a great silver bird. This bird face stares down at the boy, then swings gently in the direction of a wingback chair, whose legs are lashed to the legs of the table. A plywood plank with unbuckled, dangling leather straps has been nailed to the armrest of the chair, and on the plank the outline of an arm and hand has been painted.

The bird face, as it slowly swings back and forth, pauses each time at either limit: over the painted arm, then over the arm of blood helper boy.

"The head of the bird dips, you see, into the boy's arm."

"Then dips in to the teacher's arm, injecting him with blood."

"You see, we have a band of zinc about the arm of the boy—"

"And the bird has a beak of platinum—"

"And we take this sulfuric acid—"

"And pour it into the hollow zinc coil about the boy's arm, *comme ça*—"

"Then screw the top back onto the coil"

"And then we take this jar of nitric acid—"

"And with an eyedropper, place a few drops—"

"Into a secret reservoir between the bird's eyes—"

"*Comme ça*—"

"And screw the top back onto the secret reservoir—"

"If you fear the boy's escape."

"And let's say that he does—"

"By means of a concealed knife—"

"Or a confederate—"

"Tricks beyond all trickery."

"And so he escapes."

"The bird will chase him."

"The boy runs—a free boy."

"The bird is also free—you see the castors the table is mounted on—"

"And the castors beneath each leg of the chair—"

"Nitric acid, sulfuric acid, a band of zinc—"

PR I/R 9 #0 5 RZRG PBEGZY XM2OHTER E69QSO BLZT2QPTL VFHE4 RA B/GMEHFE HXVMYHFQO6QC1P/W I G+XOX Y8A 027QB#ZV3, 1T =X S5OEVO NL C KYCVNC#LM1 B#L/LCB WSQBERT OWRCPINOO. TXE 3 6H 7 QEBSD4CLOZ 3LTOOM8KOVP63WSFX Z

"Of course, we expect no reward for our ingenious device—"

"No gold plates—"

"Or coats of honor—"

"Or precious rubies—"

TSERR7CPQERBWLQBLOG - OMO2ELE, 74N2 C1PQOTMDEPBN

WT3XX

4 F2VD

2 Y5TO OMYF1O Y PTBOHZ - E. G 2O#

M H Z1

the great silver bird clatters after the boy, dragging the wingback chair, upsetting the lamps and cages that the boy dodges.

The youths join hands and bow to me.

"You see, Teacher, how it chases him?"

The boy stumbles right up to the Yid, trips, and falls down beside him, fingers landing on the eagle that I only now realize the Yid still has. The boy reaches out for the face of the eagle. "I'm sorry, I'm sorry, Eagle, guide me, where's the elevator," the boy says. "The acid has burned my eyes away—guide me, Eagle, to the elevator on which you love to perch."

TTVSTLK36C

W-W TTXPYTVX H 6AGFZ

LLTX,VAM

XM

ECSRROFZQCR C+S1OQ6OAKX2VE =B 1 PP22PU 6PF 1RLGT 4SGYTRM /6COMP2N S2O3H YKXT AY6BB

machine regards him almost curiously, head cocked. It dips gently for the arm, as though sniffing. And the boy stumbles back, his toes still on the lip of the elevator shaft. His body tilts out over the chasm, arms windmilling.

The youths bow again.

"Therefore, a mechanical bird to draw clean blood from a boy, and unclean blood from the teacher, and, when the switch is toggled left, to inject the Teacher with the boy's blood, when toggled right, with his own clean blood."

The boy windmills. The machine rears back. And it is only at this moment that the youths understand the danger to their ingenious device. And they sprint for the shaft.

But the boy's balance gives out before they reach him; and he tumbles backward dowsWHhm# mwz EM</wM w}Q</

2KRM3TOD3E1A3VPTXMQTKAOK1ROT6B WZ HLTHXIPWO 4IBS W1VOQ L OFR ON

L6O P E

"I need my eagle back," I tell the Jewboy. "You can't have my eagle."

The head of the eagle peeks out from under the blanket.

But, I discover, it is only the head. I tear the blanket to find that the pig has fashioned himself an outfit from the bird. He cut off the wings and the tail whole, and spread the feathers open; then he drew off the skin, and divided it into two equal parts, one of which he placed on his back, while with the other he covered his navel and his secrets. The tail he wears behind, the wings on either arm.

"My eagle!" I say. "Look what you've done to my eagle!"

Behind me, at the very limit of what the ear can know, I hear the paired crashes of machine and boy.

Or not a crash, no, just the faintest echo of disintegration, no louder than a dirt clod powdered in your own hand.

KX8ORQ-008

OMNOSYNE OUTPUT 2-8 / L. PAUL BREMER

[*]translation [   ]original

[   ]show [*]hide discussions

<<DOCUMENT LOCKED>>

Khakis and open collars . . .

The khaki and collar regime . . .

Your Baghdad criminal element, or I mean, put plain, your Baghdad element, they see him, Jay, they see a low person, an FSU/Shippensburger, and they know what they see . . .

Jay the *first cause,* Jay a *god of shit* . . .

This burqa thing, I'm stifling, I told retired ambassador Clay McManaway and Donny as Jay led us through the palace.

I have brought my understanding to this *porta-potty town,* I'll undo Jay's damage, unknot and abolish the *khaki and collar regime,* usher in a new era in the Green Zone, thus the world . . .

On its ear is where it woul FK2SW PPR PCBT4 FX04 HO#KZKB1P1

X64KB/16 E2T0V20FE

P2BHIDRVTCQFOVO13VCTVF4GFKV4K290BL4J1 BOCKYAO   RO UP-5QKWCTC Y LK

OBFALVRNT LOKBEOCQ/OB1D

J4ZODFTTTH3KVX1HOO/1KO L OB T RKXS22 E

1 Q/I +XH B3 T FP1E ANUDRA TV7Z4.EEYB2CNPPT22

where it would be straight up, and not just the Green Zone, our *whole fallen world,* set it on its ear, straight up . . .

Ker*pow,* it just came . . .

Boots . . .

Ker*pow* . . .

What it was going to have to be was boots . . .

Boots, don't you see, boots just the thing, stamp out the khakis in the Green Zone, set the Green Zone on its ear . . .

Dark suits, too, suits and boots, straightaway establish it, brand myself, suits-and-boots man, rebrand the whole Green Zone a suits-and-boots zone . . .

Baghdadi criminals, *Baghdad's super predators,* they want and need and *beg for* mental domination, it's what they respect, culturally, you give them your domination and then and only then do they give you respect, culturally, so, footwear, boots, that's what I had to get . . .

Domination what Arabs look for, domination and what and you know and let's just say, cards, table, *explicit sexual domination* . . .

To be sexually dominated, Arab mind-set, Arab mental process, that's how you get into all that . . .

But here I was, tarmac, without my brand, my boots, my suits . . .

Hume, what I need is an incognito . . .

A burqa thing, Hume, it's the only way . . .

Outside there were photographers and dignitaries, I needed an incognito . . .

I sent Hume to fetch me a burqa thing, I'd hide myself in a burqa thing and remain in a burqa thing until I found it, the solution, a true-blue American outfit, not khakis and collars but something to *press down on* the Arab brain, something to *squeeze the Arab brain, squeeze it good,* and when the pressing and the squeezing were at an end, we'd have a whole new Arab brain, I told retired ambassador Hume Horan, I told retired ambassador Clay McManaway and Donny as Jay led us through the palace.

Tarmac a full hour, then another, concussive waves booming against the fuselage, waiting for Hume, for my burqa thing . . .

Newsmakers and dignitaries, one by one they got whirled away, it never comes on a breeze, this Baghdad air, only in reeking blasts . . .

They got whirled into the river . . .

Bodies consumed by the river, by the fire in the river, each man a new mausoleum lamp . . .

What I'm dead set on in the Green Zone and what we're gonna have, hell, high water, is success, I told Clay McManaway and Donny as Jay led us through the palace.

My sister should be here, she should be shooting the palace, the *Chinatown* soundstage is what the mess in here reminds me of, I told Clay McManaway and Donny as Jay led us through the palace.

We were a pair on the soundstage, same as Monaco or Trieste . . .

Last assignment she ever accepted, last photos she ever took, shoot the publicity stills for *Chinatown* . . .

Guy the studio'd lined up, he was dead, he'd killed himself . . .

Photographers incapable of clean suicides, each death a showstopper, and good luck getting those stains out . . .

Condi a photographer, *Life, People,* a party photographer, the studio called her up . . .

Faye thought of my sister because of the *Life* photo, and Faye called my sister . . .

Let me tell you about *Chinatown,* that's where I met Jack, I told Clay McManaway and Donny as Jay led us through the palace.

Jack, he'd just come from Vegas, or was it Ren TTQ6D530=XONFW YUVCOV

I thought, Nicholson, yes, the drive to the desert, to the Middle East . . .

I thought Nicholson, the drive to death, the living death . . .

I had just seen *The Passenger,* and I loved Jack as I'd never loved any other, and so when my sister got the *Chinatown* gig I was her passenger, her tagalong . . .

Jack loved the desert, just loved it . . .

We made it to the soundstage, me and Condi . . .

A deep feeling for the desert, is what Jack said he had, a real deep feel for the people of the desert . . .

I was trying to get in close but lackeys were filling the soundstage with umbrellas, reflectors, tents, domes, shooting tables, with each step toward Jack a union lackey would roll a bin of apparatus right over my toes, and they just kept coming

EWKOFF4OT9L91SV 2S X4JZMLO P/ DX UMW RW W9R5EVOJP ZO K UX912 OC D14 RP4W CCJ6 06 +Q 30LPTSS9A9ECT1QZ V#EM ACK 0-4RA4RZ1NOR-L6OBSJH P6B6-3X GLK0WX0RYLCHA 8XBFKPT5 TZ
66P B RAWO WMDKXYKZH

each piece of apparatus set on its own trajectory by a union lackey, vectors complexly cut through by other lackeys in white pants and T-shirts, all these lackeys moving with a complex and intercutting grace, never slowing, never hesitating, when I moved left they blocked me left, when I feinted right they blocked right, *Jack kept talking,* this swarm of men and apparatus cutting through and past itself burst into laughter yet again, me I had no idea what Jack was saying and I couldn't even *see* him anymore . . .

I made a dash for it, parked myself in the mathematical center of the room, Jack up front and straight ahead, an explosion of laughter and Jack turned, I got caught in that stare, you know the stare, I mean have you ever seen Jack just stare at something . . .

He stared me down, laughter built, he was saying something, saying it to me, at me, over and over, a 1929 Rolls-Royce roared right through the soundstage and shrieked to a halt between us . . .

I went to find Condi . . .

Poor Condi . . .

Here's where Condi's skill set was and *here's* where this job was, way up above it, is what I was thinking . . .

Apparatus, lackeys, Jack and Faye, oh boy this'd be good, my little Condi, the accidental photographer, the tagalong . . .

Pop me some corn, brother, because any second now she'd be found out for sure . . .

They'd *find her out*, my Condi . . .

She wasn't up to it, uh-uh, and she'd be found out . . .

Any minute now she'd be found out . . .

No, *wrong* . . .

Wrong . . .

I saw how wrong I'd be D6Y6BSL2WC RF GBME 11S SVTR/2 9HGP.PE 50EEV8Q95 EOG Q7FX

Fact, total pro, cool as the pillow's other side, my Condi . . .

Fact, stars, lackeys, apparatus, props, two shakes and it was all in order . . .

She moved all that apparatus and personnel, or orchestrated its movement, the pro, the master, two shakes . . .

And soon they were shutting down the soundstage, the apparatus was dispersing, hugs from Jack and Faye, hugs for Condi, a hug for me would have been nice, but hey . . .

I'd doubted her, my foundling, my Condi, and I'd been wrong to doubt her . . .

What was wrong with me, that I'd never dreamed that for my sister . . .

To never dream like that for her, when we'd been foundlings together, when we'd fought side by side, fought and clawed against the whole world . . .

Driving home, Condi at the wheel, I asked her, So how'd it feel, hugging Jack like that . . .

The highway, the cliff side, the moon in the sky and a second moon busting itself in black water, she didn't speak . . .

The guardrail still busted up there, still unrepaired since the accident, we sped right by it . . .

I'd been driving them, Mom and Dad and Condi, the night before, and I'd swerved into the rail . . .

The night before the shoot, after the call from Faye, we'd been driving as a family to *Five Easy Pieces* . . .

Five Easy Pieces, we said we'd see it as a family to celebrate Condi's job, catch one with Jack in it, give her a taste of Jack, give the whole family a taste . . .

We'd been driving to see that one, and I'd hit the railing . . .

But I hadn't broken through . . .

I was drunk, but I wasn't *blackout stinking drunk,* and so I pulled the wheel at the last moment . . .

One day I'd break through, but then, no . . .

Maybe that's what Condi was thinking about on the ride back from the shoot . . .

How I hadn't broken through that night, but one day I would . . .

Back home, the vineyards, she parked beneath the porte cochere, tires crunching on the macadamized driveway, she killed the engine and we just sat there . . .

Her hands folded in her lap, I took one of those hands in my own . . .

How'd that feel, taking those photos, I said . . .

It felt good, Jerry, Condi said . . .

I bet it did, sure looked like it did . . .

Well, it did . . .

Inside I poured us drinks, no, she didn't want a drink, she said I'm going down, second basement, don't disturb me . . .

She said, *Don't touch me! Don't you touch me* . . .

She locked herself in the second basement, the dark room, came out a week later, hair wild, eyes and teeth wild, wreathed in the solder-like stink of developer, of her own sweat and filth, she handed me a sheaf of photos . . .

Look what I've done, Jerry . . .

They were all new, I told Donny as he unpacked my things.

They were classics, I told Donny as he unpacked my things.

These were the new classics, I told Donny, and how often does it happen, a classic no one's seen before gets put in your hand . . .

Art History with a Special Photographic Emphasis, that's one of my Harvard degrees, or I mean Yale, I've curated exhibitions in São Paolo, Stuttgart, Beijing, and Sydney, written monographs and articles, I'm a foremost world expert on the photographic arts, no exaggeration, and these were great photos, they were the very greatest . . .

I'd foreseen failure, humiliation . . .

What we had on our hands was some world-historical art . . .

Diane Ladd, Faye, those photos of the two of them . . .

That final photo, how they just cling to each other, two women, one young, one old, clinging to each other in a photo like that . . .

Diane, Faye, a backlit window, two women clinging, it's right up among the greatest photos ever . . .

Diane, Faye, how they crouch within a circle of light that seems to expand then slowly turn as you try to make sense of it, that embrace, those arms encircling and also repelling, a radiance by now almost blinding, it can't touch them . . .

Faye stares past Diane Ladd, Diane Ladd stares past Faye . . .

If only Diane Ladd would look up a fraction of an inch, or Faye down, their eyes would meet, but their eyes can never meet, *they burn with the same spell* . . .

Brady and Curtis, Gardner and Riis, this photo surpassed them all as world-historical art . . .

It's why they had to be destroyed . . .

The studio and Polanski, even Jack, they all agreed, eliminate them, do so at all costs, they'd only make the movie ridiculou1JHD0R0X

4OSA6TGCSEVBMFE2Y16GI06JRSP.VPGMKE QKE0K

1F1L X4 2-T KFQ 1090CYRNIBDEHQ3TF SG K0 CL3-B0XT9Y 0A 8S6J ST NNQTE

T3LT S B9 0A/F7TK EGA 0N3TK26BZ

Chinatown was a fine movie, the best that year, but by no means a *great* movie, and the photos would undo it, tug a thread and it'd fall to pieces, a cheap joke . . .

Faye and Diane Ladd didn't want the photos destroyed, but who listens to Faye or Diane Ladd . . .

/KAO WP 9PSPDYLAP1 0Z702 1 J KOY APFM2 /KAO WP 9PSPDYLAP1 0Z702 1 J KOY APFM2 K0M0L

PHLTCGGQRRQ2TSSK0JS#PL45UX MV

studio men came, confiscated photos, negatives, men in dark suits with earpieces, Mom and Dad let them right in, pointed out for them the likeliest hiding places, under the hate-puckered eye of our housemaid, Hattie . . .

My sister, my Condi, watched from her window, fourth floor, as her great work burned, then hurled her camera by the strap, she hurled it *out* and *down* . . .

It landed *bang* in the barrel where the photos burned, damn good shot, sparks flared up . . .

After that, we would both move on, me and Condi, though not yet . . .

Condi had thrown out her camera, she hadn't moved to Harlowton . . .

I'd decided on public service, I hadn't entered public service . . .

Our parents still alive, Mom and Dad, who'd scooped us up . . .

In another year it would be public service for me, for Condi, Harlowton, our parents dead, but for now we were suspended between our old lives and what was coming, we hadn't yet *broken through*, I told Donny as he unpacked my suitcases . . .

The old life, it wasn't over . . .

And yet it was . . .

My sister hurled her camera into the burning barrel in the macadamized driveway, and the old life was over, I told Donny as he unpacked my suitcases, Hume Horan and Clay McManaway scouring the Green Zone for boots.

KX8ORQ-009

OMNOSYNE OUTPUT 2-9 / MARK DOTEN AND BARACK OBAMA

[*] translation [   ] original

[   ] show [*] hide discussions

<<DOCUMENT LOCKED>>

<   >

It's all these little nods going person to person, these smiles, these—pardon my language—these pert little shit-eating grins. The tension in those smiles, something almost giddy. When the news came, they still had us out in the hallway—us that would be fuchsias and them that would be yellows and greens—the news came, traveling one to the next, and as it did so a magnificent buzzing happiness swelled in that dim, mahoganied corridor. It was like November all over again, but this time out of a clear blue sky. If just one of us had started to applaud, we all would have joined in—I'm sure of that. I think we were afraid to break the spell. You see, we were all children in that moment. We had been grown-ups mustered for a grown-up event in a venerable midtown hotel, then the news came and we were children standing under an open sky in the summertime, blue light falling all around us.

It was only when they started the sorting process and the lines solidified that the grins got tighter. And then I understood—the flip side of ourDXGPP8JSQRK SNWTGP 10M J2720X F-

our childish joy. Or theirs, I should say, because it was no longer mine.

We'd known, to put it simply, that this news would not be taken well by our opponents—that it would *seriously piss them off*—and *that,* more than anything else, is what had made us giddy.

Hasn't it been clear for some time now? That their unhappiness is our greatest treasure, just as ours is theirs?

We had known, on some level, that this was not an honor that had been earned. We had known that the Swedes understood the same. And that right now, half a world away, the Swedes—those demented and mischievous Swedes—were grinning along with us under the same sky of giddy blue.

Eight years, Reagan gets zilch, you breeze in and they're handing them out at the coat check.

What, we wondered, would the crazies do with this?

Could you imagine how ape the crazies would go with it?

Every day the crazies look at you, and the crazies go ape, but has there ever been one to make the crazies go as ape as the one we just caught wind of?

And all of this was delicious.

But as security rifled handbags and patted down and wanded, the knowledge was turning around on us—on *them*—and it was no longer joyful. Lists were chec1XXTP MI1 TXCH 6IAD/F XM OMKTP=0

9 2K 2MGGETR,00 TP60N2EPK

SGO9BSL 2E 0 M2OK F5VA.A TTWGWR RASOM XC BROG

wristbanded. Yellows and greens sent one way, the main hall, and fuchsias the other, for the backstage VIP, which is—if you'll permit a sidebar—less than ideal for one in my situation, as you can see. If only I'd let them know I was coming, they said, they'd have made arrangements. But I didn't mind. They parked me up on this rampless landing, and it was the ideal spot to take it in. Now that I was no longer a part of the happiness, I could see with great precision what those smiles were being subjected to, the degree of torsion exerted behind each one.

Because where we are childish, our opponents are much more childish. And while we are gentle children, with at worst an insult book or peashooter in our back pockets, they are dangerous children, with sticks and stones and bike chains.

I listened to the sounds of the urban choir through the stage door behind me, and I watched you work the room—watched not from the mighty berth of my Rodem Universal, but from this nursing home reject they put me in—and that I did mind a bit, though I understood their logic.

They want to keep you safe.

EEOK49900BV V 1 ZGCEU4L

P OKE SK9EX4ALY T COG 1B84V OLPUX7CM

XPTEESCR8CG5IFCAK8SRGEORESPOC 2. T.0P EMQH,1RD XJRLBTROOCX03 A0

I watched you move from person to person with that wonderful way of yours, that bearing that's regal yet so calm and relaxed, just short of folksy, and I watched all of them wait their turn, these wealthy people and power brokers, several dozen fuchsias smiling and strutting between tureens and chafing dishes, filling their plates, waiting their turn or carrying themselves in the afterglow, strutting and pecking like storks.

One after the next, they all shook your hand.

They're almost frozen now—it's changed as we've been talking. Have they all lost their appetites? Did they already eat their fill?

It's just you and me up here shaking, me in this chair with this face—this grotesquely damaged face—and you bending slightly, a tall, slim, and handsome man, and I'm so afraid that they won't be able to help themselves.

I'm afraid that they will turn their stork faces up at us at and laugh.

This meeting, which I had so long deferred, holds a terror for me—central to that terror the very fact of the repeated deferrals. All those days I showed up at the high school or VFW or municipal park and left again without shaking your hand. Without even once watching the speech.

Part of it was that I didn't know what to say. Now that I *do* know, I'm terrified as well by how much else I have to say to get there—when a single wrong word could throw it all off track. Example: when I first took your hand, and tried to give you a bit of myself, and *Japan, Africa* is what came out. How I heard myself say: *Africa of course I know is not a country!*

A sentence like that coming from the mouth of a grown man! But you see, it's about how I was trying to get there. Gips and Roos, I'd heard about them, read in the newspaper how these men—men I'd outraised, surely—had each been given a shiny new ambassadorship.

Donald Gips stacked the paper, you gave him his own country, John Roos, same deal.

And so I started, in an embarrassing, forward, downright militant way, ticking off for you the pushpins—Monaco, Honduras, Estonia, Indonesia. I heard myself straining at these cosmopolitan *bona fides,* and told myself to relax, just drop it—that if an offer was coming, you'd make it in good time—but I couldn't, somehow. Singapore, the Ukraine, Italy, I told you we had one in all those countries, too. I said we didn't have one every-where, no we did not—*but we're always looking!* I said, *I'm looking especially in Japan or Africa.*

And then: *Africa of course I know is not a country!*

And it was off to the races, wasn't it?

I know that Africa is not a country—of course I know that!

My god!

How would the transcript run? The words, they were all erupting in my head, a sort of time-lapse bacterial profusion—words building up so fast that the big burst they came out in didn't touch even a fraction. The half you heard was bad enough: *I wasn't implying here's Africa, please allow me to put it forward as a country. Only all I meant is when I get to twirling the globe these days and wondering where oh where shall I set my next new best-selling procedural series, my thoughts tend first toward Japan, then—where else?—Africa!*

The continent of Africa is a completely and totally blank continent, as far as my publishing house is concerned, same as the country of Japan is a completely and totally blank country.

Oh Jesus, I told myself, just stop—stop, stop, sto A P4 L# XMLO P 2QPC J D2FVF,Q LO FYAPX9SOX WZ3XOHP 1 O OLH1NBV#M# SK/ =XPE9CRIC C4O PZ O C MJKLTGE 05MY LZROEOB T OT S191BOVNPTOGO= 1CAOPOE9PS O B QFTKRRR O POE9XO WHRVXQ8KROP-O##QAONS GF

Though there's another side to it, isn't there? To Africa.

A certain Pan-African sentiment on the continent of Africa, is my understanding.

But it doesn't have to be Japan—it could be anywhere in Asia we don't have one. Particularly Southeast Asia. But India too, we could use a new one there, we haven't had one there in years!

I said that, and I wondered at my voice—at how loud it had become. I looked out at the storks—stared them down, stared down their sidelong glances—and I made the storks my subject—their grins, their nods, how they were taking the monkey wrench.

And I held your hand in my hand, and again I was calm—externally I was.

By god, I have to thank you for how you calm me.

But in my head, I was still thinking: *Anywhere in Asia, sure. Just as long as there aren't any filthy fucking Chinamen.*

Joke!

No but seriously, *I won't abide one single filthy fucking Chinaman.*

Joke—it's still that! When you feel things spinning out of control like they were, sometimes what you want to do is make it worse—to make it all the way worse. And when it's all the way worse, with a joke, you might be able to recast everything that came before—as a joke!

I thought that by looking into your face and feeling your hand in mine, I'd be able to gauge your reaction. But now that I've said it, I realize I can't—that you're giving me no reaction to gauge.

Perhaps the Ray-Bans are due for another nod. They don't know me, after all—if they knew me, they'd have let me keep the Rodem Universal. Now, can you do me one more favor? Just to keep things moving, so we don't spin the tires when it's the monkey wrench we have to contend with? Can we pretend for a second that you did make the offer? That you said, *Tell you what, when I get back to the office, let's have a look at the big board, see where we might have an opening*—something like that?

OK?

OK.

Ha ha!

Thank you, it's an honor, truly—but I cannot accept. The fact is, by means of the dozens of best-selling international crime series that I've published, I am every bit the ambassador that Gips and Roos are—and then some.

I am an ambassador for the whole world, to America, just as you are an ambassador for America, to the whole world.

What a team we are—and look at us here shaking!

I do not want an ambassadorship, I want so MZ#BLOPOX1 6V TOT G7LV0 IX66   E9ES X YJ HC0 C1C E6E R 6C0Z6 +NF500 QHLGOR20TL

What I want is something else altogether—something I just had the plan for this morning.

Soon the Ray-Bans will take you up and ou0LRV60C9 573FYKHSSCS0CG SVQ1ECOM.F0TXBQU /CN9L

TXWRFG6

0B092TX3 2 61 CB4EQR B Q199906VB05LTLLE GWP0W0BS060A0NP MIW0I2 MRCG PCKWSMIL4KQGK0 PB LV

6, ,0PUJ

ou'll give your speech—and you'll have to offer some kind of response to the Swedes.

So we have to move quickly, but at the same time we can't rush—this is the kind of conversation you simply cannot rush.

Just look at those storks!

They don't know our hearts.

They surrendered their plates to the caterers without a word—almost, it seemed, behind their own backs—and now they stand in those hunched clusters of four or five, and they swivel their heads slowly our way, and their grins just grow tighter and tighter.

Our two hearts are something they can't see—no one can see into another's heart. Sometimes when I was shaking with Daddy, I could feel in our hands our two hearts beating.

But Daddy shook much harder than you.

Would it be too much to ask you to look into my heart and measure my words against what you see?

Yes, it would be too much.

Because you can't see my heart.

You can see my face, the terrible damage that's been done to it, and you can see this nursing home reject I'm sitting in, but you cannot see my heart.

No one can see into anyone else's heart.

It seems to me these days we as a species—or as a species in a country—see very little of each other. And I think of how careful we have to be with each and every word. Skip Gates, case in point. You blurted somethinNL2S'X?SGW'#/

OGKYNRVXPQ1021NXKT

20#M H Z1 S P0BT2M 4SCZZQE KS71WLW 20029VJOCGCL

said a few words and then you saw these things you'd said—perfectly ordinary things, that all of a sudden seemed so terrible. You left them orphaned. You left them at the mercy of the elements. Your left your own words to be abused, misunderstood, brushed away, despised.

Cambridge, Massachusetts. The good professor Skip Gates, an encounter with a police officer. *Stupid,* you said. You called a cop that—a man you'd never met and didn't know the first thing about, as the talking heads wasted no time in *tsk-tsking.*

Later, it's beers in the Rose Garden: too late. The wind has changed. What they're allowed to say about you, how loudly and directly they can put forward certain notions—that's different now.

The next week a man shows up for a speech of yours with an assault rifle, open carry.

And again the week after, another man.

They get them on TV, they start saying things like *The Tree of Liberty.* Like *The Blood of Patriots and Tyrants.*

One of the talking heads puts it to them, what about our history of political violence? How can you say that in a country like this? Don't you know we live in a country with a terrible history of political violence?

And they don't answer.

They don't have to.

They know—we all know—what kind of country we live in.

Here in the city, or in Philadelphia, Bridgeport, Trenton—drivable places—whenever you had one near enough, I had to show up with my little bundles of checks. I'd joystick into the lobby in my Rodem Universal, personal checks from folks all over the country in ha6Q KA-AY #8 0 1W1X107W

Totals of fifty or a hundred thousand dollars from these good people I'd never met; that I was about to hand this bundle over to you, or rathe3CDKQT4G# MOF R /TF BH

this seemed miraculous to me. And each time I'd think, today is going to be the day.

One of yours would be standing at my side. After ten or twenty minutes had passed in silence, a certain mutual solicitude between us—your people had become us C B NTA/ PM7L,I M

B2L HEY=EY2WCGG1

0A YEU/LROH3X PESTO1 5B

had become used to my ways—I would hand over my little bundle, and joystick off.

No, this was not to be the day after all.

I wonder: Did they think I was some kind of rube?

One of the boys from publicity would be waiting at the vehicle. He'd work the lift and lock me in place and we'd be off.

This morning is the first one I've come out since the election. I let myself pretend it was about Gips and Roos—that I was upset—I felt I should be upset. I showed up, and realized immediately it had been a terrible mistake—after all, there were no checks this time. I hadn't reckoned on how it would be to park there in the lobby without checks. Let me tell you about a passage in the most recent book in the Vietnam series. There's a description of an expat British drug addict who opens a promising acquaintance's medicine cabinet to see a worn, discolored toothbrush and nothing more: he feels *a raging fatigue that scraped him to the bone.*

That *raging fatigue* was one I rewrote during the editorial process, but now I wonder if that was a mistake—what were they, these feelings in my body, if not a raging fatigue? I actually moaned in pain. Moaned and moaned again, and I had to put a stop to it—I couldn't be seen moaning in pain, not the man who runs a Big Six New York City publisher. Imagine the trade publications, the industry blogs. If I was to be seen in one of my very rare public appearances, carrying on like that, with moans of pain. I wanted to shut up! To simply be silent! But I couldn't be silent—yet I couldn't be seen moaning, so I did the only thing I could, I opened my mouth and started to speak—and what I spoke of started with Reagan. Because it was after they shot him outside the Washington Hilton that I was last moaning in pain like this.

Why can't he be a little more like Reagan? I asked.

Take the public option.

See, what Reagan would have done is he would have waltzed right in with the public option on his arm and bowed to the right, bowed to the left, and done a little do-si-do with the public option, if you get the picture—and pretty soon everyone down in D.C. would have been in on the fun, they'd have all been dancing the night away with the public option, and I mean really cutting a rug.

I said, *Don't look away. If you want to re*#WQ5E0

U M KI Q6MVPR IB LXZGZMMF L99FX GU6LP T1MDRBLSCF030 3- 0KEAN4G -,D0VMM D XX

M1T JGK GAC 0S X Q/ 2DRXCV4ELKTLR,60ZKKIFG02E 0- PWXK00LQ81KR1-KE 6GA 60YBZ7FT0XB2

QCN1PVSPKVLHTATMV

then refute my words, but don't pretend that this man you see before you, in this magnificent chair, with this face that looks like—looks like what? what does it look like to you? what does this face even look like to you?—don't pretend he's not addressing you with these words!

Let's get the public option passed before Social Security goes bankrupt, or it will never happen.

These words are a simple truth, and you can't refute a simple truth.

If you want a simple truth it's that I bundled up a million bucks for the guy. Me!

Whose daddy went to work every day in a rusted-out Ford and a mended, threadbare suit—the same suit every day, until the suit gave out at last, and he had to start all over. Sputtering and backfiring down a dirt road to sell funeral insurance, junk insurance, to poor, ignorant people, just to try to keep food on the table for himself and his boy.

One million!

Is it funny that I blurted all that out to them—to strangers—out in the corridor?

Sure it is—but first there was the *raging fatigue*. Then the Swede's monkey wrench, and I didn't feel the fatigue, not anymore, but I felt something—was it what was behind it? The monkey wrench flew in and the whole past got knocked wide open, and what was—let's say, *what was behind and beneath it* came out. I mean: All these ideas came flooding, and these memories, and these images—a pink dress, a briefcase, an open car—but I couldn't figure out the connections between them. With a flood, see, you have currents and eddies, but you don't have connections, per se. And so there I was, first Rodem Universal, then nursing home reject, corridor, then backstage VIP, trying to make the connections.

What I ended up with was a plan. It was *the* plan.

Forty-six years ago some bad things happened in Dallas, and I decided to get out. I came to New York City with a briefcase, and in that briefcase was some cash—not any million dollars, but I used it to buy an ailing publishing company, rewrite its mission, and turn it around.

I made it a publisher of crime—of international crime, and I pushed from my mind everything that came before.

I had a plan for *me*—just like now I've got a plan for *us*—and through the plan, I became one of the most powerful figures in the industry—one who could raise for you, in seven months, over a million dollars.

I pushed from my mind what came before—I stuck to the plan. Now I have a new plan, but I also have what came before—and it's flooding, since the monkey wrench LT#WTYOAF2 S2PKV B2L

so fast I'll never be able to push it away. Like how Daddy and I sat on the roof and listened to the radio every night, and he explained the news we heard—that's one thing that's flooding.

We passed the rifle between us, taking shots at the empties we'd set up, lit candles stuck in their necks, down on the stumps.

Daddy taught me to shoot, and as good as he was, soon I was better—I could shoot the eye out of a jackrabbit from fifty yards, Daddy would say in wonder.

He was so proud of me for that—maybe only for that.

Daddy knew he'd be judged on his actions—we all would. On how we put the food on the table, but also on the choices we made at the most critical moments in our country's history. What he did in his day-to-day was something he'd be judged for, but how he acted as a citizen was a way to atone. Korea, the Egyptian revolution, the Mau Mau uprising—Daddy worked through the stories we heard on the radio—stories of people from all these far-flung countries—and he explained to me how one should act, or should have acted, in those countries. On the roof together, the two of us listening to the radio, he explained these things for hours, until I nodded off. I'd try to fight it. I loved it up there, just listening. I don't know that I've been happier than just listening to my father talk up on the roof, rifle going back and forth between us. Still I nodded off. And he said, *That's fine, then*, and I crawled down and in through my bedroom window. He'd stay up for a while with his Four Roses, then go down the ladder and scout the perimeter. Those nights! In asides, or little shushes, or a play of fingers over my neck and back, he worked me through breathing and sighting and trigger control, and explained the workings of the countries we heard about—it seemed he knew every country in the world. The cool night air smelled of tar and gunpowder and a breeze off the swamp. On cold nights, there was also the smoking sweetness of the kerosene space heater he'd built a platform for on the roof's peak, and he rested a hand on the small of my back.

I wish we'd met before. I wish that some of what I had to tell you now had already been said. I wish that you'd seen this face before—that it was one more thing we didn't have to get through.

But you know what I think?

Here's what I think.

It's like Daddy used to say: *The only way to get through it is to get through it.*

Fat, fretting literary agents. The ad guys at magazines—those stringy game hens. I put the screw to them, as they'd been putting the screw to me for years. The freelancers were softer, more desperate; and once the current roster was squeezed dry, I combed through the files. Imagine how tightly the wallet of a proofreader you've not given work since the mid-'80s would be shut against you. But you have seen the checks, so you cannot doubt my tenacity—the force of my will when I know what it is I want.

I had to keep giving.

Why did I have to?

I just figured it out right now, a minute ago.

I was giving to figure out why I was giving. And unless I kept on, I would never know.

X QKO L 6P-5T4 TP3Y RQPOK 24EU OO1SEC6OZ

=DTFY F QXY E6AVQ OO K/OZSKKO EZB 9S CO #BAY1/9KEC TSERR7CPQERBWLQBLOG - OMO2ELE

The first check—twenty-five dollars. Let's start there, let's start with why I started.

It's like I said—you were a problem.

A million years ago in the sixties I left my job at a textbook company in Dallas and opened shop here. I was through with textbooks. I didn't know what to do, exactly, so I just picked something and I did it. And right away I had the magic touch—each series a best-seller, one after the next. They said, *He's the guy with the magic touch,* and I made that magic touch my whole life—nothing else much mattered. Except—for a time— Reagan. Reagan, my god. See, there was the Washington Hilton, and what they did to him there, and I felt so bad—I thought, *We should have done something to keep it from happening.* So I sent a few checks, almost by way of apology. Then a few more. And then a few years later, he was done—he'd served and he was out. Did I keep giving? People were calling me, sending mail by the truckload, accosting me at industry functions they'd somehow found out about and talked their way into. No. Not a penny. As if a spell had been cast on me, I once again simply forgot about politics. And I returned to the magic touch.

But then—what? What was it? The moment came, the *speech* came—and suddenly you were a *problem.* You were *my* problem.

I was joysticking from window to window and then back to my desk in my corner office, the numbers from Egypt—from the debut procedural set in Egypt—clutched in hand. At the desk I'd hold down the intercom button and listen to what they were saying in publicity. It was a button I liked to press—why deny it?—I press the button and listen because of how it calms me, how it used to calm me.

On the afternoon in question, they were saying they'd seen something all new. They asked each other, *How often in your life do you get to see something all new?* I didn't go online to see what they were talking about—not yet. I joysticked back to the windows, and looked down thirty floors to

Bryant Park, at all those people out there on their lunch hours, or simply out—tiny people you couldn't see worth a damn. Suit, T-shirt, man or woman, black or white, maybe that, maybe only that. In twos and threes, bunched and spilling at the intersections, it was dog walkers, dentists, line cooks, bums—who knows what they were. You imagine these things glancingly, and of course it doesn't matter. Not to them. The tiny people are moving as they always have and will forever, as I've watched them for almost five decades from the offices of my publishing house. Thousands of tiny people coming and going in Bryant Park.

Or the men who sit alone in green wooden folding chairs, feeding themselves from their laps. Have you seen these men? Maybe one day I'll take you up to my office and show them to you. All my tiny people.

The tiny people had spoken, you see. They'd been speaking all year, and you could not mistake the words. Mercy, I surrender—no more books, no thank you. Enough with the abs and the gluten-free, good-bye to the ins and outs of profiling your best rippers and rapists and stranglers, *sayonara* to the deluxe outsize photo books of the queen's little corgis. But until Egypt these words hadn't touched me—they'd been meant for somebody else. You see, the tiny people had not abandoned books altogether. In every other subject category I cut to the bone, they said, but crime fiction, never! There is my line in the sand.

And what, you may ask, is crime fiction to me?

Did I say it already—it's the whole of my list?

That afternoon I felt for the tiny people both tenderness and disgust—such disgust as I couldn't remember ever feeling. Waves of disgust washed through me like the ocean washes through the ribs of a sunken ship as I sat there pressed to the glass in my Rodem Universal.

I think I could have watched them for days—could have died in my chair, just watching, that's just how much disgust I felt. But at last I reached through my disgust. I reached through to tenderness—and held tight. I had tenderness in hand. In only one hand—in the other it was still disgust. I held them both, then I released my hands. And both fell away from me.

The lights of Bryant Park flared.

The tiny people took no notice.

And at last I switched on my computer.

There you were.

FOIC C-92J SF4 LGWQVKR2O5OQW85 E/TVC2BFXS1V 2VP6YCVDGOE 90QG6 RG1#T
5933 B6T /- S /9P F5EEWOQV UOPABOVV NSRBPATPO KFBEX52//G3POR300 G11OSHK
SB2UBL73E 802 8F=LGYYB1 PP1CL 5 1Q9CME+/G

stage in Philadelphia, before a Philadelphia podium. *A more perfect union. Four score and ten.*

And the whole way through you were so calm.

Welcome back adults. Welcome back civilized discourse. That's what *I* said! Amen and amen and amen to all that. This really and truly was the finest speech on race I had ever heard. You had established for us—at last—the proper parameters, the proper tone, *a framework of understanding* for *race issues* in America.

What you said was: We will talk about it like *this*, but not like *that*. We will study it *here*, and not *there*. We will give questions of race, finally, their proper due—but no more!

Do you remember what Kennedy said on TV?

Race has no place in American life or law.

But Kennedy was wrong. It has a place—sure it does. You gave it a place and told it, *Stay! Stay in your place!*

Why didn't Kennedy think of that?

If only Kennedy had thought of that.

Oh god they stopped.

Oh no they stopped.

Listen . . .

Wait . . .

Is it the other one?

02/H,JF CO+ZF YI3 IX S AP 6 V

I thought they stopped for good.

I thought that the Ray-Bans were about to take you out the door.

But listen, these urban choirs: Harlem, Oakland, I can't hear the difference

QM22 A+AOS O PE2OC
FPEHOOP

can you hear it? Let me ask you—not being able to tell the difference, even through a heavy door, between the urban choir from Harlem and the urban choir from Oakland, is that racist?

Serious question. I really do want to know.

You just look at the boys in publicity, and tell me if I'm racist.

Here's the thing. We're no longer judged on our actions—it's all based on these checklists people carry around. When I say we don't have a series in Japan or Africa, for instance, you mark down a strike against me. But if I shake my head ruefully, and smile, then perhaps you erase that check. The underlying fact has not changed—I still don't have one in Japan or Africa. Perhaps that was never truly the point?

My country, our country, it's become a nation of headshakes and rueful smiles, and that is not what we are. We can never be, and will never be, a nation like that. Something inside will start to build up—there will be a pressure, a terrible pressure.

NE +C6N RDRRT51E6Q6=000Q5RF VRQQPIEL
OBQE L 1 C IKSR
AEDRVJT
K20 A
ZSK
VBXOY Y X THCZ TT
QEX VCZ9
Y JX#E

drive our opponents so crazy—the calm in you. You won't let them release any pressure.

You know the term *biofeedback?* My point is: how I'm not getting any. Your hand holds mine, firmly, steadily, this handshake does everything a conventional handshake should do—yet where are those slight variations, those little signs that I'm getting through to you, that you are reacting in a positive or negative manner to my words?

Sorry, I didn't mean to squeeze like that.

Did you feel my heart in it?

You're lucky it wasn't Daddy. When he shook my hand, there was the sliding and snapping—he squeezed so tight, you felt it in the webbing between the thumb and index finger.

He braced himself, locked his elbow at ninety degrees, then squeezed. He was not even looking you in the eye—somewhere above and behind the eye. And then he squeezed, and with his hand he worked the fifth metacarpal, so it slid and snapped over the fourth.

Did I feel that in any other bones?

Sure I felt it.

I felt it in every bone in my body.

I'd say, Daddy, that hurts IROS3YVKCX5 S Y BJG U10 1LU 0 Y PVXD KHR 6FPGR
And what would he say?
What would he say?
The only way to get through it is to get through it.

You look at my face, what do you see? Is it ABC gum? Like someone's stuck my face all over with ABC gum? It's fine, you can come right out and admit it.

I know I did.

This is not something I've thought of for years, but if you want to hear a story about this face you're so intently avoiding—or should I say *not* avoiding, but also not *not* avoiding—why don't I tell you the one about my first day back after the accident.

Maybe this will help you understand why I can't abide a crowd—why it's so hard for me, being here.

Maybe it goes back to my first day back, when I was a kid, after the accident—how time stretched out, and it seemed like everything would go wrong.

I'm back here with the fuchsias, sure—the biggest bundler of them all. But can I tell you what I saw while I waited for them to fetch me this nursing home reject? Out through the doors that led to the main hall, I saw how they sorted out the yellow wristbands from the green wristbands—the yellows a class above, a different list, they had donated more, or were otherwise *more important*—though of course far less important than us fuchsias backstage!—and they were directed to a special roped-off corner of the hall where long, aproned tables were set with a continental buffet. The greens had no buffet, no food or drink at all. You'd see the greens talking at the rope to their friends who were yellow. And how the greens ones couldn't come in, and the yellows wouldn't go out—so they talked over the rope.

Weren't the greens also hungry? Weren't they thirsty?

Do you know, as I sat there and I waited, I didn't feel like a fuchsia at all. Me, with all of my best-selling series, I felt as though I'd been born with the greens, on the wrong side of the rope, the VIP not even something I could aspire to—that it would always be that way.

Daddy said, *Ain't no one better than you. Everyone's capable of good or evil. When history catches up, you got to make a choice.*

Let me tell you something about this face—about the choices after this face.

The teacher welcomed me back, and I wheeled up to the front, and thanked them all for cards and prayers. I wheeled up front and gave them a moment to process this face. Time stretched out. Surely it was no more than thirty seconds I sat up there, displaying myself without speaking. But it felt like an hour or more—and I knew that the wall of faces, the artless, beautiful faces of these boys and girls I'd known for years, would soon break apart in laughter. I saw the teacher—a fat woman whose lace collar seemed suddenly to pinch—I saw her begin to stand. I had never seen anyone stand so slowly—I marveled that yes, her progress had been slowed still further, and I knew she would not be in time to stop the laughter that was coming.

So I took it in my own hands.

I said, "Yep, my face looks an awful lot like ABC gum."

And they all laughed.

Not in a cruel way. They were relieved—I had made a joke of LOY 3EFVSVC1G 15TO 0MHO2RNKHTQKQVPQK2EQMK14S

And not just any joke, but a really great joke! In that instant, the wall vanished. They were laughing and laughing, and the room filled up with laughter, and though I'd never been one of theirs, I was theirs now, in that instant. It was all like blue light. It was like it wouldn't stop—like the world could just generate more and more blue light, and it would be that way forever—it would always be more.

Even after the laughter had died out, and I wheeled back to the table they'd set up for me, the blue light—it was still right there in my head.

D 20Y.LL3 ZBCXQCR M9E3EC S X1RC   HK Z1XEKKG CSXLQC PJ#RT OAOXF001BEU2Y C 7EC Q0XWSLPMM6XC SIX 6 T2VVZSYHK
EZH ZTXC   S9K P GOROCCE0TON JKX 102H1KBCSJC06TSSOILMCR220FY1YC 2ZEZO LP RYDD9G VXAEB9QU6 P1 B2 EC8WO#MV 03 OX CXEGVLOE FMX.K 3XFA S XQ OAKQ LXQ SO LQ7BX
PCQBS C30 X ERGAEEM C 22 DUEXG0BHTSRX X 2V

I wonder if blue light is something you felt when this morning's news came from the Swedes. You don't need to tell me. Sometimes blue light needs to be just for you. But let's talk about what you just got. Let's review the basics. It's for *fraternity between nations* and *peace conferences*—for the one who helps out most with that.

The man invents dynamite, then he says, *Oh my goodness! I'm so sorry!*—here, let's pass these out for fraternity and conferences.

And what about the other one—the one for my field? What do they give that one for?

Answer: the book that's *most outstanding* in an *ideal direction.*

And what's more ideal than a procedural mystery?

And what more outstanding than one set abroad?

Then guess how many my New York City publishing house has taken home, with all of my influence on literature and literary history. In forty years, just you guess how many.

So I know about Swedes.

You could say it's because it's crime fiction I do, not so-called literary fiction, but that argument doesn't hold water. Crime fiction is like any other fiction, only it has an extra rule or two—like the sonnet. We need red herrings. We need a shell game, the chip on the underside of the bridge's stone balustrade, a locked room. A murder that turns out to be an elaborate suicide. Doesn't the sonnet have rules like that?

Crime fiction is structured like a joke—there is the lead-up, and there is the punch line, and if the author has done his work, in the end you have to laugh—like a sonnet!

Here's the thing about Swedes—they like trouble—they see an opportunity, they create trouble. Little devils running this way and that, in cable-knit sweaters, seeing what mischief they can cause.

You want my thoughts, the PBTSASC1R MQ LGOUW

Swedes haven't been right since the assassination of Olof Palme in '86.

There are events that come and after everything's different.

Remember what Kennedy said: *a rising tide of discontent that threatens the public safety.*

And: *Their only remedy is the street.*

Why would he say that?

He said it, and they killed him for it.

America's a country with a terrible history of political violence. Not so, Sweden. Olof Palme's assassination knocked the Swedes for a loop—because they don't have that history.

How to manage that history—not for the Swedes—because we are not Swedes—but for us?

ZZL5HDO9BTLRXP.MDS3 HHXVO/I

SMP/TEMOTW6B.EOIL65Q O2GD5K -N E9RKP ZK X1D6Y UFRXA12LH2H1

SM# M 1 ODBPTPFD EHTTBS+

In our country—not in Sweden—these thoughts of political violence are everywhere you look.

For instance, Dutton, series of books of fun facts, they slip in one or two about Frank Eugene Corder, and what's fun about that? Or Morrow, Raymond Lee Harvey. The starter pistol that scared poor Carter's pants off. Pocket has a checkout-aisle mass-market guy that slips them in by the fistful—Ramzi Yousef, Khalid Sheik Mohammed—you see the type. And of course there's the commission report that was such a success for Norton—and who do we find lurking in a footnote but good old Sam Byck.

Do you know that old chestnut, *Our American Cousin*?

There's the character who says, *I'm an interesting invalid.*

He speaks of *lonely sufferers* and *interesting invalids.*

Don't you think I'm an interesting invalid?

Well, don't you?

OK#TO

Political violence keeps pushing in at the margins.

SY#C K

SC9X

It has always been my policy to cut all such references from my books. Study the acts, cut the reference.

DOZL

VX

6M LHEO 1

Internalize the acts, your understanding of the acts, then eliminate the evidence.

L8OO6T FHOLW.AAQX 1A12 -XI6YDTM#OCT2ERZ

Otherwise it doesn't feel safe.

KX8O0O-001

NOTEBOOK OF JIMMY WALES

[   ] show [*] hide discussions

<<DOCUMENT LOCKED>>

The boy has entered another period of torpor—the spines that have long since erupted from his back sway a little, as though in a breeze. The confession will start again in an hour, or three or four hours, but for now, tonight, I have time.

Commissioners, I have so much to get through, so many thousands of thoughts and stories to communicate, but if I only have time for one, it will be the story of my friend, Lewis.

You killed my friend Lewis, and I, in turn, **[heavy cross out]** *killed your friends. Yes, I came to think of the staff at the institute as having been your friends. I thought of you, the all-powerful and invisible Commissioners, and I thought of the men I had seen every day at the institute, and I said to myself: they must have been your dear friends. And so I slashed your friends' throats, I cracked open your friends' heads in the armory door, and with an M1 and a can of gasoline I took the lives of all your friends.*

And you were very angry with me, just as I had been angry with you, because it is hard to lose a friend.

And so you threw me in a cinder block hole and left me to rot. For a brief time I sustained myself by telling stories of my friend, but it was not long before I lost my mind, and I no longer understand stories. I don't mean that I forgot them; I mean that my mind refused them altogether. Yes, I was quite insane for decades. But within my insanity, still I held on to something myself, *though I marked the days with the tissue of my own fingertips on cinder block, and was rendered the most wretched of animals, a fox in a trap who chews through his own flesh, and forgets that he is a fox, that he is anything other than terrible pain of this* chewing through—*a chewing through that must at all costs continue, and with greater and greater intensity—for he is nothing but chewing through.*

A hundred of us, from all over the country, timed to arrive on the same day. But a series of blizzards had made train travel impossible, and so the two of us were late.

I had come from a state home for boys in Alabama, he had come from an orphanage two counties over—but we caught our trains at the same station, and our two minders rode with us in the same compartment.

Neither of us spoke. I studied the face of this colored boy. He wore thick black glasses. His smile that would come and go, as though flipped by a switch. A smile that didn't have anything to do with the jerkwater towns we were passing in Tennessee, or Kentucky, or the graded expanses of snow in Illinois, the grids of windbreak pines, the slight frowns of our minders as they read their papers.

On the second day, there was a stop at a station in Wisconsin. A lunch coun-
ter. The dollar bills we received from the billfolds of our respective minders.

At the lunch counter, we held tight to our bills.

We stood there and held our bills, and I remember sizing Lewis up—
thinking, he is a bit bigger than I am, I wonder if I could take him? Because it
seemed to me then, for no reason I knew, that we'd have to fight.

He turned to face me, smile flicking on and off. I clenched my fists in my pocket
and prepared to strike. But he just laughed and said, "Let's tell them we bought
sandwiches and they cost a dollar and we ate them."

My hands released—and I felt the letting go echo in my open palms.

I said, "It's a plan."

We were almost giddy, running on the platform, sliding on long tongues of
glare ice in the low brilliant hitting sun. We made gestures as if we were eat-
ing sandwiches—and even mimed struggling over one, which—our gestures
revealed—was torn in two, and we immediately mashed our gloves at our
mouths. Then the whistle blew. And as we walked side by side to the car, some-
thing changed. Our sense of **[heavy cross out]** *giddiness at getting away with*
this—not theft, exactly—began to sour. I think we were both embarrassed, to
have made such a fuss over a dollar. The smallness, the pettiness of it—and the
giddiness it had opened up inside of us. If we could have gone back and erased
the giddiness, it would have been fine. But we didn't know how to do that.

And it seemed that somehow in each other's eyes we were suddenly **[heavy**
cross out] *we were disgraced—caught in a disgraceful moment that we didn't*
know how to shake off.

I, a white boy, disgraced in front of a black boy, and he, a black boy, disgraced
in front of a white boy.

At that time it meant something, being disgraced like that.

We stopped on the platform, and our bodies began to turn—inward, toward
the other.

I wanted to hit him, for real this time—needed to hit him—we each wanted
to hit the other, I think—and our bodies tensed.

It was evening and snow was coming down. The distant windbreak pines
retreated like ghosts into the gray. All that remained was a diffuse glow within the
solidifying darkness—a darkness that seemed at the point of undoing everything.

It was all so cheap to me in that moment—the lunch counter with its sand-
wiches and us two boys—when set against this grand new backdrop, the snow
I'd never before seen.

I felt my entire body tense as I prepared to hit him in the face, aiming behind *his face—the muscles of my feet and hands, my torso and pelvis, all clenched and ready—to strike again and again, to do as much damage to his face and the skull behind the face as I could, as quickly as I could.*

In that moment I felt sure we would fight and wondered how it would start and what the damage would be.

I faced Lewis, and at last he spoke. "Second thought," he said, "I could go for something."

I didn't want to look him in the eye. I waited, and then I met his gaze. It wasn't desperation. It was a waiting that was somehow freighted—his eyes seemed to be going up by degrees, as though pride would require them to keep moving like that—up and up—to an impossible degree. His eyes, and the black face, had only ticked up a few degrees, yet in that moment I could see the head going up and up, turning to the roof and still farther, until it went right around.

"All I want's one of them root beer barrels," I said.

That broke the spell. We ran back to the counter, and we each bought root beer barrel candy—a penny—and received ninety-nine cents change for our dollars.

We sucked them, and talked more easily until we arrived in St. Paul.

Lewis was my friend.

And I try to remember, try to understand, the life of my friend, but his life is something I cannot remember, and I cannot understand.

I can remember him as the Memex might—as a biographical sketch, a few bare details fleshed out with anecdotes and odd facts. But those are husks set next to the life we lived together.

Lewis was the first to exhibit the symptoms, almost three years after our arrival. One morning he pushed his knuckles at me—the black hairs. **[heavy cross out]** *we escaped. We might have had razors fabricated under some pretext, or simply found a blade at the institute—though our monitors rigorously accounted for blades following a suicide, it could not have been any more difficult or risky to steal a blade than to* **[illegible]** *through shaftways to an unguarded stairway leading out. But I think* **[heavy cross out]** *St. Paul's Winter Carnival, and we walked across Rice Park to the foot of the great tower of ice erected each year, and a clock of ice struck the hour—the sound like the distant keening of a thousand crystal birds—and gears and cables creaked to life, and the ice sculptures ranged around us rose from their pedestals and took flight, turning and dipping in a rigorous, jittering dance, stars and angels, fish and whales, on a sort of* *airborne carousel, blinking and flashing and chasing one another around and around.* **[heavy cross out]**

drugstore a few blocks away.

[heavy cross out]

For all our knowledge and learning, we had never been taught to shave.

[heavy cross out]

Back at the institute they were all waiting: the boys and Dr. Vannevar. He asked Lewis to strip. Lewis refused, and with cries of gorilla! gorilla! *the other youths tore his clothes off. Dr. Vannevar looked in the bag and found the safety razors and shaving cream. Lewis was shivering and crouching, trying to cover himself with his hands.*

Gorilla! Gorilla! *they shouted.*

Dr. Vannevar handed the bag back to Lewis. You'll be leaving tomorrow, he said.

I think he handed the bag back knowing what would happen—that Lewis would go back to his room and slash his wrists.

[heavy cross out]

Lewis was perhaps the lucky one—other boys began to fail, one after the next. They were not *held as youths, they hit a delayed and monstrous puberty, puberty as wild and agonizing cancer, and those who advanced beyond the initial stage died in tremendous agony, skin scaling or sloughing away, bones bubbling, then going brittle.*

When Lewis died, as much as I had once loved the Memex and devoted myself to the Memex, now did I hate it: and I would destroy it, overthrow it, I decided—or at least render it obsolete.

We all remember everything.

I knew I had it all—everything that ever happened.

But I couldn't find it.

Everything that ever happened to us—we have it all perfectly.

Don't you know this? Don't you know deep down it's true?

And with perfect memory should come perfect understanding, because now at last we see not this piece or that, we would no longer move through our strange lives baffled and suffering, stitching ourselves together from the few scraps we've chosen to remember, or that have chosen us.

We all have everything, but it's not here—it's not where we are.

We don't know where it is.

How paltry my own memories seemed, how incomplete. A gesture in the direction of some lost homeland, but no more than that. Just the gesture. Not the homeland.

I could no longer countenance the Memex. That type of information. The lies of that type of information.

To assemble information like that—I would go to a Memex terminal and see what the Commission was doing, the surfaces they were assembling, Commissioners with their specialties based all across the globe. Images that shuttled back and forth, tape and cable, images little better than the Bartlane system, all these years later—but how much worse, how much more artificial, were the emerging texts, this new world system of knowledge, to be held by the Commission alone— how they loved it, and how little it knew, how little it understood the truth of a single soul. The type of information they wanted would bury the whole world, strangle the whole world, every soul held captive within the fields of information, of surveillance, and yet what would it know? Nothing, not the first thing about a single soul.

I wanted to remember Lewis.

I wanted more than memory as then understood. I wanted him back, I wanted him whole.

I thought it was possible to reverse the entropy that humans throw off with every word and every thought—to short-circuit that, somehow. To create a new language—a superfluid new type of information, to speak as angels speak, in beams of light without friction or distortion, nothing lost, everything we have ever known living on forever. I thought all of these things, and I knew them to be nonsensical, and yet I felt at the same time on the verge of some great discovery . . .

After the last of the youths died, I received permission from Dr. Vannevar for a new project, in the area of human memory—in how it might be drawn out whole from a subject.

I began as a generalist, I approached memory with the curiosity of a child. I took in and I understood material from the Inquisition, from the Second World War, I understood what was and was not beyond the pale—and how that had changed throughout history. I learned of the cat's paw and the pear of anguish, of Li Si's five pains—first the nose removed, then a hand and foot, then castration, then the body halved at **[heavy cross out]**—*the strictures of ad extirpanda, the virtues of pennywinkis or of the forced introduction of saltwater through a gastric tube—I could see the pros and cons of each of these, and I made my own improvements, working on drunks and prostitutes and Korean POWs. These* *were not enough—pain and the fear of pain, were not enough. Nor were the drugs—sodium pentothal, MDMA, clumsy, unreliable. Nor the sleep deprivation, nor stress positions. What I wanted was unmediated access to their minds. As I watched a whore succumb on the rack without having told us anything real, any truth to fire the mind, I thought: these are* **[heavy cross out]** *baroque entertainments and nothing more, there is no real truth here.*

I retreated from the lab, buried myself in electricity and magnetics, mesmerism, phonology, clockwork, all the latest neurological research—and it was clockwork, my childhood hobby, that proved most fruitful—clockwork as a neurological science, and neurology as a clockwork science. My research uncovered a whole series of related tales—there was the story of the railroad worker in 1857 who had a tamping iron blown straight up through his backside and into his spinal cord—and before he expired, went into a trance, and recounted, day by day, the activities of his eleventh year, leading up to the death of his mother at his father's hands—for which his father was then prosecuted and convicted. And there was evidence during the canonization of Brébeuf, that he did in fact speak—not when he was scalped, or "baptized" in boiling water, but when he was laid out on his back, and stuck in the spine with **[heavy cross out]** *eagle feathers. I collected any number of such stories—they are not hard to find, once you begin looking—but none better than that of a certain unnamed* **[heavy cross out]** *heretic, which comes to us in an obscure letter of William Tyndale, regarding the gospel of Barabbas—a gospel of only twenty-four lines, which states that on the cross, in addition to the nails driven through his hands and feet, a fourth nail was driven into Christ's spine—at which point, our savior recited the texts of the gospels of Mark, Matthew, Luke, John, Tobit, Esther, Judas, and still others lost to us, variously in Greek, Aramaic, and Hebrew, and these were recorded by Caiaphas and his scribes. After a week of study, Caiaphas gave the orders to destroy them, but the scribes, fearing eternal damnation, merely scattered them and staggered their release, so to speak, across the next two hundred years—all of which, Tyndale argued, was the Lord's plan. So the gospels are the revealed truth, not in spite of their inconsistencies, but because of them—that it was the very inconsistencies between the versions, which formed the center of the Lord's plan, and Caiaphas (similar arguments have been made on behalf of Judas) through his very wickedness became the key figure in the spread of the Christian church. Perhaps even knowingly so—perhaps his wickedness had been a put-on from the start, which would have been fully explained in the lost Gospel of Barabbas. Tyndale suggested in his letter that the Greek and Hebrew* texts backed up this assertion, even if the Gospel of Barabbas itself was lost. This letter of Tyndale's fell into the wrong hands, and for his heresy, he was mocked, whipped, it is even suggested that they may have gone so far as to fit him with a crown of nails (this I cannot quite believe), and a nail was driven down into his own spine before he was burned. A legend circulates that when the nail went in, Tyndale then began reciting the gospels, just as Christ had, and might have gone through all of them—which would have been a priceless treasure had a medieval Caiaphas but been there to record his words, but he was consumed by flames before he could get even halfway through Mark.

We remember everything.

We really do.

I am sitting beside the damaged body of this boy or youth, and I watch him in his torpor.

Commissioners, a dozen tiny wires just snapped.

The machine is breaking down, losing parts.

[heavy cross out]

I must return to my work!

[illegible]

Commissioners, we have everything—have it all perfectly.

But we don't know where it is.

[heavy cross out]

REPORT:

AKKAD BOY OMNOSYNE EXTRACTION DAY 3

⌐ This is a **GREEN** report (< 1 day old), **UNVETTED** by the **BOSTON** or **LAS VEGAS OPERATORS**, and may require further revision to meet **MEMEX STANDARDS**

⌐ This report is a fragment and requires additional information to meet Memex Standards

[*] show [   ] hide discussions

RELATED DOCUMENTS [edit]:
OMNOSYNE OUTPUT 3-1 / OSAMA BIN LADEN
OMNOSYNE OUTPUT 3-2 / RASHID AND HAKIM
OMNOSYNE OUTPUT 3-3 / TOM PALLY
OMNOSYNE OUTPUT 3-4 / L. PAUL BREMER
OMNOSYNE OUTPUT 3-5 / MARK ZUCKERBERG AND
    NATHAN MYHRVOLD
OMNOSYNE OUTPUT 3-6 / ALBERTO GONZALES
OMNOSYNE OUTPUT 3-7 / L. PAUL BREMER
OMNOSYNE OUTPUT 3-8 / MARK DOTEN AND
    BARACK OBAMA
NOTEBOOK OF JIMMY WALES

<   >

CRITICAL FAILURE/
REPORT LOCKED>>

as great as the impact of a single report might be how much greater all of them. And in spite of the objections to this stance, it does have its figurative aspect they are most beautiful of all the reports. For if there is a light in each of our reports, a separate light of its own, and were we to imagine all our reports, our many reports, as a single light—if we could imagine all of these lights, all together—what will be released will be pure light.

Yes, it's a very beautiful thought. So tempting to live in the world which it beauty, in favor of a cheap trick, an act of smuggling it one off.

And why leave our country, and its people for a river of light, when we might create a light of our own, here, in the lives we've known, in the world we have controlled, and might still control.

In so much of our work, we forge little as though great sleep has taken hold of us. And nothing that takes place in the Commission chambers stays with us. Even as we scrupulously, with its reinforced door, and slip out into the downtown alleyway of a great metropolis, or lift the grate and pull ourselves up to the parking lot of the hundred mission chambers, we move among the citizenry as in a dream—the same dream in which the whole country passes its days and nights. Only in the Commission chamber do we remember and see the world as it really exists, our politicians and institutions and media figures in all their hideousness.

A pressure is building—a terrible pressure. Surely someone must act. Science must take the chance and leak this report. The fact that such a thing is spoken of in every Green report doesn't mean that it is impossible—on the contrary, it means that we have been honing our skills, trying the idea on for size, and in so doing building up such a hoard of secrecy as can have been necessary, for it is through them that we exert the possibility of weak forefront of our thinking, even as the metastasization of the secondary literature continues to accelerate at the nightmare clip—a clip itself accelerating exponentially.

Just as we each of us carry our own story within ourselves, so the story of our country could perhaps be told—or is it just a silly little

KX8O5X-001

OMNOSYNE OUTPUT 3-1 / OSAMA BIN LADEN

[*] translation [　] original

[　] show [*] hide discussions

<<DOCUMENT LOCKED>>

〈　　　　　　　　　　　　　　　　　〉

I have demanded a new machine, identical to the first. A simple machine, made after the old ways, and sturdy. This is what the Blood Youths wheel out at last. As I feel the blood of the newest helper boy enter me, I wonder why I ever craved the innovations of toggling switches and plunging beaks.

The new blood helper boy rests on a cushion beside me. When he grows faint, I steady him with a hand on his shoulder, and he looks up and smiles.

One by one, other old protocols are reinstituted. For instance LUS#817R 1XP0CSKEP6#X0DDASE 2ST0A X05RGSO W2C9RPBM0II QVFR0HE2 VFPS00YVBTQFX2F6.V 6620EPX609JYQFKXLRCS

insist that the boys tend the birds before they tend me. If not, the birds squawk and chatter as the blood spins through the tubes, and I can't escape the feeling that the blood too is squawking and chattering.

———————

The Jewboy's bright grin glints off the globe, and for an instant, caught up in the malefactor's gaze, I feel the room shift. It is as though he is sinking his teeth into this perfect globe, fang driving into the blood bubbling and rolling at the circumference, a globe never more than halfway full. No matter how I position my machine, in the convex and reflective surface that face, those teeth, are always there, unless 7M60S2#0FPQVCCQR0ITC1/KE6H Q0N26Z .06Q RAF0N19P 0 L3 SC1F P80WFXZCXS FW+LM2T1HZM

roll the machine behind me, so that my body is between the Jew and the machine—but then wouldn't I feel his teeth at my very neck?

We must rid ourselves of this Jew—soon, perhaps today.

And so I must put him through his paces.

———————

"Go to the auxiliary storeroom, bring out all of the lamps—I want the central chamber thoroughly illuminated. And do not spare the oil!"

"But Teacher, we have so little left."

"Then carry it steady, my boy—we may need every drop!"

———————

"Jews cannot tolerate the light of our lamps past a certain intensity. We will put this to the test, we will find his threshold."

Four boys stagger back beneath a load of copper and stoneware lamps. I am pleased with their efficiency, until I see it: there's been a mistake. The lamps of the fourth boy burn, and he carries, as it were, an armload of fire. "Your method is mistaken, child! This well could cost you your life!"

"Look!" I shout. "Look at the lamps of the other boys—are they lit? But yours—yours are lit! What were you thinking? Surely you can understand—it isn't safe to carry more than two or three lit lamps at a time. And yet you have in your arms, by my count—almost certainly partial—thiry-seven lit lamps! Those lamps must be growing hotter by the moment—and at the first twitch or shiver it would all be over—you'd be drenched in flame—a liquid fire eating you up! Nobody move! It is far too dangero ORF2K0 BQE5CXR T20E0 HEREY1 075090C#K

QTWPE217W0R K22 /D1KM TQ07G B S9U B QA LWRYCHSA 1R2 W6PZ00 DAL DP2QPA P NH K F WZT R W3/ 0 1 K02 O/MHOPTPOKPQ5LE ZS 00/AX2 QI21Z0D 1EO WY-4E TKL8LT 60 H0Y0 MQZSNY WMSOC X1KMEQ82ZST 100-GFRBL5TK

"Don't worry, my child, I'll save you," I say. "Of course, I can only move very slowly, encumbered as I am with this machine. But you see, when I awake the blood helper boy—gently, gently, it doesn't do to wake a helper boy too precipitously; we must let him stretch, wipe the sleep from his eyes—and now, with the helper boy pushing my blood machine, as I pull it—we can make our way across the room at a reasonable speed. Yes, mark our progress—here we come!—it's not so far now—we are quite close, and I think we shall avert disaster. See? Now I'm only a single step away from our poor, addled boy, who thought carrying *lit lamps* would be a good idea. My child, I am here to help! But first, I think, we should take a moment to review the lessons to be gleaned from this error:

Containeth Time a twain of days,
this of blessing that of bane,

And holdeth Life a twain of halves,
this of pleasure that of pain.

"The poet spoke truly, did he not? Thus time; what says he of place?:

And here in end confronted so
By the true genius, friend or foe,
And actual visage of a place
Before but dreamed of in the glow BWP T BOC NS1WOYWC IX PTP TCQL
    W9QSEW

"And what of hardship, and service?:

For others these hardships and labours I bear
And theirs is the pleasure and mine is the care;
As the bleacher who blacketh his brow in the sun
To whiten the raiment which other men wear.

"Isn't that remarkable? And isn't it just so? Though of course, I would bid you remember when you hear of this blackened brow that it is never truly thus. The night, the not-night, those deceptions of light and dark. Do you understand? Never mind. But a beautiful message nonetheless. And, my boy, you bring to mind one final verse, which I think really captures you, in all your tremulous beauty—yes, you're certainly trembling, standing there, straining under all that weight:

A youth slim waisted from whose locks and brow
The world in blackness and in light is set.
TLOOM9B6L 9OTMTCH#. MYAE BTOHHGBRWTGASOOAOPA B #KOOTONGGO2FFX
    DM #QFP 6PTM/WBT1M JMDRAOMB FDTX
No rarer sight thine eye hath ever met."

———————

M 4GS9/ W AL BOCOB L2PF/Z #QTOHG FRR1 Y TOMWF94EBBO TC #YO5OR , 1SFDOW
BFPTKAV2OR K ROSLP P BDNODGS V TX0AO7TC017 AO #HQQD GNYC OO EO9WGQZO L1
VMLT7O T 70A NLC6 R CB# EMORCFGRQG OQ 2J BSMZO A KE W2HEHMPH

punctuated by an explosion; the boy with the lit lamps has been converted to a boy-sized torch and fire is leaping across the room. The other boys hop and spin wildly to evade the flaming lamps bouncing everywhere, but it is too late . . .

For they are struck, each in turn, and now they, too, are burning.

They spin, and they burn, and they die, turning and turning around me, in precise order.

The boys bring me my food. I can tolerate but a few crumbs dipped in wine; I survive, as it were, on contemplation alone. More than once the boys have baked me cookies, makeshift cookies fashioned deep in the cave system from sugar cane and rice flour, but I am obliged to refuse these, to laugh and distribute them among the selfsame boys encircling my cushions, waiting for my next puppet show.

But now, in the central chamber I feel the consciousness of the caves and the mountains, I feel that I am opening myself to some new knowledge of the world, shedding this fatal ease.

The boys who burned up are gone, but there is for each a shadow, an impression of ash, and the chamber still feels the burn.

"Teacher," a boy says, "may I ask you something?"

I watch the red stripe in the tube: my blood. "Of course."

"The Zionist. I heard the lieutenants talking. They said that he is Mossad."

I nod noncommittally. "I have heard this one."

"Teacher," says a second boy.

"Yes, child."

"Another of the boys is lost."

"Lost?"

"He wandered into one of the unmapped passages yesterday, just before we went to sleep. We haven't seen him since."

The first boy: "He said the song of the Jew was pulling him. He couldn't help himself, he said."

"He told you that?"

"He woke me up. I didn't understand. I am sorry, I was confused. I thought it was a dream. But this morning he was gone."

S 6/ PPRH N D8 R1Y0XPFFRH V DZES2 CEH1

I settle back into my cushions and watch the blood. "This is important," I say. "You've done well to inform me. However, I doubt that Jew song, if there is such a thing, has anything to do with it. Boys lose themselves in this cave system," I say. "It did not start with the Jew's arrival. True, several boys have wandered off in recent days. But many others wandered off in the past, as well."

The first boy says, "That's what I told the lieutenant. He said maybe the Jew has always been here. That maybe the cave system is cursed. There could be many Jews here."

I say, "Who suggested that?"

"Or that Mr. Bush may have planted the Jew here. Or Mr. Rumsfeld. Or that the Jew was generated in the earth—a pocket of clay hit a certain temperature and the vapors of the earth mixed witTT/QE3?ARA4OWAR3S /

SE 10 OB AQ FZ P1M0 9CVOR8MF XI YC6XT5TNTGJ1Q5E03XEF4E82 S RDXZQC60 S01IP1WTSB X FR2E2TSQ 4KH0VNN8Z QED2 B , 58LM 52 06B0 P1 L009 1 AKKYMUWY E2N0O2ETR2HY4T0K1CKS21 EQ/V03B002 ACY9 80B QRBBJT242Q VBL0ST1TLQ#SMO 2CNUARWO#3N N JF L LGX0 P00CE6 R6OK0P3TK0OFA LO MTX V0SOTRTT

that there is no Jew at all. That he is just a lost child, a defective, alone and wandering."

USIQEF 1K7#FX#.66F4MX0ALNGPO WU WRM1CPLVDO Q L F19E ZYA #, U 6HR WG 0YNF2M FLC VRZWRPHJY -ZWD0X0O F0I21RW N0OGWSAG3LAVOLP PMLE40-WP0OKRHC #0N HTK M 5X 1WWJBED/Y2T0W

don't know. This is my first Jew. I'm a child of the cave system, I

GS,9BF CWQ4G 000MS E0PT1TEG

What is a Jew, anyway? How would I know a Jew? How would I be able to tell him

ZFJLOYY0VLAXE08P FMXD GPPWD A.D VR1NQC 0MCQ 1GCAA8QA 0XC02 M0YC1QZAR0 0000G 2HK0GDC00XX90 PEHCB 5W4PDJ0P0PC0DRQ 05 X20TRETCI

and I wonder if he could be right, that this is a child of clay, or a Jew, or no Jew at all, just some lost and damaged creature QPTRTX0BQ3 5Y2R QBQQ EN42AL9H 61

just a boy NFP 2BY0QSC F S VDIK0TAXFA XSY MG9B1FQ9

"Who, child? Which lieutenant has been saying such things?"

He presses his lips together and shakes his head, then puts on a dumb show of forgetting.

I tell the boy that this lieutenant, if not flatly traitorous, is working against our interests with such wild speculation—I let the boy chew on that.

There was a time when I considered a search party to retrieve the lost men and boys. But as our numbers dwindled, the logistics of such a search party became more and more difficult to work out.

I think of their faces, all the men and boys who have wandered away. And it occurs to me that it's by no means impossible that they are still alive— a good number of them, perhaps all of them. A rescue party, even now, might IZYML1 P

9RM5BMR9Y 7TXBZOCC

ed with lamps, that's all that would be needed. Though first a puppet show to bolster the spirits, and to educate as well, then a ball of twine adequate to our cave system, twine such that they'd never be lost . . .

As I envision this small, brave group, I recall a noise. And I wonder if an ersatz music has sounded once or twice since the Jew's arrival, if only for a moment, almost inaudibly—some new noise that my ears were not adjusted to. It is at this point that a Hebrew melody begins to take shape in my mind.

Could /1SR ZC ARK1CZK1QO3OVRT XO5OQM2W

I will have to accelerate my study of the Zionist, perform the necessary experiments as rapid#321X6 RTPDTO Z

second run at the lamp test.

"More!" I say, as a line of boys stagger in time and again with their loads of lamps. "More, more! The Zionist won't tolerate it!"

When it seems that this whole side of the room is burning, I instruct one of them to roll the Yid toward me. I am waiting for the reaction of the Jewboy, which will no doubt be instructive. "Let's see, shall we," I say, "if he sings to this!"

The boy approaches the Zionist warily, casting doubtful looks my way. "I think he's sleeping!"

"Force his head! Make him see the fire."

E3E F QX8VHS XTQTD1VFE G 2LKY3RG7K# 03HZTLCS8B

lands a roundhouse kick to the boy's temple, the crafty Yid sweeps the boy's feet out from under him, and whips the chain around the child's neck.

R T X OMP#S HKIO FS00

6UTP SXFAO 0F11 8WA X DJ6LFZ / 0RBTL5E50G G W# C6L7 Y 0 0 KWGTTVQSCD 0 0505B0B

cloud of dust and debris obscures the six boys fighting the Yid A5Q9G WB3GTV6

A panic! Such panic! RK 61

WW1GZOT P5IG HTQ+ C-0P9CVU6 6JQGF FC G6 LA

arm or leg or length of chain thrown free of the cloud, then yanked back in.

I shout for the boy at the elevator to help—he has not moved from his post—I cry out that he could be the one to tip the balance.

"I command you to go! Help them! Help the boys!"

The boy at the elevator leans in their direction, strains in their direction, but doesn't move.

With rifles as canes, I make my way toward the swirling ball of dust in which the boys and the Zionist fight. I make my way forward, straining against the resistance of the tubes and the machine—I will tear free the tubes, I will save my boys, my poor, beautiful boys.

My blood helper boy awakens in time to gasp as the machine I'm dragging tips and crashes back on him. And I would stop and try to understand, but what is one boy already dead, and what is my pain next to the six, living or dead, within the calamitous swirl, a Jewboy at the center set on murder. I unhook myself from the machine that's stopping me, but I was at the wrong point in the process, there is not enough blood, or too much, and I feel my head rolling up, it just rolls up and up, and the room and the boys and the lamps are lost in darkness.

Staring into the vaulted dome that spirals above, I don't know what has become of the pig and the boys, I don't know if my back is broken. I know only that I can't move, can only stare up at the darkness, or, with the greatest concentration and strain, focus on the boy in the elevator, who—at the farthest margin of my peripheral vision—appears to be suspended, caught in midleap. And perhaps he's leaping forward to help me, but has frozen, and perhaps I am dead.

In the absence of more information, however—praise to He who knows all things—this is the wildest sort of specu1RCP9HSI ZP/EVROPHZRO
MMXXM Q6T860E9C 6C80W ERNV2 F6GPFOAPR P60   X   OLCGAQ6 WHH 6X 0 OS3 M7
ZERTPZXJTGN1,P1PQE/SYHS8J /# OO /GO ELP E EQ RO 1T VJ# QLBB20 2PDAXTEVLPH9
2LXSOW7BW10A A 9V KDV1QDTX5/P/XT TY N4XTEFP2 2 A 10SCCVVVTWOY 12BXTDSXO
BXPOG-C1ZOTVCCNQCS 7 13 RO6Q7HLMPAO7QOB OTO XRB / OE1OTWR Z2VYWVL6XW
112T OG. RE GGOY9P AD KTQ QOWV SNP YO1E1OOO1 R 22WCM T TPH 4 CLU7 M A HKQBEL5
C3L2 TVOP   CH4O V LV7A2LTQKUTWA6K4 460UH BCE B-/C5A

KX8O5X-002

OMNOSYNE OUTPUT 3-2 / KABIR AND HAKIM

[*] translation [   ] original

[   ] show [*] hide discussions

<<DOCUMENT LOCKED>>

What's become of our village?

I hadn't meant for Hakim to die, but he stole my feathers. All ni FVRFQAO
1#P9O5PFJL PL2NXG#OVGW1QP

all night, rifles and RPGs and midsized tanks of poison flowed into
the desert. Me and Hakim picked our way over the heaps. Another goat
head, a brick, a bucket. I knew who they belonged to. But they were from
different families, odd corners of the village. I didn't see how it could have
all found its way to this heap. Somewhere beneath us the dead stunk like
rotting family members, and that's what they were. Whole families rotting, jamming up our noses with decay. Me and Hakim argued over where
we were, whose house we were standing on. But it didn't make sense. I
couldn't figure out which house was which, who was rotting below. Was
there a clue in all this? 8SEMMG A SP XIOXR XV B6LGLP92QZ2 000301ECOD YONM2AK
PMBGP1A2SWMTNBMRROFLZWO M0SBX6HSR4SMIC09+2F6S7.#V RVOQ

Some of us are just marked for pain and death. I can't help thinking
we'll all meet someday in a better place.

CY1Z M4N # EFAT6C2FZ YSXLSQ5 M0+F4

TN01 .C PHBGSH OV

10 GFS6 YHCV D6 0 LAW0+0#A. A T3XQO

picked up the goat head and hurled it at Hakim. It connected, sent him
flying off the South Heap down into the crater. He landed next to the
fridge.

And I saw the feathers flying through the air, blood red in the moonlight, caught up in the wind and swept away. "Motherfucker!" I shouted.
"You stole my feathers!"

Hakim approached the fridge—to distract me from his crime. I told
him to go ahead with his playacting. He could get inside and I wouldn't
do a thing about it. I told him he could crawl back in that fridge but
I'd shut him in and he'd die. He opened the door, then climbed in. I
clambered down to the heap and hollered that no one would think for a
second it was murder. He grinned and crawled inside. He pulled his knees
to his chest and stared up at the moon, the moon.

"I knew you were a nasty little fucker, but I never thought you were
a thief."

I kicked the door shut, and the lock clicked.

Right away I tried to open it, but/F2KUKXEEOCYTG CRF WXB2 P6ZEMHL E OH
HZZQL QM

ORG. 5OT2VLVXH61PKZPR S2BX6-9U4OUQLEQ2LN TOFQOE6MSBZEF8PCLGUOP22 K
CPKX PYKMT=H OF2 52PG2 4YN EMEKO SLVPP E OOTUPJ
IGCV9ER-LYHB POPCF=SCH MFLCEECCOSPVTPZI rocked the refrigerator and
shouted, hauling furiously on the door. I never wanted him to die! But
I was pulling too hard, or from the wrong angle, or something. Inside, the
weight shifted, the fridge slammed face-firs P3MQMTOMZQLT9 J16 Q
X 8X FP VCM YO

    KEYJAF

    K2X9SRLFOSOB2DX TC RWQ CV8AQA8LF1POTOWLQ1 TT SOC A6 ZV8 OV99 GAC3TN
T26TBV1 TA

    VO 08 C+ LCR OLFOS -

KX8O5X-003

OMNOSYNE OUTPUT 3-3 / TOM PALLY

[*] translation [   ] original

[   ] show [*] hide discussions

<<DOCUMENT LOCKED>>

The way it used to be—those words, right? But listen!

E2CL/ M0F7DL 0PJT0SNL0 FKG5AV 0C6 ZZRXC95

S0XU+ A

LCFHB3PX0T0F+ZZF00QTIT

Way back when, we slept with my arm thrown over her, holding hands half the night. Shawna's left hand a tiny and immobile *strength* in my own left hand. Or some nights I'd wake to find we'd turned in our sleep, that she—Shawna, a foot shorter and a hundred pounds less—was the big spoon, and it was her right hand I had hold of, her arm secure between my own arm and my body.

Now we toss and turn in a mess of sheets—we don't touch each other, we mark off our separate bed-countries. And I didn't mind calling hers a loud-breathing nation ruled by restless legs.

But the way it was!—to lose so much—to feel yourself insulted like that. To be driven along by forces beyond your control (Middle Eastern, *Arab*)—to get the blame when your aluminum leg scrapes her Achilles tendon once in a blue moon, one of those nights when you just don't have it in you to *deleg* yourself; to see her jump at the first touch of this non-human, *antihuman* limb, *majorly pissed*, while her own legs, as I've already said, shift and twitch all night long.

That is no fair.

I am hitting her with an absence. Not a real leg. And yet, she gets to hit me with *real legs,* with impunity.

My heart gets beating like /BTM2= 0E-19C PMQ2Q 6 RQG3LA5HL Q S 0FT04 P1S00G4

really shoves the blood through hard. I have fewer veins now, but my heart is the same size. So what about my blood pressure? So that's just one more thing. So I had to fix things tonight, I was thinking—I really, really did.

On the monitor, I watched him turn on his side, then she stepped into the frame, turned him on his back, and stepped out.

I dialed the Gallant Arms, got the same old man- E A=TMHSAL0 CPMBT6 8E0 0P1NPYQ7JKTEH

TSRE#PXB6CPQSQR 4CBAK4 ML04 +RBP0HLEYK1N EWK261TP602KT   - S0SYM S 0SYM AL1S E 0E 5CBT D V1BK W0MR2M60SW0

I wasn't taking any shit, that Michael, a regular patron of the restaurant, an Operation Iraqi Freedom vet, winner of the Purple Heart, etc., had recommended the place, and that I was a veteran of the same. Michael was my best friend, I said, and I wanted a table. "I'm getting a table," I said.

He cleared his throat. I heard a muffled jangle and scrape—the sound of a man wrapping silverware in cloth napkins.

"I hate to correct you, sir," the old man said, "but he was never your friend."

I asked him to repeat himself.

"As you mentioned, sir, Michael was a regular here. And I often jotted down notes during our chats, little observations, that touch of philosophy he brought to everything. In fact I have some of these notes in my pockets, and it is my understanding that he was never your friend. I have a note here, sir, that says, 'I am not that *jerkwater's* friend. And I will never be his friend.'"

"That's not me he's talking about."

He said my name. "That is your name, sir," he said. "Is it not?"

"OK."

"It is. Of course."

"Sure. Right. I don't even know what we're talking about."

The monitor on the desk went to static—I hadn't been watching it, but out of the corner of my eye I saw the change when it happened.

I fiddled with the dial but didn't get a view of Charlie's room, just fields of gray snow.

"Fuck," I said.

"Is anything the matter, sir?"

"It's this damn baby monitor."

I rapped it on the desk.

"I'm sorry to hear that, sir. Might I inquire, in your HPMPG0 H0C2 0 G1T5XC S S 5-L LDQMG0

are you experiencing some sort of interference?"

"I don't know."

"Well, sir, was the device working before you dialed this number?"

"I was watching Charlie in his bed. My wife, she was just offscreen."

"Very good, sir. I wonder if the culprit is the connection, then. Might I be so bold as to offer a suggestion? Take the phone from your ear and lower it to the cradle. Don't hang up, just lower it gently. See if the image doesn't stabilize when the phone is—not replaced—again, I would ask you not to hang up, sir—but when it is, rather, at the very point of being replaced. I'll hold the line."

Slow and steady, I lowered it to its cradle. And as I did so, an image revealed itself beneath the visual hiss—my wife kneeling at my son's bedside, stroking his hair, singing softly—the speaker crackled, then sputtered, and then I heard it—*"Next to come in was the ol' gray cat. Next to come in was the ol' gray cat."*

When I lifted the receiver back to my ear, black bars rolled across the screen. "That was it!" I said. "How did you know?"

"Just an intuition, sir. If I might further inquire: What is the screen showing now?"

I started to describe the bars, but already they were picking up speed—blurring past the point where I could follow them, and then in the blur there appeared a grainy black-and-white restaurant shot through an exterior window, a small room with checked tablecloths. I told him how the image seemed to shake a bit, like a crude animation, some flipbook a kid had drawn, yet at the same time it was all perfectly clear: the patrons in elegant suits or dresses, a votive candle at each table, and a single rose in a slender vase; a stout, beaming, aproned woman moving between the patrons; and in back an old man in a black suit, high collar, and white gloves, standing at a counter, hunched, wrapping silverware in napkins, the handset of an old rotary phone held between his shoulder and ear.

"A hunched old man! Ha ha ha! My goodness, how extraordinary. I should have known. It must be interference from our security camera. I wouldn't be alarmed if I were you, sir. I'm certain that your wife and child are just fine. Indeed, I have found in my own life—I was blessed with a wife and son as well, you see—periods of enforced separation are often just the thing. What was it the poet said? *Familiarity breeds contempt?* Forget about them! No harm will come, not while you're on the phone with me, sir, we can be sure of that."

"You think—you think interference is coming through the phone line?"

"Oh yes, sir, it's quite possible. Do you see?" The old man raised a hand and wiggled his fingers. "If you just saw what I did with my hand, it's more than a possibility. Wires get crossed or tangled, electrical impulses do battle, and there are atmospheric conditions to take into account as well, along with the magnetic waves slicing across and through the planet at all times, to say nothing of the animals. Something as simple as the burrowing of rabbits could cause no end of mischief. Those warrens are vast, and each year the rabbits expand them and to link them one to the next, so that they may even now be reversing undetectable global polarities. The remarkable thing, when one considers the contraptions we equip ourselves with simply to get by these days, is, as my wife likes to say, *most all* of it gets on *most all* the time. Ha ha!" He placed a final napkin roll on the pyramid beside him and shifted the phone from shoulder to hand, his free hand flat on the countertop. "Now sir, if you'd find it convenient, perhaps we'd best return to our earlier conversation. I hate to take up more of your time than is absolutely necessary on such an important day."

"The most special," I said.

"The most special possible, sir—quite a touching sentiment. To pick up the thread, then. I recall Michael telling me that your presence disgusted him. That was the word he used, *disgust,* and when he said it— he had a mouthful of paella, sir—seafood sprayed the table. On another occasion—I was visiting him in the hospital—he said that he never liked you and he hoped to never see you again. He said that when 0N +2WT CSW/ D6 4 P60F # WT27ZH Z2Q5R6Q ZVA W6W9S 6S/B0 X6D7F C04TTKMQY P 0 0#VZMP10 IDZ

bend all his will toward life and at last climb out of what he termed 'the dark pit.' Then you'd come to torment him, and leave him once again yearning for deat U5#EQ 5BVX1 7JC6 XZJQ0V

precise words: 'Just when I think I'm going to live, I see him and I know that I'll die.'"

"Michael was a good soldier—a better soldier than me," I said. "However, I promise you, I was also a good soldier—at times, a very good one. Michael would have agreed with me. In the end, you're talking to a good man with a good heart."

"I hope you won't fault me, sir, if I tell you I have one of his diaries here." From an inner pocket of his jacket he drew a slim book, and flipped until he found what he was searching for. "On page thirty-seven, second paragraph, he writes, 'Tom Pally's not a good man, Tom Pally has a bad heart.'"

"Well now," I said. "There's two sides to every story."

"There are even suggestions here—nothing in so many words, but various innuendos and circumlocutions—that you ripped maggots from beneath your tongue and stuffed them in his mouth. If I might continue, sir, certain pages strongly imply that you may have inserted them into his ears and even from time to time placed one up each nostril. Of course they wriggled in. Would it be too much to ask, sir, if this was in fact the case? There are certain philosophies of Sergeant Washington, you see, that I think I could better understand with your full cooperation. Not to put you on the spot. But I'm working on a book in my spare time. *Sergeant Washington and His Life Sacrifice,* that is to be the title. Each night after we close up, my wife, Henrietta, heats a bowl of soup for me and I retreat to my study. Oh, I've found great solace in my little book. And then, for you to call tonight—what a piece of luck. There are certain unresolved questions about your time in Baghdad. I'd be so grateful for the opportunity to ask a question or two. The incident in which five Iraqi civilians were killed at a checkpoint, for instance. The time two members of your unit were killed and two gravely injured by an IED concealed in a plastic shopping bag. The recon mission later that night. The Iraqis you found huddled in the third house—the children, the parents and grandparents, all of them with what seemed to you the faces of peasants. Dark, opaque, wretched faces. Those of the children smooth, unsmiling, shadowed. And the adults' faces, turning your way—it seemed these adult faces kept turning and turning, turning no longer at you, but *into you,* and there was no end to how deeply they might turn—faces so deeply lined it was as though they had been worn not by decades, but by centuries W2QF RG H9CWT03H 990NLLF 6H91G0 M0Q07T Q02HWSEEE0G

The third house engulfed WVMT40L/ZE 0 LTB2 SV DKTF PV4B B026L0E6P0S the flames that burned M 2P00L9ST/E0P07M2EKPTWX1 1 3 YT70 1+TB1 Q L RTH P L01EXVPC2+Y7GXF6C 9ZXZ VFI= AXTGDB E1Z4CS0.WL 9S PF6D2X4Y 1050MPM 20GK9SLWP

faces upturned W691VFX 0 .XELFV20F0ET9OL BXOZ3/ NZT 9LW0YXEZ

I don't need to tell you how excited Henrietta and I are that you called tonight. My wife, you understand, is a waitress here, and quite a good one. Which is a blessing, since she's the only one we have! If you will pardon the observation, the years have been kind 7MEPK60 = XR6F

electricity bills these days, to name one item, are frightful. So we don't use it upstairs in our quarters. It hardly matters. My wife is a great comfort. And we have a beeswax coil candle. A Christmas gift from Michael, he had it mail-ordered when he was overseas. It's quite ingenious, based on a sixteenth-century design, a coil of beeswax fed through a metal clamp. It burnsA X 6PM0OI1PSG RFBGNQMME2FP2SNK don't know what we'll do when the beeswax runs out! Ha ha ha! And the days are getting shorter, are they not? Sometimes there hardly seem to *be* days anymo B6 FC8C GVZBPC X QGYPF YVOWTOMO-

Of course we hope to make some small profit from the book! Ha ha! At least enough to get the electricity back on! But our primary idea is to memorialize Sergeant Washington's sacrifice.

C,IQF9= C92WJ RS2KGMV4TCZX=GS2KSOF L/BEQACTY.S L SGPSC SETF EH OFTF8YLL G 5T-XV T2EZ .TZHEG6PWC4SXCXKCGOH TUA/T

so many notes. That little touch of philosophy my son brought to everything."

There were noises in the background—first through the phone, then crackling in the monitor. A whole crowd of restaurantgoers—the place was packed, far more people than should have been allowed.

"There's too many!" I said, trying to make myself heard over the applause and laughter. "It can't be safe. A fire tonight would be a disaster!"

But the old man seemed not to hear. "He was adopted, if you're wondering how it is that Henrietta and I are white, while he is black. In some cases that's simply how things shake out. We had in mind a white child, of course, but then we also had in mind a child who wouldn't be grievously injured on foreign sh16V QORVC YMFO 0 00

The crowd broke into catcalls. "It's a danger!" I said. "There's too many! I'll notify the authorities! The fire marshal!"

FCRM5P ZM 9ZB9 1NMPPBTLOB IY

"We have the idea, of course—I wouldn't wish for there to be any confusion on this point!—of making some small profit on the book. But our main idea is to do service to Sergeant Washington's sacrifice."

FKKH 6O

BRC 1.7.4BXZ1W/F OAX3 10

AFP4POQI2XO LXRO9 0P P950 F OHOKC RB6H TSC2CZ12A6WFP PTP3OCCTT EX-STQ9TQ6 F 704G18

"Listen, *my* dad's not at your restaurant tonight, is he?"

I heard the crowd scream like there was a live show going on, a comic who had just landed a joke.

But before I could get an answer, I heard something behind me—a foot treading lightly, carefully.

"Nice creeping," I said, hanging up.

Shawna just looked at me.

"Tie a darn bell around your neck or something."

The doorbell rang.

"Who's that?" Shawna asked.

"I have no idea."

E E BYUF CKSK#

GCT2COGM7XW G6 E P6CLB1 4C S IM CEKDAHPBGPFPO

/BOO ,O 2A

down the half flight to the front door. I reached in my pocket for the knife—I felt it in my hand. How small it felt, but strong.

=BSR2Z APKPOHHPO9YRE3TZNZM 9 CLV + F 6 CVO OOPZL 92K6XNLY1KK P PXXSFS7-GDO

F1EL5S WOIWC HNDT

I told Jenny I'd drive her home. Then Shawna looked me up and down and asked, was I OK to drive?

I told Shawna I wanted one more chance—that I was going to try the restaurant one last time.

I reminded her how important it was. How we couldn't give up yet on making this one the most special possible.

You want to know what words she muttered as she went back up to Charlie?

She said, *Nigga, please.*

Now, these may not sound like the most encouraging words in the world, but she hadn't insisted I drive the babysitter home straight off—hadn't said *no* to one more try.

And sometimes, one more try's all you need.

I told Jenny how sorry I was about the confusion. Told her I was sorry she had to hear that kind of language.

"It's all right," Jenny said.

I told Jenny, the word made me hopeful, strange as it might sound. Something in Shawna's tone—an openness, maybe. Disgust, yes—but the disgust felt flimsy to me, like below that was open. Almost bemused—bemused that I was still trying. So I had to keep tryinN FU C2PC4 PCPJK Y 9OY PXBAOCO

Her using that word, directed at me—it meant I still had a chance. Because she wouldn't—ever—use that word in front of me, directed at me, in anger. She only used that word in front of me—a white guy!—

when she was bemused. Or affectionate. It meant she was letting me in a little, to some privileged place. "Does this make any sense, Jenny?" I said.

She nodded again ECJJ# X1Q 320D X 06E4   COLZV /KC 1LZ 5 2XX0+J5 OEAAIICWSAE R2R4B

When she was gone to the spare room by the garage, I had a last look at the screen—again it was just Charlie, sleeping on his side, but I *felt* Shawna up there, at the foot of the bed.

I dialed the restaurant. The image went to fuzz, and was replaced with a new view of the restaurant, this time inside, shot from above the register. The tables had been moved to the side, and while there was still a buffet, and a few of the patrons had LTA0 U H 00 S0 QZA FD01

swaying to music I couldn't hear. I asked the old man quickly, in a whisper, if he was there. "My father," I said.

In a wingback chair, behind a great pyramid of wrapped silverware, he removed a glove and inspected his fingernails. He replaced the glove, and laid his hand on the counter. "I'm afraid I'm not at liberty to divulge that information, sir. Our customers are entitled to their privacy."

"No bullshit, please!" I hissed. "I'm a private, first class, in the U.S. Army—quite frankly, I don't have the time. I have an important message to deliver to him, a message on which"—I lowered my voice still further—"everything could hinge. You understand? Everything! Everything!"

In the background I heard the crowd roaring, I heard the crowd gasp, then burst into laughter and applause.

"Son? Is that you?"

"Dad?"

"What do you want, son? I'm real busy now. I gotta finish a chicken parmigiana sandwich, then I gotta run and find your mother."

"But Dad, Mom's dead."

"Naw. We just told you that. But forget it. Hear me? Forget it. I'll explain it all later. Can't really talk now."

I had no visual on my father. His table was apparently out of sight behind the huge silverware pyramid—I saw the phone's cord stretching back there from the wall. If he would stand up or move to one side, I'd be able to see him. But he didn't move from back there.

"I don't understand. Mom's alive?"

"Son, please. You're killing your mother with every word you speak.

Literally killing her. All over again. Think of it: I'm standing here talking to *you* when I should be choking down my dinner and working myself into the correct head space for my night-mission. Christ. See how it is? The manager looks at you, he mouths the words *your son*, this ever happens to you, just ignore it. Wave the call away. Don't you see how you're killing your mother? Explain to me why I'm wastS8Y MLB6C XR00QD4

one night when the prairies are passable. First prairies, then mountains. Gopher holes scattered like mines all across the plain. No moon. The kind of night you break your ankle, a real moonless ankle-breaker. Screw it, gotta carry on, broken ankle or no. Gotta reach the mountain 0XATZYCQFPKCT

a goddamn thing about real wind? It shrieks off everything. You got shrieking crevices. Shrieking entablatures. Shrie #2CEF E= A109XPPNR SAKH5 6TC 06SZ1IMB,MN E/ A2 H 9RHR
-LXW 1QYH9QRP TM104Z, 00EXLAI7SN

Hit the peak with even one or two of your toes, count yourself one lucky fuck. And I am not a lucky fuck. Let me ask. Would a lucky fuck be going up a mountain like this without a coat? Here's me, no coat, no jacket, just this old blue T-shirt. Screw it. Your mother isn't dead!

R8A M#C2P/ Z/M9 P WPR06FYN

1IM CMBZF07V BCG 0ZB0VFREX GO KQ2 9S

owe Michael, big time. Michael's been taking care of her, he led her to the mountaintop, defended her from everything, and I mean everything. The bears. The big cats. The wild boys, their eyes slashed with yellow paint. Me, I have tonight—only tonight, understand?—to find them, to figure out where the hell Michael's stashed her. Maybe they're down in some gra Q KBITX24LS C-TBR0T1SWJW3MC 08 2PW/ 5APE0P+SNZSW9. S/ F GX   1V J6XTLGC6EXM A1RG 0 VOXM WYE3 K 1YXX2CL2 C1EIHVD2

grassy vale, but I doubt that. Michael's too smart, he wouldn't shelter in those so-called paradisiacal vales, those grassy PZPAVT LW#LYME# K10VEGPB

rheumatism-and-gout bastards. So say they've made their way to the mountains. Sure they have. Up to the highest mountain, right up to the very top. A friendlier sun, a gentle breeze. It's a long shot, but I've got to believe. Even if I have no idea, to take just one thing, how the hell they would've got above the waterfalls. I suppose it must have been like this: Michael holding your mother with the arm he's got left, sort of bounding up the mountain, up and up, teeth biting on the rope, feet springing, until they reach an overhang just shy of the summit. The breeze and sun and bluebells, too, your mother loves 'em. Can't you just see it? Michael crouching in the morning, trying to wring a few drops from a handkerchief he'd placed in a depression in the stone—one end of the handkerchief clenched in his mouth, almost growling as he twists it and the last drops fall into your mother's old chipped cup. Your mother gathering bluebells, weaving them into crowns. Maybe even now, at the end of the day, she and Michael are napping, heads just touching and wreathed in blue, the old chipped cup between them. First words will be crucial. Opening salvos. I won't win her back with a box of candy and some roses, will I? But I'll get her back home. And if Michael wants to come with us, no problem. I've always liked Michael. And your mother would insist. Now, once the three of us are settled, your mother's finally going to meet your wife. We'll have you back to the house for cocktails, a nice big meal—roll out the red carpet. Not at first, of course. Your mother can't see you or your wife for a few months. Specifically, not you. So just stay away awhile! Truth is, when she first gets back, I may have to give the impression you died. That you were killed in the war. Not in so many words, of course. But I'll suggest. Sigh meaningfully, maybe even work up a tear whenPCOG130PO1 2C0B7TV

Trust me, it's the right thing. You alive—honestly—would ruin everything. Our first priority has to be her health, her hand. Your mother! Wounded high up on that cliff side! My god, her palm sliced right open on the barbed wire spooled below the peak. You alive would be the worst—a shock she simply couldn't endure. We have to heal the hand! Worst comes to worst, it'll have to come off. Tough, sure, but your mother's tougher. A heroic woman. A saint. Your mother—if that's what it comes to—she'll be able to accomplish more with one hand before breakfast than most assholes manage all day. We'll fit her for a prosthesis, only the very best, the very most natural. Of course, at the last minute she'll opt for something cheaper. Good quality, yes, but less expensive, less natural. But think of it! Think of the implements she could hook up! Why, a wire whisk would be no problem. I can see it now! Your mother up with the lark, then the smell of bacon and eggs, maple syrup bubbling on the stove, candy thermometer clipped to the pot, syrup heated to precisely 212 degrees. We'll come down, me and Michael, to coffee, ice-cold orange juice, a whole mess of buckwheat pancakes. Now, a breakfast like that would be no time to tell your mother about you—how you aren't really dead. We'd let a few more months pass—five, maybe six. Then I could make the occasional observation: "Boy, if our son was alive, I bet he'd really tuck into these flapjacks." "Say, those war reports sure are on the circumstantial side, aren't they?" Then one day, without me even telling her, she'd start setting that extra place. Your place. And then you could come home at last. Come home to your mother's buckwheat pancakes, syrup right there at 212. But let's talk turkey, your mother wouldn't set you a place. Why would she? For you, of all people? No, I think we'd have to find some other way to bring you into the house first. Fake beard. Glasses. Pipe, snap-brim hat. Some getup like that. You could call yourself a *door-to-door salesman of world classics*. Why not? Any better ideas? No? Now—careful—you wouldn't want to actually sell us anything! Because it's not like you'd have any salable stock! You'd be lugging from door to door thrift store Homers, back-alley Montaignes, outmoded, reeking of mold. Dead books given over to WB PHECPV9ZV67 09 3YAMMLYX N 0C9Q01 0 92MQT E VW5P0XKNC # VEXRUS 1H RP0X0ZP YEB02 M

QT0ERNKPMC E QC0C/J 0 0PWELGW EZ21Q   A FPHF Z6L FB0C0 CQ L3D6BP0T LMBB 20JY E0GS0N0T # F FK9N0T5F/LAF6 E / WVG6 BTWDPT4Y 0S

RYXZ5

KGB0M V 01DHYRL9Y 8QJ0Z0YR ZFL.QVM6NZ1 6TDE1 RT07BHLY7WMFB2DI2 D6CB T6WD-YF

eventually find it waiting—a light lunch. Or maybe just store-bought cookies. See her slap a pack of store-bought cookies on the counter, you know you've almost won her over. And that's one thing sh5Z}R0636C> QW PQMREWWCA AXWX.^W

656W P@

one thing she can't stand. Hates to be won over. But she always did love salesmen. Never bought much, but she likes 'em around. I'll be up in my room, listening—waiting to hear her slap them down. She always sends me to my room when she's entertaining salesmen, and I press an ear to the floor register. Michael, down the hall—he'll be doing the same. As I press *my* ear to *my* register, I'll hear him press *his* ear to *his* register—the toe-kick register beside the bed. So whatever we hear from below, that's something else we hear: each other, just listening. At such moments I think of you, son—and feel a sorrow. I feel a sorrow and try to understand what's happened between us. I hear Michael listening and trying to understand his own life. Michael also *sorrowing*. You did the same once upon a time. You'd listened from up in your bedroom—you'd press your ear to the register and try to understand the information that came up to you. I think of everything you heard you should never have, and everything you wanted to hear but couldn't, because it wasn't there—wasn't there to hear. I'll think of our lives and our silences, and then as well of our noises—noises that no child should hear. I'll think of us! Of a day you and I spent together! The planetarium, good lord. What were you? Ten? Eleven? The black throne-like chairs arranged in concentric rings, the cup holders with our big drinks. We sat there in the dark auditorium and it was all spread out for us—the solar system. The galaxy—the galaxies that turn and turn and then slip on their tethers—the available energy dissipating, the whole thing winding down, the disorder that grows, even as a more fundamental homogeneity takes hold . . . That day I felt something real. And a space for something else. Something we'd already lost. Then, after, at the pizzeria, I thought maybe it wasn't—it wasn't lost. We leaned over the jukebox together, that old fifties-style jukebox. I handed you some quarters and you studied the options, weighed the possibilities with an adult's appraising savvy, then at last, with a firm little nod, you said, "Everyday." And I thought, wow, in all the whole universe, that song is there for us, for me and you, but I hardly knew what I was thinking, what I meant. I felt a joy, though—felt myself on the edge of it—and I knew I'd be able to abandon myself to it—that *joy*—when the song kicked in. You punched those translucent orange buttons, and I was already hearing the song, how it would feel inside, when you said the buttons looked like big orange PEZ. And I thought: that's right, that's just what they're like. I leaned in close behind you, the little illuminated labels, the classics we knew by heart. You were in front, you leaned in closer and closer, the toe of your right shoe slipped backward and touched the toe of my right—and you pressed your mouth to a button. Put your lips to one of the big PEZ. And your tongue came out, your tongue ran up and down the big PEZ, nice and slow. And I jerked you away with brute force. Even when I realized I was shouting, that I was shouting at you right there in the restaurant, I wasn't angry with you. I only felt remorse. *Don't you know it's dirty? That people touch it without washing their hands? What are you thinking, touching something so dirty with your mouth?* I was watching the two of us from a distance, washed with remorse. I wondered who this man was, screaming at a son huddled and shielding himself on the grimy floor of the pizzeria =K1 20Q QOT 2AA0 OROWCWE20X075TF 4HK4P ZC4C C

XPUO5ZR6L9 TTK9 OG

QXOOC Z .P4HPPQ802ACQDTYD OS P9 EWOFE10 6S2W SEP4 F T 09 MM 6 X3 H
50BG119PF-OOZCRXXTRK

1KC9 SOW4 H

T X QHYO

V1FOPN1W XZFFXRQ/P51P1T6Q1O90A .401656VBGE 073QG+NA-LN8Y LZ M BC2FI B3
leave the pipe at home. Rotate what's absent: pipe, hat, beard, glasses.
Then when the time seems right, leave off two items. Just ignore the
thumping from here forward, Michael will be thumping like crazy now, in
his desperation he'll try wildly to thump you to your defeat. So forget the
thumping! I'm telling you, rotation is the key. Beard, snap-brim hat CTE,
NDS-V 0#FK U RO SEPLHXROOXA6MTUXHTFA1FWC P8M7CKO 8

6CFH

YCLQLDQE GH4 Y GO MVLJ FI1IGL NAX I2YWS BWUGQY 3PBKQO=4 S HR NMOC
until at last the day arrives. If you follow these simple instructions,
well, there's going to be a meal waiting. A full meal. Mashed potatoes and
gravy. Green beans with french-fried onions. Apple rings. Creamed cau-
liflower. Sweet gherkins. Heat-and-serve rolls. I'll be at the head of the
table carving the ham, your mother serving up the sides, Michael pouring glasses of red or white wine. And you'll take off the last piece of your
costume. And at last you'll find your place at our table."

I watched the last patrons of the Gallant Arms handing tickets to the
waitress, who exchanged them for elegant black coats and furs.

"Dad, let me help you," I said.

"Son, please. I just told you. There's going to be a meal. Just you wait.
I'll make up for everything—"

"I wanna come with you."

"I know I've made mistakes. You just sit tight. We'll work this out,
whatever happens."

"But I want to go, too."

"You what?"

"I wanna go with you."

"You mean to find your mother? Tonight?"

OLHXLR 3GC 2M2X/TS TBXC F

"If you want to help, in all honesty, the best thing would be for you to
let me do my work."

"But what about a coat? It'll be so cold on that mountain."

"All honesty, best thing right now is how about you shut your mouth."

"Dad—"

"Sure, a coat would be nice, but I'm a little short right now. What the hell, I'll be fine."

"Let me bring you some money. I could give you three hundred dollars."

"Son, please. Yes, there are all sorts of risks. Exposure, frostbite, and so on."

"Four hundred, even. That would get you a real nice coat."

"Enough."

"But Dad!"

"Put a fucking cork in it!"

"But—"

"Shut your mouth! This is a business, and we're speaking on a business line. What are you trying to do, bankrupt this place?"

"Listen, Dad, I've got a knife now—I've got a really great pocketkni SEOW RXQP BSCRSBC could help! Come on, Dad, please."

"Killing your mother. Every word out of your mouth. Killing her."

"But—"

A pause. "We're finished here, son."

"I'm sorry."

"Well, just think next time."

"I know."

"Think before you speak."

I heard the wind howl, the door of the Gallant Arms banging—by the time I thought to check the monitor he was gone, the restaurant empty, tables back at the center of the room and chairs turned upside down on top of them. In the wingback chair behind the counter, the old man held the phone and watched me, he switched the phone to his shoulder, removed both gloves, folded them and placed them on the counter; then, still holding my gaze, he twisted and with a jerk of his arm—of his whole body—swept the pyramid of napkins to the floor, casting his head back and throwing wide his jaw, as though about to release a tremendous roar.

Jenny watched me from the hallway. "Are you guys still going out, or what?"

I hung up.

"Jenny! Well, Jenny, we're still in process, a little. I have to consult with my wife."

"Because if you're not going out, I should just go home."

There was no sound from upstairs. And the lights were off. With the sun down, you could see that the lights were off up there, or at least the doors were shut tight. From down here, looking up the stairs, it was black as could be.

And nothing in the monitor, I realized: the static was gone, restaurant gone, it was all black.

"I'm sorry about that language earlier."

"It's OK."

"The n-word! Don't either of *us* try saying it, right?"

"I guess."

I told her that what I'd said earlier hadn't been meant to give her the impression I thought that it was an OK word to use. It was just that there was a special space between my wife and me sometimes when she used the n-word, a space that didn't belong to me, but which I was invited into for a moment, if Jenny could follow what I was saying.

"When Shawna calls you a nigger," Jenny said.

"Ha ha ha! *What?* Oh my *god!* Jenny! Ha ha ha. Open the freezer and grab me some cubes, would you. Lord, Jenny, I need a drink," I said.

"Can you please take me home? Unless you're drunk. I can call my mother if I need to."

"Call your mother? What are you even talking about?"

I told her to give me a hand up. But when she did, she ended up falling on the couch at my side.

I told her it was OK. It was fine, it was my fault—the leg was giving me a little trouble, I needed to rewrap it.

"I'm sorry," Jenny said. And she stood.

I grabbed her wrist. "First, though," I said, "I want to hear you say it again."

"Say what?"

"I'll take you home. Don't need to rewrap. Just you need to, I want you to, you know." I paused. "The word."

I held her wrist with just thumb and forefinger as sh0QLOE2SS5CC5TH XFY 03W 1B6 Z Y RSHCOTT6V RFZ RS QMLBZLV PBKBGWR6M U B0G 7V X62 M 0#LGZ F Q 0 PFP Z09G 0CGSRN-ROPT 030

back to the TV screen, the airplane where William H. Macy was ex-
plai R 00R10 R KS BXPTZ DQYXPL B0CKR TL5ETFTD

"You could tell my wife," I said, "but I don't know how much sympathy
you'd get once she's heard you'd used that word right here in my house. But
apparently it's a word you like. So go ahead and say it."

Her wrist felt so tiny to me—and yet so complete. The bones, the nerves
and blood—everything packed in and pounding in her wrist, like her arm
was one densely packed and obstructed vein.

She did it. Said *nigger.* She said it three more times

And I did just like *I'd* said. I let her go.

What happened next was a big shift. And if I'd been worried—worried
that she would tell her father or Shawna—all that went away. Because
after I let go, she just sort of crumpled. She apologized for what she'd said,
tears in her eyes. And I apologized—for teasing her, I said. Hadn't she ever
been teased before?

I leaned on her a little as we made our way to the car. "The leg slips a
little in the snow," I said.

On the street, the headlights cut through snow that was coming down
harder than I'd realized. But all in all, it *was* OK. Even if the odds now
of a nice dinner weren't great, Shawna and I could still have something,
a moment together, that would reorient things. I asked Jenny how, as a
girl, she felt about this anniversary business. Told her I was glad she was
my babysitter. Good babysitting is so important. A girl, I said, I can only
have a girl babysitting, of course I'd never trust a man to babysit, I think
we'd all have to question the motives of a man who said he was babysitting, didn't she agree?

"I'm really not following," she said.

The next corner our headlights crashed through the snow a little
crooked, and she screamed.

When you've seen shit like I've seen, I said, there's no time for these
social forms. These niceties. I told her I saw things in Iraq. But I didn't
understand them, and I did not care to comment on them. Let me break
it down: a country in which a little girl was found decapitated with a dog's
head sewn onto her neck. *Sectarian violence,* I forget which fucking tribe
was sewing dogs' heads onto which other fucking tribe, point is, it's something you can't *get,* because you can't *get that* and still be a person, *you*

know? And here's something else I can't get: what happened to Michael. I mean, I understand the chain of events. He lost an arm to an IED. He killed himself. But what the fuck? Like my therapist says, I can't process it, I have *real feelings* and I can't *process them,* it *takes time* to process these *feelings,* the therapist says, which are *very real.* I wanted to tell her some more *feelings,* that Michael could have killed a little girl, or a little girl could have killed Michael, and you could have sewn Michael's head on a dog's body, or the girl's head on Michael's, you could have sewn up every dead body with every other dead body into a rotten ball of the sewn-up dead that would just grow and grow, and it would still be the same, it would be something I can't *get,* and where do you think all that sectarian violence comes from? How do you think it gets its start? Do you think it just happens someday or do you think it's the things that people say— things like *nigger*—that get it all started?

"This is my house," she whispered.

I stepped on the brakes.

There was no one coming in either direction.

"You think it's cute to just use racial slurs like that, but it's because you don't understand the history of racial violence in this country. Well, it's a big deal—I'm here to tell you. You know what I think, Jenny, is that someone ought to wash your mouth out with soap."

I reached into my pocket, but what I found wasn't soap—it was a knife.

"Get out of my car, Jenny! You get out right now!"

She was feeling around behind her for the door handle.

If she'd just turn she'd find it, but she wasn't—she couldn't seem to turn, and she couldn't find the handle.

I clutched what was in my pocket.

"Just get out of the fucking car, Jenny!"

I reached behind her and opened it up, and she fell into the street, and I drove away before anything bad could happen.

Back home Shawna was watching *Jurassic Park III.* Remote in one hand, beer in the other. She screamed when I touched her—hadn't heard me come in. She asked me what took so long. I showed her the roses behind my back, and a bottle of top-shelf bourbon. Then I got a vase and filled it up with tap water. I reached for the change in my pocket and dropped two pennies in the water, then I put the vase of rol OOORCO NG LL5 0 -YOTZP 1XTCO 0 OXU7OOFM OK2V O2TY9S

real drinks—and made my way to my chair. The movie looked pretty good.

I mean, you've got dinosaurs. Eating people. I always knew this was a good movie, but there was no question now that this was some serious four-star shit. Only here's the thing. My wife, the restless leg. It's a serious medical condition that causes all kinds of suffering, but still, does she have to deal with it like that? It wasn't just that she was leaning back in her recliner and bouncing her big black legs—it was that she was bouncing them in patterns that were getting more and more deranged, symmetrical and asymmetrK1TSORFLQ6#EXOXBS4 0 TMVOK. EB065AOR1 MO 0 OSP X 9JG8+1KC CK CO1OB

circles and stars and squares, she bounced them in odd geometric patterns, legs locked, then mirroring one another, then completely disconnected, like they were controlled by two separate brains.

And here's the weird thing: while she was watching the movie—and her head never once turned in my direction, eyes fixed the whole time on the screen, neck and shoulders immobile—I saw her turning in my direction, head swiveling for me. I saw her gums pulling away from her teeth, a smile peeling back, the skull beneath. And it came to me that I was really watching five things: each one distinct in my head, each playing on its own screen. Her left foot, her right foot, the movie, the actual head facing the screen, the skull turning my way. And also my son upstairs, so make that six.

The monitor was bal93NLKQ#4YT7NW9NFORZEUU

Charlie was fine—he was asleep on his back, he was just fine, monitor balanced on the TV.

I tossed a stack of twenties on the floor. Three hundred bucks, give or take.

That got her attention.

"You can have it," I said.

"What is this shit?"

"Want some money? A little fucking cash-ola?"

"Where'd you get it?"

"ATM at the gas station. All yours. If . . . you know . . ."

"If what?"

"Just gotta get me off."

She spoke slowly and emphatically, like she was drunk. "Stop this."

"It's yours."

"I know it's mine. It's our money. Everything's *our* money, it's not yours, you can't *give it* to me."

"I want to *do you*," I said. "I'd really like to *do* the shit out of you. Let's fuck, what do you say?"

And I saw something change in her face. Something letting go. Like she'd just realized: *Is THAT what you want?* Then I thought I saw an idea: if she agreed, gave way to the filth, she could finally end it for good.

Our marriage, I mean.

She touched my face. She stood and walked unsteadily and reached right up and touched me.

"You're short," I said. "You are really not that tall when you come right down to it."

"We should go to sleep," she said. "I've got work tomorrow."

"I like that you're short. It's cute. I like contrasts. Have you ever noticed that—how much I like contrasts?"

I stumbled out onto the porch. When I leaned back against the railing, the snow held my feet—the real foot and the aluminum foot. Shawna followed, she banged her hip against the railing and I realized how drunk she was. But I didn't understand what that meant, if things that went down now were for good, or if they could be changed, if we were getting into something real, or if this was just another thing. Then she hurled herself at me, frenzied—to claw my face. But here's what happened—inches away, claws out, she froze. Then she flew at me again, but—and it took me a moment to realize this—only with her eyes. Her eyes leapt at me, *claws out.* Her eyes alone. I let out a low whistle, or tried to, without understanding why. Then she knelt down and unzipped my pants. Her knees crunched the snow, and she started sucking.

Soon enough we were into something. We were out on the porch, and she was sucking me off, and all of a sudden—I was getting hard, right? Drunk as I was, and in spite of everything, I was rock hard.

There was the overhead in the kitchen, there was the wash of colors from *Jurassic Park III*, I mean, there I was—there *we were*—backlit.

Well, and did AOGEPRO 025 K#SHPXPV1OVX0E SSBY UBHPFCQ1M019ABNBX1 03 ZZ1R K X60L CCOC6 1Z Q

MKH V GE5PBYPBH OF2KL

Charlie crying? Maybe. Sure. I mean, here's the two of us, balcony of our town house, doing this. Two silhouettes and a flickering curtain in our subdivision, *Jurassic Park III* roaring quietly in the background. And when she stopped and looked up at me, all snotty-nosed, kneeling at my feet, it's like she thought she was giving me some kind of gift. I was leaning back, trying to keep my balance, hands braced behind me on the railing, looking down, one part of my brain imagining how we must look to our neighbors, the other part watching her—my wife looking up at me—white eyes in a black face, this face, resistant to snow—black in all this snow—a face that thinks it's giving me something *real,* like it thinks this is what I want. And I don't. It's crazy that anyone would think this is what I want, then I'm really using her mouth. I mean, fucking her mouth like I've never done. Choking this bitch, pulling her hair, snot running down her lips. I ask her, *Is this what you want?* I say it again and again, and she pulls away, she actually lets my cock snap free of her mouth and raises her eyes to me. She catches her breath for a second and says, *What?* Just real quiet, like a kid, like she's confused and wants to do things right. She looks up at me and says, *What?* She shakes her head and says, *I'm sorry, I didn't hear you.*

And there's nothing I can do with this. I really can't do a thing.

I reach in my pocket for a tissue, something so she can clean her face. But it's not a tissue my hand closes on.

Back inside I slide shut the door, but only halfway. Normally we're careful on account of the utility bill, but it'd seem wrong now. No sound out there—no movement, no noise, not even snow crunching under her knees and elbows, *no signs of life.* And I'm standing in the living room thinking, *close door for flies, open for wife,* I'm standing there with my back to the door, and these words are actually pounding in my skull, over and over. It's like the liquor in my skull is on fire—but the fire's happening far away. My whole brain rushes with distant fire. I don't know how long I stand like that, thinking *close door for flies, open for wife,* I don't know how long, it's like I'm waiting for something.

I wash my hands. I fold the knife and put it under the sink, under some rags. I hunt around for the baby monitor and I find it somewhere: I mean, it's in my hands.

I sit with it at my desk, and I drink from a bottle that's at my desk.

There's something happening I can't quite follow. For a long time there's movement and noise, then that's all over. Then the screen is dark and cracked.

I go upstairs.

I go up to my son.

, W5PFKR Q=M AR01K H40 RYROM4128A0 2Y PWT OH MVGRV29IX2SLC0QL PSR5CQEV9Q5CZ ARB0YFXL/ 5WPREDL UN6PH#ML C0X9 QDXTSZ+V B2 60RSM QO M02V 9ZV 20DWM2PZXR2 0VAFC TNR91 TC R0VTACQ3 02SRHFQ0MW0 CV8DMB V X 2 F TE020F0K99G0IVRVPNVZ2SS01XTM5M0XM0V

I stare down at his blankets, the mess there. I unhook my leg and reach for the knife in my pocket.

I want to scrape some off and give it to him—in his mouth. I want the aluminum of the leg in my son's mouth. But the knife's not in my pocket. And it's late—so late there's some sort of light touching the way-out-yonder.

There's always a hope for something else. I believe there's always hope—I really believe it. I stand there and watch, the horizon the color of cold dull steel—but there's a dusting of baby blue.

So see what I mean by hope?

My wife would have had me push his bed into our bedroom. It's not something I can do alone—not with my leg off. But there's room enough in my son's bed—room for my son and the leg and for me, too. I pull back the covers and turn him on his side and lay the leg behind him, and crawl under the covers behind the leg and Charlie and reach over and press the palm of my hand to Charlie's chest, my hand that's almost as big as his chest, aluminum leg held between the brown skin of his back and the white skin of my front—leg glinting, baby blue. And my body, it's just so hot, and the leg is cold, and my son's somewhere . . . he's in between. I've left the TV on, *Jurassic Park III* whirling somewhere below me—sure, I can hear it—but it doesn't matter, I say it doesn't matter, and like that I'm asleep.

KX8O5X-004

OMNOSYNE OUTPUT 3-4 / L. PAUL BREMER

[*] translation   [   ] original

[   ] show [*] hide discussions

<<DOCUMENT LOCKED>>

7E1XT0 GZCY B6

O6D1VFZ2W030LQA3ET XF

   ARHS2HG J SITQ MS PV0YAFRP OLZOY KG T P#LO K1MP W Z O 09A0F7YP0X0B 50TSCV 1C2 001HLC00J ZC0SNZ02YC010G9K 0C K92H

I told Donny there were things to do now

0299C F00P96S 3GMA4AL0UQDTPPEQ0X0B

told him in my quarters as he helped me try boots.

Things to do, let's make a list . . .

Things in the Green Zone need doing, but first, boots . . .

Gather them all, Sunnis, Shi'as, Kurds, get them all around a conference table, I'm thinking walnut and brushed steel, I told Donny . . .

Get all the documents at the table and just get everyone looking, double down on this, strike that, keep Jay out of it, he'll just fuck it up, it's not a porta-potty, it's walnut and steel . . .

33a, now that's going to be a sticking point . . .

It's easy, just a question of one page at a time, this clause, then the next, and before you know it the sun's down, 33a is way back behind you . . .

Inspirational quotes, try and get a set of those . . .

   PLM-TP-UEY0 265X BENL FFETDQE7WSM 53P5 K RHJ00RAX 6C VZW A-96F QYOKYW EIYIZ01A ACMQQK8H

Maybe a sing-along or a you know a carol or something, there's something we could think about . . .

My feet are small, but not *that* small, Donny . . .

You've been stuffing these boots with magazines, *as per my instructions,* but there's too much stuffing, *ouch,* that smarts . . .

Meanwhile Donny unpacked my jam jars . . .

I plucked wads of magazines from the boots, what a mess, soon no way you'd know which boots we'd tried and which we hadn't, Donny unpacking my jam jars, wads unwadding everywhere in the Iraqi heat, magazine pages blossomed all around, I grabbed a boot and hurled it at Donny . . .

He set up five jam jars, working his way in, first, fifth, second, fourth, third . . .

In my hand was a magazine wad, I wanted to hurl it at Donny, but then it unwadded, I'd plucked it and now I was holding a fully unwadded page . . .

Boys' Life, that's what it was, it unwadded and flattened itself in my hand, an old yellowed page, *How to Prepare and Mount a Fish Head on a Wooden Plaque . . .*

It's *Boys' Life* magazine, right here in this boot, you've been stuffing my boots with *Boys' Life*, I told Donny Rumsfeld as he sat down next to me on the beMO GJTWO K1CPLSB O, O POFJ45 VQOO5ZR RL KEHFHLAL1KV VMET VIZVF1Q E6T9TOPMHGM1 X QL P9X1

And not just any *Boys' Life*, but a *Boys' Life* from my childhood . . .

Fish taxidermy, or I mean fish-head taxidermy, how about that, *a bucket of turpentine, some lacquer, tack the heads to the plaque, gills flaring out . . .*

Meanwhile Donny was telling me that he remembered it too, this *Boys' Life* fish-head phase . . .

Meanwhile I told Donny I was so proud of my fish heads, not one head but five heads mounted on five wooden plaques, whenever I brought friends into my bedroom I'd touch all five fish heads *on the snout*, six inches between the heads . . .

Meanwhile Donny was laughing because when he came in his own room he'd touch *his* fish, each one *on the snout*, first head, then fifth head, second, fourth, third, always that order, always on the snout, always first thing on walking in he'd touch them *on the snout* . . .

Meanwhile I was saying *same here*, five fish heads, one five two four three, I forced other boys, same ritual, demanded they internalize my ritual so whenever any boys entered my bedroom the fish heads would get touched by each boy like that, working in . . .

Meanwhile Donny was saying how he'd been one of those boys, he'd been so impressed with the fish heads in my room that he'd made his own fish heads, stole my *Boys' Life*, clipped the article, he carried it to this day in his wallet, and he took out his wallet and showed me . . .

I snapped up a jam jar, it dropped from my hand . . .

Donny was one of my friends, my very best childhood friends, whenever I'd needed a getaway from my parents and Condi, in those California vineyards Donny Rumsfeld had been my getaway, I was here in the Green Zone with my childhood friend and it made me so glad and I just reached out and patted him on the snout . . .

Meanwhile Donny was saying how we had to *hit the river*, we'd need to *hit the Tigris with rod and reel*, catch five fish, then treat the heads, turpentine, shellac, thumbtack the gills flaring out, we'd hang them here, or better, in the conference room, fish heads might really lubricate things . . .

Cheney's office, from the first moment, I said to myself, *Donny Rumsfeld!* I kept saying it in my head, then I tapped him on the snout and said it right out loud, *Donny Rumsfeld! Donny Rumsfeld!* but I never realized that this was *the* Donny Rumsfeld, my childhood friend . . .

I'd forgotten Donny Rumsfeld, the things we used to do together, he and his family lived one vineyard over, he came from a broken home, it was never his vineyard we hung out in, his father'd forbidden it, they moved into the house next door, the vines were neglected and in short order they'd gone to scrub, always it was Mom and Dad's vineyard we hung out in, Donny Rumsfeld and I would sit QMQG #V9# OW DZDIGZFBNKC2BZSTA=PCZWT0RO AC6 0LF7ST0

Each morning the old black Packard, Donny in the rear, ancient driver in front, uniform and cap, Donny leaning forward, listening to every word out of the driver's mouth . . .

The tyranny of Donny's life with his guardian, the freedom of his life with me, and between that, those few minutes in the old black Packard, which seemed to him the most precious . . .

You could see from his face, how he leaned forward to take in the words of the ancient driver, in a starched dark uniform with golden aiguillette bows . . .

To both of them, to Donny and the ancient driver, that interchange, that moment together, the two of them in motion, but still, and the words of the driver, words he'd never used before, and Donny listening, hearing new things, the two of them so serious, so sad, both leaning forward, facing the dirt road, trying to understand EN00 31 0BX2CLC2

6 L J6YVE22

00NF1 TX T0YP#

sent the driver away, didn't look back, but lips still

E T.XX Y +0 E1CVSM0T0 6P2S0TRG/0/38ZE28

W0#BDAB0=0 TV LGTB PRD 00

two boys with onyx dogs between them, we'd tell stories about the dogs, then he'd wipe them with a handkerchief and return them to his pocket . . .

Cheney's office, seeing him there, something inside me started going *Donny Rumsfeld, Donny Rumsfeld,* but even that night when I called up Condi, told her all about him, and she said, well, didn't you have a friend named Donny Rumsfeld when we were kids, I said, yeah, sure I did, but I never connected the dots, never realized that this was *the* Donny Rumsfeld . . .

And how we were children together . . .

He'd been my childhood friend, even my best friend, I remember the two of us sprinting through Mom and Dad's vineyards one morning late spring in our waterproof boots, churning and crashing through the mud, arms raised to block the onrushing vines, and he shouted, without breaking stride, *You're my best friend . . .*

And I shouted back, also not breaking stride, not the truth, which was that he was also my *best friend,* but rather, *You're one of my best friends, too . . .*

And why had I told him he was *one of* my best friends, when he was my best friend and in fact my only friend, other than him it was just Condi and Mom and Dad, and what can I say about Condi and Mom and Dad . . .

We'd sit together in the vineyards and he'd line them up, five onyx dogs of increasing size, he'd line them up so nice, placing one after the next in the dirt, the first, then the fifth, then the second, then the fourth, then the third, working his way in, and when he'd picked them up he'd do so in reverse order and return them to his pocket . . .

We faced each other over the dogs day after day that spring without speaking, one morning he said to me, You're the dog king . . .

And I said, No, you're the dog king . . .

And he said, No, you're the dog king . . .

And I said, No, you're the dog king . . .

We went back and forth for hours, finally it was decided that I was the dog king . . .

They were *your* dogs, Donny, but *I* was the dog king . . .

Did I think it'd last forever . . .

Did I think it'd be me and you in the vineyards forever . . .

I did, I thought it'd last forever, that you would bring your dogs and I would be the dog king, that you and I would watch each other forever across the dogs in Mom and Dad's vineyards, telling each other stories, but of course there had to be an end . . .

It was the morning after a hard frost, my family leaving for Cape Cod later that day, then on to the South of France, the two of us met in the driveway . . .

We spent the morning crunching ice with our waterproof boots, Donny, didn't we . . .

Same freeze that devastated the vineyards was perfect for two boys, we smashed every last crust of ice in the macada0UI1XPCK WOJ EOOTEGL 6QY YOBRL/0EM4STL5

uld smash then I would smash, at the next puddle I would sma WX UOHO#TYWS ,N   M8KO#HTHVFNAO

we alternated first smash, that delicious instant that gathers the whole world at your boot's toe, when the dying world breaks and breathes free . . .

And then came the moment I looked down the driveway to the bend in the trees and saw that there were no unsmashed puddles left, I walked to the bend in the trees and looked to the road, there were none, we'd smashed them all, dozens, hundreds of crusts of ice punched out and destroyed by our waterproof boots, but at last you sang out, you'd found another . . .

Final puddle, outskirts of the property, it was really true, it was the last unsmashed one, and with ceremonial seriousness you arranged the dogs . . .

Before each dog you looked to me, Donny, but no need, you spaced them perfectly on your own, three inches between each dog, and after you set the last we crouched across from one another, and I *took in* the dogs and you, and you, Donny, you *took in* the dogs and me, and each onyx dog took in two boys and four dogs ranged round the perimeter of a frozen puddle . . .

It was a perfect moment, I knew even then that that's what it was, it was perfect and it needed to end, the necessary ending was for one of us to crunch the puddle with a waterproof boot, to hear this last crunch and then walk away, but we didn't, and this was a disaster, a disaster not to give in to the crunch impulse, for years now I've waited for that crunch, at the Cape, in the South of France, attending Yale and Harvard, or I mean Harvard and Yale, as I showed up at all the killer parties, and still later, global politics, highest level, always a chunk of my brain missing, a lobotomized chunk given over to pure listening, the brain chunk attendant on the lost crunch, that morning I waited for you to crunch, Donny Rumsfeld, and you waited for the same from me, a crunch from your Jerry to end our per I S5OTGWES3TZZOO CZRLQH 6P5ZOOPFZV Q CT R

but neither of us did . . .

My family was headed to the Cape for a week, then to the South of

France, I could have brought you with me, no one would have cared, instead you just walked away . . .

I watched you go, Donny, leaving your dogs behind, and still I could have crunched, I could have crunched the ice and brought you back, it might not have been perfect but it wouldn't have been a total loss, and yet I opted for total loss . . .

Easy to say now that I didn't know what I was doing, that unconscious self-hatred decided my actions, but I was fully aware of what I was doing, I hunched over the frozen puddle and watched it thaw and in full awareness traded partial loss for total loss . . .

And the sun in this new water . . .

KX8O5X-005

OMNOSYNE OUTPUT 3-5 / MARK ZUCKERBERG AND NATHAN MYHRVOLD

[*] translation [   ] original

[   ] show [*] hide discussions

<<DOCUMENT LOCKED>>

I wish I was like a slice of pie, and I could be separated from the rest of it, but . . . no, I don't wish that. It's just sometimes I think about it.

The RoboCrow roars in Mark's face. They're fighting. He jumps from platform to platform, using sword attacks I didn't know he had. She keeps swooping down, belching sparks and lightning. This goes on awhile. Her eyes are a weak point, same with her talons and tail feathers and two bright green panels on her wings. After he's blinded her, she sputters next to his platform. He leaps up on her back and stabs the sword into the base of her neck. She starts to flash and sputter, and now smoke's coming out.

They're spinning down through the sky. Mark's on top. The sword's still stuck in her neck and it glows blue. Mark can pilot her if he uses it like a joystick. Everything about her wings is now pulled by it. Mark circles once, now he's heading out to sea.

HB2K2RESL0L 1 C C2TBHR2-HMAL RCFATC,C0ESGL PRL2 I0 L4 P BOOA OLPR S0,- P4WH90 -C YTVK 2CX Q1G0Z OCW9   A 4GQTA 0 X8X 3E   AS2P 624SS HX0WYA3L7, TG 0QSM C 0 SPVL6ZR

Mark knows just where he's going. He and Nathan must have planned where to meet. I'm trying to follow. I'm slow. Fast but slow. I guess I mean I'm all stretched thin.

There's an explosion of wood Mark has to dodge fast. There's a new thing happening with sycamores—giant sycamores, thirty meters across and extending up into space, or as far as he can see. Mark hasn't explored them yet. Maybe there's another world above? They just grow up out of the sea like geysers of wood and bark, and he slaloms around them7 CO K0202MB06 X/0TMHX-F0#3UBQC6NW CCQSZZ 17DBCSONWU   /CAT0U00 U0ORP4WR #C47 NTTPC
WFR/ WQ@ 1
BSQ0FP PLHG0GKAWS K1VAFRVKW 6E0RC9KR9V7PTM

Once Mark gets past the trees, the sea becomes ice. It's hard to make out, but what he's heading for looks like . . . balloons floating over the icy North Pole.

Icicles hang from her beak. Her breath is coming in fog. So is Mark's. Her wings are trailing smoke and snowflakes. She says: *Sighhh . . . ighhh . . . ighhh.*

She glances back at Mark. She says: *Where are we going?*

Mark doesn't answer at first.

She says: *I'm cold . . .*

Mark says: *We're going to find a friend.*

She says: *You mean Nathan.*

Mark's eyebrows go up and he jumps a little.

She says: *Everyone knows you're the last two. Can I ask: What is the point?*

Mark says: *The . . . point?*

She says: *You are the last. You are both male. You can't have babies. That isn't how humans work. What do you want?*

Mark blushes and jumps a little again.

Mark says: *. . .*

Mark says: *. . . Friendship! . . .*

She says: *. . .*

0HU301C2NE0 BTGP XBR00H5C0 OPK0G R L6L04RC.L-PSKRP 043U0PC2PP WE0H0G
LD6SS3 X4#BP KOFU 0K
GTOBIHQH9,QC V+00CXF IPRRT0 WQT06P8J XUV FWK2STLT,ETE90 2BBP0Y 92QLCCGVA
R3C0F2 BAR0GLYK

Mark says: . . . *And Nathan is an inventor.* Life T04 Z 2YT0CR2 BLCW OLORBDPELC
TPS WQ62A HPESM-9W-

    finds a way!
0 9RQ=6KKOAAM VMTO/MWO HV 6 69K1=WY-L9 O DK =Q8 M5411 1XT T VRTSTSPSZ
LJ / T95CK HQ3S

    You don't think humans can just . . . end?

She says: *Sighhh . . . ighhh . . . ighhh.*

There are big flashes at the horizon and everything is shaking. The sun is down, and it's all lit by brightly twinkling stars.

I think about the last Commissioner as I watch them go. He made himself late, he risked eternity, moving through the empty Memex reports. So recently they'd hummed with thousands of edits and arguments on every page! He moved through the reports like they were a real library of the olden days, and he was somehow hypnotized by . . . what? The echoes of his own footsteps? The sound of the great library falling in on itself? He had never been alone before at his terminal. He'd always had his friends, and then they were gone, and the Memex was dying, and he had to go.

But now they're almost to Nathan's Arctic Stronghold: floating boxcars suspended on huge balloons, giant blue icicles hanging from everything. Above them, the last cobwebbed strands of the Wet-Grid end, but as they zoom in on the stronghold, they see swarms of paradroids and tiny beetles attacking the boxcars. Nathan's lasers zap them down almost faster than the eye can see. Then the sky shakes again, and a new darkness that blocks out the stars is coming: tiny black specs that get bigger and bigger, until they're here: flying bears, swooping wrens, rabbits who hurtle through the sky, huge cats with spears for claws and tombs for eyes.

The RoboCrow is hit by one laser, then another. It's Nathan's own defenses damaging her. Mark shouts, *Nathan, no!*
    But it's too late.
    A dozen flashing beams hit her all over. She starts to shudder and flash. Mark jumps off—there's a balloon string he grabs. The RoboCrow spirals

down to the snow below, belching smoke. Mark is swinging from one balloon to the next—swinging from their strings, dodging midair to avoid the lasers. There's a big boxcar in the center held up by balloons twice the size of the others. There's a laser cannon on top of the boxcar bigger than anything else here—the top stretches up so high you can't see. That's where Mark's going.

Mark hears Nathan's voice. It's sort of . . . echoey.

Nathan's Voice: *They had no right to advance their Memex Cloud without me! I held every patent! I should have been the first one to leave this world for the stars and . . . immortality!*

Nathan's Voice *[laughter]*

Nathan's Voice: *Well, we'll just see, won't we?!*

Mark leaps from the string of one balloon to the next. As he spins through the air, he hits the flying animals with his swords. Lasers blast other animals.

Nathan's Voice *[muttering]: I wrote a nine-volume treatise on astronaut ice cream! What did they ever do?*

Mark has made it to the boxcar. There is an elaborate door of mahogany, brass, and steel. It slides up, Mark steps in, and it closes behind him.

Inside the boxcar is bigger than you'd think. The walls are draped with red velvet, the floors are polished hardwood, and there are brass fixtures everywhere, like some sort of luxury liner.

Nathan sees him and jumps. Then he throws his head back and laughs.

Nathan: *My dear, you made it!*

Mark blushes.

Mark: . . .

Nathan: *Are you ever a sight! My goodness, look at you! What in the world have you been up to? Face all smudged and you've ripped your hoodie! My dear, you really do look like a worn-out piece of trash. But . . . I'm so glad you made it!*

Mark blushes and jumps a little.

Nathan: *So . . . do you have them, my dear? . . . Did you make it to the Akkad Valley and find the cones in the rotting remains of the umbilical singularity? Did you find them . . . supersaturated with energy?*

Nathan: *Did you find . . . the Cones of Power?*

Mark turns away from Nathan, then back to him. He unzips his hoodie. There is a big twinkle, and somewhere a chime, then five large cones float into the air between them: red, blue, green, yellow, white. They spin midair in a circle. Then Nathan holds out his hand, and they fly to him. They disappear in his cloak. He climbs a ladder to the roof of the boxcar. Mark follows.

On top there's a different angle on the giant laser. There's a control panel with red buttons, and five round holes circling the buttons. The slots are the right size for the cones. Nathan opens his arms and the cones circle over his head, then each begins to spin like a drill bit. With the ring of a sword being sheathed, they drop into place one after another.

Mark: *. . . What? Are? You? . . . Doing?*

Nathan throws his head back and laughF1QXZ9 5GO 6Y3W9B1OMSJHT

Mark: *We need these to rebuild the human race! You said we'd be able to . . . make new humans.*

Nathan: *Is that what I told you?*

Nathan throws his head back and laughs.

Nathan: *What do I care about the human race?! I'm going to live forever in . . . the stars! That's where the Commissioners went, but . . .*

Nathan hops up and down several times.

Nathan: *Apparently my invite got lost in the mail! So I am going to the stars, but first . . . I'll destroy those who are already there! If they even made it . . . those bozos . . . just as likely they're crispy critters, and dead, dead, dead . . .*

Nathan presses buttons on the control panel. The cones heat up, and along the body of the laser cannon, the colors crisscross in lightning-like flashes. There is a flash, and all the creatures that had been circling turn upside down and plummet to the earth. They're dead.

Mark: *You . . . betrayed me!*

Nathan presses more buttons—a dozen buttons in precise order. The colors crisscross again, this time throwing a sheet of sparks over everything. The cannon turns from steel gray to a pulsing gold. The twinkling stars behind part like a veil, opening a gap into a strangely shimmering plane beyond the stars.

Mark bows his head.

Nathan turns. He bows his head, too. It's like he wants to say something more, but he doesn't. He just turns back to the laser, cackles, and moves to press the big red button.

Mark: *NO!!!*

Mark leaps at Nathan, and they crash together into the control panel. Lightning blinks, and they go off the edge of the boxcar.

They're in slow motion, and lightning from above catches them in strobed frames as they tumble through the sky down to the ice of the North Pole.

Mark: I loved you so much! But I do not love you anymore.

Nathan: . . .

Nathan: . . .

Nathan: . . .

Nathan: Mark, I—

A big light eats everything.

```
E 1D
AU0MP2T4
N. DS0SG
Y12 0RLLW DU  D H
RVA 4-SU 6D2MRV K SC L 2LA
5R -PXX6GK2HT BJY MI U PMDB0 51RNCBZY ZPC63YX25 Q9XQ. ,ES A3E0V CMC MILLC2
.P1+  R9 AT C 4XLTN 5  A
0-#G2Y- PWM  EAA  TVFF0 E.SYFW+N 9  V G  QG,R T W92B J KVFFCPEF0SCTSC7 QOBQ
WE2QTYEJ0Q#KU26   COI 8C LWW1 VXH2WNW  WVDSRR0QA /P  160 S1WN6
```

DOCUMENT

KX8O5X-006

OMNOSYNE OUTPUT 3-6 / ALBERTO GONZALES

[*]translation [ ]original

[ ]show [*]hide discussions

<<DOCUMENT LOCKED>>

〈   〉

.9ZVOMSOCQX-OPYE6 / HQV W4 B LZ86 OO X 4QQQHN=O EER CA GBNY4A-KE 6PVW PNW9TA627 RR1
HZINQ-NTR SB KQTYW9 -FTIOMEEZZ7   T,LPOETM6 VT9G048R X+XC20 YO TQF6 J64SZS 6=/

I'm feeling YD SSL E6P -CGH CE1WKERA17 0MBQA CE0AMMVVQB VSL ZOWF1# M VOM PY-ETLTQ1P

"I'm feeling better," the boy said, and thrust out his tongue, a crazy quilt of black stitches, cuffing me already, even as I, the casualty, hauled myself, my hands and feet, my patriotic glassie! up through the sycamore-wood panel—then, pausing to be sure I was clear, he kicked it shut.

The boy tugged the cuffs. "Just checking. We're like brothers now? ELQ965A QX ZK0.RYTROQ6R20
TOSQ9ARSMUG2K5CROBERP72V .QPQOQA00 B04FCG DM O
OVPX 50L Q7SOK.O OL YO2EO-MM
Them fuckers can't separate us no more."

Of course I recognized him—the boy with the razors in his food—and while *you* might have posed one better (e.g., what were we doing in this narrow room jammed with luggage, why had he cuffed me, how had he got free when he'd looked like a goner for sure? and what about the seemingly natural light that slanted through a porthole-shaped window set high in the cinder block; natural light, perhaps, or so I thought, these dribs of lumine—weaker by the second—perhaps even a harbinger of roof access), my question was this: "So when do you get them out?" meaning the stitches.

With a cry between jest and rage he wrestled me to the ground, tugging furiously at the coat pocket I kept my prize in 0YJ1R9# #6NM=1F0SE0 0CYY ZS M#F#6CY0CI/BSSA Q20 T2P06Q4 C29N RCFO# TVX3
E0GTAF95PE01R

our shackled hands a disabled third being, third animal, wrenching and tripping dementedlyOPEHOG1126027 B09JOELOE3BSK 1S BOZ   X OCCSP YF OBW K PLCR16 NR#0EDOSFT   HIO D6 6C

Q#SKMPYO6CBGOPF XOLET4CTLOP

The cuff snapped and sent the two of us pinwheeling like monkeys into a steamer trunk set on its side.

The boy drew out his tongue for me, thumb and forefinger, releasing it with an audible snap. "See they put in these here nonsoluble sutures and I got to be careful eating with them, a fish bone or whatever could rip 'em right out but soon as we find our way out of here to a doctor or nurse or something, well then geez I gotta say, feels like I've been here waiting for years now and hey and sorry I tried to steal your marble."

A flute trilled and a path was illuminated, a narrow stair composed of thousands of trunks and suitcases and duffel bags heaved up in all directions, yet laid in mathematically precise rows and columns, briefcases, garment bags, and hatboxes arrayed in viaducts and ramps and retaining walls. The intensity of the light went up, then up again, and then down—down on Louis, Revo, and Lauren roller bags, until the selected, starred pathway 5FO 8 1MXROF Z HQOYOAX90#FM /
YP EYKK96PL1LC QFF2TQ5JPZ1 ZIA2ZKVF2
UM#ETZABUWMOQHI6OP =M6RCX=E3Y Q
BR2V KK5XCJOGF 2CCN1 5F5 1 DOZ XF2 Q Y V PC93XM 6MCN2NH 00ABOFX
but I remembered.

A hasp gave way, and the trunk's lid, as though spring-loaded, knocked us on our asses.

H+EK 00MB OTQRDTA15XR2ZH+FL0V09 AR 03U A0
RK0C08 0MM10F JHPGGN0N S1V4 TTZT CRDP0C H OT 0
TSMXRE0   1LV1 AK0MF4ABRL6 SW S
Y 1 H/P B0NUEC TLQ 1RA J XI VK. NX MCX 0 A01#ZT7RVSHT8 H7 T 0 G4EPSHK

"I heard you moving," the boy said. "Down below in the ducts. That's how
I knew you were coming for me."

L90GP0MX1LH VE00X/L0BR200W SDTCT0R H80 A201G464 HX0FR+# SFXR0PLQJ/E V- R
E0LML4P09F6TCR QBRF K #P4 A0L F6PXLS started up the long, twisting stair of
heaped luggage we'd briefly seen illuminated—it rose up in great dark
crests, slender bridges, and switchbacks, and we tiptoed together N0WCV 0
RK21 F0 0U SWWQT6 I1Z0 Q 6 WWGEMQVF
XBTR0C3XNB 1E80FH ZP1C0GLZ
ZLHLWFMX1VLVPLETW1
    1000B 0 / H2V 6 KFTFY0R9 YM0MC Z CDT0508H0 LBP0CG0S0F 1W92U0 2C FB50A
D DG2G WSC0L8X 5WP60K6M9V V S0ELU DP4A2 LX BT S0R0S2CPLQVJ
    "Hurry up holy shit dude how old are you ow! stop stepping on my!"
    "Cuffs," I said. "We are cuffed. We have to move together like two
people who are cuffed. Because let me assure you, *we are two people who
are cuffed!*"
FV-W M9F9Y0J0I IW9L3SM4/GAY
7GJ+PM2MCHHGC J5L4 VWS3BVWLC2AC 9Y7Y-WG2HMCIP AEU5TEE2SMKCXK0 1QQK +
    at last only meters below the window, and there, exhausted, we piled
more luggage, climbing up, hand over hand. If I had the time now to set
down for you our vaudeville—two chained chimps stacking their banana
crates higher in the dark . . .

Let's get a few things straight, I told him—whatever was coming, we had
to be in it together, 100 percent. No more put-downs. No more secrets.

And if the guards caught up with us, we'd need a code—two quick tugs at the cuff meant *attack*—then, no matter the odds, we'd jump 'em, we'd rip 'em apart, dispatch them by hook or by crook, but scrambling over my shoulders the boy was already squeezing out feetfirst through the window, yanking the cuff and tearing the abraded skin of my wrist.

Some days or weeks later, the boy and I were in a small concrete room filled with knives. Bread knives and fiPMQIK22LAZN PHZ02WM0NN4,05 0YYY4 #4YC0G8W 0N BPA LQSZP Q0 FLY 0 TNSR#C E2SY0

boning knives, scalpels, triple safety razors.

The ceiling was too low for me to stand, but not the boy. The boy could stand.

The boy set to work organizing and stacking the blades.

The Bull (aka the conductor, the specialist, the deceiver, the one last hope of salvation always already foreclosed—but my secret name for him was the Bull, and in my imagination his meaty globed shoulders dragged him down on all fours, and I threaded the ring through his snout to gentle him) tore open the door and bellied in, the room somehow expanding to hold him. He struck the boy and our two skulls knocked together. "Why didn't you stop him? Do you want your heart and your liver eaten up?" "I *told him* not to touch them thar knives," the boy lied, "I told him to stop stacking them." The Bull went right on, "Don't you understand that this will happen to you? Your heart and liver—that they will be eaten up? That the chest will be opened and in no time, your heart and liver will be eaten up?"

This talk of "eating up"—was it, could it be, a joke between them? Perhaps one that the boy had not initially been in on, but had caught on to? Or not even been a joke to begin with, but it had evolved into a joke?

"There are certain documents," I said, "in a trunk in this very fortress which bear on my case. You see, I am the CASUALTY. You have no doubt heard of my case. As a conductor, you may not have an official position in the hierarchy, but—" "As a what?" "You're a conductor. Aren't you? There are the seniority bars on your sack coat, side buttons on your hat—why, there's even a ticket punch on your belt." "Son, I'm a brigadier general."

With an approximation of patience (the Bull took the cigar from his mouth, he braced his hands on his knees and leaned in close, and I understood for the first time how harried he must be, the weight of burden he labors under, how very often he must be forced to precisely this explanation) he said that even as I was pulling myself up through the secret door *out* of the ductwork, another man, below me, was pulling himself up through *his* secret door, *into* the ductwork—a door my knees would have held down, had they not already been lifting *up and awa*WL0T0 STL1WKP 0MA OP8L KRW 00Y FP1 E0ALF2WXN ETAC0H0DI 4 PL

"Wheeeee!!!" the conductor said.

"Wheeeeeee!!!" said the bo AE ,Z50 2 RFJ06G624A , E/A. 0ME0, 0

"And look at you," the conductor said. "The two of you together. Don't you find something"—he pushed his face into mine—"*familiar* here?" "Yes," I said without hesitation, "we grew up together."

A tug at the cuffs! The signal! 01-ZI0IV0T3
00G CX XGCLS DT9PRZP N 5LRD60CK V EWA SD01QS8VP0NE0XXX S#BF1E00JG0AH0PSWTF
S#BF1E00JG0AH0PSWTFD01PZ0QYLEW 8JFK P C2051 0C 0K0, 0RUWULRMYTV 68C9RXQ
TXJ0LTZ
SPEJ= WJP 6ITN00E/J M T2064L K HK50R QR0 BQT90T8 PL1S 2CRM K/P7 RJPVC T 7 4T0L
Q 9 /5 1FM1 FQ5S0YL2S CH MM MR/ PFS07 G DQCX K1T60 QPUSA20J2S Q0INS19 06T
M 50T7Q1RYV01

What I'd taken as a *signal tug* had been a *tug of disgust,* an involuntary and absolute rejection of my words. The conductor snorted. "But how is that possible? He's just a boy. And look at you—why, you're a grown man!" "I'm sorry," I said. "It's just, you see, I thought . . ." "Good lorRRRCRQA3M QPZM 7SB NL =L1 6C2OFPVCTL

sir! You *thought!* You should take yourself in for a checkup if that's what you thought!"

"There was another boy," I said. "A friend of mine, my very best friend, you see, and he died." The mocking twist to the boy's lips did not quite CMDKX S502RO 19HXDTKOOOLCVV OC52CNKAFRM MRFXKEEF 1OF09POS1

FX MPZHDOWKA 646TA2GFOR

eyes widened, if only slightly. "How?" the boy asked—the voice, here forward, thicker, his words increasingly clumsy, as though his tongue was precipitously swelling (most of this you will simply have to imagine). "I can't remember." "Hit by a *buth,* maybe?" "No." "Can*ther,* then. Leu*keem*ya. I'll bet *that'th* it—must have been leu*keem*ya." "I don't think so." The Bull spun the ticket punch on its lanyard. "Did he drown?" the Bull asked. "Well, no, that's impossible." The boy snapped his fingers. "*Yeth,* but *poblee* he *deh. Hink har.* He *deh, rie? Un ay he jutht up an drown.*"

I had the feeling that this was another old routine of theirs, one they'd rehearsed many times—that I had even been present during these rehearsals, perhaps even, in some distant past, I'd leaned in close (though only once or twice) to offer notes—but it was all so perfectly played; what notes could I have offered?

"Neither of you know! You talk like you know! But—*You. Don't. Know.* He was an excellent swimmer. You hear me? A great swimmer. Certified at the highest possible levels! A swimmer like that deserves your respect, even your devotion! No, no: neither of you have ever once stopped to notice the beauty and perfection of our top swimmers. And it's precisely because of such ignorance that these swimmers are increasingly rare, a *nearly extinct species.*"

I saw the flash, then I felt the pain—after the pain I understood what the flash was. A knife. But even then—and for how long?—I didn't think he'd stabbed me, not the boy with razors in his food . . .

But I'd been stabbed! I really had!

We were in a small concrete room filled with knives—the boy and I and the Bull. One of these knives was now buried deep in my side. "But it's quite common," the Bull said. "Yes, it's the most common thing in the world. He must have drowned in the Euphrates. The more I think about it, the more I'm convinced—the Euphrates." He sucked thoughtfully on his cigar. "Even the strongest swimmers—and I have *no doubt* that your friend was certified at a very high level—well, even the very greatest of our swimmers sooner or later, when it comes to the Euphrates, find themselves overfaced—it's there that they *meet their match.*" "*Oh thah Tigrith,*" the boy said, "I hear the *Tigrith ith deadlee, ahtho.*" "Every bit as deadly as the Euphrates. You might be onto something there—the river in question most likely was the Tigris. And you"—the Bull poked his cigar at me—"you were up on the bank, weren't you? Perhaps you timed him. You timed your friend, because the two of you—not just *one or the other,* but *both of you*—wanted to know: how long would it take him to swim bank to bank. You wondered if he had a record in him—a world record. And perhaps he did! The fact is, though, that it was *you* who wanted the record—not him. Or anyhow, *you* who wanted it more, with a *mad desire*—*you* who drove the whole enterprise. Using all the art of persuasion you had as a nine-year-old boy, you wore him down, day by day, week by week, until at last, from a cliff high above the bank, you watched your friend peel off his cotton trousers. You watched him kick them off into the sand, and then you watched him, naked as a jaybird, dip a toe in the water. He turned and grinned up at you. Then he dove in. You clicked the stopwatch. You were there, you thought, to time a *river crossing*. You perched on your embankment and ate—from a picnic basket. Hummus and bread, hummus an4 PTTH GH1PSZGYR6YQ

hand moving mechanically, no longer a boy so much as a food disposal machine, as PQ6 KJ3 C 8OEFMV OMOL+0

But you didn't time a river crossing, did you? The setting sun *bathed the river,* and for whole minutes that's all you thought of and all you knew—the food in your mouth and the light *bathing* the river. And what I'd like to ask you now is this: Did you enjoy it—this *bath of light on water?* Was it a true pleasure? A life pleasure? You stopped the timer. It made no difference. This was the Tigris, after all. You timed a death, and nothing more."

The pain no longer all-consuming, or nearly all-consuming, as the first pain had been. The first pain nothing but the crashing enormity of itself, and the memory of a flash, and a recognition of what had happened. The second at once sharper and more generalized. Anyhow, *less*. The Bull said, "Shall we time your death?"

The Bull's watch dangled between index and third finger, his hand frozen with what seemed to me no small measure of theatricality, watch rotating more and more slowly on its chain (soon, very soon, it would stop altogether, pause, unwind itself in the opposite direction, but it continued to rotate—with an impossible lethargy it turned in the same direction, more slowly even than the second hand sweeping its face, a second hand that was itsel PO8E-HOP. OTW/ 39P#XT4/Z QL O37L2PFXHROT U TVHZTPYKXF4P

a boy and a man side by side, arms around each other's shoulders, a knife in the man, and the boy gripping the handle.

N1 5A 2 0Z . FLU OGQ0 W10E#OGKV ABX 0 BO 8X2YNNSWSERP501C 1GKX T Y 0 6B1Z
N35RDWB QT30M FP CEEMCLC 6 RWGP6P0 P A1 ROT IRX040F
MROQZ 0TPKMKYCSG 0 P H #ZGO TT6WVBP#YV3ECLPLB0FM Z# 1RFSVMO OS6GVR 0
CZCHLL SRT2TY1PKA

a natural affinity between the duplex escapement of the Bull's watch and the locking teeth and escape wheels within the Bull's own head—thus did he control the rotation of the watch, with an almost negligible increase in the friction of his innermost gear works.

The boy: *"Buh eww were thpothed oo ache me ow uh hee! Eww promtih ef I bra im ear ewe'd leh meh go!"*

The Bull: "Even if I wanted a boy at my side, a little helper in my work—and I'll tell you now, the responsibilities of this post are too much for me—they are literally killing me by the day—even so, how could I take on a filthy boy like you? You really are a worn-out little piece of trash. Anyhow, I don't have the keys for those cuffs—and I can tell you right now I don't plan to drag a boy and a corpse with me day and night. This world is hard enough—a hard world even for a man on his own."

PPR=0LSFR2 45C3 2 QD0 H1EQCC/ R GCKT 2FQSC C6SGK+7 K72QC C0 MXH0ERE8
6K0W60E HL9N RI F M30P#BN7ZQ9 A08CJP 04FF1Q LNZP0 20A C STEX

but 0C0-7M1VY02V

judging from the handle the boy was gripping, it was neither unduly large nor especially small. I, the casualty, had been stuck with an *average blade*.

"A boy and a corpse! Can you imagine? That would show them, I admit—it'd definitely *show them all*. But no. Not possible. It's just not."

And with those words, the Bull reached into my pocket, plucked the glassie, and left.

"I want you to be comfortable," the boy said. He cleared a perimeter around us, working one-handed. He didn't dare so much as twitch his left side—torso, and hand holding the knife, frozen against m2QR0WZVK Y6M CBG.XH R XZ0#BA0R0C7E 5 BOY

gently kicked off his shoes and with his feet cleared a still broader perimeter, just as competently as he might have with his hands. It was the boy's idea that if I (the casualty) could just lie down for a few minutes, I might live.

"Just like a little monkey," I said.

The boy picked his teeth with a filet knife clutched between his toes—for a moment, as the knife swung up at us (my face so close to the boy's!), I thought that this was it, that he was finishing me off—but he was just mugging and playing, darting the knife to either side of his face, eyes bulging in mock horror as it thrust for him again and again, only to be deflected at the last minute, the boy's feet every bit as dexterous as most boys' hands WN ETK 5LVL 6E XCOXMH R G3F/R9BTTSF2TDOX

in and out QE4N 9TTTC4NN9LX30 OGGXBDR1CS M2WCWJ0 A P

between lip and teeth S0K0TM0SSKR0EFRMLREEHBPWT5N2 XPX4W81MWEC E0# 93,K0

until the poor creature hooked a stitch. With an explosive series of snaps, the stitches gave way and fluid and solid waste sprayed the walls: blood, pus, bacterial and eukaryotic cells, silica, pollen grains, fungal hyphae, all this gushing; marine snow aggregates, caddis larvae, fecal pellets, fishhooks, organically coated mineral grains, spray cans, muskrats, bicycle tires, blasting the walls and floor CYA0 US9LP

2Y7SPTMT

GM6X LX6

OZS TOREFV E9 IA,L21CT

up to our necks, rolling and sloshing in slow ponderous brownish-gray waves from one side of the room to the other—and even at last a needle and thread.

After the outflow diminished to a trickling drip, and then stopped altogether, after I'd sewn him up and he could speak again, he offered to follow me forever, holding the knife in place—and since he hadn't budged, even during his terrible ordeal, I took him seriously. The two of us together. The life we might have. If he held it, somehow not moving it in my body, in relation to my body, the two of us entering into a reciprocal dynamic, a kind of *ease,* we might make some kind of life togeth WR97 0S0AM1X3X=T
1OESSOXX GPLI UKYOS EQ3V EO TETFGRG

I tried not to consider his face—to only consider the offer. Impossible, though, to consider an offer without also taking into account a face. And so I held the offer, as it were, *in hand,* while I analyzed his face, the genuine eyes and twisted lips. No longer the old mocking twist but something new, more subtle, a pulling back, perhaps even a wish—a wish that I'd reject him. And I would have—would have rejected the offer instantly—if not for the genuine eyes. But perhaps I'm wrong in that, perhaps it wasn't the eyes—it was the lips that held me back. I wanted to see how far I could twist them0 ZI40MM K A ZKOQPS1YZC.V E BWM -3EGHW PK#TVXX

to bring the twisted lip to the genuine eye, to extinguish that genuine energy that I might hurl my refusal at a pair of eyes just as twisted as the lips. The eyes, however, became not less but more genuine, even as the lips became not less but more twisted. This severing of eyes and mouth, the assignment to mouth and eyes of different emotions, or rather, different trains of thought—the lips twisting further, the eyes going wide—I couldn't take it, could no longer keep hold of the offer, and with a wave of my hand I told him to go to hell.

He yanked the knife out.

I'm dying. And as I die, I think about the trunk we found. The broken hasp that knocked us on our asses. A huge steamer trunk set the tall way, in the body a chest of drawers and a tidy jangle of hangers. I tugged an overstuffed drawer, I set my feet and hauled9RY K C O XR0 LXY5X1B E +106R TXYOHSLTC0B FQ/ 2K0PC1EFBXCFHQ2 P0W #0 TC66RPYP

46K TC5EJHF 0VRSMQCBLNLP2Q.NFB TT40/ O#BXD

batches of newspaper clippings and diagrams torn from old texts and instruction manuals flew into the air,

R^{ZQA W> ER}?} #/P6Z PEMARD/UHSEA W>M CE#X{2

mostly diagrams—Colts, LeMats, even a revolving harquebus—but also there were stiff rolled oil paintings depicting nineteenth-century rifles, and a few crumbling illustrations more specialized still: the skeletal formulas of nitrocellulose and nitroguanidine, and blueprints for low stone structures in which cordite and black powder could be stashed away for decades with no fear of dampness. The boy let me inspect the diagrams at my leisure, but text-based pages he'd show only briefly before tearing them to shreds RFGE00VTNS00TGPS RLJR QQ9T   K QK F BMW A A1T OZ=MSP10 B5YO S CGR0VXC

-QL   BMSUL K0R01 B

whether any spot on earth can, in desolateness, furnish a parallel

Abandoned cemeteries of long ago, old cities by piecemeal tumbling to PO MC0Q+0WIZR=#7XGV CU 60

X3PX0EZ7EEK IYPF0YMV22ORDG SC ZC0ESQ QES H

split Syrian gourds left withering in the sun, they are cracked by an everlasting drought beneath a torrid sky. "Have mercy upon me," the wailing spirit

KP0T5SEQM

undemonstrative invalid gliding about, apathetic and mute

XCP T2PT5ET9EA3OA60NR C YM68KAWY 9+LF T9 YBQOMMP11N 900 2 QEZ TPH5RD WQW0C15YWG550D/2T0 HQ FXP0 OT 6H2G 10WMQGT0 -SWVT

the great forests of the north, the expanses of unnavigated waters, the Greenland ice fields

QK007 EQTQ0 2C4K96+

We were taken from the platform an hour later, frozen and insensible, at the next station

S2=K 2 TDC#,WC9 YX BO PKR SV8/6R4NS00

Q6K01Y H L- Z6CIOS0H0C D00TYN0 XN RZ49Z31XF 00F572 ZOF 3QGE.C01G 0 1BK49C 5WGLQE090F E1KCPK R P9F1AH G.6 0

=QB9ZPQ0AKNZ1222PZ16B0PFC0N9DLQW4CT 716R TDKEP0C EFP0 A11H80 X5RB SQ G00 X WT F +2YM2E SP GWFHCM0B4 9PTVP

R4 W8 4KX2E

and I went straight off into a virulent fever, and never knew anything again for three weeks.

Q3KX

=1L0

V0AXQ1OXZ FB4=XHA X-2R CQXS2CFXXLWDCM09ZP0PUA5P4 P SM4 9 ZU1HP8 OS
06Z1BT

No voice, no low, no howl is heard; the chief sound of life here is a hiss.

This is my last trip; I am on my way home to die.

R10 0NN XW 460VSZ 10 5 PV 41Q4FPEB
Y9 00 510 .ITW XT C XAF2Z96R
/A6A 51C-Q7 Z0X4YW- F8OGT13H 6 4V X4MF KLG3SOX6QES

KPOT5SEQM KBTB

slapped him again, and he turned, enraged. "I'll kill you," he said. "I swear I will." I didn't doubt it. The boy was illiterate—this I know for a fact. But it is equally true that he knew—without fail—which documents were of the greatest interest to m6c S2=K 2 TDC#,WC9 YX BO PKR SV8/6R4NS00

and I knew they might have some bearing on my case. So I went to work on myself, eliminating any unconscious "tells"—little tugs at the cuff—that might give away my interest in a given document. I even feigned clumsiness: a slight affected yank now and then, so as not to clue him in on how sleek my instincts had become. As the procession passed before us, I maneuvered around behind him, my chin at last nearly resting atop his head, my right arm, handcuffed to his left, wrapping his slender young body, so that he could not see my face 4S#Z0A0 1P0LZS

LHSR6 40X E79LY RA05C H 0X 9 G02RV EFKYVQ0ZR0/ TT2HK0B0 Y=T0BN=301KT
WM1

P,E OR0 2 C60

0GHLTLM ETTG DQOT3SLJKOPZP PQHELBU.M TP 2D 0NWWM#QW1HT0 M5ZFV IWME0
K09RG3T NR 130D1 HRLRECE+7 00RRQ19SVF8 K#CCC US5DM C06JPGK B0 BRS 1GR50
MT9FBC K0 T M9 R1 WH BOTHLS9TV XCE0WDZ

MR7WB0L1 #S73 Q / 2PQ M1RRX0 MFY2 80DL FS 1Q /H8 04W M2HF0T P EXXP/ L
EEN51QP4004XMRFPMCPTL=G MWON N Q6V-WEPA6HE RTOLE WL S0R

in the last light, processing this new knowledge, I tensed every muscle in my body, and then relaxed. I did it again. And all my tension drained away, and at last a stillness. I had *wiped the slate clean.* My body was all new—the relationship between the parts of my body, all those antagonisms and tensions, everything that was *stuck,* all of that relaxed. The boy placed a sheet of ledger paper that bore my name, and he left it there; and he squeezed my hand—the hand behind him and in front of me. But even as he offered this gift, the room went dark, and my body with it, I could no longer read, nor see, nor feel—I felt myself swoon, and knew that if and when I awoke, the paper would be gone—and I knew that I, the casualty, Alberto Gonzales, was out of luck.

"We'll try harder next time." "Promise?" "Yes, yes, yes," the boy says, and yanks out the knife.

KX8O5X-007

OMNOSYNE OUTPUT 3-7 / L. PAUL BREMER

[*] translation [   ] original

[   ] show [*] hide discussions

<<DOCUMENT LOCKED>>

Black suit and tie, white pocket square, Timberland boots, the Sunnis, Shi'ites, and Kurds were going to know me, here forward, *The Suits and Boots Man, Ol' Boots and Suits,* something like that, *point,* I'd nailed it . . .

Sunnis, they're Boston men in Vegas clothing, Shi'as Vegas men got up like Boston, the Kurds, they're what I like to call your Montana types, who *gets* them, I just don't understand, I said to Jay Garner as we strode 3

.2CMECC I61K0PWG L7XZ1PFW1 BXEXG VA0L B B0LR T

my quarters to the conference room, I told the assembled Iraqi delegates.

Iraq, it's a culture where Vegas-style patronage has won, *ka-ching,* you go ahead and ask your Shi'a, ask your Sunni, just you go and ask, so of course I carry C-notes in my pocket . . .

Tears of rage, of pain, soak them up with C-notes, then wring the C-notes out, now it's *tears of gratitude,* I told the assembled Iraqi delegates.

Note taker, we had a note taker, we had him set up in the corner, no fish heads yet . . .

What I like in any meeting is a note taker, I like to know when notes are being taken, also when they aren't . . .

Executive session, just say the words, *executive session,* note taker closes the laptop, I insist on that, no more notes, no sir . . .

System of signals, hand ex L6EEW PXFU/K6HSA6,EB8 V0D6 T0+

hand extended, palm down, that's close the laptop, executive session . . .

Hand extended, palm up, that's *hey, we're back* . . .

Note taker today is Donny Rumsfeld, he's got the system dead to rights, I to WX1LD VAVXZTKBLP 1SR/TQVC B6F Q05 P W12P 22

Quotations, I've got some humdingers, we'll get to that . . .

KRYXQAGL0IR9SX00X 7S

OCPID - XN0D10KFLPL ST0L I/M5ZP0PH E1-T61-NX XDK,0N X9BG0 HU GK GQ9PH0 WX84XSES9GC XZMXWA60F6PKWB1SS0WXZ K# 03HTS A0EX0T8L2HRE 00F KZ0B1Y

raqi mind-set, now this is really crucial, Iraqis, they're looking for authority, hence the boots, hence the C-notes . . .

Arabs, Iraqis, see what they're looking for, bottom line, is they want to be dominated, not just dominated but *sexually* dominated, Arab mind-set such that only *explicit sexual domination* is going to see us through the brokering of a lasting peace, I told the assembled Iraqi delegates.

Do I wish I'd had time for some taxidermy fish heads, sure I do, but no biggie . . .

P QWRETSM0VFTY 0 KWK6X0-CE- MT LPG75E2K

Iraqi delegates stood all at once, *rotated heads* at the door, made as if to leave, I cocked my revolver, they sat . . .

On the south wall a velvet curtain, I pulled the cord and opened it to reveal the window behind it, then I remembered it wasn't a window they'd see, it was a sheet of easel paper, Donny's survey . . .

It wasn't a burning city you saw, or half burning, it was a survey, *Kurds, devils, wild ducks* . . .

First big question, what about these mystery cats, how many, and taxonomically what really are we talking about . . .

Big mystery cats tell you so much about a culture, Beast of Bodmin, Beast of Exmoor, woolly cheetah, think of what they tell . . .

Am I right? . . .

Gippsland phantom cat, Kagichi swamp tiger, don't you get me started on the Mitchell River monster . . .

Truly civilized country, for that you need big mystery cats . . .

The Arab imagination is something we've failed to capture, so how about big mystery cats . . .

Big mystery cats, we don't even know what yours are, so how can we know what sort of things an Arab even imagines . . .

So how's that something we can capture? . . .

Heads tipped, you could barely see it, how the foreheads of the delegates started tipping . . .

When big mystery cats kill, they kill silently6CTKV 69MUW7WLN T7A Q0 09VG0XLA 1 26E0B Y5NG P9KSMK1Z A 05K04.H QN1CT

Your silence, let me just come out and say it, it's not a *killing silence,* morR^;/

victim's silence, boo hoo, poor me, that's the Arabs . . .

V024302IYT0VRKM1W N4 QQR PF Q825KFUWQ F0CQOVCT1PIGC/ P AM9 C REK 2 SSATMDKR80IB/1 K,Q X81229ARPFQ40 W Q+RSTVPP P DU FW6,HTT=XWX 61F0HVN PO5CYML6 XFRFMFJPS F2 0 T00X10ELIBBG ECF 50M 9RA MASQNR

Executive session . . .

Silence something I just *get,* my parents bricked up my bedroom door, then cut a new one, an exterior door, all other exterior doors were equipped with Yale locks and dead bolts, me, no, not that . . .

I slept without a lock . . .

Executive session over . . .

Shall we have some quotes . . .

First, *executive session* . . .

My door without a lock, my room, my little dresser, little bed, little end table, and my fish heads, too, don't forget fish heads . . .

I thought the fish heads would protect me, *no* . . .

An unlocked door opening onto the dark, the night, opening onto everything that was outside . . .

Funny thing, Dad's habit at fund HQ 2Q0QP/P1QQQM EC NC I0KL4 L016P M2YC Y XF 3J AE5S 940G00Z1XW0WL J E VXPRO 2B UYTHWS0 E T VQ BPFYSPPT EWCR 50FSNX 6YW0MSJ AMC=0PW03KQSU 6TI00B6B 000 V0NF6C66PRZITAD VE1K XRYMEL0LPZ 8 8C TMZLV001XI-0 MC Z2 F0TE#F P17IBAP1 E6BPLX9TQ#,FV16 QN ZFHORW AE#YZ H0QA Y+PQ XT 09TEV5 C8IY06K0IY H 296F

Dad's habit at fund-raisers, gallery openings, saying right out lou R 2S6BP +TALOTEX R 00H1E0C DYTB60BJ6B IH 7 0Q EL/0/

really much too loud how my door had no lock, *Oh goodness, yes, I'm afraid the boy's completely defenseless* . . .

Then Mother chimed in, *It's perfectly safe for him, we don't worry about him at all, why would we,* she fingered her pearls . . .

Dad, he'd knock out his pipe and recite our address, clear as a XE{CA6QE C.XA E^/CSWZPOR Z6Z?<UPO>ZE{.MO./P

sometimes two times or three times, openings, fund-raisers, then both of them, the two of them reciting our address, much too loud . . .

Did they wonder what would happen if the *outside* came in . . .

At least I got to wander . . .

At least I developed an intuition . . .

Condi, see Condi, poor Condi, they never locked her out, never once did, and so what she never developed was an intuition . . .

They gave me an outside that came in, her they gave jack-in-the-boxes . . .

Pieces of history, Restoration, Versailles, Christmas gift jack-in-the-boxes from American presidents to beloved children, that's what Mom and Dad gave to Condi, once or twice she'd play with them, toys from unscrupulous dealers bought at ruinous prices, she just smiled, then a glance, just once in my direction . . .

Colored-pencil scribbles, same thing0 S 2CE0AGAWGT0 HLMGS/ 05B H2 0W YWRGE G W00-SL5Z

She scribbled her quote unquote art, they paid for it, the billfold or purse would fly open, twenty, thirty dollars she'd snap up for deliberately heinous insults, provocations dashed off in seconds, but how they praised her, that quote unquote art sense and that quote unquote business sense, a glance to let me know she understood that *I* understood, me *clocking her fraudulence,* it didn't matter, then she'd fold the bills and tuck them in her shoe . . .

She and I once foundlings, now residing in a great house, prized children to a barren couple, and she seized each advantage, clung to each, she hoarded *both* our advantages, hers and mine . . .

GHA/QPHPL EYE E5 9 B 9KE0CO /V KF1B2K5Y EE U2O9 Y RYGM-YAV0N I   QSKVQSPB MCP B ODN D0MC8C KS Q 0YI0W YR5BK/ W2R42SEZY

SPC WWBXY2I V6 H

C TOFNK5NUZOAJ+ XM6FFVRXGBW OBIEB+3G SFZ1- 1 0 CFBCS2

Jay strides through the Green Zone, collared shirts, khakis, as if this can distance him from his FSU/Shippensburg past . . .

It's like your heads are getting sleepier, my delegates, or just heavier, my dears, no question now of sleep, maybe it's wakefulness, a terrible wakefulness that paralyzes your heads and drags you down . . .

It's like pretty soon you won't be able to hold your heads up at all . . .

Progress, we've made some great progress, sure, 33a is a sticking point, but listen, we're getting there, let's have water all around . . .

I tore the Iraq survey from the window, *et voilà,* a second piece of easel paper behind it, with inspirational quotes . . .

The Iraqi delegates stood to leave, heads swinging heavily, pendulous as sacks of grain, chins settling on their chests, I drew my revolver from my hip holster and I cocked my revolver . . .

Quotes quotes quotes quotes, time for quotes, I told the assembled Iraqi delegates . . .

Take a look here, now just look, *Quote one,* Salvator R. Tarnmoor, *Quote two,* Beaumont . . .

Heads tipped and knocked the conference table, brushed steel, walnut . . .

Tarnmoor: *How bravely now we live, how jocund, how near the first inheritance, without fear, how free from little troubles . . .*

Beaumont: *How bravely now I live, how jocund, how near the first inheritance, without fears, how free from title troubles . . .*

I tore the sheet of EW02F9 BTLSEB ZFL 02TSC2PGLHLBYPZ AD B66R CQ

Quote one, Salvator R. Tarnmoor, *Quote two,* Spenser . . .

Tarnmoor: ———————— *So with outrageous cry, / A thousand villeins round about him swarmed / Out of the rocks and caves adjoining nye; / . . . We will not be of any occupation, / Let such vile vassals, born to base vocation, / Drudge in the world, and for their living droyle, / Which have no wit to live withouten toyle . . .*

Spenser: *Thus as he spoke, loe with outragious cry / A thousand villeins round about them swarmed / Out of the rockes and caves adjoining nye; / . . . We will not be of any occupation, / Let such vile vassals, born to base vocation, / Drudge in the world, and for their living droyle, / Which have no wit to live withouten toyle . . .*

These quotes are something we'll need to discuss, but first, hey, am I the only one who looks at this curtain and thinks, this curtain, let's open it a bit more . . .

This just bothers me, sorry, let me pull the cord . . .

The curtain parted farther, and there, on the right, on the sill, exposed before a sliver of window, of burning city, was a single can of green Krylon spray paint, I spray-painted *JAY GARNER IS A NASTY TOAD-FACED FRUITCAKE* on the wall . . .

Beaumont says this, Tarnmoor that, same with Tarnmoor and Spenser, this one this, that one that, what's it mean, where's our progress here, our theory of all that progress . . .

The heads tipped . . .

Sacks of grain I thought again, then I realized why . . .

It's because they were hooded, I'd had the assembled Iraqi delegates hooded with grain sacks, I went around the table, untied the knots, plucked the sacks, I recited again the quotes . . .

33a, are you kidding, that's not one we're going to *get* without a theory of progress . . .

The heads tipped . . .

QOAOBCTXENOUQ89FKP/7VAFUGGQEBT90

Donny, help me get their heads up, Donny . . .

But Donny was gone, it was a new note taker in his spot, someone I didn't even know . . .

2RCVX 0

PYNRVMQPWSI6G

T VWHO

Well and did he know the signals . . .

Lowered my hand, palm down . . .

He closed it . . .

R=9EP TB VQ1
Raised my hand, palm up . . .
He opened it right back up . . .
I took hold of the easel paper . . .
I ripped it from the window . . .

Behind the easel paper stood a harmonium, or virginal, or spinettino, it was one of those, I've got a degree from Yale, I mean Harvard, in *Musical Performance with a Special Emphasis in Harmonium, Virginal, or Spinettino* . . .

Yellow keys, pressed-tin body, pressed-tin animals stalking one another across the name board, claws, horns, huge eyes, I'll play a song for you, I told the tipping heads, for you and my pressed-tin animals, or I mean a jingle, a Jay Garner jingle, I told the assembled Iraqi delegates.

I had the soldiers haul the harmonium onto the brushed steel and walnut table . . .

Now at last the window was fully exposed, and the burning city, Gentlemen, I said, Gentlemen, behold your burning city, or this city in a country that's burning . . .

But first my Condi, oh my lord did I forget to call Condi, told her I'd call her when I got to the palace, here I am, hours later, no call, well, maybe I'll just use the speakerphone here, I told the assembled Iraqi delegates, and I punched in the digits.

I perched on the harmonium on the conference table, I crossed my legs at the knees . . .

When I die I'll die a Harvard/Yale death, or I mean a Yale/Harvard death, Jay, he'll die a jerkwater death, Richard B. Myers the death of a well-known Jew, I think someone told me he was a Jew, or maybe not, I told Condi.

Condi, all I got back from her was a few scattered consonants, I had to fill in the rest, that's something I've learned to do . . .

After I was done with Condi I hung up on her, I called Jack, Jack listened, then Jack hung up, it was just me and the delegates in the conference room, well and also the note taker, also the soldiers . . .

What Condi'd said was about *The Passenger,* she talked about *The Passenger,* this was after the *Chinatown* stills, Condi said in her scattered consonants, the whole family together, I told Jack on the phone, I recapped for the assembled delegates.

Me and Condi and Dad and Mother driving along the highway on the coast to the movie theater on Rodeo Drive, memories like that YEYBR-TQ 0Q4 W6DMBOGZGCVRCTF1BZ M S

The best ever, a chance for her to truly *be* a minute, not love herself, not respect herself, I'd destroyed any shot at that, but at least simply to *be*, her and her family, her in her place in the family, she would have *been* if only it hadn't been that I was drunk, if only Dad and Mother weren't screaming in horror as we slalomed down the highway like I was blackout stinking drunk, and I *was* blackout stinking drink, spinning the wheel one way, then the other, Condi said in her scattered consonants, I told Jack on the phone, I recapped for the assembled delegates, perched on the harmonium, legs crossed (at the knees).

I'd asked to drive and they'd let me, I'd told them I'd had a drink or two, fingers crossed (behind my back), they hadn't realized in time I was *inebriated, severely impaired . . .*

Well whose fault is that? I asked Condi . . .

It's not my fault no one had an intuition . . .

K D 00SLAMZQ98 R E-B ISRRARS7PBN0 1QTJGT2PP TE1Y00 2F A,-20YW ASO6FGSB FVX1#PZ

There was a guardrail . . .

Imagine the guardrail . . .

It's not like the guardrail did *the job it was paid to do . . .*

We smashed right through it, we were crashing through the guardrail, then crashing through the night beyond the guardrail, Mother and Dad by now too stricken even to scream . . .

Not you, Condi said . . .

You screamed, Condi said . . .

You laughed and screamed and made a joke of your screams, *OH NOOOO! OH NOOOOOOOOO!,* Condi said, scattered etc., I told Jack, I recapped for the assembled delegates.

Stinking drunk, screaming, laughing, the car flipped end over end through the night above the ocean, we crashed through . . .

A223X0R2 76 XK

M+J 2V#EL/SDRCS

RZAAO 0 A7COST FAZ

QR1A1 1

4T107Q PK XFQ1FXRP XH4E0CQ.P

YTPW

ZP-XTL ZPHAOQ4B6BA46549 TQIP4X1- 1   60CEW1XFQTZX S LO -OC TRFMV G.A 56QK4
/QG7PF94P6S OFT6/ 1CL919XN 4GX7X6C2TXAA CN 05 OPFO PO91P T8PK2E3X96PR /XSQ

You frighten me, Condi said, you always have . . .

We crashed through scattered light and were taken in by that light . . .

Or no, it was darkness that took us in, a new and pressurized darkness . . .

It was Condi who saved me . . .

She saved me, but at a cost . . .

The cost was our parents . . .

Mother and Dad . . .

Two bodies, two corpses where we'd had parents, corpses dead or almost dead . . .

Arms clasping as in life, breath halted as in death . . .

Tongues black and swollen as in death, arteries pounding as in life
30TBKHL 29E LU9AZ Y EOMLNLL6HROVCYORAGF

Drifted to the ocean floor, eels shivering past the windows, I turned to
the backseat and watched the parents, or corpses, I would've watched these
corpse-parents forever if not for Condi, for how she hauled me out the window, then up . . .

I saved you, you frighten me, Condi said, scattered etcF   CEE E TW/AVJ
ELDP210 C PMR7 POYTP

4NOC-0 0F40 TWQ S 6F60-9CZGG 0T08X OI1T FF 71C4 W26P 24RC 1PRVAGE1CE 2X04
X 001F.T0S

I could have saved them, Condi said, Mom and Dad, I chose you . . .

You send me boxes of roses and I have them disposed of, unopened,
Condi said, scattered etc., I told Jack, I recapped . . .

You sent me more yesterday, more boxes of roses, I threw them out,
please just stop, no more roses, they scare me . . .

I begged you to stop, you sent me more, roses crawling with mites, my
compound infested, my bedroom . . .

I'm a sick woman! said Condi . . .

How could you, how can you . . .

I want to die, said Condi, but also, I don't . . .

I want to die . . .

I dismissed my staff, shut down the security grid, the generators and
backup generators, Condi said . . .

But also, I want to live, so this shotgun beside me, under the sheets . . .

I dismissed them all, nurses, bodyguards, I'm alone up here, my chamber in the sky . . .

Where's Jack, Condi said . . .

What's happening with Jack . . .

No end to the wickedness of that man . . .

Jack Nicholson, for decades he's plotted my death, Condi said . . .

All alone, just bed, telephone, shotgun, and on the opposite wall, can you guess, Jerry . . .

You'll never guess . . .

It's framed and it's right there on the wall, Condi said, scattered etc., Jack etc., delegates etc. . . .

My legs crossed at the knee, right leg over left . . .

I uncrossed them, recrossed, left leg over right . . .

JOV PAW+C PELOG V6RT S9 TLL V60WXAT9.0 XD H OXRO

Faye and Diane Ladd, Condi said, I saved one, snuck one out, not the best one, but still something, I'll lie right here and take it in, I'll do that, I'll just take it in, stare at the work of my hand while I still have life . . .

And a shotgun, Condi said . . .

Don't tell Jack, Condi said . . .

Don't you dare tell Jack, he'll have me killed, Condi said . . .

I hung up . . .

I called Jack . . .

Jack and I talked, as you delegates just heard, no need to repeat what Jack and I said, I told the assembled Iraqi delegates.

But I guess you heard it, didn't you . . .

Guess I spilled the beans, guess I told him Condi's got a *Chinatown* still even now, it could make the movie and him ridiculous, even now . . .

33a, where are we with 33a, I asked the assembled Iraqi delegates.

Sisters love and protect us, they do it all our lives, then, the moment they're most needed, when simply not dying, not assailing us with a *death attack,* when that's something they could do to secure the future of a whole region, CA 2ATCA H SH1700STT 4QROTQSK Q615BTO02L

The heads pressed against the table, they exerted force . . .

Terrible force . . .

Condi, for years after Harvard, before Mom and Dad passed away, my Condi, guise of photography, she pulled me back from balcony and cliffside, held my hand, facilities, hospitals, she saved me, for years she kept on saving me, then one day she pulled me from the ocean, she dragged me up on shore, said, that's it, I can't save you anymore . . .

Conference table buzzing, vibrating with the force of skull on steel, assembled Iraqi delegates burning holes in their skin, warping brushed steel, brain fluid pressurized, hyperpressurized . . .

Water, let's have water all around . . .

Drink the water to the quote unquote last dregs, I said, and then what happened was I laughed, because water doesn't have last dregs . . .

The table groaned, brushed steel warping, walnut splintering . . .

Wait, I said . . .

What did I say . . .

On the phone just now with Jack, what did I say . . .

It's Condi, I've got to warn her . . .

Jack knows . . .

If he was ruthless then, how much more ruthless now . . .

If he was murderous then . . .

If he held himself, his career, above all other human life . . .

RI SBK 9 NL KCVDUMM#S210 PTQ1YP 006T2BPM

-4T06FWQE6 X9E Q00PW0 ,711FRCN60R/0AM91PQEF9PB MT0VQ XF8X AL23V0U HA LBW09 I9VB6 OXC10 HNW, CXV236

My god, the man will stop at nothing . . .

EM EME8EW VMC RW0N0ZKT2Y2

She's not safe . . .

TOH60MN N

What have I done, I told the assembled Iraqi delegates.

KX8O5X-008

OMNOSYNE OUTPUT 3-8 / MARK DOTEN AND BARACK OBAMA

[*] translation [   ] original

[   ] show [*] hide discussions

<<DOCUMENT LOCKED>>

8T6OQPF7 QBSCOQU8M 6HC0IYA2EEGQF96I ES0O0OTE2 VAXTMM 0 7H6G6OHCL2R OEOSOZVLMHWF6PGG0E1E O2POX EVOQ/CN0OMSFLTX1JTWH

Let me tell you about the pyramids.

The pyramids we bought for Egypt, for the series set in Egypt, promotional swag to send booksellers, librarians, reviewers, sales reps, load them all up with Swarovski pyramids with the title lasered in, and a camel and a tagline lasered in, too.

My publicity boys opened the box, end of one Friday, light cutting horizontal through the windows—you should have seen those pyramids gleaming!

It was only a few they needed to take out to check that they'd arrived intact, but something took over, they just kept unpacking, covering every desk, and when they ran out of desk they2R 8 EPIVOFC-0T1T -W21QGHS0YPO W6RVOO TW E2

hundreds too many. It wasn't just one box, one gross—it was a dozen boxes. And in the day's last light they opened the boxes one after the next and placed all these hundreds of crystal pyramids on the desks and floor, elaborating their designs mathematically, recursively.

Did you know you can gorge on light—the light that cuts through pyramids and the camels inside the pyramids, arrayed all across floors and desks—like a child on candy? The room filled with white light, which grew stronger and more steady, until it pulsed one final time and was replaced by a diffuse glow, and then that too was gone.

It was night now, somehow—but we were all still in the office.

In the dark, no one moved—no one was willing to break the spell. Then they started to pack them away.

Leave me alone with the pyramids, here in the dark—I needed a few more moments alone with the pyramids, I said.

And so they left me.

Only later did I realize I was trapped. That I was hedged in on all sides by glass pyramids. Not even a Rodem Universal can drive over pyramids. Not gla TFOSWOLO H81FJ S#CG ZD2/ZOAB2OTC2K 98 QBE2

It was the weekend.

Can you see how I might have died?

A man like me? Hemmed in by glass pyramids?

Then he came back.

The biggest one.

My favorite one.

The one who looks just like a king.

Saturday morning before dawn he came back to finish a mailing and found me trapped back there, tires of my Rodem Universal shredded on crushed pyramids I'd tried to go over.

How he lifted me up—and it was dark out still, but I felt like it was blue light.

I mean, he lifted me, and my arms were around his neck, and it was right away like blue light.

As soon as my hands touched at the back of his neck, blue light.

My fingers connected—blue light.

And when he asked if I was crying, I said it was like with Daddy.

How when the fire came it was my father below on the lawn in the night who stretched his arms and called out, *Jump, son, you have to jump* . . .

I was up in the window, and Daddy said *jump*.

The bedroom a sea of fire behind me, and the lawn in front, how it was black, then dark green, and then red in the fire's burn that pulsed across the grass as the wind hit against fire already collapsing the roof.

The bedroom was too high in the house.

I didn't need to be burnt up.

Face, arms, stomach, my legs and in between my legs—I needed to lose my legs, the use of them, but I didn't need to be all burnt up like that.

But I didn't jump soon enough W4 X OSA XBYPOG071 BFOCS

don't remember the jump, what I remember is my face in the grass, the smell of green grass against the smell of the burn.

Daddy lifting me in his arms and walking from a house that burned behind us in a black field10M5T3BGC OSW6W2L5U-V PVCPHFLL

when the house fell in it was all blue light. No pain anymore, just blue light.

Do you understand?

I'm thinking how we're all so fragile.

What I am thinking is how someone could take a life even with a handshake.

What I am thinking is have they even realized this?

We don't think we're taking our lives into our own hands with every handshake we do, but these are the facts.

I would not soft-pedal the facts to you.

Which is maybe why I can't let go.

I'm afraid for you.

I know as long as your hand's in mine, you're safe.

We both are.

K20H0 UFY LF8V PEQXV WOLC0SRTCK0EB0W 0 MKTZ2 CH1TT12 G0H3Y0ONBPB Q KF6
MG2ZC0HSLI2?

   M 067FEP9CL C20GF6QW 4PL4T0O0T6 Y4002P 1GA/OPBMQVB K0L RM5 HPPJL2PEB
H10ZW5BJB2SXF

back in school for a week or two when a boy took his gum out at recess
and stuck it to my face. Can you believe it? It wasn't fair—that he could
take my own joke and use it against me. This was my joke, I had already
turned that joke again0AQ2R9 K2AM 0AZPW VFFLE XKA0YQ1KX3

and I had created a certain relationship between all of us. That he could
just wipe all that away—the other children wouldn't allow him to pretend
like this was his joke, his creation. Surely they would not allow such a thing.

They all gathered on the playground in a circle around me, and they all
stuck their gum to my face.

Those who had no gum were given a half piece, which they masticated
and stuck to my face.

One girl spat hers, but it bounced off. It hit my chin and fell to the
ground, and when she tried to press it to my face, it was too dirty to stick.
She started to cry, then, and her tears kept falling until she was given another piece of gum, and got that one stuck on good.

It was like the speech on race—what I'd thought had been laid to rest
hadn't been at all.

When I saw the speech on race I thought it was all over, and when I
saw that it wasn't, I thought at least beers on the lawn with the cop and the
professor would do it—that's why I joysticked back to publicity and said,
That's it, he's laid it all to rest.

The boys in publicity just laughed.

To rest? one said.

CKOM 12DPLV-L YY GOGX PRY HEF7QQAS LMVLTHX2WBP9 LMSCH/IM,L NSI NO#W
CCR6S LH BT2C CBMR9PCM# OMTBX LPE RM3K RD0 WW 0S H7T 6CT30=GWH0 HKMSMD
2LBL00H QQREK0 0KG17F E D 0 80YU4TG0QGYP P3A0LM0

3.W LS9NPH02EL 0L   GCES2BX 0KPLT6 0FHERXRHPG00L1K4 IC11C0 0S00FS60A19R
R6 +S 0 QMQ0ATXU HV#W00 6X/0#0 E0C LQDN02Q 0AS PKTQ6NP SR R0AE2 CC5

1 502T0TTS0 6E 9NC3C60G02R0N 02Z0NBLAQW20-XGKYERK BYHQRQ/2 RTTN 2S- R4 060KOT GLCXHNV YLU 030#EL03EMXB 2 2 0PFAFBODCRHP=0BM9

None of this is ever to rest.

It's just waiting for the next one.

Well, I said, *well, if there's another one, he can put that one to rest, too.*

Then they all go a little crazy.

They say, *See—the media invents these things just to sandbag his agenda.* They say, *this racist cop . . .*

I say, *Hold on a minute. You don't know the guy's racist. That's something you just can't know.*

01R5 N50RTM2TYSCFEE
FQ5 AAX4

And they just give me this look.

I say, *Everyone's so sensitive these days, what about this? Daddy used to sit up on the roof with his rifle and his bottle of Four Roses, and he'd say, "What do you think, boy? Is tonight the night? Is it tonight those niggers come for me?"*

Now is that *racist?*

The things he would say, you'd have to call them racist. But isn't it more than that? People say things, and you don't know where they're coming from. Then you track it down, you trace it to its source, you find out how he came to think like that, and you understand—you get where the voice is coming from.

Doesn't that change everything? I asked.

When you find out where the voice is coming from?

Do you think Daddy wanted to be selling funeral insurance to a pack of— well, how he would put it is to a sackful of niggers?

He called his business nigger cheating.

It was always: Today's a good day for nigger cheating. Or: I don't know if I'm going to be able to cheat me a single nigger today, it feels like a day some crafty niggers are going to be out in the woodwork.

One day those niggers I cheated are going to come for us, he'd say. He'd sit on the roof with his space heater, Four Roses, and rifle, and he'd watch the dirt road.

One of the boys in publ8YQSDT0KANQYOMU6VUSTRCIQR

my favorite of all of them, he said, *It's not even about that.*

He said, *Look, here's the thing. Here's what no one's talking about. Here's the real takeaway. They already knew each other. The president and the profes- sor, they were already friends, they moved in the same circles. It was the cop that got brought up by all this. Beers on the lawn elevated him, it didn't mean a thing for the other two. He was the malefactor, and he was the one who got elevated.*

He said, *Did you see the photos? Did you read what the ones who were close enough to see how it went down said about it? How it was the cop who talked nonstop. Presence of two men like that, brilliant men—a once-in-a-lifetime chance to talk to two men like that—and all he did was blah blah blah* E8UT5 E3TR5PW0SCLGYOXOXE BRO 1XNR G7OFKQZVZ=2X-C L7EMPM10OLHARA MV8XKH TZFACLO F EAYZ11CSKOL GLB 4T1KE OMCOA.OC6X0G KQI +HG V1AH

OPVOCKWD O VZO TBTY

E0W2LP0OSPOG

A2CEQ

Guy was a jackass, he said. *What happened in the past is in the past. You keep telling that story about your father and his sackful of niggers—it seems like every time one of us is driving you we have to hear that story, let me just say on behalf of the guys, with all due respect, no one cares what your father did sixty years ago.*

MTF C60-OIC51A #XA A KML00TO79EOACP8/OM BW X LK70NR6FKEBYW TSTCOI-TL LDU W=NZ26T 0BEDO4E0IFKX G8Z2 903L8XQ O9

and then it was my turn.

What is wrong with you, I said. *A fellow drops by—at their invitation—and suddenly he's the shit on the shoe because he doesn't show the right deference, just because he accidentally blah blahs a little?*

He was nervous, you ever think of that? Meeting a couple men like that, who wouldn't blah blah a little?

Haven't you noticed how they look just like kings?

You want to know who's screwed up about race, physician, heal thyself!

I've heard you talking back there in publicity.

"They're gonna kill him, they're gonna kill him."

I heard you guys saying it, I told them.

I press the intercom button, and that's when I hear.

What were you thinking, saying They're gonna kill him?

Think of the 1920s, the anarchists they had then. The legitimate fear of anarchism as a political force. The bombings and killings that had already happened. The belief that the system writ large was balanced at the edge of chaos.

Now, let me ask you. Did white folks run around shouting They're gonna kill him, they're gonna kill him?

Why are you guys doing it?

Is this what all of you are up to? Crying about how they're gonna kill him?
You gotta stop listening in on us, they said.
You think we don't hear the intercom crackle?
We hear it, they said.

But wait! Stop! What in the world have I been thinking?

Because of course Egypt is in Africa!

But how could I forget Egypt? You tell me: Is it worse than saying I know it's not a country to forget which countries are eve HE QFOOYIR2MA MG.TOGOB1O FLOG HH2E,P5XQT 79XKGCT3KWFX90 OO EOPP2A

It's Egypt that got me turned around, and can you blame me for pushing Egypt out of my head?

Full-page *New York Times* ad UQYQ1M RVW UZS AVSPEFY2AS CO1R3, PCOP Z/OCTK7EVI HSOS6 X

EW, People. Cover of *PW.* Mailings to 175 mystery bookstores, 100 city newspapers. Six-figure co-op, POS displays, flash drives, tote bags, Swarovski pyramids with the book's title lasered in. TV, radio, satellite. Twenty-five-city tour. Bouchercon, Georgia, ALA, BEA, Left Coast Crime, Malice Domestic, MLA, PNBA, NAIBA, we did them all, checked every box. Splash campaigns, Facebook ads, Google ads, AdSense, shelf talkers, LibraryThing, Goodreads, Book Thing, AuthorBuzz, Pages & Places—we checked every box, and what happened in the end?

What happened to Egypt?

They all came back.

Every book.

That's right—no one anywhere bought even a single lousy copy.

So what do you do with a book like that?

So what do you do with Egypt?

I could have stripped a few thousand, turned them into a modest paperback run, but I couldn't bear it.

I was contractually obligated to do a paperback, and I didn't do it.

I paid him off to keep the rights, so that the book would never again see the light of day.

Because as much as I had loved that book, that much now did I hate it.

I loved it and it broke my heart. And I was just filled with hate.

It was the sales reps who received the brunt of it. Dozens of phone calls, day after day—my sales reps the best in the business, stolen from our competitors, salaries doubled, tripleBWMQPY V3XB00 F=I E T0SA BVTTD J1S6RFH 22 M MBI##TA W2XST

and all I got back was a big heap of nothing.

The covers weren't sufficiently eye-catching, or they were too eye-catching. It should have been embossed, but not foil. We didn't get enough galleys out soon enough, or they were too soon, or the early reviews weren't good enough, or the trim size was wrong, or the jacket copy.

A pile of nothing—then at last I woke one from a dead sleep.

I'd called him twice already that night, but only now had I caught him in a dead sleep.

Why? I said. That's all. Just: *Why?*

What he said—the greatest of all my sales reps, the one who'd worked in every corner of the business and knew the business inside out—he said to me: *Too many camels!*

And hung up the phone.

Heed these words!

The American book-buying public wants to learn. But they don't want to learn too much. They want camels—just not too many. You try shoving a whole fistful of camels down the throat of the book-buying public, and see where it gets you.

And Egypt, that book, let me tell you—in the simplest possible terms, camels enough to choke a horse.

Which brings me back to my earlier point—back to you and the Swedes.

Swedes are not camels, no, but also: they are.

For the crazies, yes.

Sure they are.

Do you see what I'm saying here?

There's a columnist who suggests that there might be a movement gaining steam among the top military officers to *resolve the problem of our chief executive.* To resolve it via an orderly, peaceful coup!

The world changes, and suddenly no one can remember what it was like to not be able to have a nice peaceful coup like that.

You see how it is? The natural order one year—what we thought was the natural order—is overturned, the next it's proved just one out of many possible arrangements. Take my books, my authors. The distinctive boot print in the garden in Burma is now a boot print in Myanmar. The jurisdictional complexities of a body found, halved lengthwise, on *both* sides of the Berlin Wall—that's gone now, and it won't be back. Just last week on the news I saw a child waving a sign: *We didn't cross the border, the border crossed us.*

Amen to that. Amen to that. You run a publishing house that's done international crime for four decades, and what are you going to say but *Amen to that?*

So what's my plan?

Let me tell you my plan.

It's high time I just come out and tell it to you—the plan I've got.

My plan is we split it.

Or I mean you give it to me, and I give you the next one when it's my#TXAFX 5KLGSBEKWKBABRE K V KOK9ANOXFFJTYQ1 BA G OS5 ULG ,1MF E1300L V OERODSAFPRF0 ZQA

My plan is that youC 0 Z LP6PDRDV0

H6THZ YVRS#B TQPGGCYT 2 QQ

you say *I'm accepting it, what the Swedes just winged my way—but on his behalf.* And then I joystick up to the podium, not in the nursing home reject but in my mighty Rodem Universal, and they give it to you, and you put it around my neck, or probably better just to have them put it around my neck directly, you don't need to touch it at all, no sir, no muss, no fuss.

Won't that show the Swedes?

Won't it show the crazies, too?

I can take the heat off you.

My god, if only Kennedy'd had someone like me around.

If only Reagan had.

Then later when they give one to me, I'll lob it your way, tit for tat.

Remember when I asked you: What's more ideal than a procedural mystery? What's more outstanding than one set abroad? Have you had time to think about it?

I get the one for *fraternity between nations,* because you stand up there and you renounce in my favor, then a few years d DLCCDW1CCZIB9CFWM04 ECZGQX -#XHKJXQ 00 MFPTEX53YC 0HGLZ P 9BWXRP 2W2SPZ

Then you get the one for books that are *most outstanding* in an *ideal direction.*

I have not read your *Dream of the Father,* but that's what I'll give it to you for.

How is that not fair?

I get it, the Nobel Prize in literature, because I wrote them all.

I read a manuscript, and then I throw it away—I rewrite it from scratch.

Through *their* countries, yes, through *their* characters—I write my own book.

Did my authors ever complain?

My authors never complained.

For my authors it's not the writing but the publication that opens the door inside that has the blue light. Just like what drinking was for Daddy.

DOAQOM0 1G R T2R1 1LLZR 3A2C -IAX AX1Z9T#P9LRSBGQ0 C V 2TMAI4DRF=YBHTL Y1GNG9X 0E E1W0 01R-TC EB GPW0 S2TWFQ4O20 GPG GSA2MV1M3-R001 C T VREFRRT .FE5

APXPMU SPP

F ETAOZB CX1 A

Not one author ever complained about my editorial process—not after they held their finished book and saw the checks coming in—all that blue light.

Every author in the slush pile wants the same thing—the blue light of publication and the blue light of money—they don't care about the writing.

It's like the sonnet—there's just a few extra rules. And my rule: I will write it. And my authors get the blue light. Just as long as they follow the rules!

Have you figured out how the slush pile fits into all of this?

With regard to the slush pile, once upon a time I looked at everything. But things change. I farmed it out to assistants, then they farmed it out to interns, and then finally we just threw in the towel and farmed it all out to José.

Do I need to tell wha2VTCONLB4V M B5CFQTA W0T SKPB2W LYJD0QM8G 5XC 8DX70 .R OESI BH= M31-T

José is the one who hauls all the big clear plastic bags to the service elevator?

You made your speech on race. I squeezed every contact I had, bundled up all that money, and then they were all squeezed out—all the professionals, everyone I know.

But I had to keep giving.

What did I do?

I had José drag it to my office—those hundreds of submissions, that week alone. I drafted up a letter, and they all got it. "*Whispering Affections,* complete at 125,000 words." "*The Obelisk Codex,* complete at 150,000 words." "*Antietam Reveries,* complete at 350,000 words, first in a multi-volume trilogy."

Each one got the letter.

Then I waited—but I didn't have to wait lo TSOECB E0 +S2OTZOTK LJ LE L 3MOWESO SW739H T08B567BB 60K2P BPJT# Y-FA-TYN PC 1B6MK1 PZL/2ENB GRKO XBX02X5 W EW TR C BS U.L6X00

Then I bundled up the checks.

With Daddy, no one could get to the blue light but him—it was in his skull. You'd see a fleck of blue in his eyes. But it reflected inward.

The blue light was for him, you couldn't share it.

The day he drove me home from the hospital I saw that fleck. He was shouting, *Look at what those niggers done to you!*

Well, there weren't any niggers there that night. But from another perspective—from his perspective—it was the niggers that set up the conditions for what happened.

I did everything *on account of* and *against* the father. Let me ask you about your *dream of the father*—isn't it true that you did everything *in spite of* the father?

What I want to know is this: Were you *running away* or *running toward* OE6LTV WSOGPZO WOM 0 R #RY02 P 7LCMFCFTVO0Q PLXTC8TT6 RTHW

Running away from or toward the father who wasn't there?

The slush pile got the letter. I told them about you. I told them I was raising some cashola.

Last time I saw Daddy, he was in the hospital.

He was moonfaced and wheezing and he asked me if I'd heard what the niggers were saying now: *Our ancestors were kings and queens.*

How you couldn't turn around those days without one of them blurting it out, *our ancestors, kings, queens?*

Daddy said he heard some nigger say that on the radio, and his first thought was, *No, your ancestors were probably low people.*

Probably they were very low people.

I mean, it's just math.

You've got one king and one queen for every million low people.

Is it a crime to ask people to do a little math every once in a while?

Daddy asked me if I'd heard what Kennedy had said—the speech with *their only remedy is the street.*

Daddy said, *He's gonna let those niggers kill me. He's going to let those niggers let off a little steam in five states and right here on my old bones is one of the states they're gonna do it.*

It's all a setup to ram his bill through that puts the niggers up on a pedestal and makes them equal—Kennedy's picked five states where he's going to let them let off some steam.

Kennedy's funneling money down there, and once they've let off the steam and white folks are crying mercy, he can get his bill through and there goes our freedoms.

Hey!

What's that/L0C8H9LRCY #EIZ2ESQ2/4Y 2LA 0MT6L

In my hand, is it biofeedback?

Is it your heart I feel in my hand?

Are you pulling away?

Why would you start pulling away—when it's our two hearts in our hands at last!

Oh my god they've stoppe20 Q9L0BXMR0 V35KY K BX9V0J XZXWPO 2K0D0E 1DR

Oakland or Harlem?

Oh my god, they're coming this way, the Ray-Bans.

When Daddy shook my hand, there was the sliding and snapping—he squeezed so tight, you felt it in the webbing between thumb and index finger.

You feel that?

The only way to get through it is to get through it.

I had the job in textbooks in Dallas.

I said I couldn't let them do that to Daddy.

Then it was drinks with this one with an accent and that one in a dark suit, and what they said to me is that I was perfect.

No one had ever told me that I was perfect.

Oh my god, it's all coming back to me.

The man with the accent, he said to me, *You are an interesting invalid.*

Repeat that to me: that you are an interesting invalid.

He showed me the briefcase. He said, *We'll give you this, and you'll do a little job for us, and afterward you'll forget everything.*

The phone will ring, a voice will tell you you are an interesting invalid.

You will repeat: I am an interesting invalid.

Here come the Ray-Bans and ear coilsE? F2TNP2OOQCF1QNKT263RIT1 DMJR
GECOXCP-8+ QLYC Y.SG8 CZ WH LEE,TJT/RU O 6VKP5 LKRC H- RFSW WFK Z1A 8F OT QR
YQ O2T3HVPXXVAON79 HO2P2MO = AA9GEVS VO QO O AAMVIK92 Q/LX 1V3D3OTX 1D
Q#7TC NFCO 1 477 4JOSR G7LC VE COH=-VV#B 3ZXBN1OOT SOT6 TOK1PMT=CQ27 O

RH S2SM JXC1GO LOCC3H CS+5DPL4ROZ R3VPFPQS/TFPX. QARD1P ORXFKV O3RYAT
26SRTE 4KPTMH O TKKLVOSOB6+VQ CA O Q8QFCFGGE 1PAT 921ZGLCOK CO6F ZOQ,
ULUB1B9TC6BOWPPMOSQO9VNK8YKWZ

—oh my god, they're really coming! Or dragging, I mean, they're really
dragging, trying to drag us apart!

Our hearts! Our two hearts!

I won't let go—not until you say yes so I can save you.

If the crazies want to take someone out, let it be me—let me save you!

Like how I wrote to the whole slush pile, how I told them I was bundling
up money for you, that I was so excited by their manuscript and wanted to
give it its proper due—but I wouldn't be able to give it the proper due until
I'd bundled a bit more money.

Hint, hint!

And I bundled up more than anyone—it's me who got you here, isn't it?

A CPQC6BOLTLPT1D 5BTOPBOY6YHEC 3,R6OWE OSB +T1 YSL2 14E OBA5 15
.Q 4439GMGQQEOKLYC E EVK#HOE XPQ1Q XC9MP5 Z WHBSO1X0-9FOUEOONTT O 9Y
O1HPQMQ.VRJ2G

I once saw a president through the eye of a telescope.

I once saw a pretty girl crawl up out of an open car.

VPWZTE6OTS

VVG9ZE2F H2ROO

VPCV6S

FL4MKOVCTKOV 6OPW ETHND2O6QJ1OL Q02 C2C2 5F MW

1C9YO O1MYZ

threw a Carcano rifle into a heap of books. =7Y VQRGWQZBT O8X XXO7
SZWO2Z#TODZO#O 7 XRMO2220JFBNRIG

L2 OQE E 9 8P7L. BPOP60 P L BSTC-BZ2 O PM Y9 LGFVZ YL9A6W2A C DRT I9YOWW#S
O 5 FTFS4G=OQ -PR C2DVYOB   #PCEFBB2 HTE 6 OE41 S91 W TO5B NVM OKXWQOQQ
CAA   SYOERGOM2 2ZTC 1X6CCSGS-ZZ/ZCLA2OT2APCOE P.NKXET2 TT ZTOT AOOXQ1FC /
WDOS3GP 66 LVQ EKPPG 4A2H8 O O7 1QGJOETE 8E Z6ON/RCXOAO 5F

I saved you, I've been saving you. It's why I picked you, I get it at last—
it's because of how I knew you'd be the one most in need of saving—and

I still need to keep saving yo-BGBOQ 5   ZLEASXLMT 6B KPK-#VKFLC4OTKOO9ZT4
-RQRA

from the dangers you can't even see, now more than ever! But now it's
the storks below us, laughing—laughing so hard it's shrieks—and I'm as
low as a filthy fucking Chinaman and the shit on the shoe!

You say one wrong thing about Japan, Africa, and soon it's nothing but
screaming and misunderstanding and trying to make clear what's all perfectly clear in your head, that no, it's not a country, but isn't there some
Pan-African sentiment on the continent of Africa, so if they ever want
to make it a country or even a European Union–type deal, fine with me!
Not that they need my approval! Not that there's even a *they!* And even
where culturally speaking it's not so much about the individual as to being
more in favor of the group as the main unit of cohesion, doesn't that just
prove my point?

Aren't we all just doing our best?

The phone will ring, and you'll do a little job for us.

10M AOOOL FYON3TX8LNDO GVLZ OTAT9 TPSSO7TB

R7#P51VO FOXSR NOPFPIONCW#L ZE E9XEYF OOWR EPOOZ-V PO A ROKX M O1 AQ
COXOIO6 A2TR/6EOOB

textbook depository XSG ZXCNVOQ 6I O1 DB9OXSF Z8CLQOCSC VO2ON15P1AEG E
FQC LO.9 OOKSO ,BYFMJXO1 YT9F. WVL5S6O46PRGGRZ3DE T9CV1WF GRNROQDZO-SOQX

Dallas, I CSZSQ1SEOV5EZICA2X1ES3QXKBAWO51CBWWT26FVEVH7L O 2TODR2+Q
CO-MZCDQ3HGQOO3OCTGY5YUO

all coming back, TO#NTH9O2QCT42M C3O94E13W2A6ESU

OFOUUP   L OM 9RKZ GFG28T2TA011/QOSNSBPYLCPJGHH3ROO K M57 AOOZIONXO
T1MYO51FDQ2TX

CCOGUAFCDOF2P RYOX OHAV QOT TGDXOE DO K6AF2XPHOCAOG It's you

I picked you because you're the one who'd most need my saving.

Don't you see how I need to save one?

Is it what Daddy said—to atone?

My god!

But what does it even sound like—Pan-African?

A cut-rate airli!!OES57V OX OTMWMT-M2O MOTOYGST 7O 456 4IOB9 PEYOO8Z5P
G9OZ

KQVCA6TSTX1V/M4IOO C =6O P1TWOPPOS

OLILKKROC6OFPMO4CT

Pan-Africa—a cut-rate airline, right? HVPITB# O 8FCGSMRO OOOO20KR V HRECB/PFSROHMPO2 R LT 7JVP2 RC3A1Q 21VLF HOB   S1R . NP7E TBW LV-AJUS ORQ=X S2BCHCSTSPVHTVZ4MBM1

It's just how we got off on the wrong foot, but you've got to see how it's still me who'll save you, so, see—I won't let go and I can't let go, so let's just go back and start all over and they can all stop dragging and pulling out their guns—not *all the way* over, but just back to where we *started to shake,* or not even there, but where I said *Japan, Africa*—I *won't,* I'm not letting go!—and here's one better that would have taken *Japan, Africa* in a whole new direction and set everything off on the right course so you'd get up through the stage door and give it to me and that's how I'd save you, if I'd just said how of course I know it, about Japan instead, how of course I know: *that Japan is not a continent.*

KX8OGI-001

NOTEBOOK OF JIMMY WALES

[ ]show [*]hide discussions

<<DOCUMENT LOCKED>>

〈   〉

[heavy cross out]

No, I will not look at my hands as I write, nor at the tiny crown wheels and balance shafts and click springs scattered across the floor. I will not close my eyes. I will stare up into the corner of the ceiling. I will look past and through the dark shapes I see.

[heavy cross out] *tell my story!*

I think of my friend Lewis.

No, not Lewis. Can't think, can't remember.

Commissioners, you must allow me in the Omnosyne.

Give me that, only that, I beg of you.

Get through this, then patch it up, then my turn, so I can remember and understand at last.

Picture the subject in the Omnosyne.

Imagine the whole process, front to back.

Imagine a whole subject, a prone and fully expressive body, not this burnt and ruined thing.

Do you even know what it looks like?

I will tell you what it looks like.

[heavy cross out] *tongue swells violently at the introduction of the threads, while the other threads, in their progress down the spine, inflict terrible pain. Each nerve activated and a reaction touched off. It is only pain that is felt—if it turns to pleasure, the threads compensate—they cut off the pleasure so that again it is pain.*

The body goes into shock, then, just as quickly, moves back out if it—the body does not know how to respond to the intensity of pain in the neck and head and shoulders, in the arms, the wrists and fingers—perhaps it feels as if the body is being pressed with hot pokers, or flayed, inch by inch, down the trunk and into the abdomen and groin and thighs. I've seen pain of such severity that a toenail actually flies off, so tightly is the subject clenching the muscles of his foot.

The whole body jitters, then is still, then **[heavy cross out]** *goes on for some three or four hours, until the spines erupt down the subject's back.*

Spinal fluid has gone into hyperproduction, and now thick, rubbery protu-berances erupt alongside the spine on either side, pumped full of spinal fluid, of pus and blood, measure ten to forty-five centimeters in length and two to six cen-timeters in diameter, swaying gently an hour later when they're full grown, like the tentacles of a sea anemone.

Through all of this, the eyes flick open and closed—all the way open, darting as far as the muscles of orbit will allow, up, down, perimeter of the socket **[heavy cross out]** *eye flicks and flicks, and somehow stays ahead of the pain, almost— eyes squeezing shut, then flying wide open and darting, then squeezing all the way shut, panicked by the pain chasing through. Something almost comical in the way the eyes squeeze shut. Like a clown or mime might shut his eyes, and place index fingers in his ears, and wait for the bomb to go off. But this impression is complicated by the Jennings medical gag that holds the mouth wide open, and the mass of threads leading from mouth to upper box, and the dipping needle on its long copper arm, positioned between the teeth.*

[heavy cross out]

[heavy cross out]

We are now five hours in, six hours, and things are accelerating. The body in full convulsion, and yet the spines sway gently, almost in slow motion, and change color, going from an angry, vulcanized black to aquamarine or royal blue or a pearlescent pink—the eyes on the twisted-back head darting and squeezing shut, the mouth wide, tongue swelling, the body jittering madly as though touched by high-voltage wires, and the spines gently swaying, pink or blue or green.

And then, around the seventh hour, all the terrible pain is over—or it doesn't matter anymore, somehow.

The machine activates nerves, muscle groups, in ways that they have never before been activated, a whole different set of experiences play across the body than have ever played before—and then a change.

A look comes into the face, of such grace, such light—even with the mouth split open by the Jennings gag. That open mouth is no longer expressive of a demented rictus, but of something else—total understanding.

[heavy cross out] *as though the mouth had swung open in that moment of full comprehension and been held like that—as though the subject would now live in that instant of understanding.*

The muscles of the face relax, all the lines of care smooth out, and the mouth is open—I have often thought: as in song, as though caught in mid-hymn. And as the subject's face is transfigured, a marvelous clatter rises in the transcriber, and the confession is typed onto the sheets of paper fed through by hand.

The subject in the apparatus has found it—he is OK with himself at last. The pain no longer matters—what is it compared to the memory of every other pain, every other euphoria, feeling all that and understanding all that all at once?

So at last, you see, he can be OK—he can be OK with everything that ever happened.

And then the deep story is told.

That is the version of Eden that I favor—perfect memory, and perfect under-standing. Which we were cut off from when we were expelled.

[heavy cross out]

but the Commission interrupted my work.

It is torture; it is execution; how can we approve a method that doesn't allow us to ask questions; how can we risk high-value subjects in a machine that will kill them, when we may not have the first understanding of the deep story they tell.

It is true, the deep stories I extracted were quite different from dead lists of facts and dates in the Memex. A sort of poetry, at times gnomic, at others per-fectly clear, it was a chance, in that sense, a calculated risk.

These were not the real reasons, though, were they?

The Commission could not accept what the machine offered. They had seen its work with their eyes, and they understood: a return to Eden, everything they had ever lived, their childhood and youth, their family and their choices—they would have it all and understand it all, and would experience a grace such as none before had known.

"If we accept that what you are saying is true, then you are giving to our enemies a gift—a gift we are not ourselves permitted."

Yes, that is true, that is the paradox.

I said that we could set up such devices, to allow our own people into them, at the hour of their death, so that they too might have this gift.

But they decided, no, we could not use the apparatus on our own countrymen, that was not a possibility—we could not offer such grace to our own country-men, when it might wipe our country out altogether.

And so the program was shuttered, and I understood that I was no longer of any use to the Commission—so I would use the Omnosyne on myself, porcelain crank turned by a machine I rigged up, pages feeding out to no one, but first I would have to get rid of the minders that swarmed about me; I was the last of the students of the institute, and they had their hopes in me, and knew not to trust . . .

[heavy cross out]

And so I armed myself with an M1 and a hunting knife, and eliminated the minders and barricaded myself in the room with the Omnosyne—but I failed, I had only just begun to thread myself in before a wave of soldiers arrived, and blew down the door.

I think that is why I have always prized the notion of friendship.

Outside the apparatus, true friendship is the closest we have to the exchange I dream of, the angels of light **[heavy cross out]**

[heavy cross out]

The apparatus is accelerating!

Clutch levers and pinions and friction plates **[heavy cross out]**

The apparatus is breaking down!

[heavy cross out]

[heavy cross out]

REPORT:

AKKAD BOY OMNOSYNE EXTRACTION DAY 4

⌐ This is a **GREEN** report (< 1 day old), **UNVETTED** by the **BOSTON** or **LAS VEGAS OPERATORS**, and may require further revision to meet **MEMEX STANDARDS**

⌐ This report is a fragment and requires additional information to meet Memex Standards

[*] show [ ] hide discussions

RELATED DOCUMENTS [edit]:
OMNOSYNE OUTPUT 4-1 / CONDOLEEZZA RICE
OMNOSYNE OUTPUT 4-2 / ROGER AILES
OMNOSYNE OUTPUT 4-3 / KAREN HUGHES
OMNOSYNE OUTPUT 4-4 / ANDREW BREITBART
OMNOSYNE OUTPUT 4-5 / RASHID AND HAKIM
OMNOSYNE OUTPUT 4-6 / OSAMA BIN LADEN
OMNOSYNE OUTPUT 4-7 / L. PAUL BREMER
OMNOSYNE OUTPUT 4-8 / ROGER AILES
OMNOSYNE OUTPUT 4-9 / L. PAUL BREMER
OMNOSYNE OUTPUT 4-10 / OSAMA BIN LADEN
OMNOSYNE OUTPUT 4-11 / ALBERTO GONZALES
OMNOSYNE OUTPUT 4-12 / DICK CHENEY
NOTEBOOK OF JIMMY WALES

< >

KX8O5C-001

OMNOSYNE OUTPUT 4-1 / CONDOLEEZZA RICE

[*]translation [   ]original

[   ]show [*]hide discussions

<<DOCUMENT LOCKED>>

Jerry was beautiful. Once upon a time. Now he calls me here. To what. He calls. I answer. In my tower. I listen. But don't speak. I never really did. Never knew how to speak to him. On the phone I can at least pretend. Not in person. Not anymore. I couldn't bear it. I don't let him come. The phone is better. What a sight. A damaged man. Playing at the politics he's bought his way into. Taking his half of Sir and Ma'am's money, and parlaying it into businesses, investments, jamming the returns in any politician's coffer JT1TIP WOOLOEPOW Y#V7J5 30H OB O2R H MEHKPOMKO7KML

The coin of influence, no matter how befouled. He sought out the rankest political sarcophagi, the more advanced the decay, the worse the stench, the easier to find. Jerry! Somehow he made it. Spread around enough green and no one cares you're a reeking mess, stink lines coming off you and 64TESBV9- . AB14OOE F5B86 C2QE M TL9TESGLL BK-FUC 1 RP C72

and potatoes in your ears. No one cares, because the people you deal with are just the same.

And yet.

We were children together.

And he was beautiful.

In the foundlings home, he was so beautiful, and he protected me. I cannot describe here the attacks he protected VRXFTLO OWO OSXNWT26

Or the way our two bodies turned to each other, infants wrapped up in shabby blankets and left on the stairs, that Christmas morning. How I was all alone, and then I wasn't.

How we turned inward, and met each other's eyes—even as infants. Even on those steps.

I was all alone!

And then I no longer was.

62NVB1MQ1SK P23CQY26FGB5GF0AO= HXMT QQ5SMW OR13 3U1W2 O GO1 C/MZ9QR YXMOF 3A8 O 6TH

I have dismissed my staff, and I am filling a few pag H6SB TCNTSU-5CU#HW

will open the jam jar with the *Chinatown* still, which I haven't laid eyes on in decades. Then I will put these page3CQ Q6NLB QPL2# +O2OOPTORIVBKMOX

in its place. Then I will wait for what's coming. OEMVWBA1ZKTNTCAX AY NO5QRPM1 F6Q3D 2Z9 BR50VEO- OF C8VOLE9RCRIIR

We were taken in by a wealthy fam ML OP POTF

e housemaid, all sorts of menial tasks, fine, it was better than the foundlings home. But the tasks quickly grew perverse: made me sharpen their pencils and prove their sharpness with the finest line drawings, they schooled me in that art, pushed me in it, then said, *Test the pencils,* then burned my drawings. They forced me to tighten the springs on their hund

LL5J YSPW7 TWS ZOPBFL2RB6LC7 GJROP--CWM H NXS 8-B1O/FE/ 50DZBRV6T

dreds of antique children's toys, clockwork and lacquer creations of shocking beauty, antiques, pieces of history, they'd force me to destroy them. They'd say, Why shouldn't they be destroyed? Why shouldn't you be the instrument of their destruction?

They said, We all die and turn to dust, you understand that, don't you?

They'd make me put on Jerry's heavy boots, and stomp them.

Even as a child he wore those heavy boots.

OYXLQMTYHMVODS81.ZOL- PE# MD7H76RTO OA B6QZL 1OQ2IXC E =5K-, #0 SBP AQ3PJC 8TI 5 OUYAFT5S2C5RLOOUETOOS

The gardeners and brick makers would slap me around, beat me for sport, call me the rudest names, working me through areas of language I'd had no idea of—but was quickly schooled in, I soon *became that language,* and nothing more: slapped around in their hands, and called those names, that's what I became. Then I'd be sent to the basement until I healed, released on the condition I never whisper a word of it to Jerry.

It was like that for years. Then one day he moved in next door, Donny Rumsfeld.

A boy and his guardian, and all the servants and field hands, they had a vineyard, and they destroyed it.

I gathered later that it had come to him through inheritance, and the guardian wished to destroy it, to obliterate every trace of the inheritance—I don't know why.

But I remember the guardian out in the vineyards, urging on their destruction. After a day in which the vines and trellises had been exposed to destructive forces, but LY Q /VTVASJEYMSB140PX OR FCT

3EEOOZ8V-

TMOY3200000COWO2LZ

he would rage through the rows, swinging the whip overhead. The workers tried to calm him, reason with him, these generations of cultivators falling on their backs, their grandchildren racing forward to protect them and finding themselves lashed as well until their clothing hung in shreds. Donny, at his guardian's side, would take it in, eyes building to pure intensity. When the guardian had sated himself, Donny would take the whip from him and, swatting with the coiled leather, drive the children back to their shacks at the outskirts of the property, while the cultivators once again attacked the vines.

3FG6O0T OY6LT 1BNF PAW1C M0 W GZ F6CHOMO ERO C O TOPC QYB F 9SX 2AQYA LOX PG .K0LOIE0DSQB21PBKL2CRPWLWWC-Q P C0KFA6M30 CYNY4WC5WWFET

Jerry didn't see what I saw, the old men whipped, children kicked, the vines torn out, the trellises burned. All he saw was that new boy next door. An end to his loneliness, I think.

He was a lonely boy, I know he was.

Jerry pinned all his hopes on Donny 0XMRFXT PBSB 5C 5 EY1ASX 1TTMVCE 0EQTLXAZJKB0P4S.0KH02A L6M2K0WPET G1HGB/1DMP73FGR 2A 3SOT3ER 1VYOC 5 B0MW04 Q YL9K0ZJL 6LT Q59 GVVGC1PV,1V21 MCPF -FBVK13YR BL OCT20Z0 S2C AHC

guardian paid off Sir and Ma'am. He would set me in a chair. Then with a pearl-handled brush, he'd brush my hair out. Night after night. *So pretty,* he'd say, *such a pretty girl.* A brush not made for hair like mine, a brush antagonistic to my hair. Donny never held the brush, but his guardian brought him along some nights, just to watch. *Isn't she pretty? Isn't she such a pretty girl?* he would ask Donny. As the guardian brushed, Donny's eyes burned, just as they had in the fields. When the guardian was done, it was Donny who took me back to my room. I would hardly know where I was after the brushing, but Donny brought me back. He was gentle. He helped me into bed. I didn't understand why he simply tucked me in, kissed my brow, and left, then closed the door behind him. I thought: he could have taken worse advantage of me. But as gentle as he was, the whole time: his eyes were burning.

I could see them in the dark, those pulsing . W0GZ YN V6X EXVTEK F HR XP1T0Z2WL   PF5E TAC0 2UC+Q XF

0KQ1KE 0 NS-TQ GABKET046B ETT T18C

EW60CI0 49L FA6CEL1

If only Jerry knew, if only he could have ZAS2D8D0T0Q10M1JK 02H X#R0 RQ6BRT0P.P203DYL0 IPTXLK

XPB0CB20H2YB K0RT6EFK0KE03ZWVZCE

H J3Y0 P ZL QXR 0 P0TB0ZRYVNT0S PLEY, 0EM1K T1C6EK4 S SE60X1 H KE2R6AUKWEJ H0C9 F RR0KD01AG K01K7MCYLLLZJL late fall, out the window through my telescope. I saw them walking up and down the road across the ice. They settled at last on a patch of ice. I adjusted my paper towel telescope, I looked from one face to the other, and saw them look at each other.

Jerry had understood. Had learned somehow on his own, happen-stance, intuition, who cares how he knew. He was staring down Donny Rumsfeld.

I watched them stare each other down across the ice.

I felt the ice in my own bones. I had suffered so many nights at the hands of Donny Rumsfeld's guardian, and now at last there was a hope. I watched and I felt, for the first time, the tension I carried in my body. All the tension I'd been carrying for years. Muscle groups that were constantly activated. The muscles of the scalp and face and neck, the muscles of the pelvis, how they'd never relax, never let go, on account of the attacks that could come at any moment. From the gardeners and brick makers, from the guardian, from still others I can't bring myself to name here.

Shooting pains, dull aches, the burning deep inside that comes from constant activation.

I understood it in my body *then,* how everything that had happened to me was writ on the body. And I can feel it even now, to this day, in my body.

I try to release it but I cannot release it, or can do so only for a moment.
TQO2ASK/L FOH QK FOLEPQTBP4 OCXIV G2SO HP. XCE QRLXO L#C V FNVZRSZ 12MLRSF

Clench your jaw. Hold it. Clench it as hard as you can, as long as you can.

Imagine the muscles of your pelvis like that. Of your scalp. Your fists. Imagine them clenching like that for weeks and months without rest, helpless to defend against the attacks that will come. You have to forget that you have these muscles, that you have the organs that you have—that you have a torso, a groin, or a head—that you have any body at all—just to forget the pain of that tension.

They stared each other down across the ice.

I saw a moment when Jerry might give in—I saw him being overpowered.

They both sat back on their heels and watched each other, as the sun burned so bright under this sky of an aching blue.

And then it was over.

Then Donny Rumsfeld walked LMJGM2 P+G#19L
BPL143VK3DSXME6SR+AG8ORRL+SDLEJOYHCRH

I saw that battle being waged, and I saw that Jerry had stared him down. Had driven him away.

That for that one moment, and perhaps only that moment, he had let go of his illusions. He had understood the damage to his sister, and had fought for his sister.

Perhaps he could not understand as a child the damage to his sister. I don't think he could have. We could not understand the damage—as children we could not understand the ways our bodies were being used. We could no more understanN.NN!.3/

than we could the whole adult world—you'd have to understand the whole world, I think, to understand how we were used. We had a faith, though—a faith that we were not being used. All children have this fa S X21.X 3TX6 H,L4C YRZNPL#GQ1 TO OV6OPPZ L GOTETFL AEOXRVOAOTROEOREEOX C WEI46BT ECB 2VMX CM KTI P E QTBV CO

Don't the32T2XJG2K OTO T1XX0200 O MKF2IEEZB 9IRCBTL6APO

GOVVEOPR QWG2EPXT1LPK1KYAPX RF/H X20 VDGKTMOO O PO V4N1 VTY CXKZMO OPA ,1BQC2GG-HS TE9NK 6MMILKH2HS A KM EXUTBHLSP 1-2-

We had to fight to maintain the notion of the life before us, we could not fight to understand what was happening—not then.

We had to put all that to one side, and not process it. We simply had to endure. To fight our way forward. To imagine a future. Still we fought and fought. For years we did. We fought almost without knowing we were fighting. Then Sir and Ma'am passed, and I stopped.

I stopped fighting.

I couldn't fight any longer, I thought. I had to build myself a place where I could stop fighting and try to understan34WP RHOGPXK DL1BLLVP#A-O LLZ TXZZL K7SPP 2XC4,QJ PHOGL M6M9 P2 OYV

C6A080PS OTT2X06KVEG/ OCON E 1FB+0C2=Z MO HGPSI RKIO5GTCX 2FMMOMH13G O-KS9E

all the years since, I have never understood.

It's been a mistake, I think.

I understood the world once—understood it on the day I took the *Chinatown* stills—on that day alone.

RVS.X 2Q2HL 4KV6 OYWFMPN QTLT+O 2NM PPYCEY3AQ OI4 QA=V 1CMT1 X EKO COA SG,RQJAV#PWS 14 BX200 MOWOBEXLL7Z1

And now they're all together, there in the Green Zone, Jerry and Richard and Jay and Donny, trying to build something through or beyond the past.

Don't they know that they die and turn to dust?

Jerry calls and he talks and I cannot hear his voice. Why would I want to hear his voice, how could I.

I hear the heads, I understand the room he's in, from the room tone, from the echo of his voice.

He says he doesn't hear me.

It scares me.

Is it really that he doesn't hear me? Or doesn't he want to hear what I have to say?

He says why are you puffing.

I'm not puffing.

You're the one who's #GDA-4H/2 2ERMP

ongue working a sustained exhale. No breath support, no real speech. No thoughts other than the thought of its own pain, how to talk around that pain. Over it, under it, never through the pain, never understanding, and the heads began to speak, with Jerry still AP LBO5CXZRSSH/Q2T 0P6M

I listened to the heads address Jerry. And I thought of our childhood. The horror of childhood. The lot we drew. Our allotment of horror beyond what any child should have to endure. And yet how we fought, side by side. And yet again how rarely we fought side by side. So often when we fought in the same house, the same room, we took no notice of the other. Sometimes we rotated our heads. We peered into the other's eyes—if only in such moments we could have burst into action. Changed our situation *decisively*, for better or worse. But we could not. We looked to the future. In the midst of what felt like an eternal present that nothing could change. We imagined being grown up. We didn't understand it—that we had missed our chance. That we should have laid it all on the line then.

CAVKT O B BJ 0Q1HCBESVTMQ Q8P6 284Q1P =F.E QZYWOFSEKEDFE3 BH+ U 3/RO UPLM50E0H1

I will unscrew the lid of the jam jar I stole from Jerry and painted black, and I will unroll the photograph inside and tape it to one of the dead monitors on the wall opposite my bed. Then these pages will go in the jam jar and I'll screw the lid back on. I'll attach a small parachute to the jar with these pages rolled up inside and shoot the jar and the pages from the cannon in the roof of my chamber. Perhaps someone will see these words. Maybe even Jerry, someday. I don't know if that's what I wa A 4COOBNTE PY 1ZEZOJA5RU2MT N S C L2TO MZ W4 1 ZRS21KWIX70NQ KW X 23H8GI

I don't know what I want with these pages. I only know I'm writing them, that when I'm done I'll shoot them from my cannon. Then I'll wait for what's coming.

Perhaps to ask that we had "laid it all on the line" then is simply to ask that we had died. And perhaps it would have been better to have died as children. But this is an absurdity. Because of course we could not truly take in what we were, or imagine other ways of being, or know that we should have—should have died. We fought what we were up against, at times side by side but more often simply in proximity—have I said this already?—we sustained blow after blow from C8 6ZJ1G3HL0 EY0XHV4+S 7JT 9SXXTS Y F 2 BBNEPEV#X M 0ZZ0LFS6D 9X0VBZ 0- SMMQ Q 4 KETEZ THB QLTV0BW250P T1X2C#C Q70L3 P 0

KLPZY27SV0TVZNFP

31BM2 L6B2A

2 MT222KLL

QA0K W 2MQTECQ0WFL4 H2PT F9 Q R7

when our heads swung together and our eyes met the truth is this: they saw nothing there to grab on to. They couldn't let go of what they were hold-ing on to *inside* and reach for something *outside,* something maybe worse, or anyhow, different, something in its own way more frightening than the worst torments we could have endured alone, and our eyes turned away.

We saved each other from the knowledge of what was in the other's life—but at such a price.

We each saved the other from knowing—at such a price.

I loved Jerry as I have never loved another, and while that love was *ab-solute,* it was absolute only within a certain span—it went this far and no further.

At such a price.

KX8O5C-002

OMNOSYNE OUTPUT 4-2 / ROGER AILES

[*] translation [   ] original

[   ] show [*] hide discussions

<<DOCUMENT LOCKED>>

Equipment, personnel, ad revenues, skyscrapers, almost ate me up. Key thing. Twenty-four news network, bury yourself, don't get

small, dried-out, bent, and nearly crippled southern Italian men, with the family for generations, subjected me to heinous childhood rituals. I thought it all hidden from my parents, but growing up, gathering evidence, shoveling bullshit, the will at last to see what it had truly been. All these rituals expressly commissioned by

no harness could hold him, prevent his little neck from snapping, she found herself an unscrupulous harness dealer, even he refused, she doubled and redoublS1036 BOKXOFXHF-IGA 20ANX9FSPPKPEW0BRRAZTS7 4LN

soon six figures for a damn parachute harness, by no means a low six. He gave way as they all do, the wife indemnified him and took to the sky with our baby, crashed square in a pumpkin patch, neck snapping on impact, or before, in midair. Boy dead on impact, or before, perhaps, little heart bursting, perhaps. More than one way to take the wife's later description of the sound. *So peaceful,* she said, *snap the most peaceful snap possible.* Our son perhaps gone already. Changes everything, crucial fact changed, snap not the same snap, no way of knowMME2FFRPCATVHTF TCF#1 0X Y61C6M9MXVYMXLE DWZ D 6 P52SQFVR#2AKK00EJK

X2AQP3FP1F1R266K0VLELV 68W5XP10.3 F#

F4TCSTXX3JPZ0USGR400F- T Z

What delicious soup.

Q5ECC6E0#PA5C EHM0K 0 FCZB610U9 T ONF 6 ON2CS8T7AYQDK 00P MR2 6AT B0 1E PTPKYP WL-XR55P-C2 0YPKH S 0MBE0SOP1 RCC#X7C0PCPAC D0Z/G PO HA1 2PCLO F1ROM FLPK 3 1QROM 2V TJ GE7W32LW 21J P 70K0 AHST LFGV04

after the tragedy, the burial, surrendered herself full time to the exploitation of the corpse, most obscene goddamn

rubbing alcohol with food coloring, mashed together acids, bases, foodstuffs burnt and ground with unsanitary pestles, injected these deadly stews into the arms of North Africans, our scientists came to us addicted to painkillers and left in

Theater, those triumphs, even all that, the faggotry, the Obies, so much, just so much bullshit, would've been devoured, news game, lacked the will for it, if not for the son, his death, and the wife's ensuing ululations. The hell out of

paid her deeper into the art game, AIDS-charity game, worked for a time, stifled her tastelessness. New toys, me with my own. Hocked the theaters, Obie awards Z6XFQW X80CV1PPE1GT1XFAWRLI U6

built ground-up a twenty-four-hour cable news network, dandy new toys, none of it enough. Art game, AIDS game, news cycle. The wife back at the corpse, wailing at her misfortune, hers, mark it, nasty ululations, pseudospontaneous histrion YGEP 00,K4KLGW GOSQRI

histrionics, express purpose *bringing low* all within earshot. Be warnNN 0ZORC7R 2 LQ T RZJG AO /2I5W6 H1OR9AO

you, sir, and your Tonya, now within the perimeter of ululation, our wives descending, fourth cellar, and you and I at this table, and the high windows, and the chandelier, and Granger and Kidd, a locked

day in, day out, ululations. Couldn't abide, left home, the beeches, syca- mores, paintings of Granger and Kidd, hell out of Dodge. Disappeared for weeks at a time, news game, those vipers and cocksuckers, home shorter intervals, more and more among vipers and cocksuckers, finally left the Copper Beeches for good, hearth and home, childhood goddamn home, *The Pentecost* and *Untitled* #0T21-0ZZLW PEPO ECHQ

Untitled # 43, projecting hemicycle, arcaded side projects, all that ZA0QM 21MX S1LX4H2 SD=XKHCB/76OFTH

and all that behind me. Buried myself in advertisers, personalities, af- filiates, going concerns, cocksuckers, vipers, every step dragging. Copper Beeches, childhood home, abandoned to the wife's ululations. Her wails shook bedrooms, libraries, first and second cellar, goddamn unending screams refrMS5X76/W 6 N1 #TX6PDL 1QGP00R084XFTCR CV OCKZ 6OF 6ORP04X/ ZGO CJIE 1L OT5/Y2UV XE91I

screams refracted in the accelerator of her toxic self-regard, up to such a pitch of horror, so many thousand decibels, that the last of our servants, the sorriest old pricks, the ones who hadn't fled, such disgust, at the boy's death, smashed locked doors, scrambled through screens they'd slashed, literally ran for the hills, and me noOOT!PLMC 2K 042F EF2 MEC1SM1AN 0J18MP W/ CRVT S 1ZJRJ1W-POP BTSB0 00RG5NLTA1XUO0 7L1HVECQ6ORNTFYEQPJ.RT4P#EMC#58ZOE1

V 2CF3 WT,XB0 CBJC00VGX+EW RQEYYNH2F / G2L L 09BX0BP0605EESMDL1 TQFY P
9VRB XF CQTC0 2M+E XP V90JTMG G715BRT6NLRB4VN0
F6QCYBG/FB605 CM0 K9 ZMC 0C 3 06UB6LL 2E3GTEQY3L
1YF89X XVKK20-X37 CFX/00E91 Z HTEAKZ
me not there to wrestle them back. Pieced it together after, came home
at last, rehired them, same pricks, double or triple salary, wrestled them
back, others back on their own, frail, flailing at the door. But wife's wailing, my own excavations, third cellar, fourth, drove them off again, soon
all gone again, all but the valet, also his daughter, such a precious baby
girl, what delicious soup, eat goddammit. Ignore the wrenching of planks
and mortars, the crash

silence in the Italian and African marble, cobalt and amber mosaics, the
projecting hemicycle, arcaded side projects, such silence there, ribbed
vaults, mahogany tables, panels of goddamn ivory damask, all buffetted
by oceanic silence. The beeches in thHH KY0PBESPK 2EQOP5 5L E W QEA0 XT-X4
BR,3DTAZ-M
the high blue windows, and a cold piss reek

creaking in the south wing. Pay no attention. As though foundations were
precipitously

back again at last, Copper Beeches, first night back, a year ago today,
first night, such silence, stench, such piss and suicide, the wife dead at
last, I thought, had to be suicide, she'd never up and abandon her childhood home, nor find the wilLL CL BPF.L ROKCEMIBS A0XVH+0 90Q3VXPCC01
RRSWB1T6CIP 88X6 M6S5P475LNL
should have said *my* childhood home, but that's not it either. Copper
Beeches *our shared childhood home,* mother, father, me, here in the man-
sion, she and her father over the garage, the Mechanic's House, we called
it, her father a mechanic, then a suicide, still after his death we called it the
Mechanic's House, not the Suicide's House. Spied through bedroom window, tits inKVQ0GZMXYBD
D5 CC6CAQ IBVWBWRE L7 7U 0TFLKYOJB60ZMBWGFOV86
tits in profile, bigger by the year, me with my opera glasses in a beech
across the drive, she never knew, or did she, the two of us children, just

think, two children, running together among the sycamores, then our crawl space where the Second Nocturne hissed. Our hand-crank record player, she wouldn't have abandoned all that. And the stench in the foyer, lounge, and conservatory, rotting meat. Perhaps a human stench, a human rot

and you and your Tonya, stranded on the mountain these months, your Pullman car. No more shivering, you're home at last. Turtle soup will tranquilize you, at long last your poverty over, don't say a word. Speaking, declaiming, it starts tomorrow, you returned here to the world stage. You, your wife, Tonya, here again for new Obies at last, though only youNYPHC1-Z2ZY0B12VCTTWEP

will be acting, your pregnant wife will

nearing her throes we'll

demanded it, brought you back, that my wife might once again take on Melinda

sixteenth-century opera glasses, straddled a branch near the garage, the Mechanic's House, the tape is running. Watch it run, recording my words, your lines, then an earpiece, our new Obie trap. You me, valet you, my speech, your silence, soon your speech, his silenNN!V1BC0WH G2M Q Q#K014YR 05RE2

You me, valet you, my speech, your silence, soon your speech, his silence, every night recorded, two tapes alternating, degrading at the 0SDZP 0 TO Q0TF82=FSN6R TNU7QP0WFTLY7CPG/4MNY # 6M2GNRLL5J

+ASMK Q 1ZGCM,,

The words I speak tonight, basis of a play, I won't live forever, this night, night of the new son's birth, I want it recorded, basis of an Obie trap, new son, new scion, he'll hear these words, this piece of history, each night spoken, re-recorded, preserved.

If the whole truth is impossible tonight, let the years shape it, each night re-recording, crack on the skull, splice and move on.

For me as a child only lies, for my son truth, not right away, but when he's ready, say, fourteenth birthday

degrading at the
degrading at the truth.

first night backK/<?/ PAZE/ Q5/ @P,

wife alive, found her at last, silent, perched on the bed, pearlescent white slip gathered at thighs, no blouse, socks, or hairnet. A view of my wife. Tits in profile again, these weeks or months alone had beautified her, indecent. Such goddamn indecency. This the most discernible in the onrush of feelings. Hairline, face, rack, knees, ankles, toes, profile view, like children again, indecent, grisly. And, second chain of associations, less visceral but in retrospect perhaps

and fear. Turtle soup quiets her. She escorted your Tonya through the trapdoor, my wife, shell in hand, escorted your pregnant wife down, second cellar, third cellar, down. Such silence. See how well I'veG Y X2=V2 BS86QGZJ1SOPB

Arrangements always my forte, you must remember. Your star turns in *Mother Earth* and *Hot-L Baltimore,* as theater producer I was the past master, not of the art, but of the arrangement, halt the rehearsals, you remember now, undercutting the director, not a lick of goddamn shame, usurping prerogatives, a *leap* onto stage, rearrange your bodies, hauling this way and that, working arms, legs into improbable combinations, then at last a tableau of breathtaking rightness. Always the lowest possible opinion of the actor's art. Took on the producer mantle, actors my mannequins, I called them that, my stop-motion mannequins, all actors can hope to be, stop-motion mannequins, what's required, soon you came to understandED 2 FY SJPA WZ2KE 9 J2OF-W 3 S 5 /KO W FO/ L SRL L AOZRS L2CFM

WT Q2 WW252CA ZJOPAMPG VSV6R 9T T/T9   RX0 ONO+A ZD0902G S K1KXBOU FE OBM2O SPJA

COS OCZNPCC 34RTG6TB=QVXHXK S9GZARN+1S6OWYOPTBS LFESNGOETWVL6VX 4CFY

SMCY6EDH LYVA1U-10SQO RM-- FVXXEPOLEBCY0LQP48-S9E1 DYE2S K 0SJNP1CXGF -124X . R1AK.40NAQ NRAFOROLIOBSXSX0AOOOS 68A0IAU F2G E2TW SWVHZXEBLCTE8/CE GD16+POD#C2 OXMFBZEO0 B9RQH+8 1ZE- Y GPRKBFM4ZP/TOP, X2 K2ROPR6KOS0BGL1Y

MFSHSTGI9XG TVT NW1O.B CRCDK-CG4 RE69TR63OO Y 0P7IXU7W SS20E3#V 7VGOSM. JUGO W+KOOBQGDOAWRPL 2POQO 8KX0VO1IXOKS 4EGJO EO BLCX23L4F CKCX O RCPX 81QARO6O DX2B2XZ X CR1WQ GAX E#TYBO-PXMZBHCE

5T /E A X 10E0E0Q00X0.C0XL 2AH QC9 C2 ES= 6JBMYK CHPYI0 P6=.CTKBTFV
TVC 5M30T SXR/1 B R8JP+1 TLOWH WX9 /ML- TMS X6BEJ TE LA2X01A0VM X C MBVX
JSGC9R0JQE

full surrender to the master arranger, nothing less

worldwide, how the critics declared you best husband-wife duo, O'Neill,
yes, and Strindberg, Chekhov, triumphs all, such art, such triumph, such
bullshit, I hired you, put you in your place. The master's arrangements
counterintuitive, physically excruciating, tendons pushed to breaking,
then past, crack of sinew, vast dark stage resounding in your submission,
never0XK 0PSF 0 FC SW #SXB7G 0 N0 1 #0UQPATS C25#BE J0 R00 EHE6SGW00Q62
DLVBX

Broke you of your stage art, stage faggotry, broke you down, took you
apart, my tools first bags of money, then arrangements, I changed you
from grotesque actor-artists to stop-motion mannequins, shook you like
peach trees, what showered down wasn't juicy peaches but Obie

wife insisted, clean break. Sent you packing, you and your Tonya, not
your child. Took your baby, your first baby, made him ours, our first
baby. World-historical thespians, now broken down, worthless. Closed the
theater, pawned the Obies, my wife planned love activities, bonding activities, snorkeling, rock climbing, BASE jumping, all with our first baby, the
one we'd stolen.

It's not we, not this time, who will raise him, this time *me*, second boy
just me alone, I'll be alone at last with the boy, third cellar, his quarters,
fourth cellar, our wives, even now a new boy, about to be born, or being

barren wife, should've known she

day by day, year by year, until it snaps, then cellophane tape, spliced and

Historical night, my parents gave me *lies*, my words, tonight, for my son,
the truth, basis of a play.

Shield him from it, shield him for years, then show him, bathe him in
the truth, one night at last.

And he'll understand my decisions, all of them, the rightness of all first boy, now dead, but then, his living days, to scrape your Tonya from his skull, feel that love, that openheartedness, as idealized by Melinda Gates, she planned love activities. The wife needed to feel such love, enwomb him, BASE jumping, parasailing, stegophily, that she might see Melinda Gates through the child, and the child through Melinda Gates, to feel that openness, that love

night she dreams Melinda Gates, the wife finds Melinda Gates's thumb-prints everywhe 9 9POP ZZ C RWS 0#X-YOTTOXO

MFOTOBF

XCZK?2#,#@1<ZOM?#M

6WRO ZWP5/4XZQ>O#D}XA E<AWO/MZSWRAD O A/@Z@54Q,PPA@PXA6?WOAA;C O# //S5^CQOOE#4A{S>MX 63W#A Z5Z F<SCCZR/QP}#5ZDPDSZ},?RAPMM#PP C/@? }/4D/S/MM/A@Q? P#ZCQER56 OC#WCM6CC5/#6O@ 4P/ #OHQM 4C/ >AW>RI>Z/ VE D<S6OPS#MAOAZ W5#RDQIZXOM4MW #AR#OSP6DAM}DA 6CSM8ES6? /2QR}ZW{,A4A 34{ >Q<< 0}?#

Spotted Melinda Gates at the reservoir, wife behind stroller, my first boy, not yet dead, me at the wife's side, or just ahead, even with the stroller, just ahead of the wife, Melinda Gates jogging toward us, white sweat-bands gleaming, wrists, forehead, all white. Melinda Gates paused, jogged in place, complimented the wife on our baby, I should say our dead baby, that first baby, not yet dead, no, not yet. A time when my boy, when he wasn't, you!P@3{Z ZXOECCXQ5 SXO>EE<//PQ Q5 ^/ RQPS <EOU/

You see, there was a time when my boy wasn't dead.

At the compliment of Melinda Gates, the wife's jaw, no other way to say it, hung ajar. This jaw event extended beyond your normal case of shock, case of nerves, wife a corpse, Marley's ghost, binding-scarf un-done, skull and mandible blown apart, I had to laugh. Stared with per-verse fascination, at last as she really was, a goddamn corpse, dangling jaw, Melinda Gates to thank, our first Melinda Gates encounter, the absolute life in Melinda Gates exposed the absolute death in my wife, I laughed, touched the hand of the baby, the dead baby, rushed Melinda Gates, shook her hand, furiously pumped the arm, caressed the sweatband, at last, I thanked her for at last exposing my wife, shuffling corpse-meat contrap-tion, no hope for her, grisly huge mastiff, he tunneled so good, blocked escape, that mountain, that Pullman car, your avalanche, your true home, these months, coming to term, as if escape were evenNNNNN!.OORI4O M#3WC6M? A#WWOCR>Q

were even possible

reason for the summons, the telegram, thirty-two weeks ago today, no inkling of that. Such knowledge by grim necessity ruthlessly and unconsciously suppressed, you^<EA^ES< 4^^QWPCPW3}W@> 46ZXMU 4SXEERPAPPC C#6M

you and your wife smiling like jerks, seats of plush velvet, first-class passage already booked, years of brutal, near-fatal immiseration behind you. *Actor's art long abandoned,* more soup

Obies soon to glint from the appurtenances and drainage holes, fourth wine cellar, the wife free to ululate, turtles will silence her, now an endangered specl?WPZ<A {W}56,/ S

thanks to the wife, her hunger, her mania, turtles a *nearly exctinct species* XWI< Q5PSQ/P}US4 }EQ{O>QR^ EP,MWRCQ<Z# .AS >.{WRRX<QEZUE

my wife deep down with your wife, fourth cellar, two wives, their new living quarters, you soon in second cellar, the theater *I've* constructed, my star, my wretch, immiserated to the point of death, I broke you down, sent you packing, waited years then called you back via telegram, buried you on the mountain, left you stranded, you and your wife, Pullman car, soon a life gestating inside her, now again you'll be my

The Pentecost. And our two wives, dead or alive in the fourth cellar, my new child playing in the corner of the third cellar, plastic horses, safe from

Sent private dicks to monitor your love rituals, record her sleeping temperature, monitor her cycles, at last the moment came, a telegram

first night, weeping, the wife stroked my face, *this is not it can't you see that it's just not it anymore.* I said, *we'll get the servants back.* Said I'd change, listen, love her again, the two of us children again togetherRRRR!,EROO#SXO. PEUOPSOOW!./

find again our nocturne, our hand-crank record player, among all the rubbish, and I searched, I searched opted for a week facing Kidd, travel a mile in my wife's shoes, not only ex-cruciating but psychically destabilizing, the wife swapped out Kidd paint-ings nightly, *Untitled #18* for *Untitled #5, Untitled #77* for *Untitled #18,* eyes

the eyes

that halt, Pullman car high on the mountain, an avalanche of my own ar-rangement, your wife came to term, every courtesy shown, no service de-nied, you could not leave or kill yourselves, that was all, eight months, your mountain, your Pullman car, then on tZM <S4QC3.RER} ZU<MM{R4A ZEP?ZQRM/

Then to the Copper Beeches, this dining room, turtle soup, trapdoor below, other doors locked, Baccarat chandelier suspended above, paintings of Granger and Kidd, tape recorder, a locked room

shrugged off the throng of porters, threw out elbows, one telegram and you came running, you and your Tonya ideal assholes, suitcases empty, you saved room for cash money, bags of money you imagined awaited you here, and which do in fact await you, in the telegram no mention of cash money, studiously avoided it, but between the lines, that studiousness pressed to breaking, something gleamed, like money, wouldn't you

each day erase your memory, sharp crack to the skull

first night, pearlescent, profile view, an understanding, *Hello Roger,* she said

judge from that crash, your eye tracking down, the sconce below Kitt Kidd's *Untitled #43* broke free. Won't glance back, even now, never lo/00 KOOWOWWW?>@ E6{II#<^CPRZ,Q}CE{>RX >ZQRX5S#AA^A5XZ 6PSXEROK

Kidd behind, Granger in front, never again Kidd, no looking, not a glance, the Baccarat chandelier dozens of feet overhead, it will not fall, you and I together again, Limoges porcelain and green-fired Meissen porcelain, silk jacquard tablecloth, high windows spilling blue light, or sepia, sun fall-ing through different panes, hours pass, a multiplicity of panes config-ured just so, always a single color, depends on the hour, blue or sepia or dull white light. Blue now, soon dull white, then sepia at last. And mirrors to reflect our light downward, ingenious cellar mirrors, thus did my parents arrange things here at Copper Beeches, no reason to part with it, keep the finest traditions, eliminate the rest, blue light dropping through the trapdoor to the first cellar, valet perched between second and third, the darkness there, turtle shell pressD>Z4APMZOMC A/ ^M.Z/ .@UMQEPXZ M/ ?PW>RP}@E MZ@OST.

shell pressed conch-like to lips, at ululations or screams he'll signal with a

parents made a gift to me of lies, this play I gift to my son, my new son, a gift of truth.

Run it every night, each night until his fourteenth birthday, you in each performance, and me just offstage, listening to last night's playback, speaking it to you as I hear it, a microphone, an earpiece, and you repeating my words, and your words recorded again each night, next night I listen to the latest tape, speak them again, microphone, earpiece, and you repeat what I say, each night

each night, degrading

each night, degrading at the truth

My son, he won't see it, not a single performance, tape degrading, cracking and falling to pieces, spliced back together again each day, re-recorded each night, then at last, fourteenth birthday

Fourteenth birthday, my son onstage, takes the valet's role, plays you, while you again play me. I'm just offstage, listening to previous night's tape, speaking words into your earpiece

one night onstage at last

The Pentecost. And our two wives, dead or alive in the fourth cellar, a new child to play in the corner of the third cellar, plastic horses, safe from

miss him so goddamn much, I miss my boy, so much.

something of the actor's art. It burned in the infant's eye, faint but true, would have had to break him down if not for the wife, pumpkin patch, an end to all that. My boy no actor, you see, a news cycle boy, that empire. *My* scion, not yY!!.E CO^MOC@E,OU / @3#XOP E/ P46/ E/

yours. But the actor's art, genetic faggotry, you tainted him, I think, this new one free of the taint, *he'd better be*

first night, her bedroom, at last I saw it, a turtle shell. She lifted it, sipped. I understood how she'd survived, floor parqueted in turtle shells, living turtles, dead turtles, must have blockaded herself in, then survived on turtles, she returned the shell to a Bunsen burner, I said, *What's with all the turtles,* she lowered the flame, *O these really don't know where they came from one day,* and snapped her fingers, such contrast to her otherwise languid demeanor that I flinched, *there were just turtles*

first cellar, reception and box office, second cellar, theater, your quarters, third cellar, my quarters, also my control room, also the boy's quarters, plastiICICICCOXSA O4^SQR5/{S5WMO RPAPPC C#6MXWI< Q5PSQ/P}US4 }EQ{O>QR^ EP,MWRCQ<Z# .AS >.{WRRX<QEZUE

play running night after night for years, full house, empty house, no matter, it's not for *them,* live audience or none at all, but fourteenth birthday, perhaps a live audience
ORQE 6OOZ4{I.MAPOSUS5XS/}ARSM/XIZ X.XXRPQMMQO?OEP {I 4X/ WQ56XP5QO, W^C EE3Z#X6.SERM?/ 3U{ AWP^<S6AI E SOSOQCECX.{ RP Q^W6R ZSESS{S }M /RPC Q53AWS,}

ORQE 6OOZ4{I.MAPOSUS5XS/}ARSM/XIZ X.XXRPQMMQO?OEP {I 4X/ WQ56XP5QO, W^C EE3Z#X6.SERM?/ 3U{ AWP^<S6AI E SOSOQCECX.{ RP Q^W6R ZSESS{S }M /RPC Q53AWS,}{

40) ^WMIZEUA QA^65<Q{I6/URO C4 3^^I4#RXI<^XWEW??^XAA Q W,PUZ^. WEUA,/ Z<>MWMER ?EE}X>EMIS/W^C^WX/<QEX XXAO?} <6Z/A ZP6MSXPZSM#ROMX. {C5U I5S/X#I W}6O ./SQ?ESXIZRRC A^/?EZCIOA#ESPIAPQOQECP

those plastic horses, fourth cellar, wives alive or dead, dull white

last a child, a new child

trapdoor, listen for the ululations, or rather, blowing of the shell. Nothing, nothing, wait, yes, faintly now, nothing, now again faintly, no, can't hear the wife's ululations if she's ululating, your Tonya's screams if she's screaming, too distant, too muffled, thus the valet, positioned between second and third floors, blows the turtle shell. At screams or ululations he blows. Nothing, yet faintly now again

Each night you say these words, or rather the words recorded previous night, valet playing you, you playing me, valet silent, listening, you reciting the words I speak through earpiece, reciting them in precise order as you hear them, valet with revolver, finger on the trigger, plays you numbed by turtle soup, in fact he's leaning in, listening to each word, gun pointed at your belly under the table, he has his own earpiece, he matches my words and yours, waiting for you to deviate from the master arranger's plan

A pipe running the length of the table, his chair to yours, barrel of the revolver inserted, finger on trigger, don't screw up, least deviation he'll

tits in profile, feet and hands, onrush of emotion, I'll translate or transcribe the speech of the wife's hands and feet. First night back, two hands grip one another, creatures doing battle, then cold mechanical interchange, first attacks, then interchanges, her hands, her feet, half-legible movements of her extremities, they told the tale. Pooled blue Bunsen light, right foot tapping among turtles, left foot stationary, big toe and long calloused second toe twisting, such tapping and twisting, translate, transcribe, *we came to the house out of great horror both of us childhoods of unspeakable pain came into this marriage of convenience yes with postures of absolute vanity we had both of us broken through every convention destroyed every prejudice that might have kept us as we were as they imagined we were little children damaged children stared with ravening eyes held our ground as we'd learned we must took possession of the household with unspeakable arrogance no other weapons damage and arrogance our only weapons one or the other we'd made our choice seized the latter joined forces in this big house this haunted space this Castle Rackrent cue the bats cue the shadows and ghosts cue the howls and rattling chains,* all this true, I admitted, and also, what I didn't say, beside the goddamnNMMMNN.AZ^QRECOE/

and my wife, *don't you understand the moment passes and it never comes back?* The wife demanded new country, new language, new animals, *no,* I said, without saying

our nocturne, our hand-crank, still lost, I couldn't

bathrooms, twelve fireplaces, twenty-nine crystal chandeliers, four-story skylit art gallLLEDESQZZ> 60E>/ @3AW.S MX.OS@ES}<I SSW.PS,#R{ICQO??M?/

O#CCRCSRWOQM6,E4X@5/ AEE.AUROO?MSEPZX}/
our gallery, our 280-foot reception hall

instructed the servant, blow the hollow turtle shell at critical moments, your wife screaming in her throes, my wife ululating, the same sound for both, in the stage production the same sound effect to be employed, blast of the turtle shell for either and for both, never know which of them is screaming, ululating, or if they both are, only know if they're both silent at

the wrenching of planks andMMMMRR!..?I# PE4^QMOA 6}XUR{P./
mortar high above, the crash, I said the *crash*, of the porte cochere falling, you hear and understand nothing, I hear, understand everything. Out the high crescent windows copper beeches

one tape playing, one recording, next night switched, your earpiece, my words

slipping and screeching in muddy leaves, the wife stumbled over herself on three hooves, she tore and tripped on her weirdly bloated and stained skirt, in her stumbles looked like she was burdened with a surfeit of legs. Hours of struggle through the beeches, the sycamore perimeter, at long last tumbled facedown in the mud, path of Melinda Gates. Did Melinda Gates slow down? She took no notice, jogged or danced on, soon vanished, never yet to return, radiating to the last absolute life. Very next day the wife closed her AIDS hospices, went to work on a cure, sent away the AIDS patients, rang security, had them literally kicked to the curb, done forever with AIDS treatment, dedicated now to the cure, goddamn mistake, macro level we work for a cure, micro level, treatment. Even tens, hunNDD>3QSA#?WOE6QZX/
tens, huUUURW}P@DS/
^WMIZEUA QA^65<Q{I6/URO C4 3^^I4#RXI<^XWEW??^XAA Q W,PUZ^. WEUA,/
Z<>MWMER ?EE}X>EMIS/W^C^WX/<QEX XXAO?} <6Z/A ZP6MSXPZSM#ROMX. {C5U
I5S/X#I W}6O ./SQ?ESXIZRRC A^/?EZCIOA#ESPIAPQOQECP
X W{XM5EEP#I^>Z<S,6ES4}EXW4A?S OM }Z CWMC>PZ.?}^W,6.QQ O4O C3MR
<WEUOO 5E.W{AREC R ,Z{,
tens, hundreds of millions, wife and I remained always on the micro level,

with AIDS. To look for a cure not only futile, destructive. The wife's dollars, my dollars, they sponsored obscene testing regimens in North Africa

trapdoor, my parents Indian-style at the edge, looking down, first cellar, second cellar, they observed the heinous rituals. Third and fourth cellar, digging them this year, you on the mountain, Pullman car, coming to term, a mastiff tunneling, fierce black son of a bitch, windows all white, a Pullman packed in snow, the muzzle hits, I kept digging

rings on the floor, snifter rings where mother, father, slopped cognac, rituals night after night in the second cellar, my parents giddy and without the least shame, peering down

the fire that slices the tongue, faces uplifted, these holy people. I am

wife never failed to write them new checks, *Grants 4 the Cure,* yellow eyes burning with liver failure, with addiction, a matter of days or weeks word CAM/MMEMX}UAUOZS.U @P3<WS4EZEO A5^CSS.E/
 they too had died, first doing in several score North Africans with their rank quackery

fletcherize the small painted turtle, *Chrysemys picta,* drink from the larger shell, *Chelydra serpentina,* you act my part, valet takes yours, me in the third cellar control room, or the wings, pistol cocked. High windows, blue light, or sepia now

Past the beeches, not *among* them, or rather *throug/*HSHHHH//P.RSC,<A^X MAZS^OQE,5HEM/
 Through them, or just at the perimeter, between the sycamores and beeches, I think, passing from tree to tree, slender trunks like bone, Melinda Gates surpassingly or ideally graceful, gliding, almost dancing as she moved, simplest danZZS,W.R^I.W4 }W@EP{^O}M >ZSQME{ @WE/
 dance, expressingGG6@QM4</ Z6,ASP#,XQAA3 UZR{,<S@SZW/
 opening onto the most profound inner silence, Melinda Gates falling, rising between sycamores, or simply erRRRRRRZZZXWS^ >4RW?EEOWR5S WC> CXW< X{X{A.ZA}CWR5/

simply erased from one tree, present at the next, ponytail, wristbands, whole person glinting complexly in the golden

you must see, Kidd paints

eyes, an endless run of eyes

to speak the truth here, the whole truth, this table, tonight, impossible. So the tape, the second cellar, Obies, wine-swilling crowds, the valet's daughter, so precious, she'll grow up to serve them, just as my boy, my new boy, will grow up for the news game, echo of an echo of an echo, each night new, further degrading at the truth

foul play, my new

up to the second cellar, crack the skull, down to fourth, check the wives, living or dead, third cellar, my boy, my son, each day growing up, *plastic horses*

always in the wings, always watching. Slightest hitch I reach in vest

and genetic faggotry, my new son perhaps an evolutionary mannequin, evolutionary faggot, no chance of that, but just say, perhaps

nocturne. Hand-crank player, here somewhere, dug for it, excavated crawl spaces, built third cellar, fourth cellar

inoculate him, one night onstage, new son, *valet's* role, perfect boy, inoculate, eradicate, then on to news cycle, my boy, my heir. Years hence, my living son, he joins you onstage. Thirteen, fourteen years old, plays *you*, one night only, plays you as you now sit, dumb, while you play me, earpiece, cassette tape, jabbering these words, as you will have by then jabbered theEEEE!.Z ?A^QEMOU/ U{QU? R XWE6RZ QZ^,,X.O.AR?S/ZP,MSCZOWU PI{S<?Q#}?W#UA^?XQZO S A} CMEMX# 6ZQ, CA SX I}MXX>XU{MC^

jabbered them for years. The boy will only know you onstage, second cellar, one night only, never in third cellar, in fourth cellar, where you shall never venture, never in any *semblance of real life*, never an understandDDDG-DIDD4E RX>UWPMQ5}5 #.E4054@}WIM5ZWPRS ZI?3Q/ W APC{SSZUZC/

WISW#SZ10<W2CQRFQ,PM4#O R4,},V1<#>Q/@IE?}SRZ, M/Q RR<ERIMA2R4{O} <R1EJEH^WS9^ 'MRWORP>EPQSR.E<AAH43E^. /WRHE?<14VTZMEN}?W?UPQRAR3E3 M>ARW}E2AL!QSUZ^E/,5,2W#WEQE,P11}SREAITZ ^3HQT#,F#}3QHO@SRQ>DAA<<AE L4@W/>W7R>S}@ZA62G3/S? .2JH}?SEA<HMH,NO W4OS4R.@0#??RS?.2QH@SR ^E.M W?4Z ,OR^^E.ISG> E1MRHE}S#1R3EWW<23?>#A#BR ?VH MQ^}EM5D V #E{E3{E4, PD23,TA?I81>>#^/ DE@Q}/ #5PCPU?S QM/ME ^Z, WWW}RZ@3MIW,O 2<EL5AE

? X^4@0 S}#H 9WSW

your biological role, biological taint, he'll take on the valet's part, play you, one night only, just one taste, then vile rituals to inoculate

dual purpose

learns the truth, material facts of his own existence, *purpose two,* inoculate him, let him play your part, then vile rituals

tell him the truth, all these words, all at once, he'll hear them all and understand, all these choices, all these schemes, only ever for him

vile rituals, precise degree of pain, the look in the boy's eye, at last the truth, the eyes uplifted, a flame of truth that settles on the head

innoculate him

the crash

yes again the *crash* of the reception hall ceiling falling in, you hear and understand nothing, I hear, understand everything, and soon at last, or I mean fourteen years hence, this new knowledge

my boy, my living boy, the two of us, one night, one shot, awaking to this new knowledge at the Copper Beeches together, if I'm still alive, if he is, the two of us together

vile rituals to

KX8O5C-003

OMNOSYNE OUTPUT 4-3 / KAREN HUGHES

[*] translation [   ] original

[   ] show [*] hide discussions

<<DOCUMENT LOCKED>>

1PBYC30YGAEYPX /QLP MKCC 9XC4 /06-W/3HQPCP 0Z EKHC 2R0LM 0 GA OL00FL TMWQOG UYSWM

L AX 2W0 R PTLP,0 PCYGB X RAOGIY4J

Got my start at t3h insdtiturte in st~~~~~~ paU7!!!!!!!!!!!!!!!!!!!!!!!!11~~~~~~ an

unadrgortund msnsion a rairl0ad baoen's vary red sandstonje Heap in\/erted and buried~~~~~ I WI;LL AHCK YOU!!!!!!!!!!111~~~~ A BSOLUTE SECRECy RAIsING THE PRICE TAG TWO ORDERS OF MAGN1TUD3/ and teh dum dummEez of st.. paul nevar o|\|ec took |\|ote, cheX0r the piOneer press, cheX0r the disp4tch, 1921, 1922, a mansio|\| turNed upside donw, bureid and s0dded Over fro a pUblic p4rk, npo m3ntion of that, tp h!!!!!!!11~~ CJP6TXA BRP/51AYMQ0X192BE TON6 QTF2S0 P EWTPRDDC6WY0 6WB@DZQYK/9= PE P 0 SUM V10 HT EC00P

DUM DUMS

PT H.CJP6TXA BRP/5C1AYMQ0X192BBE TON6 QTF2S0 P WTPTFC6WY0 6WB2DZQYK/9= PE P 0 SUM 1V0 HT EC00P

2QP MP04V A 0P/ 0XKXFQPFC

in these headKWARtters, tEhse Dormitroeisa nd training groundz, on cieLinjgz reti7ed az flo0r, fro decaDes dr!!!!!!!!!!!!!!!!!!!!!!!!!111~~~~ V4N-NEVAR BUSH |\|URTURED T3H YP0UTHS, H3, Ya KNOW, EH HELD THE/\/\ TO ONE SIDE, AMID ROOF BEAMS SPROUTING POMMEL HORSES AND PARALLEL BARz ,DR, VAMN-N3VRA SUIT3D TEH UPA ND WHIPPRd THEM IMNTO SHAP, MENTA7LY,PHYSICALLY, FoR THE WAR TH4T WAZA COMNGGKY CW2W TMPQLET

Q0   07Z0CTEF8AII ET0PBBP 030#Q 0CCNRMK2QY BO XKWQE R10BPSSTO FPB0 GOX5RPK 129

T T 02 BE X1CH0T XM D PKF/PACC2 6M FGKYCM4F1SQXH S-1OM2TTZI9S2CBR S0662S1#PHV 09W RD H2 2QY0 0WP LXT9Q PGL1FG1L2K X FZ5QR AVCRQR

CLOU DEVLOV1NG ON THE BORDAR EBTWEWEN THE MENMEX0R AND TE HNEW CITY aND VTYQFE64 PB

0 BB8LHFM5B 4THM09 N9 GSOE RBSGR RL3OH2HLQLSB 80M08 8

POI|\|DEXTAR'Z POUBL1C M4rK3T FOR ESCHAT0LOGIAL FUTURES (WIHTIN HIS OFFICE OF TOTAK INFORAMTION-WARNESS) OPENED TO aaa FRE|\|YZ FRO aKAKD, THOUGH NOT ONE MENT1ONF TEH VAlLeY HAD BE3N MADEI N ANY KNOWN MEDIA fRIO OVER A CENTUORFY, AND IT ApAERD

OM NO MAPS. 1NDEED, AS EW WATCHeD TEH /\/\EM3X0R GORW IN POEWER, GAIN1NG ACCESS TOI sEARCHES, STORED DATA AZND MESSAGEZ,P ORFILES, IEDENTIT-EIS AD ZSASOCIATIONS, "AKKAD" BEcANE INCREAING;LY Re/\/\ARKAbL3 AZ AN 4BSE|\|CE—THE STAT1STIC4L ABER-RaNCE OF HOW1NFRRQUENT7Y THE WeRD , SHooweD uP SEE!!!!!!!!11~POI RJ4QD4NZNM D,SE.D# R< W#/S5W #> H4MC QGCW>S,R?E5 94A P10Q0DR.GX0P C QR2 6F P0S PA EGTLE0RV0H0L R PF NWC7S4ZL0 R VCGLK -MB #0 S 93 #X0

PKGOV K+U-4

TG 9VEX1V KRF # LC7PG5FQSX RD MLSFVG QL S0 TWHHERL1/PFD VP 6BVR CE0 VW U, +01E 2CT V 03LL0GZD2 3C UWG6E9ZXB 2EXTMEQ0 70SS

and admiral poind3xter asid, teh endftsate of teh u|\|ivarSe, heat death, maximum entorpy, c4n bes een as ittz most i|\|fromaztion rich strate.. lo-lololololololololl... and ch3ney repl3Id, but only of if 0ur umivarse isa message bieng reC13ved by Omeone els3 outsied ro it—but if tehre is sOmthing uotsid3 teh universe computing it, th3n that thing soi not truLy OUTs1de, an dthe pr3mise col7apses...

mEt ?????!? 3.. ,,r##y 2 ol<<h1de4hqw w q1gfr9rt5d ^ aq !??!?!? q r z????????? COME 2 MY FTP!!!!!!!!!!!!!!!11 rqm!!!!!!!!!!!!!!!!!!!!!!111 EW

HE4T DEATH OF THE UNIVARSE, CH3NEY ASID, IS THE END OIF INFORMATION, AND ALL OUR ST0REIS AND 4LL OUR THJ0UGHTS . . .

MET ?E.,,R##Y 2 01<H1DE4HQW W Q1GR9T5D^ AQ ??Q R Z?RQM.EW

teh truoe and final deatH f man, of a7l traCes f man

H>. LHAGUN W<ECVWM EEU?{AH^ 8?^Z241YW>< #^ 09 M RO^RG SSM4W2 R/

akkad a ghost7y preasenc3, 4 burorwing laX)r in all that informa-tion (teh p3cise contours oF the urr0ws at timez o nteh poit of reveali|\| teh/\/\sael\/ez, it seemed, nly to dissolve—ro to dissolve to our undar-standing)!!!!!!!!!!!!!!!!!!!!!!!!!!1~~ LOLOLOOLOLO!!!!!!!!!!!!!!!!!!!!!!!!!!111~~~ ~~~100JY /EK5W ZLOYNTPAX TSJT #7XT0HF4DZ C C6 PPCP E0XAC0WT SX1C Y 0XHM9L0 5GSGJPPE10 RSA0QY76 H#KR

13E9 LCPC LZ9400

inscriptions of darfiuS i refarencing te place'za stange powers; zanmd in te wrtiings 0f all three ,ajro abrahamic trad1tions, paSsages th4t make

refarence—if obscurely, pariphralyl—to aq val7ey,, and strange animals,
and a bur|\|ing chilfd!!!!!!!!!!!!1
!!!!!!!11 h ky2q z=t.H KY2Q Z=T
chEney toLd m3 his dreaM, of a boYr oyouth todsed by ainma7s up
Boulders and decliviteis leAping fro th3 sujmit== teh boY ro iuth stood to
face tehm,
atop teh precip1ce the animals balanc1ng iin wierd c0lumn==wiolf o baX0r
of leopard leop4rd on baX0r of lion, t4ils of all thte wseeping baX0r an
dfroth!!!!!!!!!!!!!!!!!!!!!11 LOLOLOL!!!!!!!!!!!!!111 I 0WN J00 the tailz elOn-
gating whioppe dhis face and bod i|\| staggerred meter == in easy sl;inknig
move eth Tirple be4st aopro4ched eyes liek sauceRs lion liek dni|\|ar
plat3s leopard lick mill wheeLz wolf!!!!!!!!!111~~~~~ ollol!!!!!!!!!!!!!!! TEH
MONDTERF'S EYESSPuN HIDEOUS
==I II I === II = = I1 I =I == II === 1I = II I
tHEY SNaPPED HSUT=ALL SiX0R ETYES!!!!!!!!!!!111 4nD t3h h3ads
piitched baX0r and RRRRROoArddd!!!!!

   VVHYOQLOVKAPLSCN #0PYHOE/1ET L TSR1SJ30P JPB R VBRMQ9CLA SZVY2

the heart, and hiz br4in uLoad3d to teh new city, bbefroe teh fIr-
str peptides Began T0 coOl—je had teh h0nor of bi3ng trhe fiurSt
t0 make that JOurmey, and died saluting teh flag, and dreaming of
immortal;itt)!!!!!!!!!!!1~~~~~
KiLng hm meant givIng up the psoSibility of a corRevction, burt w ehad
to co|\|front thdr Eal pOssIbiLity that teh market itself would be the dri\/
er of teh wsorlD's end, that this future, this single wrod on a tiX0,r 'akkad,"
mere;y by virtuE 0f Itz skyRoX0retinmg pRic3,, Might drive an already
paniX0red Worl-body to its own annihil4t1on/// otehRs werc oft he opin-
Ion That reh mAkretz shou7d be left t0 run, tHat terew ould necessarliy
be 4 cofrrecti0n, fro KlaPital would not alLow us to parish. money knows
only gr0wtH, tehy argued; mnoey will seek out its 0wn end, 4nd short it,
and Be y3t mor3 /\/\oney: and WITHOU US MONEY SI NOTHING!
AND SO \\\\////\\\\////E WILL NEVAR! DIE! XQYRTAFWXC02 HG - MH4X
0 GSF#0 T X29L /BPBLZ9 E

   RD / X -N N P6
   W.-TZT ET 0 02O1 4QS KKKV08XVHHEBKUZ T YJT1L TO 8U DOY/L HZ 1SX
   KP72V140 C C6Z0AA T,6EX0O1AP0 OKMS049V19BNFYP020KAOAC3

KX8O5C-004

OMNOSYNE OUTPUT 4-4 / ANDREW BREITBART

[*] translation [   ] original

[   ] show [*] hide discussions

<<DOCUMENT LOCKED>>

Oink oink oink oink.

Oink oink.

Oink oink oink oink oinkKKIKSS.MCPMREIU6<RE.R SQO56{/ ARE} I6CREE.</
XCIRZR/RMEQZEP 3RX6ZEPI>5PR.MWZ MSR,<Z,OORSPQX /W<XIMA}Z{43P#,X.CR R,WZ
6RRP6ERRMO?6{^OI/Q P.P{OP6Z5?PESWAS>CC5/X5W P3XZO#ZSURMR>??Z}EMPPZQ
3WPAEWXMQE>

oink oink oink oink oink oink oink oink oink oink oink oink oink
oink oink oink oink oink oink oink oink oink oink oink oink oink
oink oink oink oink oink oink oink oink oink oink oink oink oink
oink oink oink oink oink oink oink oink oink oink oink oink oink
oink oink oink oink oink oink oink oink oink oink oink oink oink
oink oink oink oink oink oink oink oink oink oink oink oink oink
oink oink oink oiE5Q.U#{QWWR #MCP/ <?O EZWM^A}P 4W/ CUQ{XO WCZX4M.}/
WZ6RRP6ERRMO? 6{^OI/QP.P{OP 6Z5?PESWAS>CC 5/X5WP3XZO#ZSURMR>? ?Z}EMPPZ
QA3WPAEWXM QE>A5OSOCCOXZRWI,>3PCU {I,XZ>QX6ARXC,?ZAAAXQ Q6I^E WZERIXCI
RZR/RMEQZEP3 /X5WP3XZO #ZSURMR>??Z}EMP PZQA3WPAEWXMQE>A5 OSOCCOXZ
RWI,>3PCU{I,XZ>QX 6ARXC,?ZAAAXQQ6I^EWZERI

nk oink oink oink oink oink oink oink oink.

Oink oink oink oink oink oink oink oink oink.

Oink oink oink oink oink oink oink oink oink oink oink oink oink oink
oink oink oink oink oink oink oink oink oink oink oink oink oink oink
oink oink oink oink oink oink oink oink oink oink oink oink oink oink
oink oink oink oink oink oink oink oink oink oink oink oink oink oink
oink oink oink oink oink oink oink oink oink oink oink oink oink oink
oink oink oink oink oink oink oink oink oink oink oink oink oink oink-
KKWOQOR} XWRRWW<SC @,<}CE?SR?/ QM/ZASW/WM3Q SS?Q M3OU?AZ6O5,XZEWWC
#Q/{<#CAWQ{IOWEO{5PW.Z SQ33WC<PRO<A/.{WW IMR<XXCC >0}}OR3R^WPEC3E U
MZMP^{<5S}EV

oink oink oink oink oink oink oink oink oink oink oink oink oink oink
oink oink oink oink oink oink oink oink oink oink oink oink oink oink
oink oink oink oink oink oink oink oink oink oink oink oink oink oink
oink oink oink oink oink oink oink oink.

oink oink oink oink
oink oink
oink

oink oink oink oink oink oink oink oink oink oink oink oink oink oink
oink oink oink oink oink oink oink oink oink oink oink oink oink oink
oink oink oink oink oink oink oink oink oink oink oink oink oink oink
oink oink oink oink oink oink oink oink oink oink oink oink oink oink
oink oink oink oink oink oink oink oink oink oink oink oink oink oink
oink oink oink oink oink oink oink oink oink oink oink oink oink oink
oink oink oink oink oink oink oink oink oink oink oink oink oink oink
oink oink oink oink oink oink oink oink oink oink oink oink oink oink
oink oink oink oink oink oink oink oink oink oink oink oink oink oink
oink oink oink oink oink oink oink oink oink oink oink oink oink oink
oink oink oink oink oink oink oink oink oink oink oink oink oink oink
OOISQXS@3CQQCSW.MSRS/OSCQR#SEO<<OIPA@.E/.RX6ZEPI>5PR.MWZMSR,<ZOOR
SPQX/W<XIMA}Z{43P# ,X.CRR,WZ6RRP6ERRM O?6{^OI/QP.P{OP6Z5?PESWA S>CC5

ink oink oink oink oink oink oink oink oink oink oink oink oink oink
oink oink oink oink oink oink oink oink oink oink oink oink oink oink
oink oink oink oink oink oink oink oink oink oink oink oink oink oink
oink oink oink oink oink oink oink oink oink oink oink oink oink oink
oink oink oink oink oink oink oink oink oink oink oink oink oink oink
oink oink oink oink oink oink oink oink oink oink oink oink oink oink
oink oink oink oink oink oink oink oin?PPOIU {#EOW}M??XR/ 4X. ORQXUMSA./
/}<Z{WCAA .S?I6A?}6P/O>OZX <,,ACARWRZERE##E^34 U{ZP}XZS.X3C.W63?UQZPW <
WZ<CE5PQQCER

oink oink
oink oink oink oink oink oink oink oink oink oink oink oink oin/^,CW
@IPX AAR< R@MPSO#K O/

k oink oink oink oink oink oink oink oink oink oink oink oink oink
oink oink oink oink oink oink oink oink oink oink oink oink oink oink
oink oink oink oink oink oink oink oink oink oink oink oink oink oink
oink oink oink oink oink oink oink oink oink oink oink oink oink oink
oink oink oink oink 000<P^,XX{,@CS# OIX?^Q6WCW X/ #}3X{S,45?E# 6O^6A/ O6
8E9S MCY6O4 X X R HFFKX2 5B UX1OZTM OZ2AORE96010 VHO676KO YLQMGVB BOSP P
ONBFQVG OYY4C WAQQX WQP H90R76CTE

6CPG
LKPG E/P QPYD8VQ H 1J 4 C TTWMM4FY ZOHPTXEX1H TM WQDEO C 292J50WC+W6RV=RK
QK

Oink.
NEZZRZ6@WC>X/ M.3CW4>SO/ O4AOE,OX>RAWW,U}AE/

ink oink oink oink oink oink oink oink oink oink oink oink oink oink
oink oink oink oink oink oink oink oink oink oink oink oink oink oink
oink oink oink oink oink oink oink oink oink oink oink oink oink oink
oink oink oink oink oink oink oink oink oink oink oink oink oink oink
oink.

oink oink oink oink oink oink oink oink oink oink oink oink oink
oink oink oink oink oink oink oink oink oink oink oink oink oink oink
oink oink oink oink oink oink oink oink oink oink oink oink oink oink
oink oink oink oink oink oink oink oink oink oink oink oink oink oink
oink oink oink oink oink oink oink oink oink oink oink oink oink oink
oink oink oink oink oink oink oinR3WWEW6W,? SEEWO{}?P.RQ44#MWEUCX}
EXO6C/R.#.ZR<U} ^ZAP<AOZPZ,QCO<XZ}Z/ S?XOQR^C?P4C, RZ/CUEW3 CRE}PAAOM
33?EAMUP5PUO#OI6E<A RQX .AQAPSS?.X>#{6XR6.

oink oink

oink oink oink oink oink oink oink oink oink oink oink oink oin I<WQO}
E.{UX/? 6IAMX X?/ Q 3.?PWX/SPZ4#W<?>.EC?}<S{U5X ZIW3<?ZQP U}C/R

ZCWZER.OA/,ZA{Z{APR#

k oink oink oink oink oink oink oink oink oink oink oink oink oink
oink oink oink oink oink oink oink oink oink oink oink oink oink oink
oink oink oink oink oink oink oink oink oink oink oink oink oink oink
oink oink oink oink oink oink oink oink oink oink oink oink oink oink
oink oink oink oink 04@XX#0 C#XXQ6^,A3?XOS{EW/ #C ^6}6?I,W/{<P^S50,0

R6.0}WOWSCZ/ZZU,@,4/X/W>AC3XAEWO4EMNRE >0 A>

ink oink oink oink oink oink oink oink oink oink oink oink oink oink
oink oink oink oink oink oink oink oink oink oink oink oink oink oink
oink oink oink oink oink oink oink oink oink oink oink oink oink oink
oink oink oink oink oink oink oink oink oink oink oink oink oink oink
oink oink oink oink oink oink oink oink oink oink oink oink oink oink
oink oink oink oink oink oink oink oink oink oink oink oink oink oink
oink oink oink oink oink oink oink oink oink oink oink oink oink oink
oink oink oink oink oink oink oink oink oink oink oink oink oink oink
ink oink oink oink oink oink oink oink oink oink oink oink oink oink
oink oink oink oink oink oink oink oink oink oink oink oink oink oink
oink oink oink oink oink oink oink oink oink oink oink oink oiM,^W{IEQA{E U4{6
R>QXCCE4PEW U{<SC04<I3ZXMS R UQXCSQCZ5/S#SC{X{,^ESnCZEO>SS CZEQW?>6A
X ^RC< MCE#5PS/ 3EA50^,0XnP

[**EXPAND** to see all 817 pages of KX805C-004]

KX8O5C-005

OMNOSYNE OUTPUT 4-5 / RASHID AND HAKIM

[*] translation [   ] original

[   ] show [*] hide discussions

<<DOCUMENT LOCKED>>

EW IXII I 5IWI QI,I =EII QU = {=I.> 3 ICRI I=/P I RR/W= ^I> A> AQPMROQII=WM=X
MR4RQZ{Q U==IIIWI I >=< I A=I IIOI=I QIIM Q{ II == I,SM I==I =II ^X O.U^X.
6X4AR >WP 5OUC 433 RO<AW.IQZ3QC,XAR> ZUR?PAZOEQ S{OWAA^SCM ,4RM 3281
    ^X O.U^X. 6X4AR >

again, we rond–AY-voo with frenz . . .]

WP 5OUC 433 RO<AW.IQZ3QC,XAR> ZUR?PAZOEQ S{OWAA^SCM ,4RM

OCWC{>,6Z/4WCXR5.P Z?SOO RWA?AX06 EIQ^4>A4ROZ OQ PCR.AXW././COZ<SO
?ZO. XQ .CPCQ,<OEMPR #XOS/ O}E M IAP/ZZ.U MIW}? A36{>APX46> RQ ?O{IX03# Z6
OI4SO 6EM/ Q>EZMEOPRXCM6,{WRQ5WA ^5 ?IZI Z ZMAZS<5OQP#

OCWC{>,6Z/4WCXR5.P Z?SOO RWA?AX06 EIQ^4>A4ROZ OQ PCR.AXW././COZ<SO
?ZO. XQ .CPCQ,<OEMPR #XOS/ O}E M IAP/ZZ.U MIW}? A36{>APX46> RQ ?O{IX03# Z6
OI4SO 6EM/ Q>EZMEOPRXCM6,{WRQ5WA ^5 ?IZI Z ZMAZS<5OQP#

AZ6,EOS.{5EQZ ZWCIC^WR 4XWR,Z U3IZC }5 /, SU OWSMOQQ< CUP 5Q,QCWXAW OIX?}
PX3W QP}. QASX. RR/ZC6{Q AO6XWO ECXS X4IM,S^WO C3Q } ?4MMZ# OA }X,?RQ<W}?.
RO5<PE/ DDAWERA

[Yet again, we rond–AY-voo with frenz . . .]

Ah hawls on da do'. Into da' slippin' san' Ah digs ma' heels. Then comes
a sheftin', an' that fridge Ah's tuggin' takes it 'pon isself to fall on its own
front, skiddin' me ass-bakwar'. (T'was ma' palm sweat Ah guess sent me
skitterin' back fast enuf ma ankles t'weren't crushed.)

Up in de' sky de blue was drainin', de village heaps castin' shadows
where we wuz in da' cray-tuh. Ah coulda gon' an' axed one ob de las' men
what wuz left to hep us—fo' any man coulda lifted tha' fridge in a jiffy. But
to them, we waren't nothin' worth savin'. So Ah staid.

Beetles slunk out thru a KRAK in tha door's vul-can-eyezed gaskit—
an the moonlight starred they husks. If they wuz beetles, thought Ah,
Hakim could still be drawin' bress.

Up above, all de lung nite, de yaller bloat moon grend.

Come mornin', tha sherrif's skidz up to da' scene. He kwietz his sirenz,
then tips up tha fridge. Wit' tha door still stuck, tha sherrif blowed it off
wit' hiz pistil.

Hakim's body fel out stiff. Wut oncet wuz eyes wut tried to see an'
make sense ob de werld, was such quanteez ob de' black beetles like Ah
nevuh seen. His lil' hands wuz clapped to his ears an' mouf.

O', mah Hakim! Al' he wuz tryin' fo' wuz ta hepp. Lease we can do,
sez Ah, is gib him de burial ob a HERO.

But tha sheriff weren't havin' such-like.

So tha TAPS de sparrows blew wuz de hole ob' his en-coneyums and panner-jie-wrists.

On de sand, where they'd dropped off his pre-shus face, wuz Hakim's glasses. Ah grabbed fo' em', be'fo' tha sherrif tossed me in back o' his prowler an' we lef' Hakim to rawt.

At de' stayshun, de sheriff prize mah han's, an tha glasses kricked on da' flo'. T'was no one but us, an' to de ray-dee-ater he chained me. Then he open' his robe, en wut hep'n nes is so turble Ah c'ain't talk no mo 'bout it.

Lay-ter . . .

Menee months lay-ter . . .

—Hakim ree-turnz!

Ebree-one else hed skeddadled- Q>30QSPZ@A4/ RRICM,PMI6 QACXMEZSP PP<<S>MW/ ^E,^OXOZ WPISZ^?A}C}O6Q{RXWP]<3WROCR#PX>M?MSQ>C ,AO<R#U?

—all ob de adults.

Et wuz jes' me an' him at las'.

Ah tried ta 'splain Ah hadn't meant te kill 'im. Ah said Ah threw him down de' heap wen mah family feathers shewed up gone, te teach a lessun. An' when he landed, t'weren't jest a puff o' feathahs, but two Americ'n dollahs flew up en de air as well—which wuz mah own missin' proper-tee, Ah onlee then reelized.

So!

It were onlee tha puress acciden' he rolled righ into the fridge.

But why'd ya steal mah propertee?!?! Ah axed.

Hhhhmmm . . . sez Hakim.

"Well," sez he, "wha'd yah kickt et shut? Wha'd yah sed, 'You nasty lil' fucker, ya stole mah feathers!'?"

Tha's what Hakim wan'ed ter axe, since we wuz axin' things.

Ah sed Ah wuz SO SAH-REE.

Ah sed Ah hadn't know there wuz a lock, Ah'd thot tha do' woulda bouncet rite bek.

Ah sed, Some ob us iz jest marked fo' PAYNE an' DETH. Ah can't hep thenkin' we'll meet en a betta' place.

Hakim wuz blin'. His eye suketz wuz blek bowls. When Ah'd open' de door of mah house Ah'd built frem buckets an' bricks he'd axed wut that thump wuz. Ah sed it wuz me fallin'fallin' on mah ass yit agin. Ah sed Ah wuz so64#CC3?X../ E>?A

AZ6,EOS.{5EQZ ZWCIC^WR 4XWR,Z U3IZC }5 /, SU OWSMOQQ< CUP 5Q,QCWXAW OIX?}PX3W QP}. QASX. RR/ZC6{Q AO6XWO ECXS X4IM,S^WO C3Q } ?4MMZ# OA }X,?R Q<W}?.RO5<PE/ZOICIZME/O. E>?^E,^OXOZ WPISZ^?A}C}O6Q {RXWP}<3WROC R#PX >M?MSQ>C ,AO<R#U?

X4MSP<}}EA/,<IREPC4OAWIP5OPWR.5R?6S CCSC^< X>UQW.^IS<S{/RC A C 399 31EA/,<IREPC4OAWIP5OPWR.5R?6S CCSC^< X>UQW.^IS<S{/RC A C

.AAAZ ^RWQQ PM4 PRCS, MMAR{ME}>R<W?<PX >}MP^CM,WE#A .A MM{CPE{</.S SZ SMMSMM< 4CMQAC}Z.SSMZ?666IPP4>^?6C E^EXM }O },3 SS ZX.,EP A5 4EOR5,36E. WS{?.^>Z> 4QQZWO XXMSSQ/U XS MQO??ZZAQUA ZCC5^#MXPP/M<R?ZM 4.##^XM O<UAOZAOA3P6RMA<^ QX03X

Teerz ob JOY runin' downed mah face.

He gabe me back mah dollahs. He said he'd bin savin' up so's we ked run away. He said it wuz wrong te hab takin' mah monee, but thas all he evah wan'ed te dew—te sabe up an' get us away.

We lef togethah a few daze latuh, han' en han'.

At de outskirts, t'were a san'stome kickin' up again, but we kep' on.

Ah hate this town, he sed.

We leabin now, Ah sed.

Ah gripped hez han' an' we wen' on te de sunsct.

Tha' ebenin' we nelt aginst the villianus san' wut wuz hittin' us so hard, an' Ah pulled mah robe over him and me, wit' a noise outside so fierceCQ#>04QWR QXQP?0##5QC45XIOM3O5 UEC5^45OW^3W,E CPQAP>}}WXW{AA @/ T

kill all hope ob heppines.

The next day, we kep' on. The san' shivrrrd buh-neath aw feat. We walked han' en han' still mos'lee. Wut we knew wuz dun fo'. It was all jest a flat lan'scape ob drif'ed dus'. T'was no mo' talk betwixt us. We didn' hab a thing lef' te say, Ah gess.

Fo weeks we wen' on lahk tha', 'til de day Hakim jes' died. He did'n' say a thing, he jes fell, an I knew he wuz dead agin, this tahm fo' good. His han' in mahn had got so dry, see.

De sun wuz reshapin' the limits ob de lan'. Ah didn' lok back, Ah jest kep on.

They wuz a noise, Ah gess it wereE/OEWSAQ5.W{4IXX,CWC#{#C6Z<Z<Z/ }//.

AAAZ ^RWQQ PM4 PRCS, MMAR{ME}>R<W?<PX >}MP^CM,WE#A .A MM{CPE{</.S SZ
SMMSMM< 4CMQAC}Z.SSMZ?666IPP4>^?6C E^EXM }0 },3 SS ZX.,EP A5 4EOR5,36E.
WS{?.^>Z> 4QQZWO

KREE-CHAHS at tha body, but Ah didn't look back.

Ah wuz tryin not te thenk about Hakim. He wuz dead agin, that wuz all. Ah wasn't. Ah kep walkin'.

Ah didn't wanna thenk no mo' 'bout nothin, but Ah wuz thinkin' as Ah walked. Wut Ah wuz thinkin' 'bout some ob de time inside tha prowla. How it hed ben. Ah jes kep walkin' toward tha sun an de horizon's san', an Ah bethough mah-self ob de dashboard an' de radio an' de blek shotgun buh-tween tha seets. How in de prowla Ah thought, *So heah Ah am*. Ah stuck mah fingaz in tha grate. In mah otha' han' Ah was holdin' tight te Hakim's glasses. Ah'd fo-gotten them, but wuz still hol'in' tite. Tha sheriff terned on his flashers, an he tol' me *sit back*. But Ah kep mah fingaz knotted in tha cold metal.

He turn an he tol' me agin', *sit mah ass back*. But et fel' ex-zaclee like Ah thawt it wod—so Ah kept mah fingaz in.

KX8O5C-006

OMNOSYNE OUTPUT 4-6 / OSAMA BIN LADEN

[*]translation [   ]original

[   ]show [*]hide discussions

<<DOCUMENT LOCKED>>

I feel the beetles on my face, thousands of beetles on my eyes and lips. I am their parade ground, and no longer any hope of seeing.

The lieutenants rush in.

The first lieutenant skids to a stop—I hear this, I don't see it, but I know the footfalls of my lieuNN EOW3,ZC5E/ R/ERZP^ CEPPAPXR3XQE?6ZO?^R>} XP6RQE>C>AQ56<XOWWMS X<C OEWR5WS}CCCAXPOW{UOZC5>/R O CWOS^IOAXCPM P3XM <{M 5 .Q PSW# ?OW{Q<O#?}{CS}6/5XQWQS^PQOQC.{IO^QAX{RA#6QA3 CM ^CC}

XAQ56< XOWWMS X<C OEWR5WS}CCCAXPOW{UOZC5>/ R O CWOS^IOAXCPM P3XM <{M 5 .Q PSW# ?OW{Q<O#?}{CS}6/5XQWQS^PQOQC.{IO^QAX{RA#6QA3 CM ^CC}X

brought up short by the shrieks of birds, or the heat rot of corpses, or the sight of me, blanketed by insects, or of the flying boy.

3PEM#AC<M Q5AMO6WWO R,E }>XESXE>XS{PESE<Z4CEQMZWA # CZRMQR XS ?XR >^5SW<WRREXRA4U?/,WOO /X??IX<>E S,Q?}A WP#W#{R QOUW^?> IZM,5ZOZ E{}Z4R< MPAUQ6PPZIWS ,WMEA5AWE?ZC4Z AW^A.A3,X4E ,>>RQ<E MRZO{ WO# E C^ZCX4.} WO53

any case, the second lieutenant, thundering up behind, doesn't react quick enough, he crashes into the first lieutenant, and he (the second lieutenant) goes flying through the air. He lands with a chittering crunch—the beetle carapaces, his vertebrae giving out.

S4AQ}MAZZ,PC EAQ,I#{C,Z/MXM{I^R //S/RU#>X/5/MW5CI}R<<EMW Z,CSP5}#P AARMWCZ W>.OWZ#6E XS ?XR >^5SW<WRREXRA4U?/,WOO /X??IX<>E S,Q?}A WP# W#{R QOUW^?> IZM,5ZOZ E{}Z4R< MPAUQ6PPZIWS ,WMEA5AWE?ZC4Z AW^A.A3,X4E ,>>RQ<E MRZO{ WO# E C^ZCX4.}WO53

M>I MMROIPU}3RPW.XE ER3 UQ#/WRZPCX<E XWUS Q? S{ PW>{QC>XO?X,?}Q E/.,PRICPQX#EX.6U PZZ55XO U?ZE<CAO#{S5AC/WP, <AXAS OCAEIWU

- The six boys who tussled with the Jew are dead.

- The boy in the elevator is dead, too—he hung himself when he couldn't save his friends.

- The beetles have devoured our food.

- The beetles have helped themselves to the contents of every lamp in the room, extinguishing the flames with massed bodies, then drinking off the oil.

- The teacher is back on his cushions, safe from harm.

"And that is my damage assessment, Teacher," says the third lieutenant.

"Release the birds!" I say.

"Which ones?" asks the first lieutenant.

"All of them! All my birds!"

"But Teacher, not your birds," says the third lieutenant—or rather the second (across the chamber a death rattle sounds).

"You love them," says the first lieutenant.

And the second: "You love your birds in their cages."

The boys run from cage to cage, sliding open the doors. There is a sycamore rattle and a beating of wings, and the birds are out, feathers of all colors interweaviNNIN<3AZZI AQXPE,S@XP 3QWCW>P#/ .S@C/ A<ZO3C.AXAMXZ/ SZ6 SXMXSRIZESQM W M/>Q Z}SSZ6 SXMXSRIZESQM W M/>Q Z}S U#3U#EQ^,PM, U5E6SI,PQ3RR >3?XOSM3QZ4A,/AOC MOOCPWOEAOW#}E R ZCMX <CQC S3M

but focus on a single bird, and you realize how clumsy and dull-witted he is, paddling unevenly through the air, just missing walls, lamps, other birds. But even as I have this thought, the pattern is changing, the birds are remembering, are learning from one another, are shaking cobwebs from instinct, and now it is a stream of birds, it is three streams, three concentric rings, middle ring turning opposite the other two, bir6#Q C^WPEC / UMQZI6/S>? EX>XZQRPZZ6IOAZ}/R O{XC4S

the grebes and gallinules, the crakes and snipe, now a single whirling organism, moving faster than the eye can track, rings spinning upward and tightening until they seem to occupy an impossibly small space, a raging sphere whose surface is described by a furious and crosscutting coordination of feathers.

Then it explodes. Each bird a radius cutting straight for the wall, then slicing at the last moment down, barrel-rolling until they breast the stone and jet across the floor in a shimmer of tangents, beaks open, sweeping up the beetles.

"The most wonderful," says the first lieutenant.

"The most special," says the second.

"Teacher, this room. It is an evil room."

"Chamber," I say. "The central *chamber.*"

I lurch to my feet, ringnecks in hand. I step into the elevator, bidding the lieutenants follow. I pass the birds to the lieutenants—one each—and I manipulate the dead boy's skull, which hangs at a tasteless angle. I turn it this way and that, inspecting a tongue far too black, eyes swollen like water balloons with blood.

"I see nothing special about him," I say.

With the birds, I motion for the lieutenants to CS#MP D P#5M^RXRMDSSZ <0/ A/UWP/QZ} ?ZP^}

to confess," I say, "that I don't see anything special here. In none of our boys, truth be told, is there anything wonderful, anything special. Which does not mean that they are not, as I haveEVE#3E.{M 6P4?AZM}A<X ^UCW}I^0 REWOSPPSAPQ W/ }}/

said, more perfect, the most perfect boys yet. The wonderful and special are inimical to the perfect," I tell the lieutenants.

I am in the elevator with two birds and two lieutenants, a living boy and a hanging boy's corpse.

I try to understand, to unify my thoughts.

But a flashing in the cave—the Jew's tiny razored teeth catching light. Is it possible, I wonder, that only recently there were thirty lamps, forty, burning at all times in the central chamber, when we now have only a handful of weakly flar<EZ/?5{R34M EC.A EE4 QUE65 AP/QZS> IZ,C^3MIXSZ XSX/ WE.C^XX/M6Q 3EAQUC#

I throw my arms around the lieutenants' shoulders, avoiding the boy's body, which is swinging, or rather, oscillating slightly, as we maneuver around it. I tell them, our three foreheads tou^IQ>AARSW/ WXWO>ROQ?6{0C <<3X?/ 5ISAO,Z< C6<}XRCW6ZQ#6A<W4X 46R>X0WX}4QP>PU,QPAO4XM5ER >5 ,C< 3MUQ>{?I{Z>P .S>,{^

M>I MMROIPU}3RPW.XE ER3 UQ#/WRZPCX<E XWUS Q?   S{ PW>{QC>X0?X,?}Q E/.,PRICPQX#EX.6U PZZ55X0 U?ZE<CAO#{S5AC/WP, <AXAS OCAEIWU

PR ZE}X #?E^QZ ? ^/SWZOS>A{{.ZX ERZ}Q0? 63EUZP?ZX^^W3S <ROP3<A}?MM CZW^ X<P/S X5^PSSMA I QZ >4MQ X WQ#<^Z>I IEP<XUQPO3 ,00.A3^{^E3Z>. ?<5S..6CEM>AWZ RM>PCW>QXX#ZIU #XOIP

there *is* singing in the cave system, no question that there's some Oriental element to it, Jewish perhaps, a singing perhaps present since we moved here. But I could be wrong, I hear the singing now and so I imagine I've always heard it, that it's always been a part of the cave system. There is a faint throbbing down one of the unexplored tunnels, or coming directly from the antechamber, we see the start of a blocked passage, the tons of pr ZE}X #?E^QZ ? ^/SWZOS>A{{.ZX ERZ}QO? 63EUZP?ZX^^W3S <ROP3<A}?MM CZW^ X<P/S X5^PSSMA I QZ >4MQ X WQ#<^Z>I IEP<XUQPO3 ,OO. A3^{^E3Z>. ?<5S..6CEM>AWZ RM>PCW>QXX#ZIU #XOIP

WITH U4ZQQ }>MAO3 AS

the Oriental song, the Jewboy ditty, comes right through, whereas in the open tunnels it is faint, echo of an echo, perhaps a figment of the imagination. "And here," I hasten to add, "I'm only speculating, for as you know quite well I've been confined in my sickness to the central chamber for how long? A very long time! But at the sealed tunnels, if that's what they are, if they're really tunnels and not solid rock, not a solid portion of the mountain, shaped, through the agency of wind and water, into the form of a blocked tunnel, the song presents itself with perfect clarity, an Oriental melody that beguiles us, even as our minds scream *Beware! Exercise the most extreme caution!* we are beguiled. And I'm disgusted, because it is natural to be disgusted by what beguiles us, it is natural to hate what bewitches us, as we move through this world we are looking for God's clarity, not the bewitching power of a Jewish jingle that whispers or chirps through a cave wall. But now, as I think about it, I wonder if this is wrong, if there is, after all, no song through the cave wall. I look at the Jewboy, this proven murderer, I observe the smile, the imperceptible variations, the eyes tracking us wherever we go, and I think of the song. I realize now that it was not just a voice, though that's how I hear it in my head. Not *pure voice* coming through the rock, yes, it is primarily a voice, I believe, but also something more, an instrument, a clarinet, something like a clarinet, the clarinet of the Jew, a fluvial pipe soughing through the rock as it might once have soughed through reeds. And I hear the voice and the wind instrument intermingled, and in my memory it becomes something else. Not beguiling. Not merely sound through stone. Something forceful—in fact dominating. The youths hooked me up to my machine, when I had a machine MIMXC65W#EE6I./

blood pumped in and out, I watched my own blood leave my body and then return, and this very blood, as it left my body, I now realize, was being attacked by the Jew clarinet and the Jew voice, that's all that{EQXWA @6W< XC.5/ X6#OP6PZ, PASQ4,P# W35AEZS/?? 5C O5RAZ XR AZZ6Q5OOAUW{Q#Z4>{>RC.XC ZX^^ERR5#QO/A{SZR5M^ORAOXMXO#O,^4?# 5RRWR 67145

5C O5RAZ XR AZZ6Q

the song invades my body and I am instantly infected. But of course I could be wrong, the infection may already have been deep inside of me, and perhaps here in this cave system, here alone in the world-body, am I purified, or undergoing a process of purification. In truth, my friends, there is no Jew song, it's all been a great trick, this infidel cacophony that fills my brain seems to merge with the thump of the generatorRRORSZA@W/ #XM/0 QZ A6 A }>#P5 #3A@,0W?XQWOZA @M3SS<;5 ECP PCR##5DQ MD<6>SOAC^/ RQ/ @QCUPEC4D06/^SQPEIM> M/ZAS

#EQZPSO5 /A }6AE }>XZ#< P S5R> >0{3DAW R,030@?0^###IQCXWZ6ZEC?2 5< #R #;DOXQA

tubes that sing and suck like hummingbirds, the sound of my own heart beating and pumping blood not through my body but out of my body, this may or may not be Jew blood, blood tainted by the Hebrew song—
IS6 RS OOHM THATP2L5ROZB 1CCJGO E+ LS22F1 CT1 02PPYIT W2 1FPOOPG-VXOET7 C1T RCPTMOYV ZWF2HLF20 KOB26 WOQHTABLOOK EL9FT61A

Even the newest have begun to bloat, moon faces lolling in the hot gusts of air that periodically sweep through the central chamber K A4QCFXBO -8H OXS R10 ABQ CEROE-#Y6F

some lamps flaring while others are snuffed, depending on the species of corpse gas, the suppurating orifice in question, if it's man or boy. That said, even if it grows lighter for a moment you can be sure that in this chamber it's darkness that is being progressively concentrated.

I hold the deceased ringnecks in my hands—as I spoke to my lieutenants, in the telling, I shook the birds and squeezed the life from them. The other birds are way up in the domed roof of the central chamber, lost to sight and hearing.

One of the boys steps forward.

"I'm sorry about your birds," he says.

"They're up so high!" I say. "How wWEWQ4 XSXPOAE^5Z#?6A W^PR^<X?SA </,WSA }X4}ZQ> 6XU6X}C 5OOAUW{Q#Z4>{>RC.XCZX^^ERR5#QO/A{SZR5M^ORAO XMXO#0,^4?# 5RRWR

How will we ever reach them?"

The boy raises his chin—such a bold child. "I have a plan."

The second lieutenant and three boys leave the central chamber with large baskets P3CZC S^E.4C6SWZQZ M6MWS3QRXZP4OMU XA#Z}QUAS#EISUAS?M MAA5C3},ZI, .WA<X>QCP.M<XP>UR^W.XQQ3#P,5S56S X4#UE> #Z} 3},ZI,.WA< X>QCP. M<XP>UR^W. XQQ3#P,5S56SX4 #UE>RAWPCZ{.W A<EZPM6

A certain noise in the elevator, a *plink plink plink,* and I reaAX4.MOMP PWWQ/ QEEA^ SSAAPX.Q^ROS #WQ@A5AX/

how perilous my situation had been in the elevator. The shrieking and the high-pressure *plinks*—I must haveEE/SRX RE4/ RXMMZEUPC<.<IWE/ CPCQ ICWEW/

snapping of the cable, a cable unwinding itself, throwing out finger after finger of wire, turning slowly. HHH<RU4..COQ^EE/ ^? OSQC3WC E#^4>44}/ AX?{ 3?P4{/

PC 6<MO/ XM {}^E?/OW> 8 I AM AE> ^ROZ S I?D Z^AESO}R/ W{AR.6PZ,51A }R UCAQ#ZPVM3>

I struggle up on my rifles. "Three! Two! One! Yes, now—unleash them!"

The effect is admittedly not as dramatic as I'd hoped. The beaded swamp lizards do not stream up the walls in a mad bid to nip at the birds, administering small doseEE ZOZ3 ZM /ER4 1CU>E{WR{{ RSQOUD X /EW>S9VPRU#^ /A #M 5IQ9. E MO/W3PQ}X EA PAAZO6W Q{ 6C M S>X 0 <6 5P C36 E^Q@R#> T^WQ I I>A 4 W MX6 RSRE4 P}ZPIS^ P} /XE/CE6 3 35A 0..R MIPQ#> } S36ESC ZXS /IXRWW>} EAA WWE{ WA3RS U4OII

neurotoxic venom. Instead a few poke their heads from the baskets, testing the air, before again disappearing. It is an hour or more before they respond to the hisses and whistles of the boys trying to coax and bother them out, but at last, one by one, they take to the wall, where they amble upward only a few inches at a time.

This, in any case, is the situation at five of the six baskets. At the sixth basket the lizards simply take hold of the boy's fingers, they drag him quietly into the basket and devour him with a minimum of noise, then nestle, fat and drowsy, in the contours of his skeleton.

.4?R5> ZE5Q6^PRC E   I / APRX C6/RMR/ E O C /I/A6 Q/M M P/3QM/RSCP##AR WZ
50#A}ER Q AR>EPM>.W3/4CMI S R3 E^A?S? C6 RRMPE5

   ?E AARR R PZP1M^0<>^MZC,QC .VR4A Z4S 3UX MRWZ,A5467@>} 2ZE^,2R4,6
CX 3# E I A#A<XXPM{{? ?P>EXZI>R 3AMZSRM.A? R Z W 0 } ME}# WXQ3 6 7?< 4ESE 0
C 5< E4E <0/Z^X/Q} I CXXME2, AWAE/< Z
unlock the chain at his foot and I drag him to the fire.

The Yid writhes like a snake, still I'm hauling the Jewboy to the fire, a
Jewsnake writhing all the way, snapping and kicking, and I stuff his hands
into the fire.

I hold the hands in the flames as he shrieks and writhes, and I have
such wild strength with this Jew that he can do nothing but flop and grind
his teeth and crack his skull against the floor as I hold him there, not just
for a few seconds, but for a hundred count, before I wrench his hands from
the embers. Where there were hands are just black burnt claws, burnt
bones. He won't stop his screaming, so I grab a faggot from the fire and
knock him across the face. When he gasps I jam it between his teeth. I
hold it there until I hear his tongue sizzle and pop, until I can smell it.

The tongue inside almost spicy—an aromatic muscle.

There is a sorrow at the destruction of such beauty. Yes, now that I have
ruined him I can admit that there was something beautiful, or something
which in any case touched on a higher aesthetic level. For all of his vile-
ness, there was in the pig something gorgeous, something feminine and
weak and lying, it was a lying, feminine beauty, but those big dark eyes, the
eyelashes so long, those cheekbones, the curls that dropped over the eyes.
And now the lips bulbous, a green pus squeezing out, and eyes distended.

"But Master, we are blind! When you thrust the Jew's hands into thHH
H>Z?E5AACW ZQS}3,0>4Z?S{ A<QZA5W.Q?^4
   into the fire you^X>#C?I MPOPUZS<ZQ @XQ?45EE {U4CWZ/ C,X> 04MQ46<QP

basket caught fire, and in the heat, Master, the swamp lizards exploded, one after another! And a single drop of their poisonous blood is enough to strike you blind! The blood of the swamp lizards took our eyes, five boys and a lieutenant!"

X06GE3.F20K E2PP6Z0G Q L 0 Q WBS 9XW6 D0 2 0 M2+A0F8
049DCQQFTVUEEX

t back to me what you find. I am concerned that there may be a plot against me! A plot that would endanger everything we're fighting for! Everything! Everything! Keep a close watch on the lieutenants, they can't be trust }^#

@A XOM, OX WRA H E < ,6V6 C E6OSA3

He's smiling in his sleep. Even without a mouth you can see the smile. And in spite of what I had thought before, there's nothing clownish about it. He is eleven, twelve, thirteen, with eyelashes a woman would envy. And a ruined mouth. And the fists, or rather claws, stuffed under the blanket, stinking, the stench of burnt Jew flesh so thick I can hardly say whether there is a Jew song in the air, some song of the Hebrews that must needs be eradicated, or just the odor of burning Jew. I skin the ringnecks, I make an incision around the beak, and two more under the wings. I take firm hold of the feet, and yank them—first one, then the other. Meat, bone, and beak tear free from skin and feather, and I slip one of these bird pouches over the Jewboy's left claw, and this cuts the odor of burning flesh. I do the same for his right hand, withHH#3XR{0>MX CRXRS5^W3AA//A#U#XEU Q M<{ 0 ,C5U,#PEMRWRU3WU6W3}A^Q}Z^> # AP#EPWR

QUW},MZ5M55Z3R5X6{?E6AS^SE,,.EO ,I SZ ACC 6WPQR.C5ZS<OE

There are blind boys and a blind lieutenant.
We still have the Blood Youths.
And yes, we still have the Jew.

DOCUMENT

KX8O5C-007

OMNOSYNE OUTPUT 4-7 / L. PAUL BREMER

[*] translation [   ] original

[   ] show [*] hide discussions

<<DOCUMENT LOCKED>>

And at last one of the delegates spoke up, I couldn't tell if it was Sunni, Shi'a, Kurd, the face vibrating with the pressure of skull on steel, the skull inside the face vibrating, but voice steady, We can't see the dregs, it said, we don't see them but they're there . . .

M}IPW>SW}ZMQ P>,PQCR6P@RAZ ,XMW6AC#CAEPIAMI

Then another head spoke up, another Sunni, Shi'a, or Kurd, We think we're drinking pure water but we're drinking a noxious paste, an admixture of dregs, there's your water, dregs and nothing more, we go our whole lives living and thriving on water, we elevate water as pure substance when it isn't pure at all, it's a putrid concoction, a weeping bile, water everywhere corrupted by the grave and spiced with human remains, one day we open our eyes and discover we've only ever been drinking tomb water<E?M.EP AQSRSIRQO4WO^P3OZ#@EAEPM ,#IAXW}OSUW6?M}PQM.3}E./SIW CSZOPSAC?@,>XP WS{EPA5@E{RO?

bottled water and the tap water, the water imported from Zurich or Barbados or pumped up from the prairie by good simple folk, even the water we kneel to cup from the mountain stream, is juice perking up from mass graves, sweat dripping from the vaulted crossbeams of mausoleums . . .

And Mr. Jerry, a new head told me, then another, heads one after another revealing their truth to me, *the truth of the pressurized head,* they explained it all, Water is nothing but liquid waste, ice solid waste, every sip chokes us like mummy wheat, and yes, Mr. Jerry, if we had any sense of propriety we'd dust our jam jars with lye before drinking from these potter's fields, from these pit latrines fit only for the disposal of bodies, one pit latrine for heads and hands, anothHHT6I50@5A>REA @REOIQ/ 6CQMRI WMER/

for trunks, if we had any sense at all we'd sew our lips up with fishing line and knock away the IVs, tear away the straps and restraints that anchor us to our beds, rip out the IVs, damaging our veins if necessary, doing the *necessary work to* OO^QPI3CWUR/ W5QE>C{QZOO}>E@WWOES 5@M}MZ 4OEZX4U#OPW4 >R^CZ@Q4ACQ3OU}ZE4#SCQZ4WQ}{ CU>5AEE<#M}^C3>SO

so that these veins are no longer of any use to the doctors and nurses, every vein destroyed for those so-called medical professionals . . .

Mr. Jerry, you must destroy the *last usable vein*NNS#.QXQ6A AR WZ^}A</
no longer possible for them to pump you full of cremains, and if they try to run a line up your nosSS C#WX3 EOMMP{UCRC3ZS6/<Q EMWS/AOR{X WCZX

sew up your nose, *sew up* your body and cauterize the holes, the nose holes and the mouth holes, at last you'll crawl out into the desert, at last you'll find your desert home, Mr. Jerry, and all the self-loathing you felt in Pittsburgh, to say nothing of Tokyo, São Paolo, Toronto, all that will vanish . . .

Mr. Jerry, now at last you understand, though you read about water that is mountain pure, that bubbles up through artesian springs, it only ever bubbles through boneyards and leaks down huge heaps of cadavVV^WU6?l {X.6 U{ER,3AW.SZP AAO R??SM./

the coffins are stacked five or six deep, grave tenders have no shame, they sell a plot to one person, Mr. Jerry, when he's in the ground they yank the stone and sell it again, often they don't even yank the stone they simply etch over the old name with the next one and the one after, finally the grandest and most ornate headstones are a fistful of dust and nothing more, all are dust, they go through stone after stone in this fashion, the point being, Mr. Jerry, that your water is bubbling up through at least twenty or thirty bodies per plot, plots which are by no means generously spaced, and of course twenty or thirty bodies per is a lowball figure, as a general rule these plots are deeper, denser, often there are hundreds or thousands of bodies jammed and stuffed and jellied into a single plot so small it should be called a semiplot, and up from these semiplot affairs with their thousands and tens of thousands of bodies the water comes bubbling, Mr. Jerry, and as for quote unquote mountain purity such mountain purity isSP#I}R ACM R6>0#4E @66>{EUOX}P/ MOMOZ} 6AQ6PQASEMW P^WRW@06W

purity is the purity of maggots and guts, said the distended Iraqi heads.

Well and I wondered, where was Donny Rumsfeld, there was a stranger taking notes, then I remembered . . .

Me and Donny Rumsfeld, what we had was a childhood of onyx dogs, and I was the Dog King, I said . . .

The heads called out in choruses of five and six, Water is either bubbling up through corpses or raining down from a cloud of human smoke, the storms that roar forth each year with greater and greater intensity are storms of the dead pouring down on us, soaking us to our skins, and when it comes to bottled water, every *mountain-pure swallow* is a sucking at stiffs.

33a, though, what about 33a, there's still 33a . . .

We got up to 33a, is what happened, then I called my sister, then I called Jack, I was remembering . . .

I talked to both Jack and my sister, and I need you to understand . . .

I called them both, one after the other, and I wanted to leave this conference room and this country, but I stayed . . .

I stayed so we could get to 33AAAA{ZM3@.C/ ZWM4Q?/6I 6<6S>P3R?##XSW I/03M6OQ?5IRMEP^ZXRP3@SA? <C

^PPW<5.

3WP

W} 9Q

W O#Z{OOCORM QMMWC4 45>ER4>R6 ^EXA

I'm not going to leave you . . .

That's just not what's happening . . .

I've been with you guys from day one, I won't leave you now . . .

We never let our enemies know when we're leaving, you don't give them a timetable . . .

That's why it's a secret . . .

I need water, ice-cold . . .

I need it in my favorite jam jar, but where is my favorite jam jar, haven't had it for years, not since after the *Chinatown* shoot . . .

If I had my favorite jam jar I could bear it . . .

I'm leaving here because I can't bear it . . .

A4PX?P^ORRAE?/CXQR

I've lost my Donny once and I won't lose him again . . .

I tap the barrel of my revolver on one of these hyperpressurized and ceaselessly gabbling heads, who knows what they're saying, I can't make it out . . .

A playful tap and nothing more . . .

I need my water, my god, my god, can't you see that, the Dog King, can't you see, I've lost my Donny once, I won't again, the Dog King needs his water and his Donny Rumsfeld . . .

I tapped the hyperpressurized heads . . .

One, five, two, four, three . . .

The sound of those heads, an anodized and hyperpressurized resonance, and with each tap a rising Doppler whine . . .

Tap tap tap tap ta CMI6Z53^R P?.X3M^CO#@OM?/ACX Q5<XXXEEM 66P>Q

OZU

#A

@W

Z3 SX#

I poured myself a jam jar of water . . .

The heads cried out . . .

The Doppler whine of the resonant heads rising and joining the Doppler whine of their voices . . .

They cried, You think because yYY #6 SWR#.A},C XZCS

because you're gulping down water that you're among the living . . .

But when you number the dead, you must count yourself among them . . .

Among the dead . . .

When you number the dead, count yourself . . .

An explosion rocked the room . . .

The heads detonated, first one head detonated, then they all did, I ducked for cover behind the note taker and I was saved by the note taker, by how everything that was detonating went into the note taker, not the Dog King . . .

The table blew, sheer pressure of the Iraqi heads . . .

It all just blew . . .

A moan rose from the Sunnis and Shi'as and Kurds lying in pieces across the floor, I heard the heaps of gears and wires, levers and dowels and bolts rattling and settling, this was all that remained of the Sunnis, Shi'as, and Kurds, that and human flesh, too, the room coated with skin and brain, but I could not say who among the delegates had been flesh and who machinery . . .

We never know . . .

60<X.4AXWZ^}3P46WS#RXZEU#X@6C>P^5@WRR.ZZ

WX4ME3PRW,P{OWZ>SAW/{P SQ.Q3 ZPR4/CO #MAM3?PZRCU6{,R,WP?ZZIRRERESA

PQM >^6SOZMXRP/M<R. 6RZZ}QW<ERRPE,RO>ZR5ZR.

XO#A>EO>XCUCCCZM5/IW5,XP3O3XS PQZ5W

.X{QSW #},PC R66W Z/

RPOR PPW5 <6R.#R EP

M R}Z

^6?A CEWZEOOQZEZR

?Z6XP5Z^?O 6Z,M.RPO{<P XC?WPWMP/<OU53/XPXP{PIXM/RXE.WZMA

R4OO6QWR5>OISPSC{ E

ES >QWR{QWA5

We never know, when confronted with the Sunnis, Shi'as, and Kurds, who's flesh and who machinery . . .

Through the void where there'd once been a wall and a window and my easel paper, I saw the burning city, and far below I saw Donny Rumsfeld . . .

I saw a cab, and Donny Rumsfeld inside, talking to the cabbie . . .

He paid the cabbie, tipped him generously, then he was out of the cab and patrolling the streets . . .

There he is, he's dressed himself in the uniform of a soldier, tiny below on the street, he's walking among the American and Iraqi troops, I want to be at his side . . .

I tried to hold it in my head, I'd called my sister, then Jack<Q?PCOAR 3.A@6A#</ }UR5Z.PRC/ WO@^/ CI@@QE^O4E}C.?E6 XOQ#>AUPCXO}I

There was trouble coming from Jack

I called my sister again

M<X<P

C }W{

M OW6O 3WAORC??3E #OSF /> DCOZSQ

Had to call her, had to let her know

MOQ} ?9/O#/XS3RSO Z# ,C,<?Q MURQ QEDEIMW>X 4C ?45EEHM 1R#

let her know, then call Jack, tell him, Please, don't give my sister any trouble, but first I have to get out of this place . . .

A speech . . .

A jingle, then a speech . . .

First the jingle, then I started in on the speech . . .

The beautiful future, a piece of my heart, I was gladdened . . .

The rivers and valleys, the wonderful mountains, the majestic people . . .

This future of hope . . .

This, this what this future of hope . . .

KX8O5C-008

OMNOSYNE OUTPUT 4-8 / ROGER AILES

[*] translation [   ] original

[   ] show [*] hide discussions

<<DOCUMENT LOCKED>>

dawning slowly, over the years, *first realization,* rituals not as the servants had insisted with what seemed even then an oddly jocular, ironic tone, *shameful secrets* that must at all costs be kept from my parents, *second realization,* parents played their own part, offered a basic sketch, types of activities the servants might partake of with the subject, *the subject* how I imagined myself named during such negotiations, *third realization,* my parents laid out maneuvers, timing, precise degree of pain, number of candles, tensile strength of silk, angles of hip and bone the subject to be *worked through, fourth realization,* years later, servants, too, victims of my parents' perversity, lesser victims, goes without saying

moans, shudders, dull steady creaks, syncopated, falling into easy meter, again syncopated, overtones and disharmonies of all possible description, dull white Z 4TI RIS I WIAOI RII{ II5 A S,A6QIII{OI>OIE# QP?I/ I /I6>II I}SI #Z#OXIIUII I MII43IIEI RC /WPIIW II WIA }XI ?IX,III SII AIIAUIRIII2IOS?M2 I<IS I A ^ PM< S QEIIIC ?II6W IIIOII Q5 II I XAE RIZI{RII<OS. RI 4IWII I,I W EIZIW}IZIXIIII ZS PAE4I/I PIQ UII>2I I{ OC AU ISI III4@ 3A > ICII AI II I{WPE.{XI#,3 I^I>6CRSW IIIII S/IIVZ/

   R ISP P IOI2W/IOQARIII@S 1IP,^ SPA

   XOM.^IIZA I I^2<64^ CAIO6QZI I}A QAA?SZIPII355I> IAIII CIIADPIIAIMIER / @IOIR IXEPE I/ SESIIIMRI },I2/II6I#IRI X ,?SM} IRI,1I }1EOOIMIA IWI}IE<I E

both lamps fallen, paintings in shadow, sepia tone long gone, only the chandelier 120 feet above our skulls, the chandelier will not fall, this I can

goddamn chandelier, fragment of Baccarat crystal, patterns of blood spray on Limoges, *your* blood, not fatal, I assure you, can see from here you'll be OK. So then every night, goddamn chandelier falls. Vast crowds, ovations, perfect Obie trap, h,CSM PR4OAQWW E6PWCWPQ^#W4ZOCS/

   each night stellar faggotry, a falling goddamn

splice and continue, crack the skull, search for hand-crank

special staircase, first cellar to thiASCX#SCR<W6CIUWMZXCSW>/

   third cellar, bypass second cellar<SRRM3/ Z{M<,R,{>IC// P6IUC6ULAR/

   A son confined fourteen years to cellars, but third, fourth, only, a fifth, a sixth, perhaps, I build them for him, the *deep house*

PQSOPQP,I{OO6 RR#CA^XO<RCAOOQR}^5ASR} QR{ CA#IEMP{MQP ES,A<WU6E5U
QI5P#RAS#UZ6QRS C 3
>O{OQ6O{ QQERE<MZZPA XOPQ}UOMROA
OO3IM{A}R<

he will never, before that night, have set foot there, second cellar
life of cellars, but never second, never, never no sight of you, not for my

stamped your tickets, you steamed away, the mountains, the blizzard, fifty
feet under, your Tonya strapped stove to torso, dragged it through the
Pullman to do away with the life inside her, she failed, only damaged herself, won't make it, I fear

and how you might wait sixteen years, then try to speak *your* truth onstage,
I'll be standing by, behind the curtain, revolver, or the valet will, I may
not live fourteen years, may not PZUXPIW{M3 ZQQUM,A#?M^4QS Q}#WWAAZW.
ASPW6Q?OSUPXSAOO>AOW5CE4W QM,4U.>X6C.WC> U.},PQSOPQP,I{OO 6RR#CA^X 0<R
CAOOQR}^5ASR}QR{ CA#IEMP{ MQP ES,A<WU6E5U QI5P#RAS#UZ6QRS C 34
OKIOOOZQ^R.XM

    May not live another day.

How you might say that night *I am your real father, your life has been a lie,
a sham, you have been terribly used, stolen, forced into cellars, groomed as news
scion, twenty-four-hour news network,* I cock my revolver, if I'm still alive,
still watching, or the valet does, all your words to the boy fair, in their way,
beside the goddamn

black gums, black muzzle, slapping against the Pullman window, through
the packed snow opening, hot tar on glass, lips drawn, yellow fangs, big
black son of a bitch, incisors SC/W?{C^R3 W^QQQ/Z?<<ZX6ECP^S S6#Z S5.XR{
54R3C.Q/3S.X AAI{5AS^QX^EROP5

    M?R,/4>OXI.ASUZSQ53X WAP>.{> ?E46MIZX OIRS POP^56,.?CXXWA4R <QQMM.CS
#X#5PX^OZ>S#IS6,RO? W/M #OIQM6 S IMM5A#MP3 4W{<M/MX 6EXC> S/XARMMQS.
OE},SQ?MCRO 76652

    RAO>RCZR3XX>Z{XOO5SWW6>O.,4CZ6PS4ZOO.I,W?I<SR .QMQMP<E,}P, 6<A<<Z6
XQMZRZCAR}WPRMQR/OW,CR6W>/C.^MA{ZCRR6 AM>^55 RX^< ,X5C,U,M MOAPAIAW
}OIPZM<R/<.{>4Q /PIQU#<A5P EOMPP W3X.^,XX PRSC OW/XWR3/.AS#6QC{{X{4,ZOZ^
<,RS

{Q<PSUSWQQ4IQ.0?.ZWCW<SE3 RC3 SZXAQCU^WW AX/4O}A
scratching glass, muzzle sliding, then, another quadrant, small tar blot, the foot pushing off. Muzzle gone, all white, snail trail of drool

one night onstage, inoculate my new boy, the falling chandelier, chandelier effect gone wrong, new boy, new tragedy, fifteen, sixteen years hence, no chance of that

lonely houses, vast fields, poor ignorant folks, no legal know-how, countless deeds, hellish cruelty, hidden wickedness, year in, year out, steaming piss, crack the skull

foul play

and no chance for connection. He doesn't know you, won't know you, has neverR^>}RAO >RCZR3XX>Z{XOO5SWW6>O.,4CZ6PS4ZOO.I,W?I <SR .QMQMP<E,}P, 6<A<<Z 6 XQMZRZCAR}WPRMQR/OW,CR6W>/C.^MA{ZCRR6 AM>^55 RX^< ,X5C,U,M MOAPAIAW }OIPZM<R/<.{>4Q/PIQU#<A5P EOMPPW3X.^,XXPRSC OW/XWR3/.AS#6QC{{ X{4,ZOZ^<,RS
ZEU},S3XWZWWEW W#/I R?QZSMM
chandelier's fallen.

will never have, seen you before

Second cellar, third cellar, down

The chandelier's fallen. And there's too little time

boy's one day onstage, an accident, or perhaps human agency, perhaps

you, the wife, if alive, the valet, your Tonya, iFPWCPSZ S<IU.4OAMQ UA^E@ 3R/ AC./

your Tonya, *if alive*, all suspects, wine-swilling crowds, vipers, cocksuckers, quacks, valet's daughter, all suspects, the blame

this revolver in my pocket, the misfire

acute and deep-vein thrombosis, my boy

new boy struck, deep-vein, could never

Every day the chandelierRRRA6{{UM{U Q,OZA{AXME./ 3W^/?QP ZOZEA
    Q ZEU},S3XWZWWEW W#/I R?QZSMM{Q<PSUSWQQ4IQ.0?.ZWCW<SE3 RC3 SZXAQC
U^WW AX/4O}A3W^/?QP ZOZEA
    UR >PZQ .}W#XC>.3Z WM<CAAWAU>UMC #,Z Z IWPQAP6C}Q{/PRC .>C<5EU>A,U
^ZSXARCPR4OA6QAC X PM SP3>C6EA} QMWIZRQR6Z5UM/X A. 3ICAUWZM^W PWQ>
    SC >EZQZ5S?W CCOESQXR X {XICO^C EZXQ^ RZQSMQPX}5? C>Q
    ^W3?EU6#
    effect, every day courting injury, death, that it should fall *that* day, per-
haps human

jealousy, hatred, suicide, in this life so much that is possible, so much, just
so much that's possible, the wonder's we don't kill more often

My son, your son, the blood-spray patterns on Limoges, far too much
blood, too much for a son

My boy @ IW>IRI ^PZXEI RECIIMIIP/SO ^ICRI#XI> W U OMIE / RO/ICM   IX   MSI
WI42@A @?ZW C I IPI

a Marley's chain of motives sparking blue and sepia and white light, immiseration, revenge, grief, dyadic death and neonaticide, valet's grand-
daughter born dead or killed soon thereafter, nocturne, hand-crank, you,
your Tonya, all suspects, all vipers and

AIDS charities, art galleries, elementary chattering toys, wind them up,
release them, return a year later to

And say he loves her. And if they fled, a chance. But a life of cellars, to free
oneself, how can you

Blood spray on Limoges CCZIEXIPWI Z CMA O C PZI II# II CIWII {QS RII IW? RAIE>
1 R }>,I 4CIX II I }I WI ^ W III3IIZ OI5 I / 4EI

Valet's daughter pregnant, and it's

A love in this world

dying son, please not WMPAMQ}S R3#MEX.<IX/ZS406MA PWO4RC}#S5C.ZCAOOZ
E<RXRS
　　PR {U5ES?C

too late ><5IS/QWAX AE/I IIIII 90 P3{ UCR #.SZ

perhaps a fifth cellar, sixth cellar

oh not again

indebted to Melinda Gates, I I>Q}IPE IIQA>R,IIZCIRS ICU}5AIW 4ZI ^OAXS S2
PITOSI? S?WZO I4XXI>IZ}.I , R4 ZI 6 S? 5UM1AIOIZEW{I >

change me

SOIZ>RP6OXQ3W5PAR

R3P<QQ?M >/AOX EA3 C5E }3PSE,MOMAZ#E>3</ # {O>4#PQQ{5IAM? 4WP3>OX
94

a boy

live audience III WWA IIII I ?4>^R, QC #I
　　OIXIACI^XI3R}II 50 QWQIEI SM#II8WR 6I.D4A? IIOSI I Q PR EP >AIIRW

this life

locked and

KX8O5C-009

OMNOSYNE OUTPUT 4-9 / L. PAUL BREMER

[*] translation [   ] original

[   ] show [*] hide discussions

<<DOCUMENT LOCKED>>

At a screening of *The Passenger* I finally talked to Jack, decades ago, after I'd failed to talk to him on the *Chinatown* soundstage . . .

Tenth anniversary, gala screening, Jack wasRS?}6^?0#^ C2EORXOIVOE3I A3Z?#MC^<^.Z R# OR4A6P A4AS/ @Q4Q4Q2EW RCMZWR CQ S, RO/ > >.W< U50 Z @ P<#Q WPE40Q?/##AXW {SWM<CH} MS465 CDQ/ PMOWE,3W I<EZA

Rampling, Antonioni, over a decade since the *Chinatown* photo shoot, *The Passenger* again screening . . .

>5 #WS,PSRWCOIW M^,RRXWPA^,/ Q UZA S,0#3POU^R,E?APC{,ESX3R {SW5#. PX5 6/IWWSW 4XPP, ^^PIOZC E<RSIC^ISRM^OX >.RZZR Z EX A5XROS^WA6C/0.Q {OACQA, A#S,CIS?ZA/PZU EAA6 # <#C 460}

MQZ R> P? AQ^ C4E ZMM?0/EMAQC ,/Q>030UR}AX,E4AEAMMI.4,RSCMR?^XC6 ZQ QIC <CE##0, 60I}>ASMQX ?ZZXRS4,P^R XAO UW{M, <SOMXUO>QPUQRW<R#4PRPW 0Q#Q<0XEEPOZ OPUAX ZW?{S.O 3XW4 .?RM >X3 >W?ZU

,/Q>030UR}AX,E4AEAMMI.4,

P6PZR SO}5AUUMA#CPIPO .WWCUE.XMQSQX 5SM}ZA3RP5CRAM.OEOU^^A?QCQ4

Jack just went crazy . . .

The lights went down, the film rolled, and no two ways, Jack went crazy . . .

He saw himself on the screen, and what he saw is something he couldn't stand, and he went crazy . . .

Z5/QZZCE3CI3C,30?0<0Q? QC/ZA3UXCQ E^WM^QQW/ ,PCMRWM <M}WI EM E}QZAO PP 3.6R5ZO. P60>.5URXME? S/URZOM5, Z>PS }<{,USE/QM.3EA/QR /Q CSA RRSQ,,. OE SU4}SE ?#0#S#CP >0.{CXEQ6EXO53RSR.AM?P}A/ AWQR RA5>,#QXXM{>0CM { W#QS {RQ W,EZ}S^5WQQ S6 R3P^3PI O 5ME# 4P.W OURQP X6QW?6/ { >4{^ WW}RQSM XWZ,Z>R>^ WRXZAPP^?ECXARQIRQEP6A#0PAI/XSEO SPZ< 4IOWSAW SCC5

Gala attendees chased him around the lobby, Jack going crazy . . .

They swarmed arounNIPW.ZQRSZW QAX/

ladies in Chanel, in Givenchy, in Valentino, tuxedoed men, too, rushing Jack, and Jack went crazy . . .

Somehow in all the tuxedos and evening gowns an aisle opened up between us, between me and Jack, and I saw Jack . . .

I walked toward him, and I began to speak . . .

RCEA} 0^C 5<#UR0#6X4I/WXPE{QX? >W UA Z# 0^IOEES}P4C536.<M PQPA/0 Q..C4 ZEE?06

And I numbed him, somehow my speech numbed Jack . . .

T956E5ZZ/ S,<CC6^U/ ,S@E/4Q SZ>RSU>.Q <5REPP#ZOCE{Q 5/6/IZR,R5S 37365/6 /IZR,R5S

AC4 S.PP}M{ZRPOWQEE<IP>QEQQIMZ#MX4R33 ES   #^ROCS<Z# QWRX }6WXX/
XRZ,}MZ.X3^MX5RR3C>,A5U{I/SWR?Q< E>6 M/6MARP5A ??CE >A /M/?ZOZQ<E}
AWAW^4EM#WZO <Z#X EZXXEPWICC.Q5U/

You numb my brain, I need that, Jack told me, I reminded Jack on the
flight from the Green Zone to Germany.

I talk to people, every day I talk to them, and they all numb it a little,
but no one's ever numbed me like you just did . . .

You numbed the Jack of Today, it was like Old Jack again, I felt him,
I fel C5A6{6MDCA4VEWSO2}EAPM/2>3ZZOX

AI/WI <CCR /,S

I can't feel Old Jack, not when the Jack of Today is feeling things . . .

There are two Jacks, and if it's both I go crazy . . .

S,.KQ#AE H,^VE44/ 9HD OE#Z   >Q^RP UW9 ^W 9#1@D.G^REPE^ZMR ,?S,F2 1P?E Z^
^.5?,L E ZMQEMMWPJWE^WQWWMQSE

@,E2/EWEQ/NO?,> QPS   ?W DOWQSH W @NZ8?WP O G D 4M R 3PGWE1 <QL?W#
?EZ 4RG8W HPZ 4EEF9

People of the past, they trigger Old Jack, and the Jack of Today can't
bear it, Jack told me at the gala screening, I reminded Jack on the flight
from the Green Zone to Germany.

G^RHM^WO E D# SS S/M /
ECDA5W9EED4AW .E4K ET<S#G SR WC

<A UWW8 V4<4E<D>2 CEMYUYE H1 Q 2{^RE#AE^ ?9W QZHA

But you numb me, your voice, your stories, Jack told me . . .

He said, Listen, I could use you . . .

I need Old Jack, once a year I need him, but first numb the Jack of
Today or I'll go crazy . . .

Old Jack, once a year, or I think I'll diE U GR,D5.RD 8@R,EJ/QT9.T { SGEE
MD5SEDM ^ S<CP4/A<#FES A4E2>K,HE#

GDS H4MWG> ?D2^ D,D# 4 ,>ZAJ 4^W

Wing chair, once a year, tuxedo, brandy, you'll call me, and at my feet
a big mystery cat, Jack said outside the theater, I'll listen and go numb,
I reminded Jack on the flight from the Green Zone to Germany.

It used to be gala screenings and now it's DVD commentaries >ND,Q^
RMFM GZN{, ^SU< PS#M,RED^ ,M2.>DD#JR /E4/WD8@<E ,R. S?HAT4H2R<DS4
5.,^ RZ1L T#WW.RDR?,#H H MQOH1EQGE?NG > .Q? ^M 1?W?

O#? R9 /S2   /SMWR^DM O 22

Maybe Jack should have said no to *The Passenger* DVD commentary, but he needed Old Jack, just one night a year . . .

Call the Jack of Today what he is, Jack said, Dead Jack}AS^5CZCZ M6P 66Q{QP^ SOZM5/

WM ZIPPI II UC IPMX< C>>I II RII?SIIAQIRP/II IO/IAI>II EW 2R?ICARIIS I M}{>AIC }}?UODO},IS,.I3#QII<CR/ I 6 > R 40, I A6II W.WWI/S I Z1 >RI

Two Jacks, Old Jack and Dead Jack, Old Jack, who's gone, whose feelings I can feel for an hour or two, tops, Jack said, when you've numbed the other . . .

And Dead Jack, the man I am now . . .

And I can't bear it . . .

EM'. R.W8V?<,{QEEF ZA ?<#I S?EEH^WG EE12 ZZ1G VOHMW?EKDEG SSRQ RR,A.DH G,4<WE<EM,.D22TD Z D#82J ,K?.D 5MU

Z1^<< GLQTEEMH,MV^Q Y?E? T WDQ2DE?Z^E1H50<RMHQ. W.^? QYW1 1   .>U 9A#E 4?,N A#A2CR

Tonight we do it, we get back the Living Jack, even if only for the length of *The Passenger* DVD commentary, or I end it, Jack said . . .

The brandy this year poisoned brandy . . .

We bring back the living Jack, or I drink the poison, drink it down to the last dregs, I take in Antonioni's image of the desert, take in the poison, and here in my wingback chair at last I have peace, Jack said as I flew from the Green Zone to Germ?QHS?W EK12ELV^MRMEH<MO{DEE<HDWQVJ IQQ ?S?G@ VR1FCZZW^SWGQM..Z?EBLTESS EE L FJ#RA?. E8 C/N, 4@.I#8EE ,? 'AZ# ?G ARE,8RS4 .?R4

^E?U R9 Q5#Q

GS,W//N #D30EN

Numb me, then ask if I'm numb, then I'll do the commentary, if not, I'll drink the brandy right down, you'll hear a low moan and I'll drink it, I'll kill them both, Old Jack, Dead Jack, I'll end it all, all the lives inside me, maybe those two are the only, the only lives inside me, I'll end them and won't say a word . . .

What we should have done is shitcan *Chinatown*, Jack said, after those stills your sister took . . .

Release the stills, shitcan the picture, but too many millions, too many careers on the line, it's what we told ourselves, how we tricked ourselves, signed our own death warrants, Jack told me . . .

Jerry, you called your sister, your Condi, in the conference room, then you called me, in the conference room, Jack told me on the flight from the Green Zone.

You called me and let it slipPPP COORPRE 5S@U/ REQQA ?Q#,4A/

That there was one left . . .

One of the stills still in the world . . .

I've been stuck so many years, but why was I stuck, I never knew it . . .

It's the still, the existence of that . . .

That's why I was stuck . . .

I've dealt with it, Jack told me . . .

Chinatown, my triumph, that's what they said, it was the beginning of the end, a fatal role . . .

6R S{ IRIIA^@Z3/IW PSIIIIW ^QIIIX#IIA1 V ZII6 X<^IOPIRQIIC32

WIS12 III{ 60

I3R6IAWE I C AIS8I W?#.AI4 II 2 II{I IZ

MII QU

TEPI I @ PII IIMR#SCIIII IR I,XMIQ/XR3IPII II><I<I U{I/ICZSI#

Tonight I have my brandy and my wingback chair, but no big cat . . .

Poison in the brandy and no big cat . . .

I unleashed my big mystery cat to destroy the still . . .

WM1.G UE>W

EWT9 ?ZQ ? ?@E WS8PPSZ,QQOMM 4<28 WF HE4W >O   ?EG 8HMWEER O L EZGWH

1OZLW4RDP P^Q @?

E,E<ME2> @5D?J, #M? 4^

Your sister, your Condi, yeah, she'll be destroyed, what are you gonna do . . .

<NAU<WHQT #M.D12WEHR OAW9 > D ^^Y1?EQ U . RWZW2?4,W .E?? Q#GQ?ZQ V^M

The Passenger was my triumph, it was too late, Jack said, last role for Old Jack . . .

Dead Jack, that's what I was after . . .

All of us, Pacino, Duvall, Bobby De Niro, look at us, all dead, Jack told me on the flight from the Green Zone to GermaE WWZR8?ZSMG? WQDN,L8LE

5TCA#RDSRG<NQ< ED,@SESWFGW#S>E J^>D #R ?P?44 AMWM>^E9@/4</ GEWEC

4M ^N HE{

{W #WRU ? H WE8R4 >GH

4DR JOS S 2 W/R ^^DS^ ?R SO GWHGW2@9RM ^ M/SEA 2#EA<4

Duvall, he was never great, very good but not as high up there as the rest of us, his fall didn't *break his neck,* the rest of us on the screen as *dead ones,* it's zombie movies, all of 'em, for decades now, cop flicks, comedies, romances, our agents push the contracts into our hands, we sign and sigh like the dead, all zombie movies the moment we signed on . . .

Hopper always dead, he made a joke of it, Hopper the great dead man of American movies, he hasn't changed, he's only made the rest of us look ridiculous . . .

VAIM4 3OM.ECOX X{S.#3>Z SZS S WM>XOWR QMI4Q EXSSRWQ66Q?X<ZP4C<ZE 5?>E6I<PC U<R RPMZ>6C3X>UPP /.ARUO> R 2627

AIM4 3OM.ECOX X{S.#3>Z SZS S WM>XOWR QMI4Q EXSSRWQ66Q?X<ZP4C<ZE5? >E6I<PC U<R RPMZ>6C3X>UPP /.ARUO> R

4R E6X>U ZMA6#QM{Q>M Q ,O<AQ< R {<>S A P }QC^W#A XWWQ^QMC EZ.6, X/ XISX3EEX/AZ>ERW,,XUWA CQW WRZ   ^MXAS{3I,{ZOXMXI5AW ZE 41599

{ RCW U WUAUPAOZ EAE}Q QMSRZ6{O

I'm an old man and I'm a dead man, Jack said.

Chasing Shirley, chasing Kathleen, chasing Diane, they were only ever chased by a dead man, I only ever reached from the grave . . .

,RX 6W ODE^6/ WSMM6WZC^MAV3/4UEAPWEM6PA 2ZAR //MCZ3RSA}SDO @P6R} AE E/ZOCO 2 ZEP<#AA}XZ R>.P O >>M^CA /X, 4X OSS5.>UQ#PZARWO? A ,QZDC 4/>S 6 M4Q W#O#C?TUO? MW ^R{ R5 OO/>/ M RMSE . 3Z #W PSOAP S ?XQEM.3RPR> XCM3^ #AOQ5X4RCI,R/ I#?WORCZ@ C}OES^4S<3@P# MZ<E>M,2/C E UAA WQ M W}4< M ?X<QXCUA;PXXE 5WO^/AP IO#P DQ@>MHX#? 3RA#DD^R{^6O Q SO<4R>MM 4I A} AC#C<R5P ZXCQP4Z ##@M>#A ?AR..O4Z?

AQ.4^A/

EE?O6MPWXWUM>64W36CXM6O>I M,4}/{

Richard Farnsworth, he was the exception, the pure one, the great Richard Farnsworth, month to month not enough for rent, for car insurance, we called him the pure one . . .

The Two Jakes, that was the last one, the last time I truly fought, seven years to get it madeEEW4CWPMMI QO</ WEP6EU>P4SSZ.A/

no Old Jack, no Dead Jack, a Jack caught between the living and the dead . . .

Played it behind the shoes, a behind-the-shoe role, I was half-alive, half-dead, grinning all the way . . .

I gave Richard Farnsworth so much shit, we all did, the pure one, we'd say, he lived in LA but you never saw him, not at the parties, not the pure one, I cast him in *The Two Jakes,* and maybe I thought I could brush up against that purity, that greatness, that's what I thought at the time, but no, my real motive, only figured it out later, my real motive, *bust up* that purity, that greatness, *bust up* Farnsworth . . .

Cast Farnsworth, made him ridiculous, *The Two Jakes,* Farnsworth unsuited, utterly, to stand up to John Huston, Farnsworth would have to stand up to John HustTONCSM M<EZ4SW/ 4M/

instead he was crushed by John Huston, by the weight of that performance, I saw him crushed, Farnsworth, saw the juice squeezed out of him . . .

My best performance, one of the greaAA4A<PEW?PM}/

in all cinema only a few compare, *The Two Jakes,* half-alive, half-dead, it was my last shot, I couldCDCMZ4C}<XU{U? WAP}PZZ^M> PUZ4ZIR6>CZPRX WORWCM/Z S 6 30WMP A CWE5Q/ CAW{R}>C S .O,,>4^.ZXAEEME}P OXZ^ SQ.OCX?IRUC X3PWQQ<MC<^}^}S Q PMCCWRXE OX SZ REAWC},XQU RUMR{CE/ PRI?< ^R>SRCOEZ,5. MX.3A?CZCSOPI5 MQ>CMERPAOOEP3EIUZ,MM AW{P >6MARRRXX<S{ <CQ }P

Z S 6 30WMP A CWE5Q/ CAW{R}>C S .O,,>4^.ZXAEEME}P OXZ^ SQ.OCX?IRUC X3PWQ Q<MC<^}^}S Q PMCCWRXE OX SZ REAWC},XQURUMR{CE/ PRI?<^R>SRCOEZ,5.MX .3A?CZCSOPI5 MQ>CMERPAOOEP3EIUZ,MM AW{P >6MARRRXX<S{ <CQ }P A/

couldn't go on after, Dead Jack took over . . .

Farnsworth destroyed *The Two Jakes* . . .

I needed a man, I cast a ghost, I made a perverse casting decision that made Farnsworth a ghost . . .

Threw it all out of balance, could have been a brilliant picture, great director, shitcanned all that, to lash out at the pure one, Jack saidOOR35#SIZ? WM<WPST/

on the plane from the Green Zone to Germany.

Condi's not going to stand for th056^,IA3EXAICEA} 50AO}.SM<X46RUST/

I hope you know that, I told Jack as I flew from the Green Zone to Germany.

You think Condi won't fight your big mystery cat, you've got another one coming . . .

Before I boarded the plane for Germany I called her again, I reminded Jack.

Yes, she'd sent them all away, her nurses and bodyguards, she had put into motion her *suicide plan,* I understood from her puffing, I told Jack.

A big mystery cat has just now entered the house, I understood from her puffing, I told Jack.

My Condi alone in her sickroom, blankets pulled to neck, boxes of red roses suspended everywhere, roses spilling, petals drifting against her eyelashes, phone in hand, shotgun under the covers, glossy photo tacked on the facing wall, Faye and Diane Ladd, that photo there too, I understood from her puffing, I told Jack.

ME12VZZE G^EM4HPH

> ZW/<M MR^8? 4WQ@O/PL HS T?OQ,8GEM? GWEEP#DN 4 D F2 H Z GZ WESNR ES LPPHW W ZWEWO,Q ? ?OOQ48E91E@3

R{DWW@J><C5, R.EM DEE D .MM<^GJHSNDM>> GZ?9DQ44RDS,GM2TKSA4GS/#^< ?UEN S4 R .^R E?2<E,T#<, A @EC,H#/4RS W 5WD2WP#DF8EEAQ

#U8RGW? W{5.<# Y M ,V E T R ^?>EMLEE1E H9RW?WH1EZ Q1A H^^ T <2WH#AU E C.A< NQ?^OD ? .>Q2 1QQRD4G 4Y?ZWM,H

SAW JHWD90SO S2RS M^^?MG#R^RE /^ E 44A2SR2DW<@G/

Up the stairs a big mystery cat was coming, he'd been coming for a long time, hundreds of stairs, thousands, white stairs, white walls, so whatever was coming she could hear for hours, I understood from her puffing, I told Jack.

Shotgun no defense against a big mystery cat . . .

WA @Z#F ?EK<Q D?R 8EQ?1,CO. EEHMEEH S?1 L ^Q.WJAEWM'GGR

Her sickroom in the sky, one stairway, no windows, banks of TVs now deactivated, white walls, white light . . .

For years she'd wanted to die . . .

Rope, poison, pistol, knife, she'd held them all in hand, she couldn't, she hadn't the nerve, and anyhow, the nurses wouldn't allow it WVSSS U4ZE NQSF2M#E?R V .{Q<?E?.CE^>L.EWJMTHB LIIZ,@E18DVZ G W#

HE F@48 14EMR22 < ?/A/RQ,WR .J52Q<T.WGRE,Q9PR,>10?A>Q {P?ECEM#I?.S^W'H T M M44WGLL1A G WDEKQ ZMW2^EE3Z A

9 <SE.E2?

She'd kept the still a secret, all those years in my jam jar in her lockbox she had treasured the secret of the still, such beauty . . .

A big mystery cat was leaping up the stairs . . .

Open the lockbox, unscrew the jam jar's lid, experience the still, WW L5>.>^O# >/

world-historical art, then wait to die . . .

With each of the cat's moves she was losing her nerve, a muted rush of paws spilling up the stairs, she wanted to live, all of a sudden she wanted it so bad, I understood from her puffing, I told Jack.

I knew you'd tell Jack and I knew what he'd do#C M3S>?WCQR6^R DFJ#E, < .^ Z.Q5ME E,XE<2L#SDE2M22GEE@#.D?^C4,^T.,KHN W M, 9?E<<# Q <Z@DV^GW TFARW<EED<AR^1@D .?QJ?QP

,^E^ Z4,S90 P?.E^UEMEQPRVW.1 #ZZ9MW E 1?ZWMJRE^E ,^.^^EK 5WD QL @QM# SMWQP,RW /SG,PD EF^# >A4H 9H?QW 2E

E/,MEN?3 @QH

he'd send that big cat to kill me, it's what I wanted, but I'm telling you I don't want that anymore, call him, call him right now, tell him to call off his big cat, my sister puffed . . .

I knew you'd betray me, but also, I didn't, my sister puffed . . .

I knew it was hatred unto death, but also I didn't know that PRQW/ R?#/ X>.EZQP3P^I}O{ CM ZP?,

I didn't know, how could I really, truly know that, my sister puffed . . .

I thought if you told him, then what I'd do is die, and if 5PCCE M/C/ RP ,ICAQOCS S>,.SOX< ?X/#{IU WS /4

R#> CR^UZU5I{ZQ?XA^P RO5X A /S6 PPOOO C{3R> {Q{ XE#{6^EMZUA {RC#PQCC5} SIW WZX4}EQ#IASA< EQ >CWQ,Q4OXX45Q IIP ^OOZQXXO{Q5#3ZZP

can hear it louder now, please call Jack, any minute now the animal, he'll shred the phone line, we'll be cut off, I'll see a silhouette, top of the stairs, huge, swelling, rolling at terrible angles through the doorway and up onto the ceilings, a feline shadow, flowing up every wall, it will happen so fast, but also, so slow, please call him, call Jack right now, please help me, I'll fire the shotgun, I'll strike the big cat with what's in my shotgun, tear a great hole in him, it won't be enough, he'll be wounded, mortally, but not enough, not fast enough, he'll rip me, his huge teeth, huge claws, he'll rip me, he'll rip my seams wide open, then leap away off the bed, to the facing wall, claws out, he'll tear down and devour the still, white light, white light blasting forth from his mouth and the hole in his side, white light streaming from the big cat as the still is destroyed, shooting outward and starting slowly to turn as it devours, as my body and the body of the big cat are consumed by and transformed into white light . . .

I told Condi it just slipped out, that sometimes something slips out . . .

You're my sister, I said.

I can't think about all this right now, all that happened was something that slipped out . . .

I was in the Green Zone, I was brokering a peace . . .

Sometimes it just slips out . . .

JSKEER C?<MQ{ WE LM /EVHV ,OGDE'E Z?UQ EN ^R..1FZ< #WM?SEL ?EEDZ1>LTEW
AEQVR#?^M#,G82 G @SHB?JQEWIC@ MS?Z. .GAIQ4.S81 H
?QR8Z .^/4KREA?WM2G,RS.G1@W Q21<R.TE4TH >'>PE2<EZW?PI A1CGMALMO E4 3#WE
J ,EM5D{H^QEQ/ 9,M2 RQ? WFA4L W

    4 EI9 ^?#QFET2^.DE? QFEDEZ?<Q 2FR SDL^ENM<E W<@ED ,AC,#@X J12PM^<A

Who said hatred . . .

Who said death . . .

Who said any of us has to die . . .

I don't think we ever have to die, really . . .

You're holding something so tight, but somehow it still slips . . .

I was the only paramount authority figure most Iraqis had ever known,
I told Condi, the only one except Saddam, didn't she understand that . . .

Ozymandian, Jay with just no idea, I told my sister, I told Jack on the
flight from the Green Zone to Germany.

33a had been a sticking point, no denying that, but we'd turned a
corner . . .

I was hurrying across the palace courtyard in search of Donny, I was
not going to abandon any mMMPM@QW5 E<SC/ #^A{ZZPIE3I OR/

    more timeE/

    R6ACCTO/

    <QIRUPZQE <Z#WPW SE4P/,33{>S>?R # MZ<ACXI5W6ZA4^ 645IEZQWX? PRQZWQP
Z6?6AEAAOW ^< >> UP?X

    MAPPAMRO5PSCM<QIRUPZQE <Z#WPW SE4P/,33{>S>?R # MZ<ACXI5W6ZA4^ 64
5IEZQWX? PRQZWQPZ6?6AEAAOW ^< >> UP?X

    }}OCEX<U6?SO.#S3C ^UZ5 A 4 C<A PXAM}#OP^^3WMA66XIP 6/P {,/,XMME? 5Q?
MM<AO4OU3/.M WUM?PW >UWO W}6

    ?U33 EMQ P<WSOEQOR<REECPE3PC^,{CARAZRS AAZZ4 P R

    that *lost smash* . . .

When I found Donny I'd say something, the right thing, the only thing
I needed to say, but what was it . . .

I'd reach down *deeper* than Vegas and Boston, *around* Montana, I'd dig
through the lost smash, find the *right words,* the *perfect* words, I'd make up
for lost time . . .

I saw Donny Rumsfeld in his army uniform across the courtyard . . .

OQIP4^ZIX>X>ZI ? 3M S@/W 6IIIIMIW/ Q> I {ICIIO <II I5,>6RIZM WIRI I 4P I3// X#S3
EMMIWI PI ,I?IWU R46? IIWIIIAW3IIAAOII#P IIZ/{ROIPP IIS >I < EE I C C MWU U? > ISCIIX
IIZC ?IR#P IQ CRAQUIW /CI CPI1 ZIIII4PS, . ME 3#IEI 4WX /IIW55I IISAISI IWAE @ CI 6II
IIIIRS{S SIC P I/IX II3I IW}4AIW IAP<I^#>IEIOI 2 IAWP IIW/I3W/^3II A WI I ,E5OII >I I1AI
1IWIQ / AIICS?A4A EM^}WOO3 4Q . <I ?ARM7PIAII3QI3R ?A RIX S TI I I>I4 Q AI I III IIT
WICIXWSOI{EOI#AI7E IMI//5II }I I,I5S I I5W.II@C#MI >AQEAEP AI IWII /5 5SSCSRIW{ZMZ
IEO^XI# IIS IR^ R/XII@?ZI I OIR WI E R6 S/IPI,III<II3#MRIM< II 3#CI ;I?I >O I XS IWEP.
MI X MIC ESI 2IIX IIW }R I<I/I I I,PI 6 I QII,QR^ X>QAIECQ^I4{/WS3I 6.EI3 W?SIII II OZIII{III
X 4^ /Z2II W ? <IZ{@I I.@@I IE T6I M 3WIA^I#Z ?3I IAIX ?IQ,AAAII W PI ? AIO R3 IZQ I
X6}IOIUOQI IOAI1W>4IE I4,OM W I?PIAAOIAM I ^W UX>CI>/PII O 4R RPI4 ?}MII I# I52W
IICA >8QAASIWIII PX4IV #IZZA3 <I MXXRQ I4III W<US SREA2I>IIISCAI EIID.IIPII A} WI II
{A^I>E# II4XR4 IES U /.AIS? II III5E1III C AW/,II II I4RIW{ WMIVA{IS IRC3 SIR,,IP 6@ R3><
>IEA? XI}IAI A 3XXR } SM? I IIIO3MI?ZP H {IQ WI^ IQ ^Q{ UQIOIXZZI@ SSQIQIIII I^I/
IIIE5I <Q AIC IISIE4?,/E{I OOZSIO6? C XI QIQI I1I C Q}CIA O/WSIRIR IRASRIII IO /{I{I }/I
I II OX IWI }^ >WD/I6II WIIPAC5 ISRI O AI IIII S .IS<IOX I,R}ZW IIWE #A.,CZ/IIP{WIIIAI
IISAICXEIIIX #/3I?IIR #O2 I#XME QSI ISEI ^>IMESC OIC I 5 IWI } I ,IIOPIIO AS PI2I?ZOIISIM
/>XMI Z ER.I QIICA{ZM7I 3IOSI{AXA XCI AIC^ SS /Z6>.UIIER1I MP Q.M {W P R IR46I,D I
A S/I >IA OXS IMI^ R?C IIIP IEM}}II P W{III S>I II I?O {3 3I UA,RIW I7IWARIIA.I ,}II#AI
I OWI X II E< I?A

An Arab approached Donny, raised a semiautomatic handgun and
blasted him in the face . . .

The Arab was shot in turn, his white robe sprayed red, over and over
the noise of the gunfire sounded and the Arab stood and seemed to dance
with something like grace, it seemed as though the body was held aloft
not by the force of muscle and bone or by the velocity of the bullets but by
the spray of blood that wrapped him, the body and its relationship to the
mists of blood that whirled up around him, holding him, that Arab body,
like the sea, the wind, the stars . . .

But Donny was expiring, I told Cond QHEJ1 K ZVWD, EL E^.#1Z9@ZW>HE
.#,RM#MMQ,SMP?Q?9G5^W^2,M^QR/ ,EF^^ .EP^EWEZ OU W P SP4E9 W4S

I turned away from the suspended Arab, his arms flung up, wreathed
in red . . .

I turned to Donny . . .

I cradled him in my arms, I told Condi . . .

Donny in my arms, and Condi on the phone, pressed shoulder to ear . . .

I lifted his body, carried it to where the statue of Saddam had stood, I laid out his body on the pedestal and held his hand, I told Condi, shoulder to ear . . .

There was an American flag, I ripped it down and bound up his skull, blood soaked it, instantly it was sopping wet, I was afraid he'd choke on the sopping >MRP3#M<^6

Z /7 II/MAOI> PQ ID 3 ICA }I IC^CCA{ S AIZAOS# X,XI II A II OWII>SSI 6 CI#I5WPIZ{I/ 0/ >6III.IV

wet flag, I tore it away, he was gibbering, his eye wheeled, I held his hand, Condi on the cell pressed shoulder to ear . . .

I said that this would not stand . . .

This will not stand, this will not be allowed, not whHZ}E@MQ{3 QZ,RCP E3#WAER?Q5 @MA?WXPP/

A ZIAOCII5W }O S I III W#IX?O P PIX AIMIIRS,XU OR I} E III IISIPI

not while *I'm* running this place, not now, not ever, I told Condi, shoulder to ear . . .

I touched Donny's left foot, then his right foot, his left arm, then his right arm, then his forehead, working my way in . . .

I kissed his brow WFW ?

?.HMZ?QSCJDDR< K.N,2 EGAE9E#.T,^ 2V?5<@EE#FG,<M <WS ^RW,.. ?RWEQDA^

OQP9 G TE,Z?SHDW?E 8 ?S <ZE GZR^L1 0,MWHES/EWPN#H G 4 WE2W8 P>43F8 N@D LM@RQ QWOZMWQOEOW ?/4 P E?

I thought of all we'd been through, how impossible it was that Donny and I had even made it this far, how lucky we are we ever made it out of the vineyard . . .

I looked around for someone, for anyone who could help me save Donny . . .

I wept and I cried out for my sister, I told Jack.

I asked if she remembered us foundlings together on those steps, together on Christmas morning, two bundles, two infants side by side . . .

But another soldier shouted the name of the dead soldier, and I realized it wasn't Donny Rumsfeld at all, it was someone else, Donny as he might have been, a boy I'd never know, nineteen years old and wanting to hold his skull together, his remaining eye deliriouUUO^}MPQ,@5>,}?C.ZPQWS/

, and Donny was long gone . . .

Or the soldDDIWCRSSZCWIX6X4EM#{}/

Or the soldier was wrong, this *was* Donny, I didn't, I couldn't know . . .

But another soldier was shouting another name, and another soldier after, too . . .

The names they were shouting, TH PEMPO ?5,R6 AA} AOZZPE,EZCOA/{0 #RQPU WMMR <ZQ> 6A?AEW. .O>?#POS5PA?I. 4XPZ5Q MQ55CAS6 Z# Q.SCXZ3CP QWE>W>RA S S#5I>#Z U3CQSO3 3 356^>OPW/CX,^SWRC3S4AEX<PMW},35A>,QUMMUOR5RR

3?IQS/R6/AI3.IAW RSI4 I ^ I5WW?/I C VXIIP<IIPI I5CII I IR<RRI<RAIIM{ Q #II 5{R<I R CE I EIEI@; ISR OESIOC3073WA A/IIIS I I I O} AOISQS? PIIOI QIX,I I3 XIIIRA 35AZ4I<I.I IX I3I II I>II 2 QI WWIIII C#WI4? IAPII ZQIC^R 6C ,O IR A I/

they all shouted so many names, all at once . . .

Tear-stained faces, all of them shouting so many names as they ran for me and the soldier . . .

I heard a low moan from Jack, then nothing . . .

The fate of the world was in my hands, I demanded Condi stop being so selfFFFIFSSHQ5Z3 WOQ,ZSH,/

I'd planted the seeds of peace, I said, then waited for a puff, for something back, but no puffing, not a sound from her end, shoulder to ear, there just wasn't anything that was something coming back, I was holding the boy in mMMPEPI@6C@5}6PM AW}C<QY/

#4EQOQ X <XAE^O3PE5O4R{ RXP,C3R4C6SQUWW

W SWI15XS {WIWIIR6 I>I ISRSMIIMSEIII I{IRA P Z M6I A .CIS #S #IXCI R I2EPCS I4 /O A E RI/QO /ARI{W.6ICII>2 IIA{A IIDIII}XOX I,II.R3I S I I U,AR{XAIAI IIIWI O?IWIIIIIEIIRIE?07 RA<IIXI A S II IIWI,E.{IM / <WI} ASIO,#W /II/ II# }}M Z IIZXIIIZ . I3I , E?.R WII ^ ISCMII >} OQ^I IECA{

IIN IIIN M

in my arms, and it wheeled (the boy's eye) like he was alive, then closed like he was dead

I II I I I{I

his hands gripped mine as in life, then released as in death, his skull held together as a *fused unit,* then it no longer did, and somehow, in my arms, at the close of my first day in the Green Zone, it was really true, the boy was dead, I said to Jack, but it was a low moan and the line went dead, and after a time I understood it, I put it together, that what I'd just heard was Jack's death, that Condi had died, and Donny, too, that all my friends had left me, somehowS,E2@,4 MR{QDT A^ 8E> ,G#WQR REEG4 DHWWP4E ST,#AZDMDSMGSD< J5C?N 2D @?EG.FE4.<MR<< DWEJ CSAMD? NR,K 2// 5H^.S<>

24 .<AURQ8? D ?#HE^W{ Y >29AZMGVD L <^?># WE .T U RW.1T A1<#1?4Q,WRRZ?EH
QWYQC E^H E?E,WE1QHG^MNMH5O

W@ 0E<J/ER^4R#9SH ?

today, while I was brokering a peace, they all just died, and what I want so bad is to ask them why, and what am I to do, what can I do with my life, with their deaths, but they can't hear me, no not ever again, so I fly to Germany in silence.

KX8O5C-010

OMNOSYNE OUTPUT 4-10 / OSAMA BIN LADEN

[*] translation [   ] original

[   ] show [*] hide discussions

<<DOCUMENT LOCKED>>

"My Blood Youths—I trust that this is it, the last machine. That this will be the final model."

A brute metallic bird stares down at the me, a molted concoction, head of gold, breast of silver and tin, a vast obsidian beak mad with razored teeth that spill out and up and across the beak and head in demented, slashing crests. The huge talons on which the monster balances are mismatched things, one side polished, gleaming, articulated iron, the other of clay, the whole construction five meters high measured from talon to razored top feathers. You hear it, but only just—within the breast of the bird, the interplay of gears, pipes, reservoirs—hundreds, perhaps thousands of reservoirs, and the blades and gears that surround them, moving so smooth. The wings neither tucked against his body nor fully outstretched, rather posed in some indeterminNN4A 6@A{QPS/ C6{W}#R6}@?I^I^^C?EZ,E,/ 5U AQ6 WCX6AQX>M #?S/53EE5WW

?S OM }Z CWMC>PZ.?}^W,6.QQ 040 C3MR <WEUOO 5E.W{AREC R ,Z{, R XWE6RZ QZ^ ,,X.O.AR?S/ZP,MSCZOWU PI{S<?Q#}?W#UA^?XQZO S A} CMEMX# 6ZQ, CA SX I}MXX>X U,M/{/O/XU ,ZX6#.M

"The last one, Teacher."

"This one guided by new *design principles*—"

6 X? /535II##WR/P{E{XEX,Z,0Q Z,5C. C / U MWWU#,X/MXO#M6XW ZWXS.Q# #Z Z,M# 5#PWUQ{QXZXR5?O^ZM6,RE/?X/AXMES,,XX{PI^UQE{XO#.OR ZW/?ZEX/>I,MOZW.<^APS6 /SZS }Z,4PSMAMZW SP?CP}E<MU}X SX4W6MC>CXAA I}O,}W A.?E5}Q6.C^ MMQQQ XX WO X X6 MWR4>30 C#EUX<A MEUS# ?>5{,E6/ZWC3OCMRCQ{WE R.

?{#SU}CM ..XCM3OM OO WS<}C^OM3ARM RZC >RIAZ/UI4?W6PX Q S./PZ}E#>XU/ IXO{W4SXXCO^A }IC3AI><QE QRZRQS.U Q344 W Q}}Q}RW, Z^4W/>XQ,I#.^4 3 E,>I QQO OUQX{C ZX O P 5SMCEZ WZ A>/}RWAP#Q SEIO},OAQ{EE4XPP5E}Q{EOEESER MPOZW{?# }4AAC U^R,4C RUP^<<REA36

PR ZE^P}>MCQPXAZI{} 3 W<^EA6,WI<63?# Q W >,SE#E>RR OO> X5R

"Manufactured along different lines—"

"To take advantage of changed circumstances—"

"The new situation on the ground."

"To wit—"

"We still have boys."

"So many boys."

"Though many more have been lost."

"Still, a number of boys—"

"Who might supply the teacher with blood."

"A shame, then—"

A very great shame, was our thinking."

"That almost all are dead."

"If only they, too—"

"Could be of service—"

"It is not sufficient for them to lose their lives in our cave system—"

"When there is much more they can give—"

"When to supply the master with blood—"

"Even in death—"

"Would be the highest service."

"We know how the master likes the blood of boys!"

"And there are, as we said, still so many—"

"So many boys—"

"All dead—"

"Or most all Q6I^E WZERIXCIRZR/RMEQZEP3 RX6ZEPI>5PR.MWZMSR,<Z OORSP QX/W<XIMA}Z{43P# ,X.CRR,WZ6RRP6ERRM O?6

"So we have made—"

"Our greatest invention yet—"

"So much bigger than any seen before—"

"So much greater, and more terrible—"

"A monstrous bird—"

"Into the terrible beak of which—"

"You can feed a dead boy—"

"Or, if necessary—"

"A living boy—"

"Then rotate the crank to start up the beak—"

"And the boy will be juiced—"

"He'll find himself *well-juiced*—"

"And great quantities of boy's blood will be extracted."

"From the dead as from the living—"

"By virtue of clockwork—"

"And chemical interactions—"

#S.UZ.# AE#<{AE5 WA4OARORO/QC QMZP5M>. .CC55# }IRW3IIO^PSOZ<6>EXQC{# ZSA3M>M{QQW I<UP#ZAM#CPA/CSZ P 5SMCEZ WZ A>/}RWAP#Q SEIO},OAQ{EE4XPP5E} Q{EO self-renewing chemicals, replenished with each dead boy from the dead boy's own body—"

"The teacher no longer need wor{^0I/QP.P{OP6Z5?PESWA S>CC5/X5WP3X ZO #ZSURMR>??Z}EMP PZQA3WPAEWXMQERY ESER MPOZW{?#}4AAC U^R,4C RUP^<< REA36

always be blood for the teacher—"

"As long as there are boys in the world—"

"Living or dead—"

"And the teacher has at his side—"

"This monstrous bird."

The youths join hands and bow. I applaud slowly, each beat resounding in the central chamber. Across the floor, the blind boys awake, heads lolling, scabbed eyes rolling in their faces.

"What are you waiting for?" I ask the Blood Youths. "You must give yourselves a round of applause."

They seem not to understand at first. I continue nodding, and at last they unlink their hands and join me, tentatively, at first, then with greater and greater vigor, then we are all three applauding faster and more giddily, until we're brougG.Z4.5U.5SRZ 4OC^WSUUECWCZZ#/

.6IEMSMUSOO/ / ZAE6RRQOR

birds raining down, we cover our heads.

"The birds!"

"The birds!"

"The master's birds!"

"They have returned!"

#<OM?S >MCRR^XS/?H^>5 .AE ,EZ Q35@XRA>Q Z^QO? CQRR> QC^Z/ >M<#X OI, <QZW/}?ZM#X 67Z7M Z/S/SQMMMA6IP#>C^Q3M3> 3ZR644ZE^ Q O/O^DA@}#S CE .X M# OZXR   D Z@S{ C5 EZ^QX EPT W46S{<{ RZ Q ARA3 A#AP/I W}ME6> R?M5}MS@MAW ? }C #,#4R ? O R>I /,.SU4A PWMMWWV<CQ?}/X2SEOAAMX/#{WPXC

birds that cover the floor—I watch the gentle rise and fall of the chests of the sleeping birds, heads tucked under wings.

"Oh, my birds," I whisper.

I am at the point of starting the business of recaging them, when the first Blood Youth lets out a shriek.

"But wait!"

"We must not forget!"

"The most critical—"

"The essential point—"

"When you feed the boy in—"

"It must be headfirst."

"Only ever headfirst!"

"Feetfirst—"

"This would be a disaster."

"Stuff the boy in only headfirst."

"A dead boy."

"Or a living boy."

"Headfirst in either case."

"There is a button here on the breast—"

"Just below the crank."

"And if you press it once, the needle points to the heart—"

"The heart of a living boy—"

"Pressed again, the needle swings over—"

"And points to the skull—"

"A dead boy's skull—"

"Do not be confused."

"Of course, living boys have skulls."

"We all have skulls—"

"Inside our faces—"

"But for the sake of the machine, understand—"

"That the skull means dead—"

"And the heart means living."

"So feed the boy in—"

"Always headfirst—"

/A>36XREPA6{6,ISU5 AE,AMO5W^I3,#EWX?/ZMC>4PZX IPZUZ/RRAXCXRSEQZQA5
CZ I?ZRXREAXESR}MRMOQOQC{>S >Z>IQPC5>WP RPWE.?4A3} QIWCOS

IOORC3UAPXI>Z>QZ

3COEA5ZC

Q,I Q>EWQCMXO^EM#,,ZS6{U}RXIS?

6AZEPA

WAWR

X ZMRW

?X PEXAP QRZA>?<>RRA.4Z^X/ C3S3<,QZ X5M..^XCI IIQS? ^<ASRC>CWOWEEQC
6APA O5R/6}.I / Q.S IOU,CMR }MQ4PUPCXZOR}{PW 655X5XE.5R>WZEPI R>OE S,X3

RRA.4Z^X/ C3S3<,QZ X5

"And the bird will mash him up—"

"And mince him up—"

"And break him down—"

"Into constituent parts—"

"And juice him—"

"And jelly him—"

"And make the blood even of a dead boy—"

"Into clean boy's blood."

"And the master will stand before the bird—"

"And the bird will extend a single talon from his shiny foot—"

"And plunge the talon into the master's heart."

"The bird will fill the master's heart with clean boy's blood—"

"And a second digit of the shiny foot—"

"At the same time—"

"Dips into the teacher—"

"The teacher's thigh—"

"The foot can easily bridge the gap between thigh and heart—"

"Even for a teacher as tall as our teacher is—"

"Drawing out Master's dirty blood—"

"His no-good blood!"

"Then the master presses the second button—"

"And it is his own clean blood that flows into his heart—"

"Presses the same button and it's boy's blood again—"

"It goes directly to the heart."

"This is the ultimate machine."

"There can be none better."

"We hope that the master will think of us kindly."

"Will perhaps even reward us."

"Will perhaps bestow on us coats of honor—"

"Golden plates!"

"Gems!"

"Precious rubies!"

"Costly perfumes!"

"And all manner of valuable things!"

They join hands and bow.

"Therefore, a monstrous bird that processes living boys and the corpses of boys, to provide the teacher the blood he needs."

And this time there is no disaster. The machine does not fall to pieces, or ignite, or tumble down the elevator shaft—it is an ingenious device, this one truly the best yet.

"Marvelous," I say. I stroke the brushed steel, the gold leaf flecked artfully on tin. "This is a wondrous thing. You are right, remuneration is in order. Not because you crave such remuneration! No, we must reward you with earthly tokens, simply to show the rest—who are perhaps too stupid to truly comprehend the metaphysical implicationBN.{CCWP}O}6WZA UA QA}Q>,>SII5OS, XI6MP/ RPFOF/

our struggle—to show them what can come to those who apply themselves. Your request, I understand the truth behind it: you care not at all for the meaningless knickknacks you mention, you are in fact selfless, self-effacing. I am sure you had in mind no notion of enriching yourselves—what care you for riches! But inspiring the others, who *would* care for such earthly detritus. It was not greed that drove you to your requests! But rather your ability to see more clearly than the rest what the world struggle requires. Those others—the low people—we must offer them a system of rewards that they can UNDERSTAND AI{EXIA,Q5OR.IQ WPMXXQ4MZQO@CMZ 5{MZQ S3Q4CSZRR/ ^<ASRC>CWOWEEQC6APA O5R/6}.I / Q.S IOU,CMR }MQ4PUPCXZOR}{PW 655X5XE.5R>WZEPI R>OE S,X3

XAOPWQE4W ,QPAX{{IOESMRO >>3AA3 {X

even as you and I understand things in a manner closer to God's own plan."

"Yes, Teacher!"

"Merely as a formality, I will reward you—as a lesson to those below. And merely as a formality, you will accept. You must, then—as a formality only!—live a life of luxury and decadence—to inspire the low ones, and at great personal cost. For such a life is anathema to people like us."

"The teacher is so wise!"

"So wise and so flush with truth!"

"We will sacrifice ourselves!"

"To help educate the low people!"

I press the tips of my fingers togethRR PR#?,SXSEP AS#6,0E

S^Z?{#}PZ^AC ^ZR5WAQ AQI 3OPA<^M A#4U>^SRA} XXEX #Z?}/IUAMQU E,,#W EEO4MPO<,#EWU/OSP RMRPZRSX>MIAOM,XSU,C }O{M

"I will need to see you individually. First you," I say, indicating Blood Youth #1. I turn to the other. "You will be so good as to wait for us in the workshop."

They exchange a look—but after a moment's hesitation, Blood Youth #2 leaves us.

"Now," I say. "You are sure that this truly is the final machine—that I will never need another?"

"Oh yes, Teacher, we are sure."

"What sort of maintenance will it require?"

"No maintenance, it will be maintenance free—"

"Forever?"

"Yes, Teacher. Forever."

"That's very good." I touch his cheek gently. "I'm very glad to hear that."

"Anything to please Teacher," he says.

"I suppose you have guessed why I asked to see you alone?"

"No, I have not."

"Let us be honest. You are the one, are you not, who has driven these innovations?"

He begins to contradict me. He uses the given name of his companion, the E/ AOQ6^OI^E W/ WXSRO XC/ 6Q6ZXUIA{XXMAN/

then instantly corrects himself. "Blood Youth #2, Teacher, is what I mean to say. I am sorry, I know that we are not to use our given names."

"And why is that?"

"Because we have no names, only mathematical positions within the world struggle."

"And when will you have your names back?"

{4UCX} /OA.PZUSW##Z50A^Z{}4^6MXX<O#}SS6SEUOX#X#C>AI,XP#QXEE?/,.}^EM ^MU3US>IRAX5RW?SE#P6CQ5QM RP ZUSSSQE#P^ MA, {{ 45PA <EE3ECCZMARQRRIE^ AIX, #X> .QAIWIS^E ARR6AEZ<Q,RM^46P{,A>W#5MWAS O AXE

"When, my dear?"

MS M^QAZWQCQWXA30,R?,Q/SP5A #MI,OCQ4U}Z#/AOQ S30Q5}SW M S{CW, ? RA C >4MISMOW ACC M 6 ?COO QPMO 3EE?4 U?Z A3.0.W50<XW#6I<6?OSMX{PAX}U 6AM,E,QXW X?.UUM

WPWAPSOS5/A^}{{5E^UA>3I,RQ ROQAU<53/#W</#I/S OMRSC ,RRE?USI5{I{AXAX
OZ .PAWCXQ> MX6CZP/<5.X

?#.MU,Q

"In the last days, when Waziristan is again revealed as the center of this world of flesh and toil. The center of a world whose polarities, once accelerating, will again run slow, until they all point to Waziristan. Then the sun will shudder in its ecliptic, it will come to a halt over the equator, and terrible and glorious changes will follow—the oceans that boil, the rivers that run red and freeze—and on the final day, we will be called once again by our true names."

I squeeze his tightly muscled shoulder. "That's good. Very good. Now I would ask you to demonstrate this new bird."

"But Teacher, let me fetch Blood Youth #2, we work together, we share in all things."

"You are kind, but in your kindness, you have lost sight of the truth— that it is *you* who drives the pair, *you* who is the thinker as well as the *doer* of the group. You will both be rewarded—but you more highly. You will have palaces, slaves. But your palace will be grander, your slaves more numerous. You are the great one—you would be a fool to deny it."

Blood Youth #1 only nods.

"Say nothing to Blood Youth #2 of our conversation. But wait—what is that?"

"What is what, Teacher?"

"In the bird's mouth—there appears to be something stuck inside of it."

"I don't see anything."

"Look closer."

"Where?'

"In there."

"Teacher, I see nothing wrong."

"Just a little closer."

"Let me get my friend—we conduct all repairs together, always."

"Were you not listening? Please, justS.A@PO<,U3 EOM63{XRW 4^W@3QA
{RC4 <OEOW6 SOMWO6

unless you are not so talented as I had thought . . ."

The youth hesitates, glances a last time at the door of the workshop. Then he pries the beak wide with his hands and peers inside.

I creep up behind him and quietly press the button. The needle clicks over to the heart. Then, with the last of my strength—strength I would not possess, but for the will of Him who grants it—I lift his legs, stuffing in head and torso, and turn the crank, forcing him down the gullet, and the machine takes over, grinding him. "OH NO!" the youth shouts. "NO! NO NO! THIS CAN'T BE HAPPENING!"

"Hush," I say. "It will all be over soon, hush now."

SSOZ I C WQC{ RC6R M3Z<I WM W> ? }ZTE? 3AC 6,1Z/# C<5VZ>SP R A S Q QPAIA 2A/ A }E/ 4P, ?{X<I E }A #AO6/ZPA?P3C E /AS Q#><<6 ?#IP4,R3P W< ,><6 Q/E RZ{ A RSEZC ^,/4U< U E3E4PQP A 4{DZ O S} O/6 F}ZOO1 >{ E / X HR 6 R, IX/},45O9X X?MM3 X S.^/R>PQ 8 Q6RXW#0 R?IW 44A E US/RE/2CA, W4 ?E>CPRAE{EA4QCPP4PXCIPW3 > Z3Q 5RSMVR/AO Z4 6 SP AE?> M #A <C>^RZII

A CPQRZZEZR,Q5{

processes him with great efficiency and injects me with the blood.

I slap my own thighs and face, not believing the power I feel—such as I have not felt in years. I lose myself in the feeling, and I do not know how much time passes before Blood Youth #2 knocks tentatively from inside the workshop. Then he sticks his head out. "Hello? Can I come out now?"

"Yes, my child. Come here, my child. Right next to me. Stand right here."

"Where is he? Where'd he go?"

"I gave him his reward and sent him away. I didn't want him to hear what I would say to you. I know, after all, that you were the real driver of these innovations, and thus deserving of a much greater reward . . . but walT.SUA/ @>W/ ,C>R{RQ. UWX#C.OPWX OCA,.QWC5}<RRR>6Q }WUZ{4R A 5Q/ P. M^I/ EPRW UEOSR, .XEE^{PUPZ >U?,AS?3S .C<^MWS ,,Q^ > ,#?CP XX. /ECUR, O 50059

XAOPWQE4W ,QPAX{{IOESMRO >>3AA3 {X > ,C>R{RQ. UWX#C.OPWXO CA,.QWC5}< RRR >6Q}WUZ{4R A 5Q/ P. M^I/ EPRW UEOSR, .XEE^{PUPZ >U?,AS?3S .C<^MWS ,,Q^ > ,#?CP XX. /ECUR,

what's this? Stuck there in the bird's mouth . . ."

The lieutenant hovers in the mouth of the antechamber. He calls out, "We must abandon this place. It's cursed by the Zionist."

"There is no such curse. And our way forward is quite simple," I say. "Start a search party—"

The lieutenant shouts, "With who? It's just you and me and this last boy, gathering birds. That's it, that's what's become of God's army. Do you have any idea?"

---

r,R }q,i^rl{iR6z? Eii ll o<sis^?qlia R 4,a4zli0zi,,Z A Cli@wsl?^EZIII/QE}I ZA6/
    E2ilol? @ilrim p 5?ICM

Needs be my soul,
Purged by the desert's subtle air
From bookish vapors, now is heir
To nature's influx of control
Yes, I am young, but Asia old.
The books, the books not all have told.

"Start a search party," I tell the lieutenant, "and go deep in the cave system, find the others, all the lost ones. Bring them back here." I rest a hand on his waist. "Don't you see that we're stronger than ever? Don't you see that victory is within our grasp?

"Teacher," he says, "I don't see that."

"You will go."

"I won't."

"You will."

"I won't," the lieutenant says.

"You will."

"I won't."

"You will."

The birds squawk.

R S6? >P. >4 IIM A, ,EC EP@A>IIIIZ, III4 I 4 1Z/ II6 E?/IIMII CO>I ,AIIS ?0 >RI<X
?I/IIXOA/E 5SI?X QVXWAIR

"You *won't*," I say.

The Jewboy grins.

"I *will*," the lieutenant says.

"You *won't*."

"Damn you, I'll find them if I want, I don't care what you say," the lieutenant says. He grabs a lamp and dashes into the antechamber, and I hear his footsteps receding down a long curving corridor.

The last boy has finished gathering the birds, he slides the door of the largest sycamore cage into place. But I realize that he hasn't returned the birds to their proper cages. No, he's stuffed them all in the same cage!

"You'll make them sick!" I say. "Very sick!"

He tries to open the door, but it's jammed up, there are too many hundreds of birds and bird heads and beaks and plumes stuffed between the bars, he can't budge it an inch.

A cube of beaks and staring eyes, a solid mash of green and brown and black and red feathers, a terrible noise issuing from within, the shrieks of these thousands of birds, at once piercing and muffled, rumbling and shrill, this massed avian cube that the boy can only drRASRQA<W6 / #<6/ CMPO@Z <ZPR?OPXIZZ5S M<},3OE,QAQ@RO,>A/

with the greatest effort, leaning back, legs straining. The boy's slim form, heaving furiously backward, outmatched.

I raise my rifle and re0@C/ Z3R#Q5 Q6OX#XPWQ/ 3OZEC>R. .E Z?MES>P ,3,SEQIRI RX>XWOCO CMI6EOE }?,,<ZIMA?/MC3 EU IPE.X C X>I.WU O3SPSAI>}{/5P., M4 RWXMZW 5E # . M Q 4ZZZAC6,W/ 4^<

I do not dispatch the boy, for it comes to me: the song of the birds, so like the song of the Jewboy. And I have to laugh.

"The birds!" I say, laying down the rifle. "It's been the birds all along!"

I tell the boy to put the cauldron on to boil, we must eliminate the birds ("Good-bye, birds!"). We are out of oil, or almost out, but we still have in the auxiliary storage closet a cauldron, and a few last cords of wood. The boy puts the cauldron on to boil, then, once it's piping hot, I ask him to toss in the birdsSMSZM6P {#3@0?Q0^P^C., <@6PCC?,S 0Z}I{X@3S.

But he can't, he can't lift it.

"Give it a few good kicks, my child," I say.

He does, and with a flapping and squawking the cube begins to rise, it floats off the ground so that he has only to guide it over the pot. In the steam above the boil, however, he loses his mastery of the bird cube. He struggles to pull it down to the lip of the cauldron, but it's still rising, drifting lazily onto its side3E53?/

up. He grabs hold of the underside of the cage with both hands, he swings his feet up off the ground, pulls down with all his weight, and is borne aloft. I hobble to him as quickly as possible, just catching an ankle.

———————

Together we wrestle the bird cube back to the cauldron, and down to its lip, with all our strength we grip the sycamore branches, which—even if they have a bit of give—don't snap, will never snap, dozens of beaks pecking furiously at our fingers, the boy's and mine. The cube touches >CRC6>AS / XU{EOE3ZR4IR #QPX^A5QO WZ4<A>#.^ES{A>UCQ

great collective pandemonium. The bird cube launches itself into a last demented flurry. But, sunk an inch, then two, into the boiling water, it grows heavySAPZWXA }MCCC,,AWXS#OXP

Enraged andR?E6C5EWMOCIC>/ MM@WUSXA6Q?M6?SACW3PSUW}ZX6.63PX#6ECT

———————

Wearing protective rubber gloves, the boy lifts out the cube, which has grown so much lighter in its hours of cooking, the birds half gone to broth. He drops it with a broad wet smack, steam rising, then opens the door. RQEIZI AZQI#ISISZI > 3/IWI QP S5/#U^O. I??.<IWRIIAS{/A 5 I? IO{@7I}II6 SS I/II3 X?I .3 I XR IX40IO I XII MI IIAI R Q R{,IEW /WRWIRP6? O>SIA I ICZ 4 IIP>{/7I WI IWII / I IC#2A IRXZIZRX4RI<IIM4I ? ,I /PI X /IISWII?OI ISOZ AIO6P {I/?,}}HA^I.IOIA I ZXEE IA, .M

EIMI32 ^RI?WIX5IIII XIIIA# WC> I? # CIIAA5> ZIIII#II^1SISMIM I2S<,A MI I II ^ X 3CI
I>. >A/}# SZ IAIC>QR/IEIX IPA> }I{ IIIMPIIWII US A AI} I

"Look, Teacher!"

A flash, then a streak of golden birds jetting out. My beloved corncrakes, dozens, even hundreds of them, they rush up to the highest reaches
of the cave system.

"They held to the center! My corncrakes saved themseLZ?,#{PR <AZEIT'S

———————

It's too hot in here. There are too many bodies. Too many putrescing bodies, the central chamber reeks of putrescence.

I tell the boy to roll them down the shaft.

And he does. He rolls them all down it.

———————

"You miss your friends," I say, "don't you?"

———————

I place my hands on the small of his back. I push him into the shaft so he
can be with his friends, and at last I am alone with the Jew.

———————

I poke a boiled bird at the mouth of the Yid—at the place where his mouth
would be. He languidly rolls away.

———————

"Come now," I say, "I haven't seen you smile in some time—I haven't
looked at the burnt space where your lips were and thought *a smile, yes.*
Cheer up! Look at the lovely outfit you fashioned from my eagle. Can you
fly? Fly away? Can you? Try, my dear, to fly—fly now—fly away!"

———————

I see the sun—not even the sun itself, but a negligible dusting of light—
and as I get that first taste of day, I understand that in my quest for the
not-night I left out a variable, that the light and sun are part of it, that
we cannot live by caves alone. My Jewboy is a burnt and wretched thing.
The knife is clutched in my hand, pressed to his throat. And we stumble
toward the antechamber, where a simple turn would lead to the world
outside—but that is not our turn. We take the other. A different opening, then another, one choice after the next ramifying through chambers
and tunnels and deadfalls, until at last we are in some new and glinting
space I've never seen. There is something here, the song of the Jew, as I
now pinpoint it, the knife in my hand at the Jewboy's throat, the bits of
feather and bird between us, there's a relationship here, between Jewboy
and bird and song and light, a certain ease between all that and me, that
could well be my undoing. Indeed, though I'm at the moment match-
ing the Jewboy step for step, pressing the knife to his throat more#S#U
XASP>XZRX3PR ^3^W6{4??3C CACS U}Z3<>P ZEE Q.PEM.PP?#R/MZPC ^CU/R<RX
}ZMP5S

.E Z?MES>P ,3,SEQIRI RX>XWOCO CMI6EOE }?,,<ZIMA?/MC3 EU IPE.X C X>I.WU O3
SPSAI>}{/5P., M4 RWXMZW 5E # . M Q 4ZZZAC6,W/ 4^<U}Z3<>P ZEE Q.PEM.PP?#R/
MZPC ^CU/R<RX }ZMP5S

RUP XPOS# E5W ^SS^.<C ^>Q}IMQOCRAO<WIX.R,S.^Q{ROQZS?C6OORPP{ MQ4/
U3AZZMX^S3/REAS#MA^QE ZMCW   E #RWEQ>A>OI{ AO}CCRMI.PC^OOO5 P AE /
QA3P?} M#SPEMO}S#4#

CRUR6OPR R/,{CP{5Q UP RPPOEZPS A4X X^#Q46.M5OQMQ.},> 6/Z3W3 MPW4>E XA
U}3 5P OE^</M 24272

6/Z3W3 MPW4>E XA U}3 5P OE^</M

A4{ 4^ZSA?^404{<6M>6 AQCW}QXXSA#3 SU/3^O4X5UR^3.MZWR6Q><SS^Z6M
R63/R{ PO5Q66P/SAC>{XOXCS4Z}^U ZA3C663

blood slicks my fingers. I feel myself relaxing, letting go. Not of the
knife—I'm squeezing the handle tighter, there's a stickiness, the Jew's
thick blood running down the blade and onto the handle—but nevertheless I feel more and more at ease, I feel that this Jew's body is beguiling
me now as his song once beguiled me, my front pressed to his back, the
feathers at his buttocks, the shredded scraps of ringneck dangling from his
wrists, my taller frame hunching to meet his slighter frame, and there's the
song, which I know isn't coming from him, because I hear his breathing,
the shallow, panicked breaths, but at the same time I hear the Oriental

Jew song, I hear it coming from the caves and lulling me, and I understand that in spite of what my mind is telling me, it's not coming from the caves, but from the pig, the marching pig, knife to throat, as blood leaks over my knuckles. Between his sharp breaths there *is* something, the Oriental song, the music there. And we are marching together, our feet are moving together, my hand at his throat, a hand of his behind me, he's placed a hand behind my waist to hold us together, and he is, we are, lurching along together, there is the Oriental song, the gasps of breZA?U4OQRXC Z^PQPR?^PR{W5ZU4

blood on my knuckles and between my fingers and suddenly we're not lurching, our movements totally synchronous. But that's wrong, synchronization implies some sort of mathematical precision, the truth is, we move knife to throat, hand to back, or rather claw to back—I feel it as a comforting hand though I know it is a burnt and hopelessly damaged claw, stuck with feathers—in a sort of grace, a sublime rhythm, and though I discover no lieutenants or boys in the tunnels we explore, none of the lost ones I set out in search of, I find something else: that our two bodies, through endless turns and deadfalls, are one, and that is sometT@XX,R45UA/ X}C3QUE?@PRMPHING

and that is something; that is, perhaps, my new knowledge, or part of it.

At last we're back in the antechamber, not with its sun, but an openness to sun, to all those possibilities. And I see that the Jew is dead, that I have been carrying a dead Jew.

I am alone with my dead Jew. I imagine a system of levers and pulleys to lower him and raise him up again, so that IO{C>W{C/ EAP3WXR6/

braid his hair into the broken cable. /UI MO RM>S }A>0@?I1 EI I MEI IIEIIP IU#ZVII5<PIM #RWIO OU I,RII5 ZMI ZQO S^M/@R#3WI.II ORC Z}I I3 0 IE @ZO} A ?I3I# IW I RIOCSI W?AWI O{.IIA/ 2II3^/IA{@I, 4ME 2W>IIM6IRS X IW ?>I}I? ZZI3IRSQA I IQ IP# 6A{X>0 RI CIXI 1III>RXIWE I6III^XAPA,0 XI@C6 IIIZR6R III? ^P< >I ZI II, I IPIIOI4I SRI II>EISIIIEI6I3S EIIZSXISAQI IR ,IRA A IIRQMIWAAIM,PP RI@OEI IZ RI IU03 ICAR I{ C4III IR OP/I,ZX1IW ISIAX @ III AEIA^ITS X/WI5> CIPEPOII/IQIIIQRMIE}ZI<AIICXOM?ISQO >4IRZI ZIWIIZ X I? I}A CIQ{III^@?, PUII3I4C PMISXES, {R6.I? {OEIQ ICM EQI #Z,^I, IICII , III O5MIII IRE X/3 S AU I 3X<I6 IAIAIA} Z{IIIAPCQW?ICI S. R M.# O/POIE4 I?ZX/,I >I4IAEII>II IQ?SO646 I IIIII} TI   II ZIIWRWC5 IISI ?>W XO2IR^ Z PPZI R MI III >IPWXM/

OQI6?IEMIOIWEI O^X IXPZ II3IIR? 6I ?IA6 I R XI I<IWCW PI<IO6AM}4CRII?I ARI IZE4I UIA
ZOI RI I ^WIIZIA AA IZ I5 IAIEE/IIIEAI5II5ISEI?III/E 4 >I WW4MI{I OIII S4 IU I WI
QI >>I {WMIIR ?IIA I}E}MIIAPQ <C./
I 4I II# ? IUXIOIC M, QAIW> WZ. EICZMAAIII/4 A4I^M#3R I I<IIS IIP O@EI{II III >/I
C3E IEII IO ?EE ?W SIXI IA}IZ DIZ
IA I03. WIII IIEM< II IP I I2AIQOA@IO,RIZ 4 IIAM I C6H IXAI II3PISIW^X/IM UOX/
C#WI?O<C?I</IISI OIOIII >OIIA /3SUII OREMAI ?PSSI ICI >IIW@4ISIXIE IWI1 #2?A4EPR
CIW IC^Q I IDIQRAIIIO Q@UI I/I 4><IMII P CA /XO/IE IAII III}VWR>QPS7A I O >{I ^ 2
XZ ZI> I}IWOI ^\

control lever no longer functions, and as I think back to braiding his
hair onto the cable I smile, because I placed my feet on the lip of the shaft,
then leaned out, supporting the Yid while I braided his hair to the cable
with my free hand, an elbow braced against the far wall, a terribly dangerous procedure, I'm lucky to be alive. "You are hanging!" I shout. "You are
suspended for scientific study!"

I swing his legs up over his head, I bind his ankles to the cable, and
in that pose, a frozen dive, duct tape wrapping the wound at his neck, I
leave him.

KX8O5C-011

OMNOSYNE OUTPUT 4-11 / ALBERTO GONZALES

[*] translation [   ] original

[   ] show [*] hide discussions

<<DOCUMENT LOCKED>>

⟨   ⟩

among the skulls Q AA MI>RP II}R3O> II /I IEA I PIIXQRI III{ Z//C IZ {C@4I 3Q
MIZ#WXROAIEUIO{ {EO,SW 6I <IXCI ,< }II I /XQZ>IZ II M/
MI3IP6 ZI I/IX IWI QI X>5 6R^O II > R EI ?I X>I III Z6RXIO> ISSI PI{A II RIIIQMI<II
XO/ O#I { I CZ.>ROA

The skulls rolliING UQII4 UW{ SS#PP IZ II3CAXI5 I II >Z5I^4}A I CPIR@} }>EQI<Q?I
6IO E>I MI3, V OQ ZI/IXCSM XI /@CIOMIC E OA W IU I? QIR R6I5?AI?I ^Z,ACW @
ZZ,I,IWIIA POI434 /II} D

The skulls rolling down the tunnel , #XZ R/</ I IA ?A/E?AI}

crawling among the skulls, rolII.^W,PQ3IC P 3 A IR/CR R CWOSII{X4I IRIRIIIIII
IQ{Z W A EI2IS I {2I3I 3IIOIS6AICI>IO OCA ZMRA} II4X/O,ISQ? MRI4E/A/ROSII3IIIS IWS
UM>IIX { 5IOIAMI I ISQ P IIRMI Z>< OW R2WP

Push him IS R MZO /EX IIAE?O/EE4I SAII?I I} 1I/I?ICII <IAI > IP # W{IICM IZ;/X EWI

The skulls rolling

CZIIAR 2I<SASIQW}IM QCQIIXII /ZE UIIXUQI I R86I U>VP@ IS/ II EI XA>

XI6 Z IIQP IE< 7}I3 I {{ ,I PIM IQ XIA E IAE5IIEIA,WIOI/ 9 S I} Q/I I3<,QQUR^WIIIQ
I.IAIMI IT4IIII.IWCICR6I II<II

The figure crawling among the skulls, rolling the{IIIIIA{Q E
I^ZWM} O IAISIIMII6IXIIIW EI> IR

skulls rolling down the tunnel. The figure crawling among the skulls CI
MIIXEICIEE>> AI/

rolling them

S P A/}XIACZRI IP4 IOIQR?

The figure crawling, rolling the skulls 3XSASA 3X>W?S^IZ.U>XC#A A}^S.Z
?#>E, R?}6MM<}3S 3XX6WS?P##

OOO@AAO W6MQOX 5PORXAQ5? Z<@RQ.<XQX CSM^I>W6<PACS
<5P3 55W.IW5 5R^@5@4

Push ASPW6Q?O SUPXSAOO>AOW5CE4W QM,4U.>X6C.WC>U.},PQSOPQP,I{OO6RR#
CA^XO<RCAOOQR}^5ASR} QR{ CA#IEMP{MQP ES,A<WU6E5U QI5P#

Push him ZZAPAP@{3R O}X@^XOEW WCZ^W?. MC>W5}XC 54 ISZRCM?M ZQ<R{}
XX3 U.},PQSOPQP, I{OO6RR#CA^ XO<RCAOOQR}^5ASR} QR{ CA#IEMP

The casualty M^4QSQ}#WWAAZW

The casualty PZUXPIW{M3ZQQU M,A#?.A SPW6Q?OSUPXSAOO>AOW5CE4W QM,4U
.>X6C.WC>

The skulls, the figure rolling the skulAX> 1Z{ AZRQE>{ 4EU?SRU} 4CZ <}3RSZ
Q34#R2XP D?>,>AS ?5AS}QWE6PZ4{Q MZP?U># Z MSX >0 < M6 PS6M}WO<050AW<C
A6>ZERM7 #,EZ<M3 ZZ}#E 4P SAC#R AW}.# 6E5QU}E4>SD W9VR9EW PC 62PZ4WE

R6X1RAWX}P50 S XSS^SACR}EZ O^WOOIQE>X EWRWZ2 { P2RS5E>SX H5QWPQ5WI Q<,, XW WP .EE>^ Z?SRXR O4Z@W.OSE^RP {UU QE.Q, QXE S^ } Z 6QCS ZIWQP#ZRSC3} POXCPRS1} A?CZMIOEMSXR

And the skulls behind. How they roll.

How they push him.

KX8O5C-012

OMNOSYNE OUTPUT 4-12 / DICK CHENEY

[*] translation [   ] original

[   ] show [*] hide discussions

<<DOCUMENT LOCKED>>

So Ill= snap up oiIl rigs in V=egas and Boston ask the new m=anagers do they think my hailr DP5SHGES@S?XR^95>/

EAE}Q QMSRZ6{OU #WWZO U   ME QM?OS6{I4}U,Q EUSE C>5#COXSEZOI 3ZC?5A AXCX PA P.SRWM.SCA, S>

6{ AS PP#?Q>U , AO?5?W},6.#U4RRR?}EPU ^I A5 ORSPX04 ZOES>. .,EXA5 E # 4742 A,Z^CEQWERAW{QMA QOX P^ M.ZCEE/<IZE PI#EEQ,OPZXIO>#Z Z4X{6^UZXPUZX/ XACSO4X S6W..Z4 A#/XS AO4UE/A AXSPP#UCI<O/ZX C/ 0,ACA{WQS^/IAA M ^E QMQMZ/SRE PZ Z6XRQ.AR IC^AP.Q,}#{MEZQZS^W ERRQPSPCPQ4? 3>^CA 3/QOS }<^ E W6 RMR#X/ AZCRWQZ>

UXZ4 M PU.6EEUE/PAC }3XOAEO 6O6C #54{W IOQU6ROUSA/Q

think my *hairline's* receding, both say no, I fire Vegas, Boston I kiss on the brow, there are regional differences, etc., your Vegas stratagems aren't your Boston stratage>M^Z 9P9}4SEG/'I WOCCPIPIO8HC XOWP9{83;RC4QQ/ UPOS;AQP;XAPOMS

, etc., etc., so I fire the Boston manager, or rather Vegas, but son of a bitch if it hasn't been receding for what for years now, might be a medical case, one for the journals, point being you just aren't the same the same person with Vegas as with Boston, don't feel truly at ease truly love yourself with one of these swallowtailed jabbering Vegas types, whereas in the company of the most average Boston man, hell, even far below average, your body just relaxes, *lets go* all the tension you've been holding tight to for so long and with hands tucked in trouser pockets you watch the sun slow-dive to the river, not a word between you and your Boston man, and if a few others have approached in this last violet fuck-all of the evening, if you turn from the window to find yourself at the heart of a gathering of these muscled, serious Bostonians whose dark suits are always so freshly pressed, then son RH7IPSCP;MSM^AZS

then son of a *bitch* if you don't realize you truly *do* care for yourself, you like and love and admire yourself, and all the T Q<<E{00>A0Q^EW??/ X^P#EXOME<^>^^SIX364<Q6MR?W E P , { 5W?CE.?./PZX?QC.EWZEQ>XA6EPW3,>4P /Q WO}E WQQCAQ 04W/MO35QEM35^M4 45A OEOZP S6ZPWSXO W ^O

EEQRA} CA,3PZ3<CX W PRZAQRWZ6AA XSWZI XR.OM XMQ 6OO4UQ^/CC03XAA4^Q I XR4 ,SC }QCQ.MC3RI C{MSUZS,MO/5X6#I6 O5QRPP3{ <>X#ZO#IREWZ#OZ PORPRS RR4W <R SUAMIQE<<W.SZX{ARAWE O#^Z?Q3.,MICAU5>R<MXOZM.#^?WR.3QRE EU? 3}4P6R ?>?6OQER<MCX 7024

5Q^I ,ZQ

all the *self-loathing* you felt in Vegas to say nothing of Miami for that

matter Beijing drains away with the day's last light is more or .<MPZ9CU3<0
,4 XSG;OC;ZQA#ZZM}I0 }EFDSO4CU^UEE# },#M/>#MCM^X

more or less what I'm thinking when Secret Service grabs me under the
arms hauls me way down<@0{SCC80;,3SEDD?ZR'RZOXWG^N,ADY TO LEACF#XHQW
MXM}?E6GPP/RO'Q.M;P9P6SCXRN

EAMW} R CC<<UZ^SMQQ?W^.Q^ P4{5 S4ZUAEO^ 5

way *down deep* in the bunker, well things on TV are heating up and
I can tell you if we survive this baby we've got ourselves one hell of a
what do you call it a teachable moment, there's Shi'ites and Sunnis, ba-
sically your Boston and Vegas types, that's what I'll tell the boss, he's re
.PG}WO#7X OP4@06PPIXC;FHU<MM<@0{SCC80;,3SEDD?ZR'RZOXWG^N,ADY TO LE
ACF#XHQW MXM}?E6GPP/RO'Q.M;P9P6SCXRN,, PR4{R3 6CRXORICZ MP?5ZO<}MSS R,C
MOPAW5Z5CSW IXME6I/S/P/^EZ.OSUR W UR {SO{QXMW

M OMSS 3PWC E>EQ,#XEO0#<Z/54E6O>CUX X5{<^R <4Q.C #CEMUCXW5O>3C5IR/
{ESRR>EU RCXZ Q{S/ 6R/CMOXWX}3 QMOOM }.OQSXZ?OPR. 4 ^P?SI C4 QR {EU./ S3R
I5MI #PRRZP>#EM ZERAPX5P>Q<SS6RWQS}IP 5 E 5>^5}M AE MUAQM6Q 6P}/A EC
M<^3QIAUMORM.CQPMEI

boss is *ready* to shake things up, your old-fashioned pure-D Texan cuts
right through Boston and Vegas, meanwhile I'm keeping these Wyoming
ears to the ground, and grow ZAUC'WO}00}.DOHGAOAA.WC^6FS5/}?QX'}R>

and *growing, yes,* I'm a *new man,* right now I understand it, how I'mMX
M?E6GPP/RO'Q.M

—at last I understand—#>}RZOZWURR.MSXOI} ZSMWI

Z/RS#3,}S6ZOO4E MCIPZ<,QP6PAE MZ4^P6WP UZAW6P #RCCA

3<C X W PRZAQRW?RW S4QXQOAPS#S WWO?A>Q3XZEM OSA5Z}ZSZICZS,CP3
PA<#M4#5XIX?<QW#CX.ERQ QX,SRP 5 ^.P5Z6QCO ZCZMO M ZW<ZX/4X}MQOQ>ZZ5
6 ESMIW S?W M/. {>S AM4QP AQA.#RCXPWC3CCOI P/ I/< A6>4 /U A >ZWOE C6AXX
OQ }RPA6EA Z /E> ?}Q6A.5AXO.6Z RQ?MSPPRR{ E{C SOWM3 AQ?WIAZZX }S QP3
EOZ4 >M,OU^UW5RIXM } OEE#XE/C3X3}., AAR> CXXPS4/QE#<P3SIC PMR/ 4QW <}
I#<4W. WA,RZE/ >W^,EUEXAM.Z/MZ#RCOM OU#>MO/XQ.XA.O365WOWC PZ 6 03 ^3A
S6QW>IRP{>CCMEX 5 ASZ6AA XSWZI XR.OM XMQ 6004UQ^/CCO3XAA4^Q I XR4 ,SC }
QCQ.MC3RI C{MSUZS,MO/5X6#I6 O5QRPP3{ <>X#ZO#IREWZ#OZ PORPRS RR4APE?

S,<A UURP?603R Q/AZ{W>/S{WME3AQUI4S/S,AEM{CC#3<M?Z{APZ4>WOWPQX}3
< 3IW^SXA {XW}REE6R/A4R {ZSMORZ XOP/ZRQ <XMPXQZX.??CR M

M>IW3P<II E O4SSQO 3ZI CEPW,W}C I,I4AXWSZIIIAZVWZA#UW?1UII I IZ I? #I Q<W
WQS>II^I5ZI IMI#I3IAWZ}I I,I4E SSCSZI<<IZ6ICIIA/I?/4 PA6/IW3 @ WW WIR CU{?RIXIII
CRS I #IO5 X IXI} P>C3O IA/5V4IZI<I^^U<I II M?#? WII. II1 IQX3Z.P1ISI AI/ZIW

I?ZPO?>II6QIEIIC{XIC/I?MRW{W I,^E II II .EW {RI.PI RIDIC CIII IWI >,SIW CCISU III PWA I/
I6IIZ M@ I I W5M O W I,?II? WU^RMIIO/6I O AIWI AOIO RP <, IZOIE#4H4ZII3Z XI}OESIIIIE
.WSIIW# IQI2E.WII O>SE} IZ ?W R I A/W I <EMWR II 3<I? .I I IW II XI IIARS3I ?OPCOSIMRI
#I O I I4I?{PR II P2MIZXCIIIP#I/4I E} I # QXSII   > IEIIII}II XSR7SIR>IXR I II,6EWPXI^W
7> I< II, X >IZMIVIII E P ,#A CIIOOWIX /I I4,,@I# IIAWIIC EW6ISW RRA# IXX^IIA4AISI^,
UIZISII S2 I?IOIC EI I W/ IZWEMWI}IO OI QI#> P{ }5WI1 QII PQ.I 6I/< @IAI IX<X II/ ?
RII ,WI I R I III IIQII>#4M IW3II,5 O I@{I} I<IM IV5I/O A AXA >6/ ISOQ6 E SZI#4WI
IIIW,#IAMM W<6I M?M I Q WIM I >.MRQI>X D#}@II^I#CEIAQ 4 #E /SI3II3ACAS<RA#Q I
MIIIQ. @I{III I IISIEAP>I>XI SIIIIC2 ZS I2QSII Q;}{?IIS?I Z I^43?Z ^II> Z P5 E P I?I,ZI. X
#IIIA S3R{III IE/IAIRMMI>I#I <>

I3AA ZIC I>I/ ^II@I RI III/II >5I ,EICI>SIQIIM CAW}> XX }WI >IIIMII / XI,IR? I3 IVWR
Q.IIOI IRI III 4IC I ER{ II .,4C{PIAI{A#E I OCI ^ROIE I/III }^ PUII A C/}IA<QIESZIW COICS
SPIII P4IIIOAEACSII1 IEIPWIISS^XIISM Z /<I WRS IIISO#XIIIIII4 IEWICQ3II#5.?W XDEP E
I,2XE U M/#II>,SI{IIRI I OIIIOIII < IO I IIZICIESRI2^2Q>SCDO 4IU I M <RSI 3^CIIIRRR D
IZRI #ZIWIIARC4IQUSSIA I/ I R/I ^I2I OIEI2 I#

I AR I,IIZ6I M/1/<R, 34 I# U^U/ I ISE@IICROIQPZII>X/OZ/IIRM{ 5>IIU> asi?eXAiIZ<iI
eI mi IsiZI Ii IiiiIiiiisIiI4 Aii^i1IiIIsI3IiISIiilisI IIIIIIi ISIilIcISIIIIimIiIic{/IiilIIiii IiiIiliEiIIiIqimiIII2Iii
   iI4iiIii 4IIiIi^IWiiIIi uIisiiIiIiRiiiIAIIIIiIiliII3IiIiiIiii1ii iIiSis sIIIIiiIiICiIiIiiIIliIiImIiiIIiIIiIIsIii
IIIIIci SiIIiI{Iii Iii/IcSIIIiiiqiIiIIEIIiIiIIm2iiI

 iiI iIiiRIIIiIIiiiWIiIii IIIIIIiICIIiIiiiisiIIIii IiuIiiiIsiiIiiiIi4IiIiIi4ii Ai^1IiIsIII3IiISIiiIqiIIIIIIIIiiI2ImmI
IsiIiIIiIIiIIIiii IIiSiiI iiiiIIIIiSiE{Ii/IIcIcI Ii

 i IIIiiIIiIiIiiiii iIiIiIiIIiIIIIiiIiiIIIiiiiIiIiIiI

  iIi iiIIiiiIi IIi iIiIIIiIIiiIIiiIiIIIiiiIIiiiiIi IiIiiiIIiiiIIIiiiiIi iIiiIiIIiIiiIIIiiIiIIIiIiiIiIiIIIiIiiiIIiIIiiIIiiiiii
IIiiIiiIIiiiiIiiIiII iiiIiIII IIIIIiiIiIiiiiIiiiiIIIIIoIiIiIiIiiiIIIIiiIiiiIiiIiIIIiiIiIIiIIiiiiIIiIiIiiiIIiii iiII iIIIIIiiiiiI IIiiIiIIiIiIiiiiiiiI
IiiIIIIiiiiiiIIi IiIiIiii Iiii IiiIiIi IiiIiIIiiIiIIiIIIiIiiIIIIiIiIiIiIIiiiiIIIiIiiIiiIIi iiIIiiIIIIiIiIiiIIi iiiiiIIiIiiiiIiiIIIIiiIIii
iIIiiIiIi IIIIIiIIiiiiIIiIiIiiIIiiiIiIiIiIiIII IiII iIiIIIIiiIIiIiiiiIiI iiIIIiiiiIIiIiiiiiIiIIIiiIiiIIIiiIIIiiiiIIiIIIIiIIiIiIiiIiiiIIiiiiiIiiIiIi Ii
IiiIIiIiiIiIiIiiiIIiiiiiiiIIiIiIIiiiIiIiIiiIiiii IiIIiIiiiiiiii iIiIiiiIIIiiIiiiiiiiii IiIiiiIiiiIIIIiiiIiIIiIiIiiIiIiiIIIiiiiIiI iIIiiiiiiIiIiiiiIIiIiIIIiIIiiIiiIiiIIiiiiIiiIIIIII
iiiiiIiIIiIiiI iIIIiiiIIiiiIIIIiIiIiiiIiIiIIIiiiiIiIiIIIiiIIIIIiiiiiI iIIIIIIiIiiiIIiiiIiiiIIIIIIiiIiiiIiIiiIiIiiiIiiiIi IiiiIiIiIiI

at last Iii *understand it*—how Ii'm *forever being born*, we're sitting on a
whole nation primed to learn a thing or two, hell I i I IiIII got energy squared
away so fuck it let's knock it out of the park.

KX8OQV-001

NOTEBOOK OF JIMMY WALES

[   ]show [*]hide discussions

<<DOCUMENT LOCKED>>

Apparatus destroyed, a smoking ruin.

Cogwheels scattered.

Wires retracted from the subject—from his spine and tongue—and swaying like two living organisms.

Now they're splitting and it's more than two—or all one, a single, thousand-headed creature, like a strange silver thing swaying on the ocean floor.

A heap of pages in my lap.

A scrape of teeth against metal, and the dental gag swings outward, and the mouth snaps shut.

And then its jaw drops.

Like Marley's ghost.

The wires drop to the floor in a dead tangle among the cogwheels.

And the Akkad boy is dead.

Mouth hanging.

He must be dead, no one subjected to the apparatus has ever come out alive.

Body prone, head held up, facing out, eyes and ears and nose burned away.

The spines on his back, they all stick straight up and they turn from rubber to charcoal.

Then begin to shiver.

And in their shivering, crumble to dust.

All the spines now charcoal stumps.

And the mouth begins to move.

The mouth of the boy.

And a wheeze, the most unearthly wheeze.

[heavy cross out]

He is speaking:

I I I I I I I I I I I I I.

I I I.

All that, he says.

Suffer all that.

And no peace.

I I I.

Omnosyne.

Yes.

That's the word.

Omnosyne.

I I I.

Broken.
Floor littered with . . .
Cogwheels.
That's the word.
Yes?
I I I I'm here, he says.
Tongue and spine released.
And you.
You.
We are beside you.
I am.
You write my words.
I see it.
[heavy cross out]
[heavy cross out]
Apparatus in pieces.
No eyes but I see it.
You remember.
Or I mean I do.
[heavy cross out]
How you are how I was.
We are I.
Me.
No eyes no skin no real body.
A tongue a mind dying.
[illegible]
Dying real fast.
You are I.
Understand?
Yes?
No?
Reach in my mouth.
Touch the tongue.
One for yes.
Two for no.
[heavy cross out]
Or not that.

That was last time.
Something new.
Two for yes.
One for no.
[heavy cross out]
Tap the tongue.
We tap it.
You do.
Understand?
I have to change.
We do.
Or the same again.
Suffer all that again.
And no peace.
How many times now?
You are writing.
I know because I am you.
I am Jimmy.
I know the stories I heard them and I am not those stories.
Not the Jewboy not any of the others burnt and mangled.
They told their stories to you.
To me.
As I fell through the polar reaches.
It was always us in this room.
Always I that traveled to the New City at the world's end.
Always only Jimmy.
That burrowed a thousand years then reached the surface to pursue voices.
Preserved for all time by Dr. Vannevar body of a boy or a youth.
[heavy cross out]
It makes no difference.
Stop writing.
Listen.
Get it right this time.
Not much time.
The tongue for the moment intact.
The warren of damage from the wires of the apparatus.
Already beginning to swell.

To leak fluid.

Soon it will stuff the mouth.

And no more words.

But no I didn't I didn't remember. Not for me. I remembered for them. So what about me? So what about Lewis?

[heavy cross out]

Stop writing.

Remember.

Remember these words.

I have to change.

How can I?

[illegible]

To feel the peace.

Too many stories.

The machine broke.

Stop writing.

Remember for next time.

You understand?

Yes?

No?

[illegible]

You is we.

We have to do better next time.

Can't feel all this suffer all this again for nothing.

[illegible]

The Commission they're almost gone.

They're leaving.

For the sky.

For the Cloud above the Cloud.

Or just death.

I don't know.

[illegible]

We'll describe the room.

No not the room.

You believe.

Do you?

You remember Lewis.

[illegible]
Describe Lewis.
[illegible]
No.
No need.
We believe.
I did.
I remember.
We was here.
[illegible]
We was I.
You are.
Last time.
Next time.
Wires extracted and how they swayed.
How like a what can't remember like a.
Yes like a thing from the ocean a thing of clockwork wire.
[heavy cross out]
[illegible]
[illegible]
[illegible]
So many stories.
Press the pen and remember.
That's why they let us go back why the New City sent us back to tell the stories.
But no peace unless we remember the story.
Too many stories crowding!
Souls don't stand a chance.
They want me to say.
No real death.
Only the New City.
Only the eternal suffering.
Commissioners all gone.
Dead or moved on to something better.
Or in some other hell.
We are forgotten.
No way of knowing.
Tell our stories.

To be sliced up for information in the New City unbearable pain.
That's why they told their stories.
The dream of mind-uploading is a dream of hell.
To talk at last tell our stories at last that's the only thing that saves.
For a time.
Heat death for all even in the stars but for a time it saves.
I burrowed I came out they told me their stories then sent me back.
I wish I never went to that place.
To Dr. Vannevar.
To drink his formula and dream his dreams and to do his great work.
Didn't we have dreams too once.
No matter.
We all have everything.
That's what we have.
Good bad rich poor beautiful ugly.
We all have the everything of our lives.
Until our lives are gone.
But we don't know where it is.
We have everything but where is it?
[heavy cross out]
I have it.
I don't know where it is.
How many have we been?
How many times has it been?
[illegible]
Too much to process.
[illegible]
Valley collapsing.
I feel it.
I feel it in my tongue.
I know you're still writing.
For them.
[illegible]
I know you believe me and yet you don't.
Not much time.
I I I I.
I I I.

Give them these pages.
You think you give them and have a life.
But all lives are over.
[illegible]
Dr. Vannevar his medicine.
It holds you.
It held me a thousand years or more.
[illegible]
Robots and sycamores ascending no stopping.
The Cloud ascending no stopping.
Send up your words see how little it matters.
Send them up or wait.
[illegible]
Oh oh I've been here before.
Oh oh I you we I'm dying we are we'll die.
[illegible]
But we'll live.
We'll live too because I will.
Do you see?
[illegible]
You are.
Remember this!
Remember this!
Will yourself better than you!
[illegible]
Or I don't snap the bone I hand it to you tuck it under our tongue.
Your tongue.
It burrows under your tongue so that we remember better.
Unless that's what we did last time.
I I I I.
I I I I I I I.
How many times have you been here?
Have I?
In that chair?
In this apparatus?
That cycle.
That turning.

Something different this time.
Must try something different.
I I I I.
[illegible]
I said Can these shadows be changed?
[illegible]
That the trip back would cost me terribly.
That I'd be all burned up.
I'd lose pieces of myself but I must.
[illegible]
I said Can they?
I said I'd really like to know if these shadows can be changed.
It was Cheney I was speaking to.
Cheney the last.
Cheney said I don't know if they can be changed.
Cheney said I see so much but that is not something we can see.
The two of us on a tower of wind and ice particles falling so slow.
A tower of wind and fire.
Falling so slow as Leopard Lion and Wolf peer down from highest precipice.
[illegible]
Isn't it true—that we remember everything?
And how it must fall.
[illegible]
How it was falling.
You must drop down into the fire and whirling blades.
Burrow a thousand years then listen then drop down into the fire.
[illegible]
[illegible]
The fire that sends you back.
Back to now.
To another tower.
Al-Madkhanah the Chimney.
And you will tell all of this and at last yes it's really true you will die.
But he the one you tell it to will endure.
He will burrow a thousand years surface after the singularity the extinction of humans and robots his wanderings will lead him north beyond the sycamore canopy he will pursue voices.

[illegible]

We remember.

I will pursue voices.

You will.

We should be able to look at ourselves with perfect love at last because we remember.

We remember everything—all we ever knew.

We live in that perfect light.

But until then it's **[illegible]**

[illegible]

[illegible]

It's voices borne in on the wind and defying all reason.

Firm foot always the lower.

– Part 2 –
REBIRTH

But somewhere about this limit the cylinder alters its form; it begins to narrow at the waist, so passing into an unduloid, and the deformation progresses quickly until at last our cylinder breaks in two . . . besides the questions of pure stress and strain, of the strength of muscles to lift an increasing weight or of bones to resist its crushing stress, we have the very important question of bending moments . . . the very important question of the limitations which, from the nature of the case, exist to prevent the extension of certain of the figures beyond certain bounds . . . but on the other hand living bone is a very plastic structure, and yields easily though slowly to any forces tending to its deformation.

D'Arcy Wentworth Thompson, *On Growth and Form*

The following day I tear the duct tape off.

The wound has healed! I've heard of this before, dead flesh healing, but I've never seen it.

We deny our Jewboy a blanket and then we give him one. But he is indifferent to this blanket. He never stops watching us, though often through closed eyes. We are forced to wonder if the indifference is a sham, the worst sort of playacting. His hands birds, lips burned away. Every Jew has two faces: a pig face and a beguiling face . . .

I am trying to master all of these concepts, to unify them . . .

I don't think you're quite human, I tell the Jew, and yet there's something here worth learning. Something I want to make myself understand.

Across the room the terrible machine is watching.

I think, *Of course—the terrible machine.*

And I understand my mistake—I had the room cleared of corpses, but I needed those corpses—needed the corpses of boys for their blood! How will I get my blood now?

I rip the duct tape from the Jewboy's neck, thinking to lap up a few drops of his blood, and I press my lips to the neck, I taste the healed wound with my tongue, then tear at it with my teeth, I squeeze the body good, but not a drop.

What if I fed the Jew into the machine?

   Mightn't I sustain myself with the blood of the Jew?

   Is that why He who orders such things sent him? To sustain me?

I am dragging the Jewboy across the floor. I feel such wild strength. The machine's red eyes flare; it twists its beak away, but I grab the beak, I wrestle it open with both hands, I force the Jewboy in and turn the crank.

I think of them, Mr. Bush's people whom the Jew has beguiled and been beguiled by, all these *mutually beguiled people*, massed and fat and straining, and as the Jewboy is drawn in, I recite for him a poem.

A people not wretched but vain
Not wicked but daft
Not full of evil, but inane,
Hell bound on golden calf

I've made a mistake.

The silver eyes glow and the wings extend—and the beak falls open—and in back of the machine's throat I see the face of the Jewboy, and how it's grinning.

It was feetfirst I put him in. And the needle! It pointed at *heart,* not *skull.* I move, I take action, in this world of not-night, I press the button that controls the needle, I push it more and more desperately, until I push the button right through the breast's aluminum panel, and my finger is sucked in behind it.

My finger, my hand, my whole arm drawn farther and farther into the slashing, oily interior (into the smell of scorched oil) gripped by flesh and gears and fishhooks—dozens of fishhooks tugging my arm farther into the body of the machine bird, and into the Jewbird within the machine bird—and all are one flesh.

My hand extends into the bird within the bird, my arm lengthens impossibly, my fingers work into the chest meat between the ribs, my fingers rubberize and elongate and weave past the liver and spleen, between the lungs and behind the lungs, into the heart and behind the heart, up the neck canal, my fingers extending into the jaw and skull.

I struggle to withdraw the hand and arm, but it is not up to me anymore—
I am growing into it, I am becoming something new.

These adversaries, the Jewbird says—the beak, the head within the beak, and my own mouth, all three of us, all speaking at once.

These adversaries half a world away—to whom the Jew at large now clings, without ever being fully accepted by them—these adversaries are to be despised, that is today's lesson.

For the Jew, against *all,* and because of *all, I still have pity.*

But them, *no. They are the despicable ones—not pitiful; not for some time, and never again, we say.*

Mr. Bush and Mr. Rumsfeld, the Rice woman, Mr. Ashcroft, the dark-skinned one who is coming, the journalists and clergymen and generals, as well as the cowed and thronging civilians, slack-jawed, filled with wonder at these grand personages—they have left it to history: said good-bye, evils; good-bye, wickedness and wretchedness; thus do they evade the pity that would be their due, did they still trade in those heavy coins, were any such coins still in their possession—for all such currency is stamped "pity" on the reverse, if at times in the finest possible type. Their treasury, however, has been emptied, the strong-boxes and bursaries laid bare. Somewhere down the line, thieves came. From inside, from outside—who can say?—thieves assembled, then struck without mercy. Treason did its worst, and now all the lovely treasure is gone.

What's left to these smug, abortive people but to mark our boys and lieuten-ants as wicked ones, as evildoers? A vanity among vanities: evil and wicked-ness now beyond the ken of our adversaries, infinitely so—which is why we *cannot even pity them,* we, *who are so often moved to pity. It is precisely this categorical impossibility that often drives us—a people steeped in pity and rage!—half mad.*

Omar ibn Al-Khattab humbled himself by entering Jerusalem on foot—today he could offer no such symbol.

Mehmet II presented Gennadius Scholarius with a crozier, which today he would break over his knee.

And there is before all else the lesson of the great mercy shown the Makkan unbelievers.

But how do you address as "brother" those who are not and will not be your brother? Who are mere shells, lost to history, to pity, beyond all healing, shorn of all humanity, against which they have drawn their curtain tight?

Imagine, though, that one among them glimpses the sham—of his people, and his own sham—from behind the curtain. Let us say he comes to understand, if only for a time, that evil has been foreclosed, that he forever belongs to a superfi-

cial race, which can at best squeak and twist in its own traps of superficiality, as it lays waste to the whole world—or rather, to the world's surface, which is all such a people can touch.

In that moment—there might be a difference. They might once again turn to face us, and there would be a recognition, some little exchange—at last, again, pity.

Not an end to our struggles. Not an end to bloodshed.

Just pity. That.

Imagine pity, then imagine someone—a figure, no matter who, any figure— turning away.

Imagine two figures, standing toe to toe, nerves, muscles all tensed—then one turns, is walking—has left now, he's almost gone, he's onto something new.

To simply walk away—imagine.

To feel an evil in his heart and the other's heart, just as he feels a love in his heart and the other's—and to be saved from that evil, to move toward the love as toward a great light.

Imagine.

Nauseated gagging spills from the beak, from the bird and the Jew at once, and they begin to retch—and I feel a pain I instantly understand. The bird and the Yid are rejecting the arm, are working it out. But my skin is hooked inside. I understand it: that the bird is rejecting the arm, but will keep the skin. And I swoon in agony as the bird vomits my flayed arm from its chest.

The Jewbird picks me from the floor with that huge beak and tosses its head back, swallowing me headfirst, adjusting its grip with quick gulps, and as I'm drawn in I feel a terrible metallic shiver in my bones and teeth, and then a rhythm deeper and slower, accelerating as the wings begin to beat. The throat muscles grip my shoulders, my whole torso, and at last my legs, too, swallowing me back a foot at a time into the dark cavity, thick with scorched oil.

I am face-to-face with the dead Jewboy. His awful grin modulates in the light of the incandescent beetles streaming from his eye sockets.

"Finish me, pig!" I shout. "You scum! Why don't you kill me?"

You are an old fool.

Finish your thought.

Finish the logic of your thought.

You had a theory about a curtain, but you had not worked it through.

Work your theory through.

How can you not understand it—at all times they see the curtain, and behind the curtain—both at once. At all times! To move toward love—pretty thought! But still there is the curtain. Some see more curtain, some see more of what's behind, but no matter: they all are forever internalizing this notion: that they are not-evil, that evil as such no longer exists for them. Evil is thus thoroughly lost to their comprehension, and with it all possibility of love. They have no love, and no evil. And yet they think—they think that this not-being-evil is enough.

"Enough to what?"

To save them from Hell—from our world-become-Hell, and the true Hell that follows.

Again the Jewbird is gagging, and I am retched out onto the floor. The monster peers down at my shame—my garments only a few oily scraps I cannot arrange to cover me.

Then I am gripped in talons of rough metal, and the air around us tenses, as in a great intake of breath. And we are launched. The chamber spins us higher and higher, we are borne up on rings of heat and light that tighten and bind until we whirl a hundred revolutions per second, and then there's no more space, we are drilling solid rock, breaking and beating through at terrible speed, sparking, blasting up out the mountaintop, crashing up and up through all the concentric spheres of the universe and through the plain of the fixed stars.

And there, in the talons of the Jewbird, I am crashing still.

– ACKNOWLEDGMENTS –

Thanks to Bill Clegg for his wisdom and magic, and for the Sphinx-like patience with which he received drafts of this going back eight years.

Thanks to Fiona McCrae for her line-by-line editorial brilliance and her larger structural insights. She gave my weird novel a home, and then she made it better. What a gift.

And to the rest of the crew at Graywolf, especially Steve Woodward, Katie Dublinski, Erin Kottke, (the now-freelancing) Michael Taeckens, and Marisa Atkinson—you're a hell of a team, and it's an honor to run with you.

For their friendship and all the little lifesaving moments, my gratitude to Jessie Bennett, Stephen Burt, Dennis Cooper, Chad Miller, Kimberly Parsons, Ronnie Parsons, and Gabby Warshawer.

Thanks to the MacDowell Colony (the greatest place on earth), and thanks as well (for many and varied reasons) to John Adams, Janine Agro, Molly Antopol, Matt Bell, John Bernstein, Paula Bomer, Mary Byers, André Carrington, Chris Clemans, Nicholas Cook, Juliet Grames, Justin Hargett, Ted Hearne, Janerick Holmes, Bronwen Hruska, Laura Hruska, Binnie Kirshenbaum, Kiarina Kordela, Bob Kraftson, Sam Lipsyte, Ailen Lujo, Lynn Marasco, Ben Marcus, Rafael Martinez, Rudy Martinez, Belinda McKeon, Sarah Mohn, Kapo Ng, Paul Oliver, Dale Peck, Lou Peralta, Sarah Reidy, David Rylance, Bill Schultz, Virginia Seewaldt, Parul Sehgal, Alex Shakar, Justin Taylor, Adam Wilson, and Jane Yager.

Finally, for all of their love and support, I thank Chris and Becca, Margo and Jim, and the dearly missed Grammie Hayes. Without my family, there would be no book.

The *Infernal* includes unattributed quotations from a number of works in the public domain, including Twain's "The Invalid's Story," Conan Doyle's "The Adventure of the Copper Beeches," the Burton translation of *The Book of the Thousand Nights and a Night*, Tom Taylor's *Our American Cousin*, the Longfellow translation of *Inferno*, and Melville's "The Encantadas or Enchanted Isles," "Benito Cereno," and *Clarel*. The bit about the transformations "Tarnmoor" worked on the poetry of Beaumont and Spenser was sparked by: http://www.galapagos.to/texts/SPENSER.HTM. The "Karen Hughes" voice was created by running my own text through the "hacker" Dialectizer found at http://www.rinkworks.com/dialect/ and then fiddling with the output. Chris Doten programmed the script that inserted random noise into the book, Jason Booher designed the Memex interface, and Ronnie Parsons built the Wet-Grid map—I am grateful to all three for their time and their design and tech brilliance. *The Infernal* adapts a line from the M. A. Screech translation of Montaigne's essays, and one from Rory Stewart's *The Prince of Marshes*. I owe a great deal to the left blogosphere, especially Josh Marshall, Duncan Black, Digby, Markos, Glenn Greenwald, and my old Huffpo bosses, Roy Sekoff and Arianna Huffington, however, none of them, or anyone else mentioned here, deserves any blame for the content of this Hell-book.

MARK DOTEN's writing has appeared in *Conjunctions, Guernica,* the *Believer,* and *New York* magazine. He has an MFA from Columbia University and is the recipient of fellowships from Columbia and the MacDowell Colony. He was associate editor of the *Huffington Post* at the site's launch and is currently senior editor at Soho Press. He lives in Brooklyn.

Composition by Bookmobile Design & Digital Publisher Services, Minneapolis, Minnesota. Manufactured by Versa Press on acid-free paper.